SCORNED FATE
series

SCORNED VOWS

VICTORIA PAIGE

Editor: Erica Russikoff, Erica Edits
Proofreader: Judy Zweifel, Judy's Proofreading
Cover Designer: Deranged Doctor Design

Author's Note

I've taken liberties in renaming the New York Five Families and the Chicago Outfit, creating my own world and rules. If you love angst, you're in for a treat. This is not a dark romance but is morally gray. It does contain profanity, explicit scenes, and sensitive content.

For a more complete list scan below.

Dedication

For readers who believe that even villains deserve love.

PART
One

CHAPTER
One

NATALYA

A woman kissed my husband, and I ran away.

Instead of a blushing bride resplendent in tiers of tulle and taffeta, I was a dejected one hiding in a room reserved for our bridal party. I sat in the middle of the couch under layers of misery.

I was in an arranged marriage. I wasn't in love with my groom. But seeing a woman kiss him where my lips had been earlier did its job of crushing my hopeful, romantic heart. That one day he would fall madly in love with me. That one day we'd have that happily ever after.

"What are you doing here?"

Crying muffled my ears, and I didn't hear the opening of the door. I inched closer to the end of the couch away from Mamma, as if that would save me from the scathing whip of her disapproval. I was too battered to stand up to her high standards, especially since I was sure my sobbing had ruined the carefully applied makeup.

"Nattie!" Her imperious voice lashed my back. "Everyone is looking for you!"

Her hand touched my shoulder, and I had no choice but to turn around.

"Why are you—" The look of horror on her face only confirmed what I suspected. "*Dio mio.*"

I conjured up a smile that would satisfy Mamma's societal sensibilities, but the continued censure on her face told me I failed. "Do I look that bad?"

Her mouth tightened. She hauled me from the couch and marched me to the row of chairs in front of makeshift mirrors. "If someone found you this way…"

She let it hang. The silence weighed more than the words she didn't say. Everything should be perfect for my mother, Elena Conte —former beauty queen and wife of the don of the most powerful criminal organization in Italy, the Galluzo mafia.

"Is this about that woman?" She grabbed the cotton balls, drenched one with eye-makeup remover and started to scrub away the evidence of my tears. We had a team of makeup artists, but I was certain Mamma didn't want them to witness my humiliation and gossip about it after. For Mamma, pride and appearances were everything. I spied my reflection, and I looked like a cousin to a raccoon rather than the society bride they expected me to be. While I subjected myself to Mamma's ministrations, I closed my eyes and twisted my rings. Even without seeing the giant diamond of the engagement ring, I was certain it taunted me.

"It's bad taste that she's here," Mamma sniffed. "But I hardly saw anything inappropriate coming from Luca."

Luca Moretti.

My husband.

The morning started out full of hope and excitement. Anxiety was present, but it was more rooted in the unknown. I didn't know how to react when I saw him with his former girlfriend or mistress or whatever one called her nowadays—the woman a mobster kept on the side.

"I told you to expect it."

Bitterness tinged the laugh I forced out. "What, Mamma? Give me a break, okay? It's my wedding day. I didn't expect to get slapped with the rules."

Slapped was putting it mildly. I had just returned from the restroom where I refreshed my lipstick in anticipation of the cake-cutting, the garter, and the throwing of the bouquet. At the mouth of the hallway, I spotted Luca talking to his consigliere. I lingered for a few seconds to admire my handsome groom. And then *she* sashayed in. She just walked up to him and greeted him intimately with a kiss on the mouth and her body pressed against his. I couldn't pin down the emotions that tore at my chest. It was humiliation. It was hurt and betrayal. Betrayal to myself because I indulged in girlish dreams. Betrayal from Luca, because as his wife, I deserved respect. He'd been an attentive fiancé. Naturally, I had affection for him, even infatuation. Deep infatuation. Our whirlwind courtship was a series of dinner dates, flowers, chocolates, and an array of extravagant gifts.

In an arranged marriage, those who were fortunate found love. And I had hoped. It was too soon for it to be love. But today was supposed to be the beginning of our life together.

It was supposed to be perfect.

Mamma spun me around and glared the thoughts out of my head. "Daughter. Hear me now and understand. You married a powerful man. Women love powerful men. I told you this. It's inevitable they will stray. I taught you how to keep them. Obviously, that redhead wants to see if she can steal him from you, but remember, you are the one wearing the ring. As long as you have the status as his wife, that's all that matters in the end."

Mamma had hammered this abysmal outlook into matrimonial life since the time I had my first period. She scoffed at all my romance novels, which was why I hid them from her.

"Give him children," she added. "A son preferably."

I winced because all they had was me, a daughter who was a replica of her mother. She tried to mold me in her image. When my skin was too pale, she'd make me wear the brightest red lipstick. My brows were too thick and dark for her liking, so they'd been tweezed or bleached to within an inch of my life. I was a natural brunette, but I'd been blonde since I turned sixteen. I didn't even remember myself as a brunette anymore.

As usual, when Mamma was in her element of applying makeup while on a lecture train, she didn't notice she'd insulted herself by failing to provide Papà with a male heir.

The door to the room opened, and my maid of honor, Sera, who was Luca's niece, stepped in. Most of my relatives weren't able to make the trip to Chicago for the impromptu wedding. I worried about Mamma's health with how fast she had to organize one, but my marriage to Luca was supposed to prop up Papà's organization while it recovered from my cousin's attempted coup.

When Sera saw my face, I had nowhere to hide it because Mamma had my chin in a death grip.

"She's gone," Sera said. "Luca had her escorted from the premises."

Mamma paused in her makeup application as if she couldn't believe what Sera said.

My jaw dropped open. "He did?" A tiny flutter of joy wrapped around my heart.

"Of course he did." Sera fixed a stray hair from my face. "Luca was furious. He was so sure the reason you're late for the cake-cutting is because you saw him with her. He was about to send a search party for you."

"Well." Mamma's neutral expression was in contrast to the wide smile I couldn't keep from my face. "Don't get your hopes up too high, Natalya."

Sera glared at my mother and made a face.

But I was used to Mamma's habit of diminishing any joy I might have felt when it opposed her beliefs. Her bleak forecast into my married life had no effect on my elation that Luca had sent his ex-girlfriend home.

"There." Mamma backed away from the mirror so I could see her handiwork. At least she waved her magic. I looked glamorous again, and my swollen eyes weren't apparent unless someone stared closely.

The second we returned to the party, a hush fell over the ballroom, and I wanted to retreat. I wasn't used to this much attention. It was a small wedding of maybe a hundred, but I didn't know eighty percent of the people attending. Most of them were guests of the Morettis, and very few were ours.

My newly minted husband was talking to Papà when he saw me. And from across the room, he strode toward me with purpose, as though he knew I was about to slink away.

There was no man more beautiful than Luca Moretti. His face was like chiseled marble under the light of the ballroom, making the slight slant of his dark eyes more pronounced. Sharp angles shaped his strong jawline, made more distinct by the shadowed hollow at his cheek. I knew from the first time he kissed me, he was too sensual and sinful for heaven. He was Lucifer molded into a three-piece suit.

"*Tesoro*." His low baritone warmed me all over. "Where have you been?" He took both my hands and pulled me into his arms. He whispered in my ear, "I'm sorry about Jessica."

Without waiting for me to answer, he kissed me in a way that was less proprietary in public and certainly more scandalous than one would perform in front of my mother.

His tongue swept inside my mouth, and I was helpless to protest, but my battered pride welcomed the intimate gesture. To hell with what Mamma thought about appearances.

As expected, she made a disgruntled sound while Sera laughed.

"Save that for the wedding night," our guests shouted. "We want cake."

～

"Ready to get out of here?"

After suffering through smiling, eating cake, and dancing, I shot my husband a relieved smile. "Yes, please."

"Then let's go." Luca helped me from my chair and linked our fingers. I could feel Mamma's frown follow us all the way to the exit, but I ignored her. Apparently, she had less power over me when Luca was by my side. I also ignored the heckles that erupted around us. My husband told me he forbade any wedding pranks under threat of dismemberment. I, for one, was glad we didn't have to go through that custom.

I was all small talk and smiles until we got into the elevator. In its confined space, my whole body turned rigid and my heart gained extra beats. Luca himself was silent. The numbers changed floors more quickly than I'd like. Despite the kisses and heavy petting during our courtship, Luca never went further, and I wasn't sure if he would find my inexperience lacking. His mistress hadn't simply been a woman who was beautiful and of no consequence. She was an heiress and a constant subject in Chicago society pages, a bomb-shell frequently on the arm of powerful and dangerous men.

Men like Luca.

It was rumored her choice of men was to spite her family.

"You okay?" Luca's voice was a rumble of concern.

I wet my dry lips, afraid they would crack with the slightest smile. "I guess I'm a bit nervous."

"Nervous?" He paused. "You're…not." He cleared his throat. "You're not a virgin, right? I thought you told me this already."

I laughed and tried not to wince at the high pitch. "I'm not. Don't worry…"

"Good."

"I'm surprised you weren't looking for one," I mumbled, staring straight ahead.

"It hurts the first time, and the last thing I want to do is hurt you." His voice softened and called my attention. His mouth tilted at the corners in a reassuring smile, which calmed the roiling of butterfly wings in my stomach.

"Yes, well. I'm just not very…experienced."

"Believe me, baby, you'll have experience in no time." His drawl washed away the apprehension, only to be replaced by heat that suffused my cheeks and caused a twitching between my thighs.

The elevator doors slid open, and we both stepped out. I concentrated on the swish of the voluminous silk on our way to the room. My nose twitched at the pine air freshener, momentarily dispelling the seductive scent of my husband's woodsy cologne.

When we arrived at the door, Luca stilled. I kept my eyes down and felt his boring a hole through my head. Before I could force myself to meet his gaze, he swiped the keycard and let us into the room.

"Go ahead and freshen up." His tone was brusque.

In the bathroom, I stared at myself in the mirror, not knowing what to do. Maybe take off the wedding dress. I could only manage the top buttons, and I wasn't sure if my flaming cheeks were from the effort of unbuttoning the dress or the knowledge that I needed to ask my husband for help. "Luca."

The pocket door opened, and he appeared in the mirror. I wondered why there was even a door because there was a see-through glass wall along the bathtub that overlooked the bedroom.

He leaned a shoulder against the frame and looked damned fine doing it too. "Need help with your dress?"

"I can't undo the rest of the buttons."

"I'm sorry if I was insensitive and didn't ask if you needed help."

"It's okay."

He came forward and his breath fanned my nape. While he made a deliberate task of undressing me, his fingers brushed bare skin. "From the looks of this, I think it's the job of the groom to remove the dress for you."

My lungs forgot how to process oxygen and suppressed my speech. The buttons slowly came undone, and the dress fell into a heap on the tiles.

"Oh." I sidestepped out of the pile and turned to face him, but my eyes fixated on the discarded gown. By this time, I was certain my cheeks had taken on the shade of fire-engine red. Intimately aware that this was the first time Luca had seen me in sexy lingerie, delayed modesty had me rethinking my choices of lace ivory bustier with matching satin garters and opaque sheer white stockings. When he hadn't said anything and remained motionless, my modesty turned into mortification. What if he was conservative? Sera assured me her uncle was progressive. She even helped me at the lingerie boutique. I tried to distract myself and bent over to pick up the dress, fighting the urge to cover my cleavage in one last attempt at seduction.

"Leave it," he said hoarsely.

"But it's a Vera—"

"I said leave it."

"But—" I glanced up and gasped. I was staring at his erection.

"See what you do to me, Natalya? You're so pretty looking up from down there, baby."

My eyes darted back to the bulge behind his trousers. "Uh…do you want me to—"

Luca hauled me to my feet and caged me against the counter, pressing his hardness against my belly.

"Hell no," he muttered. "Our first time won't be you sucking my cock."

CHAPTER

Two

NATALYA

"I need to freshen up," I squeaked.

Luca's crude words shocked me, but it was his intent gaze and the hard proof of how much he wanted me that set my pulse racing.

"Just one kiss," he muttered against my lips. We were both breathing heavily against each other. The energy radiating from him exposed his fraying control. There'd been rumors of his psychotic temper I had yet to witness. Even when he rescued me from Frankie, he'd been cool like 007. If he was Dr. Jekyll one way, then I couldn't wait for Mr. Hyde to come out and play.

The lipstick made my lips dry, so I licked my bottom lip. A groan escaped him. Huh. So I licked it again. In that split second, he captured my tongue, forcing my head back in a devouring kiss. A tiny sound came from the back of my throat and his groan gave me the confidence to return his kiss. He set me on the counter. With his hands everywhere, excitement ignited my insides and raced below my pelvis, ending with pulsing wetness between my thighs.

He kissed me and kissed me. His hand delved between my thighs, and unlike our previous encounters, this time he pushed my panties aside and plunged deeply with a finger.

My gaze sharpened in awareness, and it took me out of the warm haze. I never liked it during gynecological exams. It was an unusual intrusion, and I couldn't decide if I liked it this time. I certainly hated it when my boyfriend tried. But with Luca, it didn't burn. It was just unfamiliar. Luca broke our kiss and buried his head in the crook of my shoulder. "Fuck, you're so tight and wet."

In, out, in, out.

I was so embarrassingly wet, but I was still deciding whether I liked him fingering me. The pleasure at the top of my mound was returning, and I was desperate for it to reach a peak. I'd attained orgasms by rubbing my clit, but sometimes I'd rubbed myself raw only to be frustrated. The best one I'd had was unexpected. It was when I rode my boyfriend's leg in a session of dry humping. He'd been paranoid as hell about pregnancy. Even double rubbered while we rubbed ourselves to completion through our underwear.

Luca must have noticed my inattention because his gaze narrowed. I realized my breathing was shallow. He extracted his finger and stepped back to search deep into my eyes.

"Are you sure you're not a virgin?"

Was now the time to admit I wasn't sure?

"I'm not. My boyfriend—"

"Enough. No mention of another man when I have my finger deep inside you."

He plucked me from the counter and carried me bridal-style toward the bed. "If you say you're not one, I'll take your word for it."

He laid me on the mattress and surveyed me. "Fuck, you're beautiful."

My whole body heated under his regard. I'd never seen that hungry look directed at me before. He shed his jacket, unknotted his tie, and slipped it from his neck. Weighing the tie in his hand as if considering something, he looked at me before tossing it on the floor. He removed his vest and unbuttoned his shirt, never taking his eyes away from me.

"I need to prepare you before you can take me."

I nodded, mesmerized when the broad expanse of his chest and tattoos were revealed. I'd seen him without a shirt when he took me to watch him play basketball with the *family*. He had powerful legs from his years of playing soccer and broad shoulders from swimming. When he took off his shirt after the game, I could only gape at his chest, the intricate ink tastefully covering his skin, and the ridges of ab muscle. That was the first time Luca had stirred me sexually. After winning the game, he was all covered in sweat and pumped full of adrenaline when he came right to the bench where I was sitting and kissed me. I had spasmed between my legs.

And I was feeling his raw sexuality right now. I rubbed my thighs to control the throbbing between them. Primed and ready, I could make myself come, but I wanted him to make me.

Naked from the waist up, Luca approached the bed and sat on the side. Kicking off his shoes, he turned to me and smiled. It was a smile that was reassuring and confident. He reached over and put a hand between my clenched thighs. I spread them like a wanton I'd seen in those R-rated almost pornographic films. His eyes followed the trail of his hand up the leg straight to my damp center.

Without another word, he got on the bed and settled between my legs. In the shadows and light of the room, I marveled how the muscles flexed over his arms and shoulders while he braced himself with his elbows.

"I'm going to sample every inch of you, *tesoro*," he whispered.

"Shouldn't I get naked?" I whispered. I loved it when he called me his little treasure. He smiled briefly but didn't answer. Instead, he lowered his head to kiss me again. Luca's tongue plunged and teased my own. When he centered his erection between my thighs, I undulated my hips and ground my pussy against it.

I was desperate, drowning, and falling at the same time. Desperate to chase the promise of pleasure. Drowning in sensory overload. On the brink of falling off a precipice. I needed to come, but I didn't know how, and I needed that release now.

He chuckled briefly when he released my mouth. "Ah, Natalya. Patience. You're trying to rub yourself to orgasm, but I'm going to give you my mouth."

I inhaled sharply when his fingers returned to play between my legs. He released the hooks of my bustier, freeing my breasts. His mouth trailed down my chest and his tongue licked a nipple before swallowing it whole. He kissed me over the fabric. He went lower and lower, blazing a trail of sensation below my belly.

And then he was there. His nose nudging against my pussy. Inhaling, breathing me in. His tongue probed the soft skin at the juncture of my thighs, and I tried to close my legs, but he coaxed them apart. He murmured to me in Italian. Telling me I was so pretty. Telling me I smelled fantastic. Then he was nudging my panties aside and my back came off the bed when his tongue, hard and hot, plunged inside me.

"Luca!" I moaned.

A rough hand landed on my torso and pushed me back down. The assault between my legs continued. He used the fabric of my panties to give friction and alternately licked and sucked my sensitized flesh. A finger joined his tongue. My clit felt swollen. I was building, building until I exploded in an onslaught of pulses. Oh my God, was this what it was supposed to feel? Luca kept eating me.

He was relentless in his attack, feasting like a man starved, and the more I opened my legs, shifting the angle of my pelvis, the more the pleasure peaked and pulsed. I screamed to the ceiling, blinded by the wave that crashed over me and took me under.

I was suffocating in countless sensations.

"Stop." I was a mindless, boneless heap. "Enough."

I was still pulsing when he left me. The mattress shifted, which made me look down. Luca was on his knees shoving the rest of his clothes away. My jaw unhinged when I saw his erection.

He smirked. "I didn't want to frighten you into changing your mind."

"You're huge."

Even in the darkness, his shaft stood menacingly against the darkness surrounding his groin.

"Well, naturally," he said cockily. "But you're ready." He positioned himself between my thighs and fell back on top of me. His cock crowned at my entrance.

My breathing hitched.

"Relax," he gritted. "You'll be fine. I prepared you. I'll go slow."

The uncomfortable pressure continued to push against my opening. I kept my eyes on Luca's face, watching him take me. A frown appeared between his brows. "You're really tight."

"Maybe just put it in," I breathed, suddenly wanting to get this over with. It was starting to sting. The pleasure of earlier left my body, and I'd grown stiff. He withdrew, and I panicked he would stop, so I clung to his shoulders and rounded his ass with my legs. I didn't want to be a failure on my wedding night. He plunged back inside, but my relief was short-lived. It was like a knife had split me wide open. I cried out in agony.

He paused. He was scowling now, his mouth curled in a snarl. "You lied."

I shook my head.

"You're a virgin."

"I'm not," I sobbed. "Not in the real sense."

"Your pussy says otherwise."

I didn't answer. I had tried everything except penetration sex; I felt hypocritical to call myself a virgin.

"Natalya," his voice commanded. "Tell me the truth."

"What difference does it make?" To my horror tears scalded my eyes and rolled down my cheeks. Whether it was from the pain or embarrassment, I wasn't sure. "Can you finish, please? And get it over with."

He cursed. "It's too late anyway. I would have prepared you better." He resumed moving, but he was gentle. The area between my thighs grew slicker, but I knew it was a different wetness. Soon, the scent of metal reached my nose.

"You should have told me." He rocked gently and wiped the tears from my eyes. He kissed the tip of my nose. "It'll be better next time. I promise."

"I know," I whispered back. As the pain faded, relief filled my chest. "It's hurting less now."

He nodded tightly, jaw clenched, and sped up his thrusts. He was watching me, and I forced a smile on my face. All I felt was a dull fullness now. His eyes squeezed shut, and he stilled. A brief flash of agony crossed his face before he groaned and warmth gushed inside me. It was oddly soothing.

He collapsed on top of me. And at that moment, we were in sync. Our heartbeats, our breathing, our nakedness. A sheen of sweat cloaked our skin, and the smell of sex surrounded the room.

Finally, Luca looked up. "I'll run you a bath."

"You don't have to. I'll take a warm shower."

He shifted and glimpsed between us. A triumphant grin formed on his lips. "Should we hang the bedsheet as proof of your virginity?"

Mortified, I said, "Please don't."

He sighed. "Why didn't you tell me you were a virgin?"

"You said you didn't want to hear about my boyfriends."

A satisfied smile touched his mouth. "Well, now I know they didn't get very far…"

I averted my gaze. "I don't feel that innocent."

"To me you are, *tesoro*." His fingers guided my face back to look at him.

"I just don't feel so innocent," I repeated.

He scanned my face, and I tried to look away again but his fingers prevented the movement. "All right. But I won't touch you again tonight."

I didn't know whether to be relieved or panicked. "I'm sure I'll be fine—"

"Natalya," he said softly. "I'm not a monster." But he followed the words with a devilish grin. "I'm not a saint either. But we'll save all the debauchery I have planned for our honeymoon. It'll be much more fun if you enjoy it."

"I did love it when you had your mouth down there." A blush scorched my cheeks.

"That's a start. Now, let me get you into a bath." He pushed off me and stood. In the contrast of darkness and moonlight, the lines of his muscular frame were so stark, I couldn't help the sigh that escaped me when he headed into the bathroom and presented me with his fantastic ass.

I was so looking forward to being debauched.

CHAPTER
Three

I had been to Paris many times, but with Luca, he had opened my eyes to experience the city of love through a different lens. The food was tastier, browsing through the art of the masters in the museums was more interesting, and the walk along the Seine was more romantic. He also fulfilled his promise that next time, the sex would be better, and it was. He made love to me over and over, worshiping my body each time. Still, I felt his restraint. He was too gentle for all the promise in his eyes and the power behind that body that sometimes I urged him to take me harder.

His response was always, "Not yet."

It had been a week since our wedding.

Luca owned the apartment duplex that was part of a Haussmann building at the 8th Arrondissement. The interior was retro modern. The walls were white, and the trimmings were darkish brown. Deep orange and blue furniture provided a splash of color. Hollywood icons of the golden age were depicted in black-and-white photographs juxtaposed with colorful images of pop art. Luca mentioned he bought the property from a successful film producer of '50s cinema, and since it was decorated by a world-renowned interior designer, he left it as it was.

"But you're my wife now," he told me. "You have free reign to do what you want with the place." Then he added with a wink, "Just don't bankrupt me."

On our flight to Paris, he'd given me a black credit card and another one that would access our joint bank account. Seeing my name on the card, "Natalya Moretti," gave me a sense of a new life. A new life where some things would never change. The building had top-notch security, and his men were always in the background. A reminder that we were not the typical newlyweds and Luca was the don of the Chicago mob.

Mid-January in Paris was chilly, almost freezing. And though I basked in the coziness of renowned dining establishments, I was feeling wifely and suggested eating in tonight.

I was making bouillabaisse.

Luca and I went shopping for ingredients this morning at Rue Montmartre and I couldn't have enjoyed shopping for ingredients more, like haggling with my basic French over the price of seafood at a poissonnerie. Fortunately, Luca was fluent, but he didn't step in unless he had to. The last time I'd been in Paris, I was with Mamma to attend a fashion show. We stayed at hotels. I couldn't care less about clothes or fashion or the high society Mamma surrounded herself with. I went along because it was an armor I put up to hide my true interest.

I went to NYU to get an accounting degree because, according to Mamma, if I wanted to go to college instead of finishing school where they could prepare me to be a don's wife, that would be more useful. As if all I aspired to in life was to mind the household budget and raise children. I didn't need an accounting degree for that.

Since we'd arrived in Paris, Luca probably was away from my side for a total of five times. Tonight, he went to meet a business partner and said he would be gone for an hour or two. It was a reminder that even though we were married, he was still the head of an organization with dealings he kept from his wife. He was allowed to keep his secrets because I had my own.

To everyone, including my family, I was a meek and obedient daughter who was now the new bride of the Chicago don. The latter I aspired to be, the former was a lie. My one act of rebellion in my teens sent my mother to the hospital with a heart attack that nearly killed her. Up to this day, she loved to remind me of my role in her almost demise. It took years for me to understand it wasn't my fault, but I had to build an alter ego to keep the peace.

Luca was my knight in shining armor in more ways than one.

When he saved me from the clutches of a deranged Frankie Rossi, he was like an avenging angel, barging into the room, shooting at thugs in the hallway before he barricaded us until help arrived.

I couldn't keep my secrets forever and I hope once I'd established my life with Luca, I could build another layer to protect myself from the people after me. Frankie Rossi didn't hold me captive simply because I was Vincenzo Conte's beloved daughter. It was because he discovered I was the hacker who disrupted their human trafficking operations with the Russians. No one else knew except him and my asshole cousin Santino. They were both dead. I was safe. For now.

I checked the time on my watch. Luca wouldn't be home for another hour. I walked to our bedroom and hauled out my carry-on. I unzipped the bag and extracted my beloved laptop. A hacker had many devices, but this was my main one and the only one I hadn't destroyed when I realized I'd been compromised. I booted it up and logged on.

I received a message from my contact simply known as Doriana.

"That was a wonderful dinner, baby," Luca said into my ear. As was our routine after dinner, he stood behind me with his arms wrapped around me while we stood on the tiny balcony overlooking the Paris landscape. I wished we could stay here forever.

"Thank you," I said. "I hope I won't suck as a wife."

He turned me around and tipped up my chin. "You're perfect, *capisce*? You're more than I could ever hope for. I hope I make you happy?"

I smiled. "Don't I look happy?"

"Maybe you're being influenced by your surroundings." His dark eyes sobered, and he sighed. "When we're back in the States, I'm going to be a very busy man."

I put my hands on his chest. "And you have me to make it easier."

"You're so young…" He caressed my cheek with the back of his fingers. "I feel guilty for plucking you out of college and denying you all the fun you deserve."

A feeling of unease crept into my voice. "You said I could continue my degree."

"I know what I said, but with everything that's going on, you might have to stay at my mansion near LaSalle."

"And you'll be in Chicago?"

"That's where I need to be."

"But I want to be there with you."

His face hardened briefly before he dropped his arms from around me and headed inside.

"Luca?" I followed him, where he poured us more wine. He handed me a glass. I accepted without thinking and took a sip.

"I want you with me as much as possible, baby."

"Then no more nonsense about sending me to the mansion." I lowered my wine and stepped into him. Luca's eyes darkened. He usually instigated our sexual encounters, but I'd gained enough confidence to seduce him when I wanted sex.

"Because." My fingers lowered to his buckle, slowly working his belt free. I palmed his cock. He hardened rapidly. "Who else is going to do this to you?" I kept my eyes on him. His face was a blank mask, but I knew he did this when he was fighting for control. And it thrilled me to make him lose it. I lowered the zipper and gripped the length of his erection behind his boxer briefs. "Oh, you're so hard."

"And you're my little temptress," he hissed. "What are you going to do to convince me?"

I smirked and dropped to my knees.

I was looking up at him, and one of his hands dug into my hair, while the other brought his wine to his lips like I was of no consequence, a woman used to service him. Was it so wrong that I found it so stimulating to feel debased like that?

Freeing his erection, I swallowed the tip and wrapped a hand at the base. Luca was long and girthy. His cock was veined and beautiful like the rest of the man. His fingers tightened in my hair and my scalp stung. I paused, not taking all of him. I wanted him to force me. I withdrew and licked around the head.

"You have to do better than that, pretty girl." He shoved my head down, and the tip hit the back of my throat. My gag reflex was strong. My eyes watered and I grew wet as I let him use me. I kept up with him, trying to choke me on his cock. This was the side of Luca that lurked beneath the surface.

He yanked me away from his cock and forced me to look at him. "Are you sure you're ready for harder, baby?"

"Show me."

Something flashed in his eyes, and a slight anxiety dropped in my stomach. He forced me back on his cock. I was growing so wet with his domination, I couldn't believe I enjoyed getting used like this. He was as hard as an iron pike. Suddenly, I was off his cock, and he hauled me from the floor, dragging me to the living room where he pulled me down to the floor in front of the fireplace.

"Don't be gentle, please," I begged. "Do me hard."

His mouth curved into a snarl. "I believe you're ready, wife."

I was on my back, my panties were gone, and he tossed my legs over his shoulders and put his mouth on me. He devoured me with a savagery, making it hard to catch my breath. I didn't last long. I was so aroused from sucking him, and I climaxed. But Luca wasn't done. After wringing me out and making my voice hoarse from screaming, he shoved my knees up to my ears and entered me. He pounded into me as if he hated me.

"Is this hard enough for you?" he growled.

"Yes. Yes," I cried.

"You like it when I treat you like a slut?"

The word burned my ears, and I stared dazedly up at him. "I don't know."

"Let's find out." He continued thrusting away, and I…loved it.

And I loved it more when he stared into my eyes and rasped, "Look at you,"—he bottomed out at the hilt—"taking all of me like a good girl."

When he grunted his release, he fell on top of me, crushing my breath.

He was breathing hard. We said nothing for a few moments.

Finally, he raised his head and searched my face. "You okay?"

The stoic facade was gone, and the familiar warmth of my loving husband was back.

"I think I am." I carefully flexed my legs, but my limbs were like Jell-O.

He was still staring at me, studying my face, when he pushed off me and tucked himself back in. That was when I realized he was still fully dressed. I found that strangely gratifying, too, that I could make him lose control where he couldn't be bothered to take off his clothes.

He gave me a hand up, but then his phone buzzed on the counter and he walked toward it.

I was left with cum trickling down my legs. If this was the slut treatment, I wasn't too keen on it, like I was just another fuck and not a recipient of cuddling or a warm bath. Conflicted, I marched past Luca and he watched me pass him like he didn't just fuck my brains out.

Fine, I was rolling with the slut treatment. I should stop overanalyzing everything my husband did or I would lose my mind. Entering the bathroom, I shifted my thoughts to the faux fur rug in front of the fireplace, making a note to throw it in the washer. Maybe I should remove it all together from there except it provided a nice buffer against the hardwood floor.

Depending how often we came to Paris and how often Luca decided to fuck me blind in front of that fireplace, we might have to change the flooring. I winced. I'd hate to rip out the hardwood floor.

Smiling briefly at my wifely duties when it came to interior design, I stepped into the shower. I was rinsing the shampoo from my hair when I heard something.

"Luca, is that you?"

"Who else would it be?" his amused voice asked.

Clearing the suds from my eyes, I saw a blurry image of him through the glass of the shower. "Well, just making sure."

"No one will get past the first-floor security."

"That's good to know." I rinsed the soap from between my legs. "Is everything okay?"

"Yes, just Carmine wanting to know when we could meet."

My heart squeezed. "I'm so thankful for you helping him out like this."

"It's no problem. I told Vincenzo, I'd do it."

My poor papà. He didn't have a son to take over, but at least his daughter married someone who could help him train his successor. My crazy cousin Santino knew exactly who to target when he wanted to take down Papà and wiped out most of his inner circle. To maintain control of the Galluzo, Papà needed the reputation of someone like my husband. I could feel my whole body blushing. Even through the fogged-up glass, I could feel his gaze piercing into me. That he could switch this on and off intrigued me. The wildcard, the maverick. These were monikers attached to Luca Moretti.

I turned away from the glass enclosure as if I wanted to hide the wide grin that broke across my face. *My husband*, I thought smugly. Not only was he super alpha like the way I loved my romance heroes, he fucked a lot like them too.

"You're going to turn into a prune, *tesoro*," he drawled.

"You're still here?" I teased.

"I love to see my wife…getting wet."

And just like that, my poor pussy, which had been pounded to oblivion, pulsed with a different heat that had nothing to do with the shower. Would I ever get enough of him? "I love your dirty mouth, *caro*."

"Part of the package."

I peered at him through the misted glass. He had crossed his ankles and arms, leaning a hip languidly on the counter. He'd taken off his shoes and was barefoot.

"I can't wait to sample the rest of the package," I said with all the sultriness of a bad porn star. I had to stifle a laugh.

"Are you seducing me, wife?"

Turning off the shower, I squeezed my hair. I needed to touch up my brown roots soon. First order of business when we returned to Chicago.

The shower door opened, and I was engulfed in a towel. Now this was more my speed. I loved Luca's attentiveness.

"I'll get your clothes wet," I breathed against his mouth.

His intense gaze made it difficult to say anything else, and it wasn't because he locked me tightly with his arms.

"I don't care." His eyes fell on my toiletry bag. He wrapped the towel around me and picked up my birth control pills. "You're still taking these?"

"Yes. I mean, I wasn't sure..." When Luca had been courting me, we did mention children when it was time. I remembered telling him I wanted to finish college first.

"I want a child," he clipped. "A son."

"Uhm..."

"Right now," he continued. Walking over to the toilet, he started emptying the pills.

"Luca!" I screeched. "What are you..." Those were all the words I could manage as he flushed the pills and chucked the container into the trash, then he whirled on me, determination in his gaze.

Closing the short distance, his hand shot out and yanked me toward him. "I want a son." The carnal heat in his eyes ravaged me.

"I don't know if—"

"No if, Natalya—" Roughly, he spun me around, bent me over the bathroom counter, kicking my legs apart.

"You can go again?"

I heard his derisive chuckle followed by his zipper, then he lowered his mouth to my ear and said, "I'm not fulfilling my duty in this if I can't perform, no?"

Before I could digest his words, he shoved inside me so hard, we both groaned. I was wet as hell, and because he had just fucked me, he slid in easily. He grabbed my hips and pounded into me. I tried to grab at the corners of the counter, but my hands kept slipping, not able to keep up with his forcefulness. I couldn't even understand what this was. He fucked like I was a receptacle to slake his lust. But that was my mind trying to frame this and I should just revel in his possession. I gave way to the instinct that was as old as time. The instinct to mate. Soon, I was rearing my ass into his hips as he drilled into me harder. Our sounds bounced off the tiles. His grunts, the slapping of flesh, my moans.

His fingers came around us to rub my clit, and I flew.

I came, almost blacking out in its intensity. He went over the edge, his cock pulsing deep inside me, shooting cum.

My husband's domination of me was complete. Enslaved to his lust.

CHAPTER
Four

NATALYA

As much as getting me pregnant seemed to be the directive in Luca's brain, making love to me was not all that he did. He excelled in the romance department too. Of course that led to more sexy times, which I guess contributed to his goal of putting a baby inside me. Although if I were honest with myself, sometimes he fucked me as though he didn't care for me, but then he'd turn around and do this…

We were sitting at a well-known café in front of the Arc de Triomphe, the famous Paris arches and a symbol of this beautiful city apart from the Eiffel Tower. After our drinks had arrived, Luca got up and disappeared. I saw him talking to one of his soldiers, Tony, who handed my husband a box of chocolates. I recognized the exquisite packaging of mint bows and an espresso-colored box. It was from the chocolatier I loved whose establishment was beside the restaurant.

"Oh my goodness," I said with glee when Luca returned to our table and handed me the box. "How did you know I was going to ask you to stop by later?" I had eaten the last piece this morning.

"I pay attention, *tesoro*." The smile he shot me made me giddy.

I hurriedly lifted the cover of the box, and my heart rolled under my chest when I saw it was the copycat selection of what I had bought. I picked up a cocoa-dusted one, took a bite, and let the decadence enrobe my tongue. I lifted my chin and puckered my lips.

Luca laughed, a rich, indulgent tone as melty as the chocolate in my mouth. His mouth fastened on mine and we kissed for a while.

A clearing of the throat broke us apart.

Our server Francois returned to take our orders.

"Ready to order lunch? Monsieur, madame?"

Luca ordered the bistro steak; I ordered the duck confit.

When Francois left, Luca took my hand and played with the diamond ring and the wedding band. "So, what do you want to do this evening?"

"It's going to rain. Paris is lovely in the rain," I said with a dreamy sigh.

My husband's beautiful lips pouted in the little-boy sulk that was so incongruent with his entire persona and yet it suited him. I also welcomed it because it closed the distance between our ages.

"Surely you're not suggesting we walk in the rain like that movie last night?"

I took a sip of my wine, happy he actually paid attention to the movie we watched. "That is exactly what I was suggesting."

"It's going to ruin my suit."

"If they're worth that exorbitant price tag you pay for them, they should hold up."

He arched a perfect brow. "That's not how it works. And I'm wearing expensive shoes."

This time, I was the one who pouted. "Please?"

His gaze lowered to my mouth. "What do I get out of this?"

I leaned in to whisper in his ear. "You can fuck my mouth any which way you please."

He leaned back and watched me with hooded eyes and a lazy grin. "I've created a temptress."

I speared an olive from the antipasto plate, and with elaborate flair, sucked it into my mouth. "Hmm, this tastes good with the chocolate."

"That's an abomination, *tesoro*." He made a disgusted face.

"Salty and sweet?"

He regarded me carefully. "You couldn't be pregnant already?"

I stilled, and my heart dropped before my mind dismissed the impossibility. "It doesn't work that way. It's only been a week since you went caveman over my pills."

He leaned closer, saying softly, "But I've gone without a condom from the beginning. And we've been fucking nonstop. That would make it over two weeks."

My heart continued to pound. My period was due to begin soon, which meant the first time we had sex had been my most fertile days. I gulped. "It's still too soon to say."

Francois returned to swap out the empty breadbasket with more French baguette. Then he inquired if we needed anything else. When Luca and I gave a negative response, he disappeared again.

"But not inconceivable," Luca said.

"Unless you have super sperm."

He smirked.

I rolled my eyes before looking around because it was ridiculous to bring this up in a crowded restaurant. "I'm going to get my period tomorrow and I'm very regular. So if I miss, there is a possibility."

"You said you're very regular."

"There is that fact, Monsieur Moretti," I said coquettishly. "But with the stress of the wedding, the wedding night, the traveling…all have been known to disrupt it. And can we not talk about this here? You're trying to get out of walking in the rain."

Luca sighed. "You're hell-bent on dragging me to do it."

I batted my eyes at him. "Won't you do it with me, my love?"

I'd been in the moment when the endearment fell from my lips. A noose strangled my throat and shut down my vocal cords. I couldn't take back the words or make light of them, but then a charming smile stretched his mouth, and elation filled my lungs. Right before he picked up my hands to kiss the back of my fingers, I thought I saw a flash of contempt in his eyes.

He kissed my knuckles. "Of course, baby."

Even when he met my eyes again and they were full of warmth, that passing expression unnerved me.

Francois returned with our orders and for the rest of lunch we talked about things other than pregnancy and Paris in the rain.

We did not walk in the rain that night. Something came up, and I knew it wasn't something deliberate on Luca's part because Dario Falcone, Luca's consigliere, and my cousin, who wasn't really my cousin by blood Carmine Calabrese were involved. I heard my husband talking to Carmine on the phone. It wasn't Luca's usually calm derisive tone, but there was a bit of agitation. I doubt it was because he broke his promise to me.

Carmine sent me a text apologizing for intruding on our honeymoon. Luca told me not to wait up for him but he made sure I wasn't alone for the night, leaving Tony and Rocco to keep me company. They were an odd pair. Tony was tall and skinny with a head of salt-and-pepper hair, while Rocco was a head shorter and stockier. He reminded me of a bulldog. He also had a shaved head. Tony was more talkative than Rocco. After a reasonable amount of time in their presence, I told them I was going to bed. I hadn't contacted Doriana since that night Luca threw out my birth control pills.

My husband had kept me busy, and tonight was the only night I could boot up my laptop. I also brought out my DEC-phone. Doriana's Encrypted Channel. That was the only way we communicated by text other than through my laptop. Booting both devices, I logged in to a gaming chat room and entered the code.

The Wi-Fi in this apartment was secure enough, but not for me. Once Luca had given me access, I was able to modify it to my needs, and most importantly, access the audit trail to remove my digital footprint.

I smirked. Because I was that good.

I brought up the message from Doriana (D0R15N7). My own Dark Web handle was Chimera (Ch1M3R2), not really an uncommon username on this secretive layer of the internet since a chimera was a mythical creature made of several animal parts, and in my case, identities.

Doriana: Are you available?

Chimera: I'm here.

The time and date of the job was ten days after our scheduled return from Paris.

While I waited for a reply, I opened the packet that would give me the job details like time, event, and type of network security. I could usually hack through most of them, although they were getting more sophisticated. The key most of the time was to search for infrastructure weaknesses of the software they already used. Hacking took time and practice, and I'd been out of practice since Santino kidnapped me. Also, I was suffering a confidence issue because I got caught. But I still had the two hundred million dollars stashed in Swiss accounts and cryptocurrency. Doriana wanted me to hold on to the money because we'd been compromised at the same time and she was trying to keep her eggs in different baskets until she was safe.

The only two people who knew about the money were dead. And Doriana, of course, because she was the one who set up the heist.

The chat pinged.

Doriana: Finally.

Chimera: I told you I was lying low.

Doriana: So, can you take the job?

Chimera: I'm surprised you haven't given it to someone else.

Doriana: The Friar is on standby.

The Friar was my rival on almost every job. He was an egotistical hacker, but Doriana seemed to enjoy working with him, too.

Doriana: I was giving you another three days because he's been monopolizing all the jobs.

I grinned.

Chimera: I'm honored.

Doriana: So, are you taking it?

I looked at the images she sent me. God, these teenagers couldn't be over sixteen. The pictures were from missing persons' reports. Doriana's contact within the human trafficking watchdog organization provided most of the info. The time between the snatch and the time of sale was roughly six weeks. They were being groomed for some sick motherfucker with money.

Chimera: I'll have to pass on this.

There was no response for a few seconds and then...

Doriana: Why?

Chimera: I'm not in a position to do the research.

Doriana: You're being watched?

Chimera: You can say I'm being watched, but it's not what you think.

I was married to a crime boss. I was possibly pregnant with his baby and the man was attached to me at all times. Until I had a clear-cut vision of post-honeymoon life with Luca, I couldn't commit to anything.

Doriana: Damn. I really hope you'll reconsider.

Chimera: I'm sorry.

Doriana: Let me know ASAP when you're clear.

Chimera: Will do.

I was so engrossed in the chat and looking at data, that I hadn't heard the footsteps and voices until they were right outside the door. My heart leapt into my throat. It was the damned acoustics of this room. Sometimes it had its advantages, but during times of subterfuge, it was a liability.

When the door started to open, I closed the chat window and brought up a real estate website. Since I was sitting crosslegged on the bed, I tucked the phone under my butt.

Luca walked into the room. He paused and looked at me. "Watching a movie without me?"

"Looking at real estate."

He grinned and walked to the closet. "What's it going to cost me?"

"I haven't decided yet," I replied in a petty tone.

Luca loosened his tie and started rolling up his shirtsleeve. Sigh, I could watch this man all day. He epitomized sexy in a rumpled-suit kind of way.

"Carmine and Dario came back for drinks. Since you're awake, why don't you say hi to them?"

"I guess I could." I snapped the lid closed on the laptop and surreptitiously snuck my DEC under it before putting them on top of the suitcase. I let the phone fall between the suitcase and backpack.

"I've never seen you on your laptop," Luca said.

I shrugged. "The iPad is easier for most of the things I want to do."

"Hmm..." Luca snagged me around the waist and hauled me against him. "Are you still mad at me for not walking in the rain with you tonight?"

"I forgive you."

"I also don't want you getting sick," he said. "Just in case you're pregnant."

Our lips were almost touching. I laughed lightly. "You and your obsession with getting me pregnant."

"We need to put more work into it."

"We have guests, Mr. Moretti." My tone was flirtatious.

"I should send them home."

"Come on, we can save that for later."

I gave him a chaste kiss and tried to extricate myself.

"You're still mad."

I wasn't, but I was anxious for him to forget I had a laptop.

"I can't stay mad at you." I nipped his lower lip. He groaned and claimed my mouth, his fingers digging into my butt cheeks and hauling me against him. He was hard, and I was pleased I was getting used to seducing the hell out of him.

Laughing inwardly as we broke apart, I said, "We have guests."

"So we do." He kissed my forehead. "I can boil water for tea."

"Yes, please."

After making sure I was decent for company, I walked out of the bedroom. The guys were in the living room. Tony and Rocco had left.

Carmine stood and walked over to me, giving me a hug and a kiss. "You're glowing, cuz."

"That's because I take good care of her," Luca said. "Put that in your report back to Vincenzo."

"When did you arrive in Paris?" Without waiting for his reply, I nodded to the other guy in the room.

Dario tipped his chin before lifting a beer to his mouth. His eyes were riveted on the soccer game playing on the wide-screen TV.

Luca frowned at his consigliere.

Yes, Luca. *What is wrong with him?* That was disrespectful, but right now, I didn't want to rock the boat. As Luca's consigliere, Dario was his adviser, making him a top man in the organization. He had the boss's ear. Dario had never been warm to me. But maybe I compared him too much to Carmine. When I wasn't looking, I felt his eyes watching me like a hawk. But he'd look away when I met his gaze head-on. I wondered if he was trying to keep me off-kilter.

Carmine was the one who voiced the awkwardness in the room. "Don't mind him. He didn't get his way."

"Which way is that?" I asked.

"We had a meeting with the Russians," Luca said. "It's all settled."

Code word for: This is not your problem.

Carmine got the message as well and patted me on the shoulder. "What have you been up to while we stole your husband away?"

"Oh, huh, looking at real estate on the internet." My words stumbled over each other.

My cousin regarded me for a beat and then he gave one clap to get everyone's attention. "You know what? I haven't seen this apartment. Care to give me the tour? I detest the team playing on TV right now."

"Sure…" I looked at my husband. "Luca?"

"Go ahead." He didn't look too happy. I wasn't sure if it was at Dario or Carmine, but I was sure it wasn't because of me.

Carmine escorted me from the room.

"What do you want to see?"

"That's a nice portrait of Jean Mansen," Carmine said, his hand on my elbow guided me further until we reached the black and white room. "Luca seemed eager to get rid of us, too."

"Why doesn't Dario like me? He couldn't be more obvious." In the beginning I thought it was because we were strangers and it took him a while to warm up to people, but he hadn't changed. He was Luca's best man at the wedding.

"Does he need to like you?" Carmine asked. "Let's go here." He pushed me toward the balcony.

"Ugh, it's too cold!" I protested. It wasn't. I loved this weather, but I knew I was about to get a lecture and was trying to avoid it.

He pushed me outside and then closed the French doors behind him. Still, he spoke in low tones. "Dario likes nothing to do with the Galluzo. One of the Galluzo clans killed his father."

I gasped. "I didn't know that."

"That's twenty years ago. He should let go of that shit. It was a fair war. But what I want to know, cuz, is why you brought that laptop with you?"

"I could be looking at things on the tablet."

"Don't lie to me."

"Then why do you even ask? You know I can't go anywhere without it."

"Are you doing anything illegal?"

"You know I gave that up a long time ago. Everything is so advanced now, they'd eat me alive." And my nose grew longer.

My hacking adventures started when I hacked the computers at an elite secondary school and changed my grades and a few of my friends'. There had been an uproar and Papà became concerned. He'd never been interested in the minutiae of my education, but he demanded to see my IQ and found out it was 149. By no means was I at genius level, but it was enough to cause my parents concern.

Papà paid a large amount of money to strike my transgression from record. Santino was the one who *took care* of the problem, which was why unto this day, even if he was dead, I hated him for killing my friends, the school administrator, and the teacher. Mamma also never let me forget it. She didn't directly reference people being killed, but she always said I would get someone hurt by trying to be too smart. I didn't know why everyone was in an uproar about my skills. It wasn't until Carmine explained I was a security risk, and no family would want me in an arranged marriage.

"I know you're lying. Santino told me he suspected you took their money." The money in question was the money I siphoned from the big sex trafficking auction Santino organized with the Russians without my father's knowledge.

"Well, he was wrong."

I was used to this game with Carmine. He looked out for me, but admitting anything could land me in trouble with Mamma because he was close to her, too. One could say he was our mediator. And he usually kept her off my case. But he wasn't able to intervene when Mamma suggested holding me back from attending college for a couple of years. Which was why at twenty-two I hadn't finished any higher education.

"I told you, *cara*," he said gently. "Once you're sure Luca accepts you as you are, you can do as you please. You need protection so no one can exploit you."

I breathed heavily. "He's a good husband."

Carmine chuckled derisively. "So far, I'm not seeing the wild-card nature that everyone is wary about."

Maybe because no one lived to tell it. I thought about Frankie Rossi's demise. Santino teamed up with crazy Frankie in hopes he could torture the information out of me because my cousin didn't have the balls to do it maybe because he'd known me since I was a child. No one outside of me and Luca knew who killed Frankie. Maybe he told the De Luccis, but the Galluzo didn't know and certainly not the Rossis.

"Me too. He's moody, but so are all mafia bosses."

"If they're not moody, they're not to be trusted."

I laughed. "Are you talking about yourself?"

Carmine looked at me affectionately and tucked a hair behind my ear. "You don't trust me, *cara*?"

The French doors opened, and Luca stood there, glaring at me and Carmine. "I thought you were going to show him around?"

Shit.

"I'm just indulging her a view of Paris in the rain," Carmine said smoothly, catching some of the drizzle that fell on us with his fingers. "Since you denied our poor girl that romantic experience."

If Luca's glare had physical momentum, Carmine would've toppled over the balcony and plunged to his death.

"And it's not your place to give it to her," my husband growled, grabbing my arm firmly and drawing me inside.

"He didn't like the pop art," I cut in hastily, trying to give a valid reason on why we abandoned our tour. "But how did he know I wanted to walk in the rain?"

The two men locked eyes. Carmine's eyes danced with amusement while I could sense Luca seething. I might be naïve in many things, but this was too obvious to ignore.

"Oh. I see." I tilted my head in Luca's direction. "What did you tell them?"

"Fuck," Carmine said. "I don't want to cause problems. Luca thanked us for saving his shoes from the rain, that's all."

Luca scratched his brow. "It was no big deal. I could buy another pair of fucking shoes."

"I think I'll go to bed," I announced, and extricated myself from my husband's hold. "Please give my excuses to Dario." Then I added under my breath, "Not that he'd care about my absence."

Once I got into the hallway and out of sight, I could hear Carmine laughing despite Luca's cutting remarks regarding his big mouth.

"You should just be honest with her," Carmine said.

My steps quickened, desperate to return to the bedroom, cheeks burning from a combination of humiliation and disappointment. I was sure Carmine softened the blow of what Luca really said. He always did that. He'd cause mischief, and then when it went too far, he'd fix it. No, I would not stay mad at my husband because I was hiding something worse from him. I was feeling guilty too, but I wasn't risking anything until I was secure in his love. When I reached our bedroom, I tucked the laptop and phone into the backpack.

CHAPTER
Five

It was seven days after the "walking in the rain" incident. The rain continued with brief lulls of sunshine, but there'd been plenty of opportunities for the activity in contention. Every day Luca suggested it, but if I couldn't be honest about my geeky alter ego, I could be honest at least about how I felt about his token gesture.

Today he asked me again since we were leaving for Chicago the next day.

I forced a smile. It was a small one, probably still tinged with hurt, but I said, "You know you don't want to."

"I'm trying here, Natalya." He pinched between his brows.

I shrugged. "Maybe next time we come back?"

"That might take a while. There's a lot going on in Chicago."

"Then maybe we should have cut short our honeymoon and returned sooner."

"Don't be ridiculous. What we're building here is far more important."

"Building here? You mean us?"

He looked further irritated. "The merger between our two families. That's what."

I shouldn't be hurt. Ours was an arranged marriage to strengthen the alliance between our families. Our honeymoon in Paris was so magical, but in the last week I had been feeling anxious.

Ever since I found out that he told the men about my romantic whim, things never went back to normal. A wariness sprung up between us. We were like opponents circling each other, but I knew what was bothering me the most.

I'd fallen in love with my husband, and I wasn't sure if he loved me back.

Sometimes I saw love in his eyes.

Sometimes I thought I'd imagined it.

And how could I forget that flash of contempt I saw in the restaurant?

So yes, things weren't back to normal because I didn't know what our normal would be after we returned to the United States.

But I was determined to make this work. Luca was known in the underworld as a silver-tongued devil who could charm a snake, as well as cut off its head in the same breath. I was a recipient of that charm, and married to that power, and I needed to return his cutting replies with understanding. I was a don's wife. I couldn't distract him with my petulance, especially when he had a lot to deal with.

I stepped into his space and wrapped my arms around his neck. "Well, then after? Paris will always be here. It's not going anywhere. And maybe…" I smiled impishly. "You'd be so in love with me then, you'd be begging me to indulge you."

His eyes gleamed predatory, making me shiver. I loved those

primal displays because they usually led to him fucking me senseless and owning me with his body. The hint of it disappeared to be replaced by tenderness. I was getting used to my husband's mercurial moods. No wonder his enemies were wary of him, and I couldn't believe Carmine wasn't aware of this when he could read people well.

Luca caressed my cheek gently. "I'm sorry, *tesoro*. I didn't mean to snap at you." He locked me in an embrace, his hands lowering to my ass, fingers digging into my butt cheeks to lift me up against him. "Tell me how to make it up to you."

We could easily have sex again. I was sure that was the tension I felt radiating from him. And as much as I loved having sex with my husband, and the many ways he brought me pleasure, I loved nothing more than just sitting beside him and watching one of my romantic movies. I had the perfect one in mind.

"Have you ever watched *Casablanca*?"

"Are you sure that's what you want to do on our last night?" There was an indulgent, almost puzzled look on his face, so despite the hardness growing against my belly, sex wasn't all my husband wanted either.

"And for you to make me hot chocolate." I played with the collar of his dress shirt.

He lowered me to my feet. "You've been eating a lot of sweets lately."

"Yes…"

"It's been a week since you missed your period."

"Oh, you've been counting?" I teased. I knew it because he'd already bought the pregnancy tests.

"Yes, I have, and I'm very sure I've successfully made you pregnant."

"What if it's not a boy? Will you be disappointed?"

"Then we'll try again." He grinned devilishly. "You enjoy the process as much as I do."

I laughed. "Yes, I do, but before we end up doing something else, you owe me a movie."

Two hours later, Luca was making commentary on Humphrey Bogart's character, Rick.

"He made the wrong choice."

"Right?" Tucked contentedly to his side, I finished my hot chocolate even before the movie started and I had Luca make me a big bowl of popcorn. "But then, if it were a happy ending, it wouldn't be a classic."

Luca leaned forward to grab his beer, emitting a brief chuckle. He was eating the leftover boeuf bourguignon I made the other day. The drapes of the picture window were open to the Paris landscape —a partial view of the Eiffel Tower, gray skies, a light drizzle, and the haunting fog were the perfect backdrop for enjoying the acclaimed black-and-white film.

"So would you have made the same decision as Rick?"

"That's a loaded question, *tesoro*, but I certainly wouldn't be leaving a woman who looked like Ingrid Bergman behind to the other man."

As the end credits rolled by, I snuggled back into him when he sat back. "If you were Rick, what would you have done?"

He glanced down at me with amusement. "I think you forget I'm not an honorable man."

"So you will not let me leave with another man?"

"Let me answer this correctly," he said. "Because I do not want to sleep on the couch on our last night in Paris."

I laughed. "It's a simple question."

"No, it's not," he shot back. "For starters, the situation is different. And like you said, it wouldn't be a classic if Rick left with Ilsa and left that poor schmuck of a husband behind."

"He had an honorable cause."

"And I'm not honorable, so at face value, if I were Rick, I would have left with Ilsa and abandoned what's-his-name to deal with his cause. And I would have had no guilt."

"Not even a little?" I pulled away so I could take in his expression more clearly.

He tipped his beer bottle at the TV screen. "In most movies, I'd be considered the villain."

"Or an antihero. If you look at the top films of the AFI, The Godfather is one of them," I said. "The most interesting people are faced with moral choices and they are faced with doing the right thing."

Luca smiled at me faintly and brushed the hair out of my eyes. "I hate to disappoint you, baby, but I don't care whether or not I do the right thing."

"You give yourself so little credit," I said. "How can I forget you saved me from Santino and Frankie?"

"And I used my niece to do it." A hardened edge entered his voice.

My gaze dropped to my hands, remembering how Sera had almost died. "I'm surprised she doesn't resent me." I looked up. "I'm surprised *you* don't resent me."

A wry smile curved his mouth. I couldn't tell if it was one of regret or one of resignation. "The end justifies the means."

It wasn't the answer I was hoping for and I couldn't find the right words to say.

Luca tipped my chin up. "Let's do that pregnancy test."

A puff of laughter escaped me. "Why are you so keen on getting me pregnant? We've got all the time in the world."

"No, we don't," he said. "Remember what awaits us in Chicago."

I wasn't suggesting again that we should have returned sooner.

Anxiety and its best friend doubt planted an enormous seed of mindfuckery in my gut. But in my gut also sprung hope. Luca must care for me. There were things he didn't have to do like watch endless romance movies with me, and how could I forget how he paid attention to which chocolates I liked? A child would bring us closer. He loved his niece. Surely he'd love his own baby and the mother of his child.

"Of course." I pressed my lips against his. "Now let's see if all your hard work paid off."

CHAPTER
Six

Fuck me.

She's pregnant.

Natalya glanced up at me. "You're going to be a father."

I smiled despite how her words sent every cord of muscle cringing with anxiety. She buried her face in my chest and I hugged her close, even when there was an overwhelming urge to tear myself away.

I kissed the top of her head. "Thank you, *tesoro.*"

And as my wife sighed contentedly into my chest, guilt formed like a raised welt on top of the anxiety. But I smashed, stomped, and squeezed them into my end-justifies-the-means compartment.

My eyes met their reflection in the mirror.

There was no joy, and I tried not to flinch at the devious calculation I saw in them.

For three weeks, I played the doting husband. I was so good at it, sometimes I fooled even myself. I'd been saddled with a weak woman controlled by her mother, but her pedigree was everything. My goal was to make my wife fall in love with me and win her loyalty. I'd accomplished that in under a week, and now whenever she looked at me with stars in her eyes, I'd been anxious to accomplish my next goal.

A child would solidify the alliance between the Morettis and the Contes. After Santino wiped out most of Vincenzo's inner circle, Natalya's father was desperate to have a direct descendant who could keep his line alive and take over his position. Carmine was acting underboss for his kingdom, but he didn't have enough support among the different clans. They saw him as an outlier, a bastard son of a soldier of no consequence, but he had the education and the mind of a politician, which was what Vincenzo needed to manage the Galluzo. He tapped me to help Carmine learn the ropes of high-stakes negotiations with other organizations, specifically the Russian mafia. I smothered a groan that I didn't need that headache, but the ambition of being the most important man in the underworld was too tempting.

"What's wrong?" Natalya asked. Her luminous eyes radiated adoration and a little apprehension that heightened my guilt.

I struggled for something to say. "I never thought I'd be this overwhelmed."

She laughed into my shirt. I liked her laughter. Like her hair, it was all sunshine, and it lifted the cloudiness of my moods. That was another thing that pleased me in our union. She didn't irritate me too much except that time she suggested walking in the rain. I only indulged her romantic notions to get her quickly with child. Now that I'd accomplished the task, it was time to pull back.

After a few seconds, she lifted her eyes again, merriment still etched there. "Just wait until you have sleepless nights with the baby keeping you awake."

Fuck.

"The horror." The grin I shot her scourged another welt on my conscience. And once again, I forced my conscience to justify my actions. It was too soon to tell her I didn't intend to be around to do all the raising. I had no desire to be attached to the baby or the mother. I would take care of them, and I would love them in my own way, but not to the point of weakness. It was okay if they loved me, but I wanted loyalty more than anything else, and with women, to gain loyalty was to first gain their love.

Sera was the perfect example. I had her loyalty until she'd gone and fallen in love with a De Lucci. The only way to get my niece to do my bidding was to threaten the man she loved.

My first duty was to the Moretti crime family.

Natalya, as my wife, would understand this soon enough.

CHAPTER
Seven

"This was built in 1893," Luca said.

I'd seen pictures of the Moretti mansion before. I didn't want to be here. I'd envisioned a life with Luca in Chicago, not here. My husband assured me there were enough things to keep me occupied.

"It's very beautiful." I couldn't keep the sarcasm out of my tone.

He gave me a long look before sighing. "You're not excited?"

"I just don't understand why I can't stay with you in Chicago. I don't even know what your penthouse over there looks like." During our whirlwind courtship, he'd been in New York doing the wooing while I'd been staying at the De Lucci mansion. And in the days leading to our wedding, he set me and my family up at the Ritz.

"It's not conducive to your pregnancy."

"I'm barely four weeks pregnant."

"I will repeat one more time," he said in a tone I'd heard him use when he wanted the last word. "Do you think I don't prefer living here instead of going to every seedy underground establishment with Dario and Carmine to make sure your father's business stays intact?"

I didn't know if I was being selfish and thought my marriage to Luca would be different from Mamma's, who seemed content with Papà's status and money. She preferred to be away from Papà. Maybe after ten years of marriage, I'd feel the same, but not right now. I didn't want to be separated from him after our wonderful time in Paris. I stared out the window without answering.

At my silence, he continued, "I gave you three weeks. That's more time than I've given any single person."

"I sure hope so," I retorted. "Because I'm your wife."

"Goddammit, Natalya," Luca snapped.

I flinched. It was the first time he'd paired my name with that expletive.

"What do you think is happening here? Surely you're not ignorant about being a wife of a boss. I expected better from you."

"And I expected better from this marriage!" I raised my voice and quickly said, "I'm sorry."

"You're being emotional because of your pregnancy," he said. "I forgive you."

Fuck you, Luca. "That's probably it." I surreptitiously wiped the tears from my eyes. I doubted tears would work with my husband, and I detested using them with histrionics like Mamma. How could he bear to be separated from me when he was at my side in Paris almost every waking hour?

"I'll stay overnight." Luca's words made me feel worse. Now it sounded like he was doing me a favor, and I required so little. "Then I'll return to take you to see the doctor in two weeks' time."

"What am I supposed to do for two weeks?"

"There's an entire house to make your own." He took my hand

in his and kissed the back of my fingers. "Make a home for our family. A house you will be proud to call your own. Casa Moretti is yours now." I looked at him finally, and feeling my gaze, he cast me the brief, charming smile I'd loved from the beginning. It did a little to lift my spirit, but not the angst that I wouldn't be seeing him for two weeks.

Iron gates of the estate opened automatically to a long tree-lined driveway. The property was expansive, decorated with perfectly manicured lawns and Italian gardens. And even as I rebelled against the idea of being left alone, guilt also plagued me. Were my ideals too modern for a mafia bride? Maybe living with Sera at the De Lucci mansion for a few weeks had skewed my views. She was Luca's niece, after all, and I could see how she was treated as an equal. Not just tucked away to mind the household, she was involved in business, granted it was on the legitimate side of things.

I tried to drum up excitement. The house was gothic looking and reminded me of *Jane Eyre*. Hmm, I glanced over at Luca. Was he my Mr. Rochester?

The Escalade came upon a roundabout with a tiered bronzed sculpture. I didn't have time to get a good look at the figurines because the mansion door opened. I recognized Angelo "Ange" Moretti, Luca's half brother from their father's first wife. He was Luca's underboss. Ange was forty-four, ten years older than Luca, and barrel chested compared to my husband's broad-shoulders-to-trim-waist proportions. Ange reminded me of the guys who lifted heavy weights but were terrible about their diets. Trailing Ange was Martha the housekeeper of Tralestelle. Her hair was almost all gray and was gathered in a nape bun. I'd met her once. There were two younger women behind her in maid's uniforms. They were not familiar.

Luca stopped in front of them while the SUV carrying Dario, Tony, and Rocco parked behind us.

We got out of the vehicle and Martha immediately came forward.

"Pleased to see you again, Mrs. Moretti." She actually curtsied and introduced the girls Yvonne and Nessa.

"Call me Natalya, please."

Ange shot me a brief nod and immediately pulled Luca aside and whispered in his ear.

My husband leaned away, and I watched his strained face turn more forbidding. Remorse and self-righteousness warred inside me. In my head, I could hear Mamma lecturing me. I was married to a powerful man, and I shouldn't make it hard for him to perform his responsibilities.

"We'll talk later," he told his brother. "My office in twenty minutes." They were already heading inside the house, leaving me forgotten with Martha.

The older woman's gaze followed them, annoyance clear on her countenance, but when she turned to me, she was all smiles.

"Tralestelle mansion hasn't had a mistress ever since Luca's stepmother left."

"Beautiful name." In the stars.

"You should stand in the middle of the garden when the night is clear." We followed the men into the house. "We're far enough from any major city or town, so the lights don't pollute the view."

"The estate is quite isolated."

"It's on twelve acres of land."

As Luca, Dario, and Ange veered toward a hallway, Martha led me up a sweeping staircase that was reminiscent of the one from *Gone with the Wind*. The gold and red carpet had the faded look not from being tread on, but from the passing of time.

At the top of the stairs sat a blue-gray cat with golden eyes. He surveyed us with a curious bored expression only cats could muster.

"That's Mrs. B, and she rules the household," Martha laughed. "You'll need to show her you're the new mistress."

Before we reached the last step, the cat disappeared ahead of us.

"That looks like a British shorthair."

Martha made a humming, positive sound. "Emilio's first wife bred cats. They're all feral now and like to stay away from the mansion. Once in a while, one of them will acquire a taste of fine living and lord it over the household."

I laughed. I didn't mind cats. "How many rooms are in this house?"

"Twenty. Emilio enjoyed entertaining before his Junior died."

"Emilio Junior, right? Sera's father?"

"Yes." A sad smile settled on Martha's face. "The boss pinned so much hope on his oldest son." Then she lowered her voice conspiratorially. "But if you ask me, Luca was the smartest among all of them. He also inherited his mamma's compassion."

"Stop feeding nonsense to Natalya," Tony said from behind us. "You're making the boss sound like Mother Teresa. Don't listen to Martha."

"But that's an interesting perspective," I said.

"She saw only the boy who came home from school and went directly to check on the family of feral cats in the backyard," Rocco added. Those were the most words I'd heard from him in one sentence.

"You can tell a lot about a man by how he treats animals," Martha told them.

"I agree with that." I thought Santino was a psycho from the start. When he came over to visit Papà and we were in the backyard, he'd shoot rabbits for sport. When I cried to Papà, Santino said they were nothing but vermin.

"Luca likes animals more than people," Tony said.

"It's because humans are stupid," Martha replied.

I couldn't agree with her more. An idiot with a gun was dangerous. I'd known many of them.

The corridors of the house were wide and tastefully ornate, with exquisite woodwork. Like most houses of the mafia, paintings hung on the walls. I wasn't an expert in art history, but I wouldn't be surprised if some of them were originals.

"These are your apartments. Luca said to put you in his room."

Inwardly, I felt relief. Usually, when it was an arranged marriage, the groom might give time for the bride to adjust. But after three weeks in Paris, I would say we had fully adjusted in the activities of the bedroom.

Rocco and Tony put our stuff in the closet. A closet that took up an entire wall. I could see a row of Luca's suits in charcoal, blue, and black, arranged neatly in columns.

Luca's bedroom was very masculine. The bed had modern lines, quite unexpected given the rest of the house. Constructed of dark wood, the bedding was dark blue. The off-white walls blended into the drab beige curtains of the tall windows. Middle Eastern rugs, probably Persian or Moroccan, covered the parquet wood floor. They looked expensive.

After the two men left, I turned to Martha. "Did Luca say I have free rein to redecorate?"

"Well…"

"What did I tell you, *tesoro*…" Luca's amused voice came from the doorway. "You have my black card." He turned to Martha. "Thank you. I'll take it from here."

When the housekeeper left, Luca walked into the room and shed his jacket, then he loosened his tie and started to unbutton his shirt. "This is probably not your taste."

I crossed my arms. "Are you talking about the room or yourself?"

"Oh, baby." He smiled derisively. "I know I'm very much your taste."

He walked into the closet.

Still pissed at him, I resisted following him to where things might lead to a quick lusty romp. I'd be satiated only physically, and in the end, sex would not fix my hurt feelings of becoming an abandoned bride.

I walked to the windows to check out the estate.

My breath caught. The perfectly manicured geometric shapes of the evergreens and hedges showed they employed a full estate staff. There were fountains, rows of flowers, and varied topiaries that gave relief to the overall greenery.

Luca came up behind me. My body went stiff when his arms came around my waist and drew me into him.

"It's beautiful, no?" He rested his chin on my shoulder and I made myself relax a little.

"It is. So you grew up here?"

"Yes. I was a handful."

"Oh, I don't know. Martha said you have a soft spot for cats."

"I wouldn't believe everything Martha says." Irritation entered his voice. I sensed he didn't want any soft underbelly exposed. He turned me around. Luca had changed into a dark T-shirt and sweatpants.

"Is there anything in your wardrobe that isn't too somber?"

"My ties?"

I rolled my eyes. "We need to give you some color."

"I don't want to take too much time thinking about what to wear," he said. "Dinner will be informal tonight." He kissed the top of my forehead. "We'll eat in the kitchen. Say, seven?"

I'd been picturing ourselves having an afternoon snuggle and relax from our transcontinental trip. But I guessed he couldn't wait to get back to business.

He raised a brow. "Anything wrong?"

"No." Where the hell was he going?

"Good. See you later, baby."

He let me go and headed for the door without looking back.

When the door clicked behind him, I stared at it for long seconds, then my gaze scanned the room to take in my new life. The large emptiness and sterility of it made me feel so alone and discombobulated. Nothing diminished the glow quicker than knowing I was going to be installed in this strange mansion while he was ninety miles away.

He said he had a lot to do in Chicago. Why couldn't he give me a chance to prove that I could be his worthy mafia bride and offer support while he did it? After all, it was to help Papà's organization. Besides, didn't he say what we were building between us was more important?

Something brushed against my leg, and I nearly jumped in fright.

It was Mrs. B.

"Meow." Her tail was languidly swishing behind her, eyes looking up at me expectantly.

I picked her up. "Your master is confusing."

She began to purr.

Luca

"So how is Natalya adjusting?" Dario asked, looking away from his conversation with Ange when I stormed into the study. I went straight to the bar, poured myself two fingers of scotch, and tossed it back.

"She doesn't like it." I poured another inch of Glenlivet and took a slower sip this time, facing my consigliere and brother.

"I thought you had convinced her?" he said with an amused tone in his voice.

"You want to say something to me?" I challenged.

"As a matter of fact, yes," Dario said. "I told you she wasn't the meek little woman her parents and Carmine made her out to be."

"About Carmine," Ange interjected. "Are you seriously going to saddle me with that *stronzo*?"

"Yes." I started rummaging through the drawers and found what I was looking for. My emergency pack of cigarettes. I offered it to the men. Ange shook his head. Dario took one and smirked.

"I knew you wouldn't last." Dario picked up the lighter I tossed at him. I reached for the bronze ashtray and slid it his way.

"Natalya isn't meek and I don't want her to be." I took a much-needed drag. I felt better already. Studying the burning tip of the cigarette, I said, "I merely overcompensated."

Dario chuckled. "I can see that. I didn't recognize you in Paris."

She was easy to pamper, and if I were honest with myself, I enjoyed it. And that body of hers. Fuck, I'd never had pussy grip my cock that hard. But today, she was pissed at me. No doubt about it. I saw the heat in her eyes when I loosened my tie, but she didn't act on it. I didn't want to encourage her further either. We had our fun in Paris. "I'd given her an illusion of power. I need to correct that."

My consigliere leaned forward. "I don't like where this is going. You should have shown her exactly who you are from the beginning."

"Don't worry. You see how she is with her mamma. She's malleable. She'll adjust to what I'm capable of giving her."

"She's twenty-two. She's probably infatuated with you," Ange scoffed.

"It's more than infatuation, brother, I can assure you of that."

Dario's chair creaked as he leaned back and crossed an ankle over his knee. "She's in love with you?"

"Did you doubt I can accomplish that in three weeks? She can't bear to be away from me."

"But you want her to get used to being away from you," Dario said. "You're manipulating the poor girl."

"You're suddenly having scruples now?" I took the bottle of scotch from behind me. "Here, have another drink and get that stick out of your ass."

"Maybe I need to shove one up yours."

My eyes narrowed at Dario. "You may be my friend. And I like you. But I've shot people for less than what you've said."

We locked gazes for a moment. We grew up together. Dario had seen what I was capable of, but he and Ange were the only people I'd allowed saying shit to me like that. But what he just said rubbed me the wrong way. I didn't like the hold Natalya seemed to have over me. Not one bit. I couldn't wait to get away from her. Clear the Paris haze that had been clouding my judgment.

"And I'm your consigliere. It's my job to challenge you," Dario replied evenly.

"Look. Natalya is important to this alliance with the Galluzo." I let that statement sink into both men. "In fact, she's the only one holding it together, but that can go south quickly. I need her on my side." Because how do you get an addict further addicted? Give them a surplus and then take it away. They would be your slave for life.

"Then why do we need Carmine?" Ange asked.

"Because I promised Vincenzo I could clear his debts with the Russians. We'll be working closely with the Galluzo to repair the damage Santino inflicted on their organization. Carmine will be picking up the reins after we throw him into the deep end with the

Orlov." Vasily Orlov was the pakhan—the boss of Russian Organized Crime (ROC) in Chicago. The man who claimed Santino owed him a great deal of money and had been creating trouble for Vincenzo.

Dario choked on his cigarette. Ange grinned like Mrs. B who swallowed a canary. A smile touched the corners of my mouth while I studied the burning tip of the cigarette. "You need to be careful with him, Ange. Don't bring him to sit-downs that have nothing to do with the Russians. He has a tendency to say the wrong things."

"Jesus Christ!" Ange groaned. "You're getting back at me for the last shipment screwup, aren't you? This is punishment, right, little bro?"

The *little bro* comment didn't bother me when it was said among the three of us. Ange refrained from using that diminutive nickname in front of others. Although everyone knew how Ange had fumed when Emilio named me boss instead of him. "Maybe. But we need this to work."

Ange's face turned ugly with a sneer. "Why, so you can have control of the Galluzo, too?"

"That's ridiculous. Who wants control of that mess? It doesn't hurt to have leverage."

"Like being married to the daughter of the boss," my brother scoffed. "Isn't she too young for you? How can she manage this house? How can she manage you? I already see the petulant pout I only see in teenagers when they don't get their own way."

"She'll learn. You forget she grew up with the Galluzo and you know how Elena is. She made sure Natalya is prepared."

"Growing up in it doesn't mean she's ready. Look at your brothers. They denounced Pop, changed their last names, and fled back to Italy to rejoin the archaic nobility of your mamma's relatives."

A chill descended into the room. Ange knew better than to bring up my two older brothers and to ridicule my mother. My mother had been a contessa. She was too good for this life but she fell in love with Emilio. Sometimes I wondered if Pop married her so he'd have the money to keep up with this estate. Chicago, like all the American mafia, suffered a blow when the Feds used RICO to go after the gangsters.

"And you're forgetting if it wasn't for Mamma's money, we wouldn't be sitting in this mansion right now. Or are you still salty that it isn't you living here instead of me?"

The chill turned downright frosty.

Dario broke the ice. "Let's not dig up old wounds. We know the boss of the family stays at Tralestelle regardless of what money takes care of the estate."

"It continues to thrive because of the sweat and blood of my men," Ange argued.

"You still believe that?" I stubbed out my cigarette. "Haven't I shown you the profits from our real estate business? Your capos couldn't keep up. We have no money to launder. I'm thinking of expanding our online bookmaking business."

Ange sighed. "If only we started moving product."

"If you mean cocaine and heroin, the answer is still no. We're profitable with real estate and there's less risk involved."

I grabbed the folder Ange had laid on the table before I gave in to the urge to go for my gun and shoot the tip of his left ear. The myth of my crazy personality stemmed from an incident when I was barely eighteen. I shot the bastard from the Polish mafia who was lying blatantly to me, Junior, and Emilio in a private room of a popular restaurant. I'd been arrested and thrown into jail without bail as I awaited trial. Prison taught me a lot of things and it made me tougher. The eight months I spent in confinement worked in my favor because I thwarted several attempts to kill me. In the end, I was acquitted. At that time, going to jail was a rite of passage in the mafia, and Emilio hadn't been too worried about his succession because Junior had been a capable underboss. But when my eldest brother died, that was when Pop told me to curb my temper and not cost him another twenty million in payoffs and legal fees.

I flipped open the folder. "I'll tell you who the problem is. Orlov. Tell me where we're at with him before our meeting tomorrow."

CHAPTER
Eight

NATALYA

I spent the rest of the late afternoon in the kitchen getting to know the people who would be my companions for an indefinite period.

Nessa was the dark-haired girl in a staff uniform I had seen earlier. In her late twenties, she was Tony's niece. She did not speak because of an injury to her vocal cords. She preferred communicating with a notepad but also used an app on her phone. Her job was to cook the staff meals. Yvonne was Slovenian and seemed friendly if chattiness was a gauge of friendliness. She was blonde and twenty-six, her position was only temporary until she got her green card. Her goal was to work in one of Luca's Chicago nightclubs.

"I thought all I wanted when I got back was a juicy burger." I popped some fried okra into my mouth.

Nessa scribbled on her notepad. *They don't have burgers in Paris?*

"One day, Luca and I wanted a simple burger and went to the nearest McDonald's."

Martha made a disgusted sound. Nessa covered her mouth and made a laughing sound.

"The patty was like a hockey puck. They had beer, though. The French don't do fast food well." I lifted the cover of the enameled cast-iron pot. "This looks good. What is it?"

"Chicken and dumplings," Martha said.

"Oh, I've heard about this."

"You've never had it before?"

"I spent most of my life in Europe, although I visited the U.S. frequently. It was mostly in the bigger cities," I told her. "I did spend the last two years in New York."

"You're so young," Yvonne said. "You couldn't be more than twenty."

"Twenty-two," I replied with a trace of defensiveness. I'd always been ahead of my class and skipped grades. My parents took pride in it until the hacking incident and held me back from college for three years. Now that I thought about it, I wondered where I would be now if I hadn't done it.

Luca and Dario walked in.

"Where's Ange?" Martha asked.

"He had to leave," my husband said in a way that brooked no further probing into where his brother was. It was an interesting hierarchy where the boss was not the oldest son. Carmine had told me it had caused a lot of friction between Luca and Ange.

"Something smells good in the kitchen," Dario said. "How are you liking it here?" He was directing the question at Nessa.

She smiled big and put her hands over her chest.

"The employees were tired of English and Italian food," Luca said, taking his seat at the table in front of the counter. "If only Martha tried to learn new things."

"I am not here in a position of cook. You fired the French chef Sofia hired." She looked at me. "Emilio's third wife."

"I know who Sofia is."

"It bears repeating," Martha sniffed. "I can't keep all of Emilio's wives straight."

Dario and I laughed.

"That French chef was a snob, and he gave Emilio a heart attack with all the butter he put in his dishes."

"It's the stress." Martha put a bottle of wine on the table. "Sofia should have helped him ease it more."

"Let's not talk about Sofia. She's happy in California now." Luca scowled at his housekeeper. I met his beautiful stepmother at the wedding. Mamma told me I was lucky I didn't have to deal with living with in-laws. Nonna—Papà's mother—lived with us for many years and she clashed with Mamma often on how to run the household down to what to prepare for dinner. And for all the fierceness with how Papà ran the organization? He was a coward when it came to mediating between Nonna and Mamma.

Luca looked around the kitchen, and his scowl deepened. "What's everyone waiting for?"

After dinner, Luca and I retired to the family room. A fire was already started there, and it reminded me of our apartment in Paris. Bookshelves were built in beside the fireplace. I walked up to browse the books, thinking about my own that were still in boxes. "This is an impressive collection." I looked at the authors and titles. Charles Dickens. Hemingway. Sun Tzu's *The Art of War*. Several versions of the latter. Papà had copies of it too. It was the code of every warrior, he'd said.

"My grandfather and Emilio liked to read."

I turned to him. "And you?"

Luca was on the couch with his legs spread in a relaxed position. He twirled the scotch in his glass. "I didn't have much time. I played sports, but when I read, I preferred biographies. I didn't care much for fiction."

"Oh…"

Luca pointed to the far end of the library. "My mother was a romance book collector. They're all there. The ones behind the glass are rare editions or something."

I returned to the couch and sat beside him. "I'll check it out later. Do you mind if I add my books?"

His brows knitted. "Why would I? You are the mistress of this house now. If there's no room, you can replace them with your books."

"Oh, I would never—"

He caught my chin and speared me with a stern gaze. "Listen to me. You are the queen of this estate. Act like it."

He let go of my face and stared at the fire, taking another sip of the amber liquid.

"Did I do anything to offend you?"

"No. I just have a lot on my mind and I don't have time to bring you up to speed on what you need to do at Tralestelle. I give you carte blanche."

"Be careful what you wish for. I might just bankrupt you."

He glanced at me, smirking. "That's my girl."

"You don't have to worry about me. Martha and I will do just fine."

"Nessa is not the problem," Luca said. "Yvonne was a favor to one of my capos. Martha said she's not pulling her weight." He glanced at me. "Think you can handle her?"

"Martha will help me."

"You need to assert yourself."

"Yvonne is four years older than me."

"Age is no excuse. You. Are. My. Wife. Do you know how old I was when Emilio sent me to collect on a debt?"

"Luca…that's different."

He exhaled heavily. "Whatever. I'll be back in two weeks. Let me know if Yvonne bothers you, I'll have her transferred…or fired."

I didn't answer him. Luca didn't say anything else. He looked exhausted. I got up again and walked over to check out his mother's books. Martha said she was a kind woman. Of course, it helped she loved romance novels. I wondered what kind of husband Emilio was. Obviously, he had no problems replacing a wife since he'd been married three times.

I peered behind the glass display. They were antique-looking, leather-bound editions of *Pride and Prejudice* and *Jane Eyre*. I picked a book below the glass display. I wasn't familiar with the author, but the cover art certainly got my attention.

I glanced back at Luca. His head was thrown back and his eyes were closed.

I walked back to him, a tenderness blooming in my chest. He looked less fierce in sleep. So handsome.

"*Caro*," I said softly and shook him.

He shifted on the couch and murmured, "Not tonight, Jessica."

Ice water splashed away the warmth I was feeling. He didn't mean it. He was asleep. Should I let him sleep like that on the couch? No.

I shoved him hard.

"What the fuck?"

"You wouldn't wake up," I snapped.

"I'm tired." He scrubbed his face and then glared at me.

"Well, at least I did my duty and you won't be having a crick in your neck tomorrow morning from sleeping at an odd angle."

"Woman…" he muttered.

"I'm going to bed."

Luca didn't follow immediately. Just as well. Unlike at the wedding when I was in tears, this time, I was more territorial. She couldn't have my husband. I put my hand to my stomach. I would give Luca his son and I would become the most important woman in his life.

I was finishing up in the bathroom when he came in.

"No one wants to be jarred awake like that," he told me. "Careful, baby, you're lucky the alcohol and food relaxed me and I didn't have a gun."

"Oh, so now you're threatening me?"

He took a step behind me. "What is wrong with you?" His eyes reflected in the mirror could cut me to pieces. "I fell asleep on you. So what? If these little things bother you too much, we have bigger problems."

It took all my energy not to lash out at him. It wasn't his fault he said another woman's name in his sleep. Because of this, I didn't want him to think I was irrational either. Swallowing my pride, I said, "You said Jessica's name when I tried to wake you up."

He stilled and mouthed, "Fuck."

My blood boiled again, and I pushed past him. "Exactly."

"How is it my fault?" he said. "I was unconscious, and I certainly wasn't a virgin like you when we married."

I spun around and poked him in the chest. "What if I said another man's name in my sleep?"

He smirked. "I know he didn't get far."

The arrogant bastard. "Yes, but what if he gave better orgasms than you do?"

A dangerous gleam entered his eyes. "Then he'll be swimming with the fishes."

"See!"

I grabbed the pillows and a blanket from the bed and walked over to the couch in front of the bedroom hearth.

"What the hell are you doing?"

"I don't want to sleep beside you right now."

"Natalya." His voice was stern. "I'm giving you some leeway because of your age, but don't test me."

"Stop using my age as an excuse to treat me this way."

"What way?" he roared. The sudden increase of volume in his voice told me Luca was at the end of his patience.

"Like my feelings don't matter as long as it suits you."

"Are you saying I should apologize for saying something in my sleep? For all you know I might be having a nightmare."

I paused at this. "Maybe."

"What exactly did I say?"

I blew out a breath. "Not tonight, Jessica."

He crossed his arms. Indignation, apparently, was a shared feeling between us. "And for that, you gave me a rude awakening."

"Obviously, she's still in your subconscious."

Luca spread his arms in a helpless gesture. "I give up explaining to you. I'm not making excuses for my past sex life." He turned away from me and slammed into the bathroom, leaving me stewing in my decision whether or not to sleep beside him.

But my pride had pushed me too far. By the time he came out of the bathroom, I was snuggled cozily on the couch.

He muttered a stinging string of Italian profanity. Suddenly, I was rethinking my impulse of sleeping on the couch.

I could feel him standing in front of me. His stare was like lasers penetrating my closed eyes.

"This is ridiculous." He scooped me up. "My wife sleeps with me."

"I rest my case," I retorted.

He lowered me onto the bed. "What now?"

"You say I should sleep beside you, yet you have no problem being away from me for two weeks."

He rounded the bed and got to his side. "I'm not arguing with you. I need my sleep. If you want to return to the couch, be my guest."

Ha! Because I made a good argument, but I didn't get up. Somehow making my point and proving him to be a double-standard asshole sat well with my conscience. I stared up at the ceiling of the room where I would spend an indefinite amount of time. Until Luca decided I could join him in Chicago, I needed to make the best of my stay here.

I was thinking of my plan and then I fell asleep.

I woke up the next morning to find Luca gone by my side. It also occurred to me that was the first time we hadn't made love at night. Maybe I annoyed him too much for him to be amorous, and it bugged me he might seek his needs elsewhere.

Jessica was in Chicago.

Luca and I didn't talk about the mafia custom of having a *goomah*, an accepted practice of having a mistress. I should concentrate on using my time wisely. Mamma's words came back to haunt me. I wanted to be more than a wife. I wanted him to love being with me. Was that too much to hope for? He gave me a taste of that dream in Paris. How dare he take it away? I'd been prepared to love him enough, knowing what awaited me as a mafia wife. I'd prepared for him to take mistresses eventually, but somehow after what he showed me in Paris, I wanted more.

I wanted everything.

Our own family outside the mafia.

For him to love me in return.

That I was enough for him.

I could work on attaining that goal if I was with him.

I should give him what he wanted for now. Maybe he would

miss me. It was only two weeks. And with that resolve, I dressed quickly so I could see my husband off.

Luca was having breakfast in the main dining room, and he was scrolling through his phone. He was in his dress shirt and tie.

"I didn't hear you get up." I took my place beside him.

He lowered his phone and picked up his knife and fork to cut through a stack of pancakes. "You were out of it," he said brusquely.

"You should have woken me up." I picked up a biscuit and started to tear it apart.

He eyed me warily before returning his attention to his plate. "You stayed awake for awhile. I don't want you losing sleep."

I raised a brow.

"The baby."

I rolled my eyes. "Luca, it's not even the size of a pea."

"Your vitamins should arrive today." He shoved a forkful of pancake into his mouth.

"What?"

He finished chewing before he answered, "I've made an appointment with the doctor in two weeks."

"I'm surprised you're not so adamant about seeing a doctor now, since you seem to have planned my whole pregnancy already."

"I'm practical. I don't want to waste time if there's nothing to see, and according to the family doctor, your sixth week of pregnancy will get us the most use of my time."

I didn't know what to make of his justification, but whatever. Fine with me. I could be practical.

Nessa came in with the coffee carafe.

I smiled at her and nodded.

Luca wiped his mouth with the napkin. "One cup only."

That's it. I glared at him. "If you insist on micromanaging my pregnancy, then maybe you should take me with you to Chicago."

"I'm just letting you know I care about your health and the baby's," Luca said in a way that made me sound like a shrew. "I've left instructions with Martha."

"I'm not a child."

"Leave the coffee," Luca barked at Nessa.

The poor girl lowered the carafe and hurried from the room.

"Then don't act like one," he said.

I met his eyes. "Is this about last night again? I'm over that."

Luca studied me for a few seconds, but I didn't look away. His gaze softened. "Good girl. These things are not worth fighting about."

I tore another piece from the biscuit and stuffed it into my mouth before I choked on my lie. He pushed the sausages toward me. "Have some protein with it."

I did so dutifully. I liked how he cared for me, but there were a lot of quirks about my husband I didn't understand outside our chemistry in the bedroom and outside our time in Paris. I wouldn't be able to figure it out if I defied him at every turn.

Luca finished his breakfast and sipped his coffee while scrolling through the phone.

"What time do they need you in Chicago?" I asked.

"Not until this afternoon." He smiled. That familiar indulgent look in his eyes made me preen. "I want to spend more time with you."

I gave him an answering smile.

CHAPTER
Nine

NATALYA

It had been ten days since Luca left for Chicago. In that time, Martha helped familiarize me with the accounts. Boring stuff, but not unexpected. It did give me an excuse to work on my laptop for hours at a time. Before I reconnected with Doriana, I got the Wi-Fi password from Dario. This enabled me to get into the admin account of the network. It was secure enough, but not from me.

I worried a bit, but Dario mentioned in passing that the one in Chicago was more updated. God, I hoped so, and I believed him because online gambling was one of their more lucrative businesses.

Tony walked in with several packages that came from Doriana. I'd always used a mail-forwarding service to maintain my anonymity, even with her. It was for her protection and mine after what had happened with Santino. I wasn't sure where the leak came from and that made me more wary.

"This looks like serious stuff." Tony had been left behind to babysit me. "Should I tell Dario to send his guy?"

Among the packages was the router that would split the house network into two. And I could modify one of them and make it visible only to me.

"Oh no," I said, panicking a bit. "I communicated with the seller and it came with easy setup instructions. I might need your help when the television comes, though."

Tony shrugged and left me to it. It took me almost all afternoon to get it up and running. Doriana did not send easy instructions, but I bugged her no end on our DEC-phone.

After Luca's customary check-in that night, I got down to work. Admittedly, being away from my husband gave me the opportunity to explore the part of myself I had put on hold. Within the walls of the mansion, I felt free and secure enough to re-evaluate what the hell I wanted to do with my life. I didn't regret turning down Doriana in Paris because I wasn't psychologically ready. With a routine being established, I could micro-step back into my alter ego and see where it would lead me. I logged in to the Dark Web and brought up our chat window.

Chimera: You there?

Doriana: Welcome back, hooker.

Chimera: Glad to be back. How did that job go?

Doriana: Like taking candy from a baby.

I laughed manically.

Chimera: Were they crying?

Doriana: For sure.

Chimera: So nothing for me?

Doriana: What? There's always something for you.

That something appeared in my notifications.

Doriana: All the information is in the packet. Same organization, different group. This one is stateside. It wouldn't be for a couple of months.

Doriana and I chatted a bit more before I signed off. I opened the files and studied my mark.

~

Luca

"That was a fucking waste of time." I shoved out of Vasily Orlov's club. I could have been home fucking my wife.

"It wouldn't have been if you gave in a little," Carmine said, walking alongside me on my right. Dario was on my left with the rest of our men behind us.

"What do I know about Santino's money," I said. "Those Russians are bluffing, thinking they could swindle the Galluzo into a deal they made with Santino without Vincenzo's knowledge."

"The boss said it was okay to negotiate an amount with them," Carmine replied.

"An amount," I scoffed, patting my suit and digging for my cigarettes. It had been torture to be away from Natalya, but it was necessary for our marriage to last. I would get used to it. She would get used to it. Maybe two weeks was too short. It was too little time to adjust to being without her after spending every waking moment in Paris.

I lit up and dragged smoke into my lungs to calm my aggravated nerves before saying, "They wanted me to throw in my cargo plane."

"It doesn't cost you anything. The plane would be making the same trip," Carmine said. "You can carry their seven passengers."

"But we know what it is," Dario said. "And we don't touch that."

Carmine laughed. "Don't tell me you never looked the other way."

"Not when it comes to this shit." This shit was the sex trafficking of minors. I had no desire to be involved in that part of the Russians' business. The less I know about it, the better. If it were drugs, and they wanted to use my ship, I'd let them. I never took a cut from it, but it was understood that I would ask a favor in return. People had a choice when it came to drugs. But I drew the line when humans were used against their will. A muscle twitched under my eye. Especially when they were minors.

"Vincenzo wants an update soon," Carmine said. "He wants to be clear of any debt owed by Santino."

"Tell him we're working on it." Carmine irritated me, but he'd also been useful as a statesman since he was less of a hothead than Dario and Ange, or me. I could also pump him for information on Natalya, on how to handle her, and he offered it, albeit cautiously. Though it confused me, since Natalya seemed to trust him and appeared fond of him. Why would he offer me ammunition to use against her? Unless he didn't want to piss me off and he wanted the Galluzo-Chicago alliance to work.

If I could pull this off, I'd come out with more leverage than ever. I couldn't complain either because I ended up with a very passionate wife.

My mind was so consumed with my imminent return to the mansion, a roar from Dario turned me rigid.

"Watch out!"

My consigliere shoved me out of the way just as gunfire exploded.

·   ·   ·

"I want them found. I want them dead," I growled into the phone.

"Carmine and I are looking," Ange replied.

"Look harder." I ended the call.

Dario was sitting beside me in the Escalade. He gave me a few moments before saying, "You're bleeding."

I glanced at my sleeve. "It's just a graze." But it stung like a motherfucker. Probably took a chunk out of my biceps too. We were already in our vehicles when the cops arrived. The perpetrators had the audacity to strike at us in front of Orlov's club.

Suspicions pointed away from the Russians because Orlov made it clear violence was off-limits at his club, but I wouldn't put it past the motherfucker to engineer the whole thing. Except, it also did him no good if I was dead. He wouldn't be getting his money.

I shoved the SUV into gear and rolled out of the parking lot. My men followed behind me.

Carmine was with Ange on the trail of the blacked-out Explorer that'd done the hit. Might as well get him some street cred with my brother.

"Maybe I should drive," Dario said. "Because you might pass out."

"It's just a graze," I repeated. "I'll let you know if I'm about to black out."

I chuckled. Maybe I was dying from blood loss. My phone on the dash rang. It was Carmine.

"We lost them, but we got the plates."

"The plates are useless," I said. "Probably stolen."

"Yeah," Carmine said. "What do you want me to do?"

"Tell Ange to continue looking. I'm going home."

I could feel Dario's raised brow.

"You're still going home to Tralestelle?" Carmine asked, surprise in his voice.

"Of course. Keep me posted." I ended the call, grabbed the phone from the dash, and turned it off.

"This is not the first time I've been shot at," I muttered to Dario. "But it'll be the first time I'll go with my wife to the first checkup."

That was a lame excuse. I wanted to fuck Natalya, especially with the adrenaline coursing through my veins.

"What happened to making her get used to being away from you and yet worshipping the ground you walk on?" my friend asked.

I ignored his sarcasm. "She's been busy. Martha reported that she'd taken over the household budget with no problem. Tony said she overhauled all the appliances at home in two short weeks." If that was her way of getting back at me while I was gone, then she could have at it.

Dario chuckled. "Have you checked your credit card lately?"

I shrugged. "She could spend all she wants and not bankrupt me. The point is"—I cast him a glance—"I'm rewarding her for good behavior."

"I hate to tell you this," Dario said. "She's not a dog."

"Should I drop you at the corner?"

"I'll shut up."

"I'll be back on Monday."

"You can work from there, you know," Dario said. "Spend some time with your wife."

"Maybe."

It was almost one a.m. when I arrived at Tralestelle. I was surprised I didn't get pulled over by a cop as I was racing home, way past the speed limit. Tony met me at the door. I informed him what had happened and to be on alert.

My wound stopped bleeding, but my fucking arm was sore. I

didn't care, though. My body was fired up, and I couldn't wait to sink into my wife.

I remembered her jealousy over Jessica. I didn't even remember that dream. I pushed my ex-mistress out of my mind and took the stairs two at a time. By the time I entered the bedroom, I was hard. I started removing my clothes—tie, shirt, shoes. I unzipped my pants and walked over to Natalya's side of the bed.

The moon illuminated her form. Her face was half covered by the blanket and all I could see was her blonde head.

I sat down. The mattress shifted, and she started to stir. I peeled the blanket away, and before she could come fully awake, my mouth was on hers, and I climbed on top of her.

Her initial struggle died away when she realized it was me. I kissed her fiercely as I slowly wedged my hips between her thighs. My cock was already rubbing against her.

When I tore my mouth away, she breathed, "Luca…"

"Miss me, baby?"

"I did…but you smell like a bar."

"And you smell like heaven."

She twitched her nose.

I chuckled deeply. "I don't think I can wait to be inside you."

She pumped her pelvis against me, rocking against my cock. "I don't think I want to wait either."

I didn't waste another second, but more than sinking into her, I was dying to taste her. I let my tongue trail down her body, over the coolness of her silky sleepwear. When I parted her legs, the scent of her arousal saturated my nose.

"No panties?" I nibbled her inner thighs.

"I was thinking of you…"

"Are you saying you masturbated just now?" I planted a kiss closer to her pussy.

"Yes."

"I should punish you." I licked around her slick and perfectly swollen flesh. Her hips squirmed, and I flattened a palm over her pelvis to keep her still. I lapped her hard, I licked her slowly, and I tunneled my tongue into her and made her come over and over until she was hoarse. I bolted up her body and pushed inside her. Her back arched and her eyes closed.

"All your orgasms belong to me. Got it?"

"But you were gone so long and I missed you." She breathed as I started to thrust inside her. I said nothing. I couldn't tell her how I nearly got shot because I was thinking of exactly this. Of how I wanted to be here with her. She couldn't be my weakness. As those thoughts ran through my head, I pumped faster, until finally I went over and emptied two weeks of need inside her.

CHAPTER

Ten

NATALYA

"Oh my God!" My shriek bounced around the room.

There was blood on the bed.

Luca shot up to a sitting position, eyes on alert, before they narrowed at me.

"Woman, how many times..." His gaze fell to the bloodied bedsheets and then to his arm. "Oh...yeah."

Relief hit me hard, but on its heels came fury. "Oh yeah? That is all you have to say?" I scrambled off the bed and inspected my legs. They were smeared with blood. "You made love to me while you were bleeding."

My husband seemed pleased. He leaned against the headboard and cocked a knee. He hadn't even bothered removing his pants when he fucked me. "Sounds primitive, doesn't it?"

My chest was rising and falling, heart and lungs competing for space inside my rib cage. "What happened?"

"You don't want to know."

"Oh, I sure do." I padded over to the clothes strewn over the floor and collected them one by one. Blood soaked the sleeve of the dress shirt. "Did you even have that looked at?"

"It stopped bleeding by the time I got here. Dario poured whiskey over it and taped me up."

"Obviously, you started bleeding again." I returned to his side. "Show me." A crusted-over spot covered his biceps. "You need to have it cleaned."

"Will you do it for me, *tesoro*?"

"Don't get charming with me, Luca Moretti," I snapped. "Why wasn't I informed that you were shot?" I left him on the bed and marched to the bathroom.

"I didn't want you to worry." He followed me and went to his side of the sink, splashing water on his face, then started brushing his teeth.

I said nothing until I rinsed my mouth. "You should shower. You stink like the bar and cigarettes." I exited the bathroom, and walked to our bed, and I stared. Our marriage bed. The first time he came home to me and he was bloody. It was like a baptism of fire. I wasn't sheltered. I'd experienced this scenario many times with Papà, including incidents involving our soldiers. They called the mob doctor. I blinked. Bloodied floors, people hustling, men screaming in agony. If Mamma could handle it, then I could too.

The shower turned on. I gave in to a heavy sigh and removed the sheets from the bed and balled them over. The blood had bled through. I was surprised there wasn't more evidence of Luca's life, but Martha mentioned the mattress was changed recently. I shook my head. Maybe from the many blood stains. When I returned to the bathroom, it was to see my husband's naked form getting sluiced with water. I'd felt the scars on his body beneath those tattoos.

"Won't you come join me?" the devil invited. "Let me wash my blood off you."

I had to grin at this. "You know it's more than your blood." I could feel his crusted semen on my pussy. Usually, he cleaned me up after, but we fell asleep right after we had sex.

I opened the shower door and joined him.

"Thank you, baby," Luca said.

We were on our way to my first prenatal checkup. "For what? All I did was pour peroxide on the wound and tape it together."

He linked our fingers and kissed the back of my hand. "I still appreciate it. My wife taking care of me."

"Is this a common occurrence? Drive-by shootings?"

His grip tightened. "It happens…occasionally." He cast me a quick glance. "You handled this morning like a champ."

"What? You expected me to be hysterical?"

"I didn't know what to expect. I thought you were too sheltered. Too innocent."

"I'm not."

He squeezed my hand. "Good."

"You seem to be in a good mood this morning," I commented. "Despite the rude awakening."

The corners of his mouth tipped up. "Why wouldn't I be? I fucked my wife twice."

My cheeks heated as I remembered the way he went down on me in the shower before lifting me against the tiles and pounding into me again.

The doctor was in the college town of Red Oak between the mansion and Chicago. When we entered Saint Clara Hospital, the receptionist greeted Luca by name.

"Wow, do you own the hospital or something?" I asked.

"The Morettis are big donors," he said shortly. "The women in the family usually manage the charities, but with Sofia and Sera gone, it's another opportunity for you." He smiled at me briefly before we got into the elevators. He punched the button for the third floor. "I will not force you if you don't want to. I could always hire someone to oversee it."

"We'll see."

Luca gave me a tight smile. I couldn't decipher if he was pleased or not. I wasn't going to commit to managing charities. I'd done enough philanthropic work with Mamma, and despite my exposure, I preferred to be in the background rather than meeting with people and asking them for money. It was more thrilling to steal from these criminals and give it back to the people they ruined. Did that make me a criminal, too? A vigilante? Maybe both. It was nagging me what I was keeping in the attic from my husband. It was probably why I didn't press him too much on his Chicago business. I worried that we might have a conflict of interest.

If he was cleaning up Santino's mess, then I might be the key to some of it, but until I knew where both families fell on the human trafficking scale, I wasn't ready to reveal myself.

When the elevator doors slid open, a nurse was already waiting for us. "Doctor Kingsley is waiting for you."

As we followed the nurse past other people in the waiting area, I could feel the glare on our backs.

It made me uncomfortable that we were led straight into an examination room.

"Did we get ahead of them?"

"Don't feel guilty," Luca said. "It's Doctor Kingsley's day off. She wouldn't see us on her regular shift because she was already fully booked. After a generous donation, including an upgrade to all these." He waved his arm at the equipment. "I think we deserved it, don't you think?"

My lips flattened. "Maybe."

"Baby," he said. "Get used to this privilege. I might not make it to all your checkups, but I want you to receive the best care."

"I guess Doctor Kingsley knows what you do?"

There was a rap on the door and a blonde woman in a doctor's coat who appeared to be in her forties stepped in. "Yes, she does."

"And she's an expert at eavesdropping," Luca said dryly. "How are you, Rachel?"

"Busy, and busier." She returned Luca's sarcasm before she grinned at me. "Don't mind us. Luca is like an annoying younger brother. We grew up together. My mother used to work for the Morettis."

"Oh."

"His father sent me to medical school."

"Are you...?" I started.

She lowered her head and whispered conspiratorially. "One of the mob's doctors? Yes, I am. I'm also their shrink, hence my double major in psychology. So if Luca is making you crazy, you make an appointment with me."

I laughed. Luca muttered a not-so-nice word in Italian.

I immediately liked Dr. Kingsley. Though I was one who got easily bored in school, I respected the kids who strived to get out of the life and turned to education to do it. But I guess when your education was mob-funded, there was a price to pay.

As though reading my mind, Dr. Kingsley said, "I could have easily opened a practice elsewhere. I've paid my dues, if that's what you're wondering. I just don't want to miss all the drama." She brought up the screen. "I'm doing the interview for your records." She looked at Luca. "I told you it was necessary. Even you have one." She shook her head at my husband's answering glower. "We'll only do what's important. If you need to be hospitalized elsewhere, your allergies to meds and everything will be on record. Your husband is paranoid. He thinks the enemies will exploit that."

"It's possible," Luca grumbled.

"Yes. But the risk of not putting it in the hospital network is bigger given what you're up against."

I thought about the bloodied bedsheets this morning and my gaze met with Luca's. I bet he was remembering the same.

The questioning didn't take long. I told her I had breast soreness and an aversion to cleaning polish. My taste for salty and sweet had increased. I gave her a rundown of my family health history, what meds I was allergic to, and answered no on pre-existing conditions. Afterwards, she drew blood for their lab and confirmed with the urine test that I was pregnant.

"Let's see if we have a fetal image, shall we?" the doctor said. Luca and I exchanged glances. His face was blank, but mine was probably etched with anxiety.

He squeezed my hand and bent his head. "It's going to be fine."

Warm gel was applied to my flat belly. Then the bulbous probe started gliding across my skin, pressing, probing.

"There it is," Dr. Kingsley said. "This is the head." She took some measurements.

My throat backed up as I saw the tiny speck on the screen. Tears formed. "That's our baby," I whispered.

When Luca didn't say anything, I glanced at him. His eyes were still riveted on the screen.

When he tore his attention away to look at me, it was a look full of tenderness and it chased away part of my anxiety.

"I never thought I would be one of the emotional ones to see our baby when it's the size of a bean."

Luca put his arms around me. "It's amazing." His voice was gruff, as if he too was fighting back emotions.

The doctor grinned at us. "You haven't seen anything yet...or should I say…heard." She split a look between us. "Do you want to hear the baby's heartbeat?"

My emotions had hijacked my voice. I could only nod vigorously.

Soon the rapid pitter-patter of the life growing inside me filled the room. Doc was right. I burst into happy tears.

~

Luca

Natalya burst into tears, and to my horror, I felt the back of my eyes sting. To hide my emotions, I tucked Natalya into my chest and stared at the floor. I rubbed her back to soothe her, but I wondered if I was soothing the uncomfortable compression in my chest that I felt more than the sting of the gunshot last night.

Thankfully, Rachel left us alone.

The baby's heartbeat pulsed around us. From the floor, I raised my eyes and fixated on the wall, on a framed drawing of a fetus at forty weeks. Reluctantly, I returned my gaze to the ultrasound screen again. Rachel said she puts Natalya at eight weeks judging from her last period with a due date in October, the exact date I'd forgotten now because of the roaring in my ears. That bean-sized speck that looked like all head and body was going to grow arms and legs.

My wife was crowding me and breathing became difficult. The air in the room dissipated and the urge to loosen my tie made me curl my fingers. Natalya was the one who gave blood, but I was the one feeling dizzy.

She pushed away from me, and I forced myself to meet her

eyes. The hopefulness and happiness reflected in them tightened the invisible band around my chest. I pasted a smile. "Happy?"

She sighed. "I'm sorry I broke down." Her hand swiped down my soaked dress shirt. "And I'm sorry I got you wet."

I kissed the top of her head. "That's okay, baby. When we go home, I can change."

"A baby, Luca," she croaked. "What if it's not a boy?"

That made me smile because I had no problem in the making of them. "Then I'll keep you pregnant until you give me one."

She gave a watery laugh and rested her head on my chest.

I needed to get out of here.

Natalya

What did I do wrong?

Things had been perfect this morning despite finding blood all over the sheets. Luca had been his charming, relaxed self. He let me mother him while I patched up the gash on his arm. He was even eager and supportive when we went to the doctor. When he told me we would continue to have babies until I gave him a son, my thoughts immediately made plans for renovating the rooms at Tralestelle.

But a dizzying one-eighty happened after our late lunch in Red Oak, where he announced he was returning to Chicago instead of staying over the weekend. He was a roller coaster full of exhilarating highs and unexpected plunges. He loved me. I saw it in his eyes right after the ultrasound. He might not be aware of the way he looked at me, but it was there, etched so clearly. The problem was when he had time to think about it. He was fighting it, but it was too late for me.

I was in love with him and I would fight for him and our baby, even if the person I had to fight was him.

As I watched Luca's Escalade drive away, I refused to surrender the joy that this day had given me. He was making dumb excuses about returning to Chicago, but I knew better. In this relationship, I was the patient one. I had all the time in the world to learn what made the man I loved reluctant to fully commit in the marriage.

"He cares," Martha said behind me.

I stiffened. I forgot I had an audience.

"Stop interfering, old woman," Tony scolded.

I turned around and faced them. I gritted my teeth at the matching expressions of sympathy on their faces.

Behind them, the massive house mocked me.

I was its mistress. I should act like one.

"Oh, I know," I said. "He was romantic enough in Paris." I narrowed my eyes at Tony. "I'll just notch this down to mafia men not wanting to sit in their feelings."

Tony scratched the back of his head. "I couldn't speak for the boss, but he's never had a wife before and his mistresses knew better than to expect things from him. He just doesn't know what to do with you."

"I'm not difficult," I protested.

"You're not easy either," Tony said. "Maybe it's the age."

"Tony Romero," Martha snapped. "Natalya is the easiest mistress this house has ever had besides Luca's mamma. Believe me, I know. She doesn't micromanage."

I shook my head and walked past them, leaving them to bicker. I didn't micromanage because I had enough business on my plate. "I'll be in the attic," I called behind me. "If you all don't mind, I'll be watching my romance movies all day. I'm not joining you all for dinner."

Nessa ran ahead of me to stop my progress. She scribbled on her notepad.

I read her message. "I don't need you to cook anything special. Just make me a sandwich."

Her mouth drooped at the corners.

I put my hand on her shoulder. "Tell you what. Surprise me."

Her eyes lit up. She nodded and dashed into the house.

Martha came to my side. "You're spoiling her."

"As long as she gets her chores done, I have no problem." My eyes followed Yvonne. She was always on her phone first thing in the morning and almost all day. One time I caught her in Luca's stepmother's old room, trying on a Chanel suit. She must have felt my eyes on her and said, "The blood won't come off the bedsheets. It's probably ruined."

"Did you try hydrogen peroxide?" I quipped before leaving Martha to handle Yvonne. It was her job to manage the staff and she had done so for thirty years. I didn't see a need to interfere except with the books. I went straight to the attic. Mrs. B, who I hadn't seen in a few days, followed me up the steps. The cat enjoyed spending time with me in the attic and was the only one who knew my secret.

I hadn't been up here in a couple of days because I was too excited for Luca's homecoming. Doriana didn't need me for the next week or so anyway, and I'd already scoped out the Russians. It was a straightforward job. They were not the cream of the crop, and admittedly, I was put out that it wasn't more of a challenge. But fair was fair. I left Doriana hanging after I lost the safety of my identity when Santino grabbed me. Maybe she was just feeling me out too. After all, trust went both ways. She had to be sure I wouldn't compromise her.

The big-screen TV was the first thing one would notice upon entering my new attic domain. I grinned inwardly, wondering what Luca thought when I ordered three giant televisions complete with home theater equipment. The third television was for the staff. Their quarters were at the opposite end of the mansion from where I was located. Although it appeared to be generosity on my part, it was one of my ploys to keep them preoccupied and I subscribed to cable and popular streaming services.

The servers and network equipment were in the closet at the moment. I made sure the delivery came in with the home theater stuff, but I had special bookcases on order which were designed so I could tidy up all the wiring.

I loved attics more than basements. I couldn't believe how perfect this space was. It had sat mostly empty because the basement was used mainly for storage. It took only a day for Tony, Martha, and Nessa to clean it up.

If the view of the estate looked awesome from Luca's room, it was magnificent up here. The thunderstorm a week ago had been a sight to see.

While *Pride and Prejudice* played on television, I grabbed my laptop and sat on the couch. Mrs. B jumped up and sat beside me. I absentmindedly patted the cat and contacted Doriana to tell her I had everything set up for the job.

As I waited for her reply, I did my usual scans of software technology forums, keeping track of any reported bugs or weaknesses that could be exploited by hackers. It took an effort to ignore the heartache in my chest, and I used the happiness I experienced during our doctor's visit to keep it in check.

By the time Nessa brought up my food, I was nodding to sleep on the couch and my laptop had gone into screensaver mode. My playlist of movies had shifted to a rom-com.

"Thanks, Nessa." I accepted the tray.

She wrote on her notepad. *Are you okay?*

"I'm fine," I replied. "A good dose of a light movie is all that I needed."

She glanced at the screen and then back at me, before shifting to my laptop.

I stiffened.

One of my mother's lectures blared in my head. "Don't let the staff get too comfortable or they'll stick their nose in your business."

And my business could get people in trouble.

"Go ahead. I'll be okay."

CHAPTER
Eleven

The days began to blur, and before I knew it, weeks and months passed. I was five months into my pregnancy, and I was getting used to Luca being gone.

When I'd been three months pregnant, I attempted to see my husband in Chicago. I tried to surprise him at the Moretti Shipping Line offices, only to find out that he was in Vegas and wouldn't be expected until the next day. I ended up an emotional wreck and couldn't stop crying all the way back to Tralestelle.

I didn't even merit a phone call from him, telling me where he would be traveling.

Even Papà gave Mamma that courtesy.

I became dizzy the next day and wasn't feeling too good. Martha lectured me that stress wasn't good for the baby. At least she appeared to be pissed at Luca, and Tony didn't make any excuses for my husband either.

When I wasn't feeling any better that afternoon, I panicked and made an appointment with Dr. Kingsley. Since it was an emergency and she didn't have an open appointment, she had to check me over after hours and declared I was fine, maybe dehydrated. She was also of the opinion that I should not stress over Luca and think of the baby. Surprisingly enough, I didn't hear from Luca and was relieved that no one ratted me out regarding my brief excursion.

Luca returned for my eighteenth-week checkup where we would find out the gender. Dr. Kingsley didn't mention the incident. When she declared we were having a boy, Luca kissed my forehead and congratulated me, then he dropped me off at Tralestelle and returned to Chicago.

It appeared he was no longer interested in our baby either.

Even his daily phone calls had dwindled to twice a week.

I touched my stomach that was only now beginning to show a bump. I'd shifted to wearing maternity pants. There was no use trying to look sexy because Luca hadn't touched me in two months. I was a new wife and about to become a mother, but I'd lost my shine and appeal to my husband. I saw it in the way he barely looked at me and offered me half-hearted compliments. My heart could tell the difference.

I questioned whether I'd imagined the love in his eyes during our first prenatal checkup. I clung to that hope, but after months of being frozen out, even I had my limits.

The sound of an approaching storm broke my reverie. I was in my usual position on the couch, with Mrs. B keeping me company. I guessed she sensed the turbulent weather. The cursor on the laptop blinked at the end of Doriana's last message.

"We're a go. Auction is still at 11 p.m. EST."

I pushed my emotional turmoil away and focused on the job. Seven lives were at stake. Four girls who were barely sixteen. One eighteen-year-old. And two boys who were fourteen.

My stomach threatened to throw up my dinner. I had the identities of the buyers. Two Saudi princes. The other three were oligarchs. Five major buyers. The others were lesser players and didn't get first choice.

It was eight p.m. Chicago time. Which meant I had two more hours to go. I favored denial-of-service attacks, which slowed down the servers. No payment meant the girls and boys would not be sold and Doriana had another group involved that rescued them.

Usually, after one of our jobs, I'd see confirmation from the news where the auction was taking place that a human trafficking ring had been busted.

However, I was going to use the method I'd employed when I stole Santino's money. I was diverting their payments by exploiting a weakness in their network security software. My program was already in place. I already had all the identifying information the assholes were going to use.

Sometimes, I wondered if I bit off more than I could chew. I was going up against powerful criminal organizations. Granted, my husband was one scary mofo in the game, but he didn't know he was protecting me against all that.

The sound of rain splattered on the roof, and lightning streaked across the night sky.

I had hoped I could have shared this part of me with Luca by now, but he made it extremely difficult given his own preoccupation with the Galluzo wasn't going so well.

From what I heard from Carmine, Papà was getting impatient, but I didn't blame my husband if he refused to give an inch to doing business with the Russians when it came to human trafficking. That was something we had in common. He had his battles. I had mine.

A soft knock sounded on the door. "Come in."

It was Martha. "You're sleeping up here again?"

I nodded. I had stopped sleeping in Luca's room since we found out we were having a boy. It had become unbearable and lonely, bringing me nothing but despair and a rip in the heart each time I woke up to Luca's unslept side of the bed.

"I can ask Yvonne to make up another room for you."

"Don't worry. I have plans for a baby room. I'll probably move in there when the baby is born."

"That's not healthy."

I laughed bitterly. "Did you even expect Luca to have a healthy relationship ever?"

Martha's eyes lowered. "I had hoped."

"Don't," I choked. "Not tonight, please? I have a lot on my mind."

The older woman smiled sadly. "There are spotty storms all over. A particularly strong patch is rolling in."

"I love storms." And rain. Especially Paris in the rain.

Martha said no more and closed the door. I blew out a breath and flipped to my network sniffer that I'd already connected to the Russians' auction site on the Dark Web, deciphering the packets that were coming through.

A few minutes later, the lights blinked.

Shit.

Mrs. B jumped down from her comfortable position on the couch and headed to the door.

"Great, you're abandoning me now too?"

"Meow."

"Fine." I let the cat out.

I walked back to the couch and picked up the DEC-phone and the signal was atrocious…

A loud blast sounded in the distance that didn't sound like thunder.

The power went out.

No. No. No.

It should shift automatically to the generator.

But even then what if the internet was down?

My DEC's hotspot was not working.

I waited.

And waited.

Dammit. It was time for my backup plan.

After checking with Tony, who said the generator was still having problems, I checked the clock. I had an hour and a half before the auction went live. I needed enough time to set up.

The stairwell that led to the attic was far away from the staff quarters. I had a go-bag ready, and all I needed was my laptop and the DEC. Earlier, I parked one of the older vehicles, a Ford Explorer, outside. I sure as hell was thankful no one had moved it into the garage. I threw on a raincoat, bleeped the locks, and made a run for the SUV. The other problem was the gates. I had to open one side manually and get the SUV through and then get out again and close it.

By the time I was on my way to Red Oak, my sneakers were squishing uncomfortably. I made a mental note to get myself rubber boots. At least my body and head were dry.

I gritted my teeth as the Explorer fought against the downpour. My windshield wipers flapped so fast, I thought they were going to fly off. I spotted a glimmer of light up ahead. It felt as though I was about to break through a tunnel.

The rain abated like magic, and I was clear. When I was five minutes from the college town, I remembered the smartphone. I didn't remember putting it in my go-bag. I probably would have left it anyway because I knew Tony could track me with it. That was why I selected an old Explorer from the fleet because I was hoping it was too old to have tracking on it. The last thing I needed was the stress of someone following me. I would face the firing squad later. I had an excuse, albeit a lame one.

It was Friday night, and the streets were busy with college kids a week before their break into summer vacation. When I reached the twenty-four-hour coffee shop I had scoped out months ago, I had forty-five minutes to set up. It wasn't too crowded, but crowded enough I would be inconspicuous. I found a cozy corner, threw my bag on it, hauled out my laptop, and fired it up. Next, I put the DEC on the stand and was relieved it was at full bars.

I connected to the hotspot and installed my shields and redirectors and then connected to the Dark Web. I had a script already set up to do all the IP hops to mask my location, and then, boom, I was in the Russians' auction site.

I reactivated my sniffer and waited.

The crew who would rescue the kids should be in position before I did anything. Then we would let the auction go as planned.

Two hours later, I had a hundred fifty million dollars split in numbered accounts and probably a bunch of pissed-off buyers. The Dark Web exploded with heavy chatter. I backed out and cleaned up my trail.

Shutting off the laptop, I swept all my devices into my go-bag, zipped up, and slung it over my shoulder and left the coffee shop. Times like this, I was glad my stomach wasn't in the way yet. Depending on what the next job might be, I might have to beg off. This was cutting it too close. If the generators had been working, I wouldn't be this stressed. Luca would soon be spending a bundle on a new generator.

I was about to leave Red Oak when I remembered my alibi. Chances are, Martha would have already checked on me. The storm had passed, and I had the windows down on the way back to Tralestelle. A cool breeze replaced the mugginess that preceded the thunderstorm. Exhilaration was like wings beneath me. Not only because of the refreshing weather, but the successful mission.

The DEC pinged with a thumbs up from Doriana. One day I would love to meet her. Assuming she was a woman. I gave no indication I was one, too.

By the time I turned on the street of the estate, my stomach clenched. The gate lights were bright and glaring. Beyond it the mansion was also lit up.

I had no way of finding out what was going on because I didn't have my regular phone. I hurriedly tucked away the DEC.

I punched the button for the automatic gates. If they were waiting for me, that would have alerted them. I hated I put the entire house in an uproar.

When I saw a row of black SUVs in front of the mansion, I was ready to throw up.

No. No. No.

This wasn't happening.

Luca stormed out of the house and raced down the steps. Dario was behind him, followed by two more men I didn't recognize.

The furious look on his face almost made me reverse the Explorer and drive away.

I barely cut off the engine when he ripped the door open.

"Where the fuck have you been?"

CHAPTER
Twelve

"I had a craving," I squeaked, shrinking away from my husband which seemed to make him angrier.

He grabbed my arm and pulled me from the vehicle. Immediately, he released me, his hands suspended in the air as though he didn't know where to put them. Finally, they gripped my shoulders, but his thumbs rested on my neck.

"A craving." A slew of emotions crossed his face. "For what?"

"A milkshake and french fries." My mind raced at how pathetic that alibi sounded now in the face of his fury.

"A milkshake and—" He lost it. And I knew he lost it because he immediately dropped his hands from my shoulders and stepped away from me. He slapped a palm on the hood of the SUV. "You went out in the middle of a storm to get a milkshake and french fries!"

"Pregnant." I shrugged, trying to act nonchalant with a bit of airhead. "And I like storms." I couldn't meet his eyes then, because mine were drawn to his knuckles. There was blood on them.

Panicked, and knowing what my disappearance could mean for my minders, I asked, "Where's Tony?"

My husband's chilling smile escalated the anxiety that was already rattling in my gut like pebbles in a rinse cycle.

"Now you're concerned for him?" His eyes flashed colder, but his fists clenched despite the bloody knuckles. "When you didn't even think about it when you went for this...craving?"

"What did you do to him?" I took a step toward him, but he turned around and stalked inside.

"Luca!" I yelled and ran after him.

Passing Dario, I asked, "What did he do to Tony?"

But Dario's gaze was equally censuring, and he didn't utter a word, merely flattened his mouth some more.

Luca continued walking without a backward glance. I ran ahead of him and stopped his progress.

His face was sculpted in taut lines, but his eyes were expressionless. "He failed to do his job, *tesoro*."

The way he said the endearment dripped with malice. The pebbles spun faster.

"I swear to God, Luca."

"Swear what?" he hissed at me. Lowering his head, he enunciated, "You think I'm in the wrong here?"

"Wrong? Let's talk about wrong," I shot back. "You leave me. You don't treat me like a wife. You don't treat me like someone who is pregnant with your child. It's supposed to be one of the happiest moments in a woman's life, but you do nothing except make me miserable."

An unnamed emotion flickered in his eyes before hardening to stone. "What's the matter? You need romance?" he sneered. "You think every day is going to be like Paris?"

"I know now it won't be. So don't come here mad at me for seeking my own happiness."

"You've been gone for three hours. What else have you been doing besides satisfying your craving?" He crowded me. "You better not have done what I think you're implying, baby." His voice was soft, but his words were threatening. "You brought back the milkshake and french fries. Could that be your excuse when really you're meeting another man?"

I laughed. Probably the worst reaction given the situation. But his accusation was so absurd, and I could only think of giving him what he deserved.

"You dare laugh at this." His gaze transformed from black ice to dangerous. His fingers gripped my arm, not painfully, but tight enough so it was uncomfortable. He hauled me against him.

"Maybe I want to be around people my age," I taunted. All the hurt and my guilt for lying to him made me reckless. "Maybe older men are too confusing and they have too many expectations." My voice rose. "Maybe I'm just sick of you!"

"You may be sick of me, *tesoro*. But you *are* married to me. Till death do us part. Especially…" He splayed his fingers across my womb and it made my whole being go cold. "You're carrying my child. You think any frat boy will be interested in a woman carrying another man's child?"

"Did I say I went out to cheat on you?" I asked. "I just wanted to remember what it feels like to be in college. The fun of a Friday evening after classes. You promised me I could go back to school. Instead, you hold me captive in this mansion."

"Captive?" His mouth curled in derision. "You have no idea what being held captive is, but I'll give you a taste. You are not to leave this house except for your checkups."

"I refuse to be a slave to your tyrannical rules."

"After this last escapade, I'm not taking any chances."

"You think you can control me? I have every right to leave this house."

"You're under a strange assumption that I'm giving you a choice." He nodded behind me.

Two of his soldiers hauled a bloody Tony to the center of the foyer. They shoved him to a kneeling position.

A gasp sounded behind me. It was Nessa whose horrified expression probably reflected my own.

"Tony…" I choked, then I turned pleading eyes to my husband. "I'll do anything."

"What do you think I'm going to do?"

Anxiety became full-blown fear and sent spikes into my throat. I lost the ability to speak like Nessa.

A malicious gleam entered Luca's eyes. One I'd never seen before, and it frightened me.

I started hyperventilating when he drew out his gun and pointed it at his soldier.

"No," I finally gasped. "You can't execute him for my mistakes."

Sounds of a scuffle broke out behind me, and I saw Nessa trying to get to her uncle.

"It was his job to protect you."

"It was my choice, Luca."

"Again. You have no choice."

"It was one mistake." My voice was a strangled whisper. I was too choked up to speak clearly. "He won't do it again. I won't do it again." Even Papà gave second chances. I understood the workings of the family. True terror filled my chest.

"One?" he scoffed. "You think I didn't know about your field trip to Chicago?"

I swallowed. "You didn't say anything."

"I was waiting for you to come clean, but you didn't, did you?

Everyone wants to hide things from me, including the good doctor, but what everyone seems to forget is I know *everything*."

He lowered his arm and looked at me. "Go to your room and think about what you did."

He tipped his chin to his henchmen. They hauled Tony to his feet and dragged him away from our sight.

Luca took out his pack of cigarettes. "Why are you still standing there? Go. Unlike your irresponsibility with your latest escapade, I don't want to harm my child with smoke."

Maybe you shouldn't be smoking in the first place. I turned away from my husband. This stranger who could easily turn from avenging angel to cold tyrant.

I went straight to the attic, fearful I'd left things lying around when I bolted in the dark. My regular phone had many messages.

Martha sent me three.

Tony sent me four.

Luca sent me seven.

I concentrated on the last four messages from my husband.

"Where are you? Tony is looking for you."

"Baby, answer your damn phone."

"*Tesoro*, I'm getting worried. Please tell me where you are."

"If this is about the baby, we can talk, but please come home."

The tears finally came. I wasn't sure if it was from relief or the confirmation that my husband was a master manipulator. My husband was Lucifer. Would he have shot Tony? I was finally seeing what made other mobsters wary of him. He would shoot his own people to make a point. And the people around him would let him do it, for Dario and Martha stood by with resigned expressions on their faces.

A rap on my door had me stiffening.

"Come in."

Nessa opened the door. In her hand was my paper bag of fries and the drink holder, carrying my milkshake.

She walked in and closed the door behind her.

"You should have just thrown them out."

She signed something I didn't understand, but she was clearly angry.

"I don't—"

She yanked out her notepad and scrawled on it. *Your husband is an asshole.*

"That he is."

She cleared it and wrote on it furiously. *Where were you?*

"I don't answer to you, Nessa."

She contemplated me, her lips thinning. *I have your backpack.*

Shit. I forgot about it.

I don't want Martha or Mr. Moretti to see it.

"It's really nothing," I hedged. "I wasn't lying when I said I missed college life."

Next time, don't get people killed.

She didn't know how much her accusation stung. It was history repeating itself. Thankfully, it didn't get too far, otherwise it might have been better if Luca turned the gun on me.

"I'm really sorry," I said and then looked around me. "I'm not leaving the four walls of this mansion until Luca finally decides he doesn't want me anymore." My voice cracked at my last words because I know despite how much I hated my husband, it couldn't erase the yearning of these past few months. Paris seemed so long ago. I longed for the tenderness I'd seen in his eyes when he saw our baby's first sonogram.

Since then, my husband had continued to pull further and further away.

At first, I thought there was hope in seeing his fury and that he cared for me. But in the light of his text messages juxtaposed with the way he treated me after when I came home, I realized the endless cycle of stupidity I had let my heart fall into.

I still loved Luca.

But he still didn't love me.

～

Luca

"Don't you think you went a bit too far?"

I tossed back the scotch and glared at Dario. "She fucking scared fifty years off my life, not to mention there's a lot of chatter about the Russians right now. It's not safe to leave the mansion." Where I fucking expected she would be.

"Carmine said their auction got hit again and an estimated hundred fifty million dollars had disappeared. Of course Orlov was saying it wasn't theirs, but we know he has several factions to hide his human trafficking business."

"That business is bad luck," I said. "They blame me for not carrying the passengers to another location."

"And as your adviser, I'm telling you, you will regret it if you'd done so. You made the right call. It's not who you are, Luca. As much blood is on your hands, the blood of children will not be one of them."

"How's Tony?" I was uncomfortable discussing my morality on the subject. Drugs I could overlook as long as I wasn't profiting from them. But if I wasn't as cutthroat as the other players in the underworld, I worried they would see that as a weakness. I couldn't let Natalya become a weakness. That was why I was harsh with her in front of my men. I didn't need them reporting back to Ange how I almost tore the house down looking for her. Which was why I threatened Tony, or I would have locked her tight in my arms, maybe even broken down and told her how I was losing my mind not knowing where she was. Then she had the gall to taunt me about our age gap? My wife needed to learn her lesson.

"Martha is tending to him. Broken rib, maybe."

"Does he need to see a doctor?"

"He said he'll be fine," Dario said, tapping his fingers at the edge of the table.

"Is there something else you want to say to me?"

"Do you believe what Natalya told you?"

"I do not wish to discuss what my wife said."

"Your reaction to her saying she might be with other men begs to differ. You were jealous."

I chuckled derisively. "That was not jealousy, my friend. That was pride and possessiveness. No woman makes a fool of Luca Moretti, and especially not in front of my men."

"She might hate you, you know."

"She loves me and misses me," I said confidently. "She thought I didn't know when she tried to surprise me in Chicago. Good thing I was in Vegas, otherwise I'd have no choice but to punish her for defying me."

"Are you not being unnecessarily cruel? Martha says the poor girl is lonely and watches romantic films all the time."

"I'll make it up to her. She's easy to sway with a bit of romance."

"Which you negate every time you two get close." Dario leaned forward, watching my reaction. "That girl doesn't know which end is up or down."

"Keep them off-kilter until they realize it's for their own good," I said. "When the baby comes, she'll be busy. Then I will have fulfilled my bargain with Vincenzo to have a male heir and direct descendant."

"But will he be your heir, too? Do you mean you're going to hand over your son to the Galluzo?"

Guilt nagged at me. "You make it sound so archaic. If one of my sons chose to join the Galluzo, the Moretti name would be powerful. Emilio would be proud. Junior might have died, but he should rest in peace that he'd left Chicago in good hands."

"Sons. You're treating Natalya like a brood mare."

"I'm getting tired of you needling me." I checked my watch. "Call Tony. It's time to put the man out of his misery."

After a few minutes, Natalya's bodyguard walked in. "Boss."

"How's the face?"

Tony grinned, and then winced. "Hurts like a mother."

"Good," I said dispassionately. I poured scotch into a fresh glass and shoved it at him. "You know Natalya could've gotten hurt driving in that storm."

He took a healthy sip before saying, "Yeah. I should have known she was up to something when she checked on the generators."

"What time was this again?" Dario asked.

"I don't know…around nine thirty…maybe fifteen minutes after the lights went out."

"The lights came back in another half hour," Dario said. "Nine thirty. She couldn't wait that long and had to get away?"

"The vehicle she used was the Explorer." I leaned forward. I'd been so blinded by my fury and worry about her missing that I missed it. Everyone missed it, or it was becoming clearer because her lame-ass excuse about the milkshake and fries just didn't fly.

"The vehicle was already parked outside," Dario pointed out.

"She planned this little road trip," I said. "It didn't matter if the lights went out or not."

"But if the lights didn't go out, I would have known she was missing," Tony said. "The alert at the gates would have notified me."

"We'll never know, will we?" I told Tony. "And I've terrorized my wife enough tonight. I will not push her." She already thought I was a monster, probably lumped me in the same category as her father and Santino. But she loved her father, so, in my opinion, she should love me too. I just needed to give her time to adjust to my nature and the way I run the family.

"I'm really sorry I let you down, boss."

"Last chance, Tony. I should reassign you, but the bruises on your face will make my wife think twice about defying my rules again."

He nodded.

"So don't let me down again. Next time, I might have to shoot you for real. Get out of here."

Natalya would drive a man to drink. Dario told me to go to my wife and stop hiding behind a bottle. I scoffed at him. I wasn't afraid to face her.

When I arrived at our bedroom, she wasn't there. For a second, I thought she disappeared again, and my heart spiked into my throat. Then I remembered Tony telling me a while back that my wife had started sleeping in the attic.

Natalya dredged up too many emotions from me that made me uncomfortable. Dario said I was jealous. I refused to accept that was what I was feeling. It was a sign of insecurity. Insecurity was a sign of weakness.

But my wife continued to surprise me. She let me believe she was a meek wife these past few months, then she pulled a stunt like this. Not that I blamed her for using my own tactics of making my enemy comfortable before I struck them where it hurt.

The student was learning from the master, but I had a few more tricks up my sleeve. This game of earning her loyalty was backfiring, and the baby was due in four months. Vincenzo was eager to visit his daughter and hinted that when the baby was born, he expected me to invite them.

I didn't want my father-in-law anywhere near my wife until I had her undying loyalty.

But I did have it. I had it under duress. Natalya was too kind-hearted to let anyone pay for her sins, and this incident only gave me ammunition to hold over her. It was a tightrope to navigate. I didn't want to make the mistake in Paris again, giving her all the romantic notions that our world revolved around each other. That time had served its purpose. She was pregnant.

The attic door was unlocked. I didn't bother knocking, but I opened it slowly. And there was Natalya, sleeping on the couch. She looked like an angel with her blonde hair flowing over a pillow. She had changed into pajamas I'd never seen her wear.

The cat was lying beside her. Was it healthy for cats to be beside pregnant women?

"Shoo," I told Mrs. B.

She hissed at me and took off. I was taken aback. Usually, Mrs. B rubbed against me first, but it seemed I had fallen from favor.

I walked to the edge of the attic and looked out the window. The moon had emerged from the clouds, casting its beams across the estate. I rubbed my chest because of the sudden stab I felt there. I could see why Natalya liked it up here. My eyes wandered over to the big-screen TV and the bookcases on each side, the light of the moon shining on them. I pulled out a book and inspected it. My wife's head was full of romance and heroes, yet she got stuck with the villain.

I wondered if she went to Red Oak to look for her blond-haired Adonis when she realized she wasn't getting the hero treatment from me. My mouth twisted in a sneer, refusing to acknowledge that it was jealousy. But in leaving my wife alone, she built her own world up here. One I was not a part of. Not sure I liked that development either.

Returning to her side, I stared at her. It annoyed me she could sleep so peacefully while my thoughts were rampaging through my head. But pregnant women seemed to sleep more. Dario had the audacity to drop one of those "Expecting" books on my desk. I shoved it in the drawer for the longest time, but finally cracked it open when we found out we were having a boy.

I should wake her and tell her she should sleep in our room. I'd had too much to drink, and I didn't want to risk dropping her, hurting her and our child.

Leaning over, my arm reached out to feather her cheek with my fingers and wake her, but my hand recoiled and I straightened. If today had proven anything, it was that I wasn't in control of my reactions when it came to my wife.

A weakness responsible for my brother's failures as boss.

A weakness that got him and his wife killed, leaving my niece an orphan.

A weakness that would not be mine.

CHAPTER
Thirteen

"Luca wants you at the breakfast table."

I was horrified to see Tony this morning. His face was black and blue and he had a split lip. No wonder Nessa hated me. I was surprised and relieved Luca didn't storm up into the attic and demand I sleep beside him. I was outraged with what he had done to Tony, and I doubted I would have stomached sleeping beside him.

"I'm so sorry." My apology came off lame because in my soul, I knew I saved seven minors from being auctioned off.

My bodyguard shrugged. "It is what it is. The boss couldn't fire me because I'm part of the family. I slacked on my job."

He gestured for me to walk ahead of him.

"You must hate having to babysit me while there is much more interesting stuff to do in Chicago."

"I consider this secret service stuff," he chuckled. "Guarding the wife of the boss is a privilege."

At the bottom of the steps, he tipped his chin at the man standing by the wall. "You know Rocco—he's going to help keep an eye on you. I'm sorry, Natalya, but from now on you'll have a guard wherever you go in the mansion."

Tony turned away and went outside the back door. I was tempted to follow him, but I knew better.

Rocco's face was inscrutable, but I could feel the disapproval emanating from him. And as we headed to the dining room, we passed the other staff, including Nessa, who didn't even bother to look at me.

I'd gone from mistress of Tralestelle to its prisoner, where everyone hated me. They saw me as a spoiled brat.

When I entered the dining room, I saw Yvonne hovering over Luca and exchanging flirtatious words with him.

"That's prime Italian breakfast sausage. Never frozen, according to the delivery man yesterday." Yvonne giggled like a schoolgirl. Was it my imagination that her uniform was unbuttoned to her cleavage, and she was wearing a short skirt? With full makeup and red lipstick, she looked like the star for a chambermaid porn movie.

My husband, for his part, only smiled, but when he saw me, he held my gaze while saying, "Thank you, Yvonne. You could add that to your duties."

What?

"Mr. Moretti?"

He grinned at her. "Being in charge of the deliveries."

"Oh." She laughed and had the gall to touch his shoulder. "Of course."

"Thank you, Yvonne," I said. "If you will excuse us, I want to have breakfast with my husband."

The other woman glared at me, but she knew better than to defy me in front of Luca.

I took my seat next to my husband. Surely, he didn't expect me to ask permission before sitting down, even when he exuded the chill of an iceberg that would give me frostbite.

"I see you're handling Yvonne better." He wasn't looking at me, but taking a bite of said sausage.

"We've been fine. She's never crossed the line with me." I poured orange juice into a glass.

"Good. You're learning."

While I filled my plate with frittata, my peripheral vision caught Luca putting down his knife and fork. He was staring at me.

I reluctantly met his gaze.

"I'm waiting," he said.

"I'm sorry for last night."

His eyes searched mine, and I forced myself to keep from flinching. "And I do not forgive you."

"Then why are you waiting for me to apologize?" I asked.

"I don't see remorse in your eyes and only more defiance."

My eyes lowered and stared at the knot on his tie. "I will not do it again." Then I lifted my chin. "You assigned me another guard. Is that necessary?"

"I need one who you won't wrap around your finger with your guile and manipulation."

I laughed derisively. "I'm the manipulative one?"

"I don't hide mine behind big brown eyes and fake innocence."

I couldn't say anything to that because I was far from innocent. "I can't help my age and how I look. It's people's fault they under-estimate me."

"So I'm learning." His gaze pierced into me. "I won't have a repeat of last night. Understand?"

The saliva dried up in my mouth, and I had trouble swallowing or saying the words. So I gave a brief nod.

Martha came in and set a bowl of granola and yogurt in front of me.

"This is a lot of food."

"You need to eat more," the older woman said gently. I was alarmed when the back of my eyes stung, realizing that I was on the precipice of falling apart. She was the only one who had shown me sympathy this morning.

I croaked, "I'll try."

Martha squeezed my shoulder, then shot a disapproving glance at Luca, before leaving the room.

We resumed eating in silence. The clink of the silverware was an awkward sound in the room. I didn't mind trying to eat what was in front of me, because Dr. Kingsley wanted me to put on more weight. But if all Luca wanted from me was an apology, then silence was better. I was afraid he was going to probe me about where I went.

Luca finished eating and picked up the napkin to wipe his mouth. I kept my eyes on my plate, but I was very aware of the man beside me. He leaned back, regarding me, and began tapping his fingers of one hand on the table.

I glanced briefly at him. "If you need to be somewhere, you don't have to wait for me to finish eating."

"No, I prefer to get this out now," he said with determination.

My spine stiffened for an imminent attack, and the orange juice sloshed in my stomach.

"Are you sleeping okay?"

I reared back at the unexpected question. "Yes."

"With your pregnancy, I don't want you stressed. Setting expectations of each other will be better for us going forward."

"You expect me to stay at Tralestelle and play housewife. I get that."

"As your husband, I'll provide for your needs." His tone was matter-of-fact, like he was reading aloud a boring editorial in a newspaper. "I care for you, Natalya, but I think you're clinging to a notion that one day I'll turn into one of your romance heroes."

"I think you admitted you're more a villain than a hero." And I wished I believed him when he declared it so. Instead, I painted him as the misunderstood antihero.

His face remained stoic, save for the tic under his eye. "Good. Then my next words won't be a problem. Listen up because they're important, and I don't want to repeat myself because the truth might hurt."

Why did I feel like my heart was already breaking before he even uttered his words?

"Just get it over with," I rasped like it was my dying breath.

"I care for you, but I will never love you." Even in his same lame monotone, the words shattered my heart. A carnage so huge the fragmented pieces trapped the anguished sob in my throat.

And he went on in his bland tone. "I will never love you in the way you imagine in your romance novels." He was so oblivious to the fact that he'd just obliterated every romantic notion I held dear.

Big tears formed and spilled down my cheeks.

I exhaled in a fractured breath. "I'm getting that."

His hand reached out to touch my cheek. I flinched from his touch.

His jaw clenched in determination. "I'm sorry if I hurt you, but I think these expectations need to be set now before the child comes."

"Are you going to love our son?"

"Of course. But I should think of him with the future of our families in mind."

"What if I don't want that life for him?"

"Don't be ridiculous. You agreed and have full knowledge of why we entered this arranged marriage."

"Yes! Because you could help my father. It had nothing to do with our child." I brushed the tears from my cheeks, anger drying them up.

Something flickered in his eyes, and then his expression warmed. I did not trust that warmth anymore. I was tired of his mercurial expressions. I married a manipulative bastard.

"At least we have chemistry, no?" He smirked.

"Chemistry? You haven't fucked me in two months."

"You didn't seem receptive, and I didn't want to force you."

"Oh, please, Luca, that's a lame excuse. You don't want to fuck me because each time you do, you feel closer to me and that scares you."

"What did I say about expectations?"

"This is why you stay away from me."

"I'm a very busy man, Natalya. Be glad you're safe here."

My stupid heart wanted to press him, but he was still fighting it, and frankly, I wasn't sure my trampled feelings could handle his rejection and ridicule.

So I asked the question *expected* from a concerned wife. "What's going on?"

"I really don't want to involve you in the mess that Santino left behind, but the Russians are blaming Chicago for one of their failed business deals that had cost them an obscene amount of money and shut down one of their lucrative sources of income. Aside from Rocco, I have five men assigned to protect the estate."

"How about my checkups?"

"As much as possible, Rachel will visit you here. I have a portable ultrasound on the way."

"That's overkill."

"I protect what's mine, *tesoro*." He put his hand on mine and squeezed. "I do care about you. Please believe that."

My insides were still in tatters to believe anything out of his mouth. "Whatever you say."

"Now," he said, ignoring my caustic reply. "I don't want you to get bored."

"There's not much else to do on the estate. You've got a full staff."

"There is," he said. "You know we're having a boy. Why don't you get started on the nursery?"

My mouth fell open, and for the first time this morning, a burst of joy exploded from my heart. "I can do that."

"The one beside our room, maybe?" he suggested. "That way, it will be close by when the baby cries."

"Okay."

"And I've said before, you have my black card. Use it."

As was routine before Luca left, I walked him to the SUV. There were more mafia soldiers than usual, and I had no doubt that the auction I broke up yesterday was the same one giving my husband a headache now.

He seemed to be in a better mood because he thought I accepted his expectations. He was right though. I had to think of the baby.

"Take care." He gave me a chaste kiss on the lips and got behind the second row of an Escalade in between another two.

I watched his convoy leave before I turned around and walked back into the house. He was an expert at evasion and distracted me with the nursery talk. To my credit, I recognized this after the initial thrill, no longer blinded by the fact that he was simply giving me a bone.

Things would change once the baby arrived because I would not accept anything less than unconditional love. I only had to look at Luca's niece to see it. Sera and Matteo had a love meant for the history books. Sera told me how Matteo wrecked his beloved Jaguar to save her from my deranged cousin in what could only be described as a movie-worthy moment. Then she told me all the things Matteo did for her to earn her love. That sunset proposal was everything. I wanted a passionate love like that.

My laptop was still with Nessa. I went looking for her in the kitchen, where she was busy putting away the staff meal. There were still a few men in the kitchen eating, so I checked out the room that would become the nursery.

Rocco didn't follow me once I turned in the direction of our rooms on the second floor. There was no exit there unless I climbed down the trellis beside the balcony. Our bedroom door was open. Yvonne was probably cleaning it. I was about to walk past it when she came out.

My hackles rose at the obvious mockery on her face.

"Are you done with the room?" I asked.

"I'm taking my time," she said. "It appears you won't be using it anytime soon anyway."

I stepped toward her. "No, Yvonne. You can't take your time. Nessa is swamped in the kitchen. Go help her."

"The kitchen is not my assignment."

"Your assignment is what I or Martha tells you. Don't make me repeat myself." I walked away from her before I ended up scratching her eyes out. I remembered the way she flirted with my husband.

"Have you checked the latest Chicago gossip?"

Sighing, I turned around. "I'm not concerned—"

"Maybe you should," she said coyly as she closed our bedroom door and started walking the opposite way. "Then you will know why your husband doesn't share your bed."

Pissed at myself that Yvonne's malice hit the mark, I hurried to the bedroom I would be converting into a nursery and whipped out my regular phone, bringing up the Chicago news site. I didn't see anything at first until I scrolled all the way to the bottom and saw a picture of Luca. I clicked on it.

It was an opening of a new club.

He was there with socialites and politicians. I recognized an alderman that was at our wedding and the city mayor. So, Luca was busy with new club openings? There was nothing strange about it. Clubs were common for cleaning money.

But the photo at the very bottom caught my eye.

Jessica, Luca's last girlfriend, was in a picture with him.

The caption read: Former girlfriend cozying up to the Moretti Shipping Line CEO. Where is Natalya Moretti? Has the shine worn off for the bride and groom?

Though a lump formed in my throat, I clung on to the logic that they moved in the same social circles.

I closed the page, but of course I had to check something else. I entered both their names in a Google search.

I wished I hadn't. I wished I hadn't let Yvonne goad me into internet stalking. I wished I had maintained my ignorance because there was nothing I could do from here.

"Moretti with former girlfriend in Vegas hotel opening."

The timestamp of the news article was around the time he went away and I didn't know. I was suddenly light-headed, and I ran to the bathroom and emptied the contents of my stomach. Since breakfast was a few hours ago, it was mostly bile and the dry heaving hurt. My world caved in.

I wished there was technology or a magic pill to make me forget all the heartache. Forget this life and its bullshit expectations. Forget my love for Luca.

Instead, I read four other articles where they'd been seen together. The tabloids speculated they arrived separately to be discreet because although mafia men could keep mistresses, they shouldn't blatantly disrespect their wives.

I sank to my knees, unable to support myself. The phone clattered on the tiles. Was it possible for something to hurt so much that I couldn't cry? It was as though I had detached from my emotions.

An insistent flutter low in my pregnant belly pulled me from the prison of my thoughts. It brought a smile to my face. It might just be my stomach's upheaval from the dry heaving, but I'd like to think it was my baby letting me know everything was going to be all right.

CHAPTER
Fourteen

NATALYA

"Luca…" The fullness in me felt so good.

"You're so tight and wet," he groaned, thrusting gently but steadily into me from behind. We were both on our side, with his left hand under my giant eight-month belly. His fingers rubbed circles over my clit. I exploded in pulses. Luca withdrew and immediately moved over me. Ropes of cum splattered down my butt. Some of it hit my face.

I shifted on my back. "I'm already at thirty-eight weeks. It's okay if the baby comes now."

He grinned at me while still milking his cock. "I know. But I like marking you." Luca closed his eyes and shuddered. When he'd squeezed every drop, he gave a satisfying exhale and got off the bed. "I'll run you a bath."

I stared at my husband's fine ass, not regretting using my pregnancy horniness to make excuses for him to fuck me. Two weeks after my escapade to Red Oak, I had quit going to the attic and moved back into our bedroom. I wasn't sure if seeing Jessica in those pictures precipitated my decision, but I couldn't demand Luca's fidelity if I was neglecting my husband, could I? We also had an impending trip to New York to attend Sera and Matteo's wedding and Luca informed me that we were staying a week. As it stood then, I didn't think I could survive being around my husband with this rift between us.

So I decided to ask him if he had a mistress without sounding needy, just practical. I still remembered his surprise when he found me waiting for him, sitting up against the headboard.

Luca paused at the doorway probably disbelieving that I had returned to our marriage bed. He had a guarded contemplative look about him as he carefully shut the door. He walked into the closet, not saying anything. After shedding his jacket, he emerged. While he was unbuttoning his shirt, he asked, "Are you moving back in here?"

"It's getting harder to go to the end of the hall and take the steps to the attic."

He removed his shirt and put it in the dry-cleaning bag. "I was getting concerned. I guess it's good exercise, but there are better ways to get that." He tipped his chin to the window. "We have a beautiful garden and fresh air."

I crossed my arms and cocked a knee on the bed, letting my sleep shirt slide down my thigh. He probably got an eyeful of my pink panties. "I do that too."

Alertness stiffened his body. "There's something else?"

"I'm horny, Luca."

He prowled toward the bed. "I had wondered if there was any truth regarding pregnant women and their need for sex." The corner of his mouth tipped up. "I was beginning to think it was an outright lie."

"You were waiting for me to ask you?"

"You were the one who abandoned our marriage bed and moved to the attic."

"I didn't like sleeping in it alone," I said. "I didn't like waking up in it alone." I shrugged, attempting to remain indifferent. "But I don't see why I can't demand sex from my husband."

"Demand?" He circled the bed to my side. "You can demand sex from me any time."

"That's kind of hard if you're in Chicago."

"If you're going to use sex to make me feel guilty about my duty to family, think again. Do you want me to fuck you or not?"

I steeled my spine. "That depends. Are you fucking someone else?"

"Are you accusing me of cheating on you?" he asked.

"It's not considered cheating in our culture, is it?" I shot back. "It's the right of made men."

"And you're okay with it?"

"I don't know, Luca. Is it a part of your expectations?" I asked. "Because it's only right that I have mine."

"If you let another man touch you, tesoro, I'm going to hunt him down, make you watch as I cut him to pieces." The threatening gleam left no doubt he would do it too.

"I saw pictures of you and Jessica." My voice wavered.

"Are you spying on me?"

"Spying? No. It's hardly spying when it's all over the tabloids." I was exaggerating. It was not a headline but buried in unverified stories.

"I can't avoid her. We go to the same events."

"She was with you in Vegas."

He sighed heavily and sank to the bed and then held my hand. "When did you see this?"

"The day you left when we had our chat at breakfast about your expectations."

He looked away, cursing, and then back at me again. "And you waited two weeks to confront me?"

"I was deciding."

"You stressed about it for two weeks before you tell me this." His voice rose.

"You're stressing me right now."

He looked away again and muttered an expletive. Standing up, swiping his upper lip with the back of his hand, he glared at me. "Be thankful you're pregnant because I would very much like to wring your neck."

"Stop using my pregnancy as an excuse to avoid discussions."

"Avoid discussions..." He threw up his hands. "What is there to discuss? I'm not hiding a mistress and I will not apologize if she's at the same event as I am. This is ridiculous."

"It's not ridiculous if the papers make fun of your wife."

"I don't read the stupid trash that you do. Taking them on is not worth it. But I will look into it, and if they make false accusations, then I will fix it."

Was I sentencing a lying reporter to his death? "I don't want you distracted with the work you are doing with Papà."

I'd heard from Carmine that the Russians were playing hard-ball. "I just want to know that...that..."

"That I'm not bringing home any STDs?" Luca asked.

My cheeks heated. His eyes softened, and he sat beside me again. "I will never endanger my wife with something like that. And I vow to you I'm not sleeping with Jessica or anyone else."

"It's just that I can't believe that you would go that long without sex."

"I'm not ruled by my dick, and there is always the use of my hand." The warmth in his eyes morphed into unmasked heat. "I

love watching you come. I love watching you take all of me. The way you throw back your head, open your mouth and moan...even when I have my cock buried deep inside you, I want to take it out and put it in your mouth." He trailed his fingers down my body, lingering over the curve of my belly, before wedging them between my thighs, seeking my wetness. "Now, I very much want to please my horny wife."

After that talk, our sexual relationship heated up. Big-time. Apparently, Luca had researched different positions that would work for pregnant women. Doggy style, standing, even in the bathtub in reverse cowgirl. He was still remote when we were around other people. The bedroom was our safe place, or so I told myself. It probably was for him too, after he made sure I abided by his expectations that he would never love me.

The sound of the rushing water turning off ended my rumination into the past few months.

Luca exited the bathroom in all his naked glory, his cock relaxed yet still formidable. When I lifted my gaze to his, there was a cocky tilt to his smile.

"Don't tell me you're not satisfied," he said in mock offense. "Do you need me to lick you?"

I shifted my thighs together. "Maybe?"

He gave a shake of his head. "The water will get cold. I didn't make it very hot. How about after? If you still require the services of my mouth?"

He bent and carried me to the bathroom. This had been our routine after I returned to our marriage bed. He enjoyed carrying me around after sex. If not to set me on the counter and clean his semen between my thighs, he'd lower me into the bath. He didn't always join me, but tonight, he got in behind me. And I leaned against him. My enormous belly bobbed in the water. He put my hair up and twisted it in a knot. He asked me to teach him how to do it when we were in Paris. Luca didn't want my hair getting wet, knowing I was going to fall asleep after the bath and he was right. My eyes were drooping.

He kissed my shoulder, sending goose bumps across my skin.

"You're going to be late," I said.

"They'll wait," Luca replied.

"But you said it was the most important meeting with the Russians."

"I've got time. The meeting isn't until midnight."

It was only six p.m. It had been a rainy day. Luca and I had spent all afternoon inside our room because he was going to be in Chicago for the weekend. I was getting more of him than I had been after he defined his expectations. I wasn't sure if I was happy with the status quo. Maybe if he hadn't shown me his caring and consuming side in Paris. Maybe if he hadn't made me fall in love with that man. I wasn't sure if it was an illusion, but the realities of his responsibilities were something I couldn't ignore or pretend to be ignorant about.

This could be our new normal.

Hot sex in the bedroom, cold husband out of it.

He wasn't exactly cold…he showed affection, and he showered me with gifts, even thoughtful ones. Tonight he gave me a beautiful locket. He told me I could put our baby's picture in it.

"What did Rachel say at your last checkup?"

"Baby is fine. I told her Mom is not, and is ready for him to come out."

My checkups were rarely in town anymore. Luca had an ultrasound machine installed in the nursery. It was overkill, but expense wasn't a concern for him when it came to my needs, as long as he didn't come along with it.

Ugh, I wished I could stop being bitter about the situation.

"Is that why you keep seducing me?"

I laughed lightly. Luca was, in a way, correct. More often than not, I initiated. I couldn't help it. My husband was one sexy beast, and if I were honest with myself, I loved his broody remoteness when we were around other people. Plus, I was ruled by hormones. It was the perfect excuse to enjoy my husband.

If only he hadn't told me he would never love me.

I trailed my fingers up his hairy leg. He growled in my ear, "Don't get me started. I have to go soon."

"Didn't you promise to lick me?"

"You're a temptress." He nipped my ear. "And I'm always starved for you." His hands cupped my breasts. "I love these. They're so heavy. You're very beautiful when you're pregnant. You have no idea," he murmured. "I should have thought about having a photographer take your picture. I've seen those in art galleries."

"I would love that."

"Maybe the next baby," he said.

"Luca, I still have to deliver this one."

His hands lowered to my belly again, splaying his fingers wide. "This is just so fucking sexy. I made this."

"You contributed a single sperm."

He emitted a deep chuckle. "Come on. I have work to do."

He helped me out of the tub and toweled me dry, then he lifted me up again.

"I don't know how you could lug me around like this."

"You weigh nothing."

"I'm a hundred fifty pounds."

"And I can squat three hundred."

"You should be careful about your back. You're not getting any younger."

He laid me gently on the bed, but his eyes promised retribution. "Are you calling me an old man, *tesoro*?"

I smiled languidly. I didn't even think I could stay awake. I was falling asleep when Luca got between my legs, put his mouth on me, and wrung out an orgasm that wasn't as intense as the earlier ones, but was enough to relax me.

I fell asleep before he left the room.

A stab in my belly woke me. At first, I wasn't sure if it was a dream. I glanced at the clock. It was one in the morning. Everything was dark and silent. I needed to pee. I rolled to my side, and with difficulty, got up. I was transferring to the recliner after I did my business. Padding across the floor, I almost made it to the bathroom when water splashed down my legs.

It was as though my vagina dropped a water balloon.

Heart pounding, I hit the lights, and indeed my legs were wet. Stay calm. Stay calm. We have a procedure. What is the procedure?

Stay calm!

I splashed water on my face and brushed my teeth. God knew when I could do that again. Halfway to the bed, a jabbing sensation made me hunch over. That was not a cramp or gas. Gritting my teeth, the first thing I did was call Dr. Kingsley. After a few questions, she told me to go to the hospital.

Then I called Luca. It went directly to voicemail.

They were still in a blasted meeting? I texted him and Dario. Then I called Tony.

"Yeah."

"I'm in labor."

There was a pause and then…"I'll tell Rocco to meet you in the room."

Minutes later, the knock sounded on the door, and I heard Martha's voice.

Tony must have woken everyone.

Martha came into the room. Nessa followed, and she smiled at me. She had somewhat forgiven me for getting Tony in trouble and hadn't been giving me the cold shoulder anymore. I guess it also helped that I learned ASL, so she didn't always have to resort to notepads or the phone app for communication with me. Together with Martha, they'd been helpful in getting the nursery set up.

"Have you timed your contractions?" Martha asked while Rocco went to get my packed bag. I was walking back and forth to add extra toiletries into another bag until Nessa signed for me to sit. We'd all gone through this fire drill before at Martha's insistence, so when the time came, we weren't running around like headless chickens. I sat on the couch, my legs spread in an unladylike manner.

"I just had that one, but Doctor Kingsley told me to head to the hospital. I called Luca and Dario and left them messages." I winced, getting more uncomfortable by the second.

"Tony has pulled the Escalade out front," Rocco said. "The others are ready to escort."

They helped me up. "Luca...please try to contact him." I didn't know who I was addressing.

It was Rocco who answered, "Tony is trying to get through to one of the capos." We made our way down the hallway. "The boss had strict instructions to keep this on a tight phone tree."

Confused, I asked, "Is there a threat against me?"

Rocco shook his head. "Not particularly, but there are high-stakes discussions going on right now."

The Russians and their money and the big loss at the auction a few months ago. The money I had sitting in several numbered accounts. Doriana told me not to move it yet, saying that she'd been under several cyberattacks. I hadn't communicated with her since I stopped going into the attic, and Luca had spent more time at home.

Many times I wanted to come clean to my husband, but we were too deep in opposing directions.

Both Martha and Nessa held on to my arms as we navigated the staircase. Another contraction hit me. Not as strong to make me double over, but just enough for me to make an agonized sound.

"Oooooh…" I moaned as I lumbered into the SUV. "I can't wait for this boy to come out."

Rocco got in beside Tony.

Martha and Nessa piled in from opposite sides of me.

"So Yvonne is in charge at the mansion," I joked. I couldn't wait for her to leave for Chicago and be with her boyfriend and leave the house. She was toxic, and I avoided her as much as possible. I was just glad Luca and I cleared up the Jessica problem.

"Heaven help us," Martha said while Nessa made the sign of the cross.

∽

Luca

The air was charged in the Kometa gentleman's club. Vasily Orlov owned the club. He was the Russian mobster who'd been my nemesis since I kicked his ass in Igra Bossov—Game of Bossess— seven years ago. It was an underground fight held every five years. He'd been angling for a rematch and had been heckling me to fight in the last one. It was a big moneymaker for everyone involved. However, the losers tend to be sore losers, because all organized crime bosses had egos the size of Antarctica. They should abolish the competition because it had done nothing but cause friction between organizations.

But the Russians loved it.

Beside Orlov was Peter Koshkin. Koshkin and I were allies, and I considered him a good friend outside of business, but inside of it, friendships had no meaning. I helped his bid to overthrow the previous leader of the Moscow Cadre, smuggling the needed weapons to his soldiers.

Now Koshkin was pakhan, the head of the Moscow Cadre which was the center of Russian organized crime.

On my right were Dario and Ange, and on my left were Carmine and two other capos.

With Orlov, my patience was in short supply. We both had Chicago officials in our pockets, and all we had done in the previous months was block each other's licenses and real estate deals. Tit for tat. It was fucking petty playing chicken. He just wouldn't let this thing with Santino go, but I suspected his stubbornness had everything to do with his previous loss to me in the games.

I didn't want Koshkin involved. For him to leave his Moscow lair meant that this had gotten his attention.

And fuck had we gotten his attention.

After Dario received word that the DEA was about to bust one of our ships when it got to port, we dumped Koshkin's drug shipment that was supposed to have gotten to Orlov.

Sure enough, the agents swarmed the pier when the ship arrived.

"We all know why we're here," Koshkin said. "My half billion in product is in the Atlantic Ocean."

The cost was really fifty million. Koshkin mentioned its street price for effect.

"Now where am I going to get the money to pay off the Colombians?"

"I already talked to Rodriguez," I said. "He's aware of the situation."

"That's not the only problem," Orlov retorted. "I have no product to sell."

"Koshkin isn't your only source," I said.

"It's the highest quality," my Russian nemesis insisted. "Credibility is important."

"My money is missing." Koshkin split a look between Orlov and me. "There's still a big hole in my bank account." He leaned forward. "A hole that needs to be filled to support the organization. I'll accept twenty-five million from each of you, but this war between the two of you must reach a resolution now."

"Koshkin," I said. "This shipment of drugs is merely goodwill on the Morettis' side." I didn't want to make an enemy of Koshkin, but this was exactly why I didn't like doing shit like this. "There's a signed agreement with my father that where a raid is a possibility, the interests of the Chicago crime family come first." I tipped my head at Dario. "We have the agreement here if—"

"I am aware of the agreement, but your father had the arrangement with my predecessor."

"Who I helped you oust."

Koshkin's eyes narrowed at me. "Are you calling in a favor?"

"When I helped you gain control of the Moscow Cadre, I didn't do it because it was a favor." My voice had sharpened. "I did it because I thought it was right."

Dario cleared his throat, warning me of the escalating tension.

"So, you're saying I should let you off the hook for losing my product," Koshkin said.

"We are going around and around on this," I said. "I'll tell you what. I'll pay the twenty-five million, but you will never use my ship again. There's a rat in our organizations and I don't think our businesses and risks align. Chicago doesn't make money from your drugs. We do it for goodwill, but it's causing more problems and risks than I'm willing to take."

"We don't need him," Orlov said.

"On the contrary," I countered. "You seem to think you need my planes to ferry the depraved business you have going on."

Koshkin stood and slapped his hand on the table. "Enough. This thing between the two of you needs to be settled now. Moretti, may I request Chicago leave the room while I confer with Orlov?"

I shrugged. "No problem." I could use a cigarette break.

As our group left the room, we went to another part of the club where it was quieter.

"I told your father's consigliere before it's bad business to move drugs for the Russians," Dario said, scrolling through his phone. He froze in the way that called my attention.

"What is it?" My phone was still turned off, and I loathed to use it most times anyway. I preferred people to tell me things face-to-face.

"Fuck," he muttered.

I'd been in the act of lighting up. I took out the cigarette and repeated, "What is it?"

He came to my side and said in my ear, "Natalya is in labor."

I reared back, blood draining from my face, my fingers mangling the cigarette. "Now?"

Carmine joined us. "You heard? Tony texted me. Natalya—"

"We know." I scrubbed my face. Emilio hammered into me the possibility of this very scenario. That made men put the entire organization first, even when it was his wife giving birth. But every instinct was clawing at me to storm out of here and go straight to my wife.

"You can't show weakness now," Carmine said. "If Koshkin finds out you ditched him because Natalya is giving birth, he'll not see you as a boss, but someone who is controlled by his wife."

"I hate this bullshit," Dario growled. "A man's wife should come first. That's why women are treated like crap in the family."

Ange's face was inscrutable through all this, until he said, "You want to change the code, Dario?"

My brother was expecting me to uphold the code. Damn everyone to hell.

One of Orlov's men appeared at the door to our room. "Koshkin wants you back in there."

I nodded. There was no telling how long negotiations would take. I was sure Koshkin would want to go for a drink afterward.

Words scaled up my throat with difficulty. "Go to her," I told Dario. "I'll finish up here."

"Are you—"

"As my consigliere," I cut him off. "Isn't that what you're going to suggest? If I let you handle this, then we'll not only be at war with Orlov but also Koshkin. That's not what we need right now."

Dario nodded. "As your consigliere, I agree with your decision."

"Natalya will understand," Carmine said. "She was born for this."

But as my footsteps made their way back to the clubroom, they wanted to head in the opposite direction. To my wife, who was about to give birth to my son. I hadn't prayed to God in a long time and had neglected to visit a church in the past few months. But I prayed now for the safe delivery of my son, and that my wife would be okay.

Natalya

The door to the delivery room opened, and my heart expanded with hope. Only to deflate quicker than a popped balloon.

I expected to see Luca, but it was Dario.

He hovered at the door and talked to Martha.

"Where's Luca?" My voice cracked with exhaustion and emotion. Both of them turned toward me. The usually stoic Dario wore a face full of apology that made my eyes brim with tears. The time between contractions was closer. Dr. Kingsley said I was almost there. But my whole body and mind fought against my son's imminent birth. I clung to hope that Luca would hold my hand through this.

To witness his son being born.

He wasn't coming.

Because he didn't care.

"Something came up," Dario said. "Please believe that it's really important."

Tears continued to roll down my cheeks, and I looked away. As much as everyone around me was supportive, I must have nagged them to death to get hold of Luca.

I should have known nothing had changed.

He set his expectations, didn't he?

The end all of all contractions stabbed my belly. It was pressure more than pain but I cried out. Martha rushed to my side.

"That was less than five minutes. Is it painful? The epidural is not working?"

"It's working," I whispered because the pain was in my heart, and I wondered if the pain of childbirth would have been better. The latter was fleeting, but the former would leave deep scars forever. I just knew it.

"I'll get the doctor." Dario hurried from the room.

Not long after, Dr. Kingsley appeared.

"I hear we're ready," she said cheerfully.

But my idiotic heart was still in denial. My whole body was fighting the birth of my son.

"Luca's not here yet," I cried. Martha helped me to a sitting position and scooted me to the edge of the bed.

"It's his loss, honey." The doctor affixed my feet into the stirrups and looked between my legs. "Yup, your son is coming."

"No. Not yet." I glanced at Martha, still clinging to hope that in all this frenzy, I didn't understand. "What did Dario say? Luca is just delayed, right?…Ahhh." The blunt pressure was the strongest yet.

"Listen. To. Me." Dr. Kingsley gripped my knees to command my attention. "Forget Luca. He'll not be on time, and your son isn't on his schedule. He needs to be born now."

I trembled as I fought for control and bit on my lower lip to keep from crying for my husband again. I found myself nodding.

"Remember those breathing exercises?"

This time I exhaled a raspy, "Yes."

"Okay, Natalya," Dr. Kingsley said. I took in a lungful of oxygen and started the fast pants I'd learned during my birthing exercises with Martha. I also did it with Nessa. Never with Luca.

"Now, push."

CHAPTER
Fifteen

LUCA

It was four-thirty a.m.

The elevator doors slid open, and I stepped onto the floor where my wife and son were resting. Guilt held me motionless. Negotiations with Orlov took another hour and, as expected, Koshkin wanted to celebrate the truce. I had intended to have one drink, but Koshkin insisted on another. I didn't refuse because they would ask me where I was rushing off to, and I didn't want to tell those assholes my mind was elsewhere. That my thoughts were with my wife and son. I didn't want any of them to know that they mattered more to me than the deal I made with them.

Duty and security for my family made me stay.

Ange remained in Chicago while Carmine accompanied me to the hospital. He had walked ahead, but when he realized I was not following, he stopped and pivoted in my direction. "What the hell, man? Your son is waiting!"

I exhaled sharply and forced my lead-weighted feet to move. The fucker was finding humor in my situation. He slapped my back. "Congratulations again."

Dario headed in our direction the second he saw us. "Congratulations." He shook my hand. "Big boy. Almost nine pounds."

I nodded briefly. Tony had already texted me my son's stats.

Moretti soldiers from the mansion packed the hallways. "Some of you should head back," I told them. "There's enough people here to guard the queen."

"She is your queen." Tony came forward and extended his hand. "Congratulations, boss."

It did not escape me that not all the men came forward, and none of the women tried at all. Martha and Nessa, especially, awarded me the kind of glare that left a sunburn.

I brushed that off. "Martha, how is she?"

"She cried for you," the old woman accused. "She called for you, Luca, while she was giving birth to your son."

Fuck.

"Not now, Martha," I snapped and struggled to ignore how those words punctured my insides, depleting me of the effort not to lose it. "How's my son?"

Nessa made a sound and huffed off. Martha's eyes followed the younger woman before returning to me and emitted a resigned sigh. A sigh that was full of disappointment that weighed down the guilt even more.

Fuck them.

"Go on in, but don't expect any welcome there."

She left me standing at the door.

I gripped the handle and contemplated my hand-crafted Italian shoes for two seconds. They mocked me because it was a reminder of my first failure as a husband. Worrying more about ruining them than making my wife happy. But failing to be here for my son's birth…I breathed in uncertainty, and exhaled determination. I was going to fix this. I opened the door and walked in.

Natalya was lying on the bed. The lights were dimmed. The crib was on her left side.

I walked up to the bed.

She wasn't sleeping. Her eyes were partially open but turned away from me, staring at the crib. She must have heard me outside.

"Natalya…"

A tear fell from her cheek.

That single tear almost sent me to my knees, and an uncomfortable pressure formed in my chest. "I'm sorry I couldn't be here."

"Go see your son." Her voice was lifeless.

I leaned over to touch her, but she flinched and inched away from me. My fingers hovered, wanting to tip her face to look at me.

"Go." Her voice was more forceful. "See your son."

"Natalya, this is ridiculous," I said. "You're not married to just anyone. You married the boss of the Chicago family. You knew how important this evening's meeting was going to be." My frustrations of the night were bleeding into my words, and I couldn't filter them.

Finally, she turned to face me and I wished she hadn't. Because her eyes were as dead as her voice. It was as though she was not seeing me. Her face was expressionless, and if it wasn't for the tears that rolled down her cheeks, I would have thought she was catatonic.

"You're right. I'm sorry."

"What? I wasn't asking for an apology." I threw up my hands. I wasn't going to win this argument, so I went to see my son.

He was so tiny and helpless, but the sight of him stole my ability to breathe. I swayed, dizziness hitting me. It must be the exhaustion from the power play with the Russians hitting home too. My fingers curled over the crib for support. I glanced over my shoulder. "He's beautiful, *tesoro*."

She didn't answer, but her expression changed from lifeless to something akin to sadness. I wasn't sure, but what I was sure of was I didn't like it either. When this moment was supposed to be one of the happiest of our marriage, despair shrouded the room. I swallowed. "Have you decided on a name? Salvatore? Elias? Enzo?" Elias didn't have Italian roots, but Natalya was fond of that name and mentioned it the few times we were talking about baby names.

"Elias," she said. "If you don't mind."

"Of course, I don't mind."

Finally, she smiled. Again, it wasn't one of pure happiness but resignation, as if she'd given up all hopes of joy.

The pressure in my chest intensified into a persistent stabbing ache.

Guilt.

Self-loathing.

Unworthiness that I didn't deserve my beautiful wife and son. "Do you want me to bring him to you?"

"He's sleeping."

"Did you breastfeed him?"

"My milk won't come yet," she said listlessly.

"Natalya…"

"I'm tired, Luca. I don't have the energy to hear why you didn't come sooner."

I didn't offer further excuses. She wasn't receptive. She was lying down, but it looked like she was about to sink into the mattress with the weight of her hopelessness. Still, I tried to muster up a self-righteousness that I had done the right thing by staying in Chicago. What I did was for the good of both of our families, especially the survival of Galluzo.

Why couldn't she see this?

But at what price? a condemning voice in my head taunted.

I forced a nod. "Okay. We'll talk later."

I was halfway across the room when her words stopped me. "Talk about what? Your expectations? I think I can extrapolate from experience."

Extrapolate? An interesting term coming from my wife. "Get some rest, *tesoro*." I cocked my head to our sleeping son. "He will need you."

I exited the room and closed it gently. Then I leaned against it, closing my eyes and shaking my head. That encounter was more draining than being in a room full of mobsters.

"It's about time you got here."

I opened my eyes and glared at Rachel. "I don't need to hear it from you too." I walked in the opposite direction from where everyone was gathered because I knew a lecture was coming from the doctor. I had had enough of judgmental people who didn't know what it took to run the family.

Nessa cast me one last disapproving look before she went into Natalya's room. Fine. Everyone was closing ranks around my wife. Great. Just fucking great.

"Where were you?" Rachel asked.

I entered the stairwell. The doctor followed as I had expected. She was one of the few people who I let psychoanalyze me because she knew me when I was a pimply faced boy who took in stray cats.

Besides, she was the family shrink.

I leaned against the wall. The itch to light up clawed at me. "The Russians. Koshkin is in town."

Rachel held a clipboard against her chest. "His timing sucks."

I rubbed the top of my mouth, still disbelieving at the string of events. "What were the odds of Natalya going into labor at the same time I would be tied up in the most crucial negotiation of the past year."

"It's not a secret that Natalya is pregnant," she said.

I kicked at the steps in front of me, letting them take the brunt of my caged frustration. "She's going to be okay, right?"

"Physically, she's fine. Mentally, psychologically…"

My foot stopped kicking, and I braced. "Do you need to talk to her?"

"Oh my God, Luca," she exclaimed. "She needs you. She and your baby need you."

"They have me."

"How many checkups did you attend?"

"A lot," I snapped. "What is this? An inquisition? You knew exactly what I could give."

"You take a wife and you treat her like this?"

"I treat her just fine. She's got everything—more than most wives have. You're reacting like Natalya. Life as a don's wife differs from the fairy tales she consumes. I expected her to know better."

"And you're using that excuse not to do more," she retorted. "Don't you want to see her and the baby healthy?"

"That's an absurd question. Of course, I do."

"The way things are going between the two of you, she might be susceptible to postpartum depression."

My jaw slackened. Fuck. "Junior's wife had that issue."

She touched my arm and squeezed, then handed me a pamphlet. "I just want you to be aware of the signs. She's subdued right now, but at least she's responding positively to the baby." She blew out a breath. "Can you stay at home and be with her for the first few weeks?"

"Yes. All sides agreed to concessions. It might be a Band-Aid to the situation, but it gives me some breathing room for a few months at least."

"Maybe it'll be good for Natalya's parents to visit?"

I nodded grimly. "Yes. I'll call them right now."

CHAPTER
Sixteen

My tiny human cooed as I wrestled him into tiny clothes. He had a head of dark hair, his skin was all pink, and downy baby hair covered his body. I wasn't sure if that was a sign that he was going to be as hairy as his dad.

"Do you need help?" Martha asked after packing all our stuff alongside a slew of baby gifts. It had been two days since I had given birth and I was ready to go home.

"No, all done," I said. I planted Elias into the infant seat that Luca brought in this morning.

"What do you want to do with all the flowers?" she asked.

"Just leave them here. I told the nurse to donate them to charity care."

Luca walked in. "Ready, baby?"

Tony, who was behind him, took our things from Martha and signaled for her to leave with him.

"Depends on which baby you're referring to?" I gave a slight smile.

Luca's eyes grew alert, and he took tentative steps toward me and our son. "You." He searched my face. "I—"

"I don't want to talk about the other night. I don't want you to apologize either because, given the same circumstances, you would have done the same."

"It was a fucked-up situation," he said, and then added quickly, "Not the birth of our son."

"Listen, before we go home, I want to set my own expectations, and I hope you'll give me this," I said.

"I only want what's best for you and Elias," he responded quickly.

"I'm going to sleep in the nursery—"

"Except that," he responded more quickly.

"You should be relieved that you don't have to do nighttime duties."

"We could hire a nanny."

"No. We have Martha and Nessa."

"Nessa is mute. I'm not sure we could consider her reliable care."

"I trust her more than a stranger."

Elias started crying. We both stared at him.

"See, our boy senses that what you're suggesting is wrong," my husband told me.

Glaring at Luca, I bent over our son, unstrapped him, and picked him up.

"I was told that it's not a good idea to pick him up whenever he cries."

"He's two days old, Luca. Don't compare him to yourself."

"Excuse me?"

I turned away from him, bouncing my son gently in my arms

while I looked out the window. "Manipulative." I faced him. "The truth is, I feel like I must protect him from you."

"You think I would do something to hurt our boy?"

"You've hurt his mother." My voice caught, and then I shook my head. "I know. You're probably wondering now if you've married someone too young or who has her head too much in the clouds."

He took a step toward me, dark eyes intense. "I married someone perfect for me. She just doesn't feel it yet."

I didn't know whether to be offended or flattered. Did he mean I should just get with the program?

His eyes scrutinized me some more before he sighed. "Let's get you home."

It didn't take long for Luca to see the logic of my rooming with Elias. After two weeks of Elias screaming his head off in the middle of the night, denying both parents of sleep, Luca relented.

"I don't know how a tiny thing could have lungs that could scream the house down," he groaned.

I pushed up on my elbows. "Are you or am I going to check on him? If I am, I'm going to bring him in here."

He rolled on his back and threw an arm across his forehead. "I need to get up in a few hours. Could you do it?"

Figured. Couldn't say I didn't see this coming.

I was at the door when he added, "Please consider hiring a nighttime nanny. I don't want you exhausted."

Fuck you, Luca. I left the room without answering. In the hallway, I saw Nessa.

"I'm sorry he woke the entire house," I said.

Nessa shrugged and signed. *He's a baby.*

She tipped her chin to our bedroom.

"He said he needs to get up in a few hours."

She shook her head, and I emitted a short, derisive laugh. We entered the bedroom together.

"You have strong lungs, my boy, and ooh." I scrunched my nose. "What is that smell?"

Nessa helped me change diapers. Not that I wasn't becoming an expert at it.

I settled into the full-sized bed equipped with a side crib.

"You can go back to sleep," I told Nessa.

She signed. *Are you sure?*

"We'll be fine. Thank you."

She nodded.

When Elias started fussing again, I gave him the pacifier. This time, he settled down and finally slept. Exhausted, I followed him into slumber.

Time flew when you had a newborn, and you couldn't tell your waking moments from the sleeping ones. Luca tried again to get me to sleep in our room, but I told him it was better for Elias if I stayed with him in the nursery, at least for the first few months. I didn't know why he wanted me there anyway since I frequently smelled of breast milk and baby vomit. He also insisted again on hiring nannies. This last time, he must have lost patience and went on a tirade—which I ended zoning out half of what he said because I was sleep-deprived—but he ended with "…stop acting like a martyr."

I stared at him for a beat before saying, "Shut up, Luca." Then I turned around and left the conversation. He let out a string of profanities I ignored. Ever since the birth of my baby, we never had the chance to talk about anything deeper than Elias's daily routine.

How he was breastfeeding, how he was sleeping, how he was pooping.

One could say I was operating on autopilot, and the most feeling I got was when my breasts were too full of milk.

I'd totally cut off whatever bond Luca and I had created in favor of one with Elias. I wasn't sure if we even had a lasting one. It certainly wasn't strong enough for me to feel anything viscerally. I really wondered if we'd lost something that night Luca failed to show up for Elias's birth.

My parents arrived the night before, and my mother wasted no time siding with Luca.

"Honestly, Nattie, why did you move out of your bedroom?"

"Because Elias needed me more, and it's tiring to make the trip to the nursery when I can just roll over and put a pacifier in his mouth."

"Yes, but you're giving other women the opportunity to slip into your place."

We were in the living room. Elias was four weeks old, happily sleeping in the bassinet and happily unaware of the adults in the room. It was the first night I felt human. At least my parents' visit affected me enough to look presentable instead of ignoring the baby spit on my shoulder.

Mamma, to her credit, helped look after Elias and gave me time to shower. I even had time for a long nap.

Martha and Nessa were running around, preparing for the first dinner party since I married Luca. It was to welcome Papà and to celebrate the birth of my son. I told Luca he was crazy, and I didn't have the patience to entertain guests right now. He said to leave it up to him.

I wondered why we hadn't entertained since we got married, but I figured it had something to do with his trips to Chicago. He'd done enough entertaining there for sure. I hated how my mother's words made me insecure all over again, and I wished I could just avoid her. But I couldn't.

"I can't have sex with him for another two weeks anyway. I don't even feel remotely sexy."

Mamma's nostrils flared when I mentioned sex. I inwardly smirked. I wasn't an innocent anymore.

"I'm just saying," she huffed. "Even married, your husband is considered a prime catch. He's one of the youngest bosses of such a powerful organization, not to mention he's handsome. There are many women willing to keep him warm at night and be his mistress."

"Mamma, please stop talking. I'm too exhausted to even care."

"You say that now." Her voice pitched low. "But when those bastards start to appear and challenge your son's legacy…then you'll care."

Carmine walked in. I was never more relieved to see him. "Why haven't you come around to see me?"

I rose and ran toward him, although I was probably trying to get away from Mamma. He gave me a hug and an affectionate peck on the cheek. "Chicago was busy."

"So, you're the one keeping my husband occupied?" I teased.

"It was tough…" He looked at Mamma. "But we have cause to celebrate now. Vincenzo wants you to bring Elias to the study."

"Oh, you guys are done with the business talk?"

"The Russians are appeased for now."

"Well, I hope it's forever." I sighed. It was nice having Luca home. We had a weird normal going. I guess it made sense that he was not sleep-deprived when he had mafia business to conduct.

When we entered the study, Papà turned toward us, and a smile broke across his face.

"Ah, you look beautiful, Natalya." He locked me in his arms. "I was worried when I saw you last night." He glanced at Luca. "I was afraid your husband wasn't taking care of you and my grandson."

"Vincenzo, you know how hard it is in the first few months. Natalya was a difficult baby too," Mamma told everyone. "She was colicky."

"I wouldn't know, *amore mio*. All I saw was my little angel." He bent over and picked up Elias who was awake but quiet. My son was looking at Papà intently. "You recognize your nonno, eh? He's heavy." Papà looked at me. "He's going to be a big, strong man."

Elias was a greedy baby. I was having a hard time keeping up with him. My eyes met Luca's across the room. His jaw was clenched and I was taken aback by the way he was scowling at Papà.

"Now you see why Luca worked so hard on that Santino deal?" Carmine asked.

"Carmine," Dario said in a warning tone that made me pay attention. We were past the small talk.

"What?" Carmine's eyes landed on me. "Surely you know."

"What do I need to know?"

Luca came to my side and gripped my elbow. "Nothing. Baby, why don't you—"

I yanked my arm away. "Wait a minute. What do I need to know?"

"It's nothing," Papà said as if it truly was nothing, and continued to rock Elias around. "But I'm sad you don't get to come live with your nonno when you turn eight."

I was still confused, or maybe it was the lack of sleep. "Please explain." I was looking at Luca, but he was not looking at me. He was skewering Carmine with the most scathing stare, and the rush of pebbles weighed down in my gut.

Carmine scratched the back of his head. "It's of no consequence now."

"I will decide if it's of *no* consequence." My voice rose shrilly.

"Relax, dear daughter," Papà said. "It was a stupid bet. The one men make when they are drunk. Luca had too much scotch, and he said he could get the Russians to cave, that he'd even bet his firstborn."

"It was not a serious bet," Luca said.

Papà raised a brow at Luca. "Yes, but we did talk about it the next day. How it would be beneficial if you and Natalya give me a male heir? Oh, don't look like that, Natalya. We are all family. The Galluzo is your legacy. Imagine your son running it one day."

"What is this about living with you when he turns eight?"

My father shrugged. "He can come visit."

"That's not what you really meant." I turned to Carmine. "Tell me the truth."

"Vincenzo has grand plans for his grandson," Carmine said. "It would be ideal to expose him to the organization at a young age."

"I don't see why that's so bad," Papà said. "Don't you want to restore the Galluzo to prestige again? That will happen with Elias."

"What if that's not what I want for my son?" I shook my elbow free from Luca and took Elias from Papà's arms and backed away from everyone in the room.

"Our son," Luca corrected, taking a tentative step toward me. "I handled the Santino problem. That was the deal."

I cocked my head and shot him a warning look not to come closer.

"And if it wasn't? What will happen?"

"Then I'd die trying," he snapped. I shrank further away from them.

Instant remorse crossed Luca's face when he realized he'd lost his temper, and he tried to soften his expression. "Baby," he said. "I would never let Elias go. It was your father's wishful thinking." He cast my father a pointed look. "Tell her, Vincenzo."

"*Sì. Sì.*" Papà rocked back on his heels and cast me a sheepish grin. "Wishful thinking of an old man past his prime. Come on, *bombolina.*" He smiled his father's smile that used to make me feel like the princess of his kingdom. Then it hit me. It was because he was rarely around, but when he was, he made me feel like I was his most treasured possession. It was exactly the way Luca ruined me by giving me Paris. Seeing both men standing side by side, I realized that I'd been manipulated all my life. And that didn't include what my mother had done.

The change in my expression caused an alarmed one to descend on Luca's face.

Yes, my dear husband, I was seeing another layer of this marriage and it was making me sick to my stomach. My baby and I had been pawns this whole time.

Mamma, who'd been quiet until now, inserted herself between us. "Is it so bad if we raised Elias? Many parents would be happy to have the help of the grandparents."

"In my old age, I'm slowing down," Papà added. "I would like to play with my grandchildren." He looked at Luca. "Kinda like Don Corleone in his old age, huh?"

"Real life is not like the movies," I said, but my eyes were on Luca. He flinched. "I've learned that the hard way."

Taking Elias, I left the room.

I heard Papà ask someone, "What did she mean?"

CHAPTER
Seventeen

LUCA

"Keep him away from me," I told Dario.

"Will do." Dario nodded to where our guests had arrived.

What a clusterfuck. If it wasn't for all the time I spent making him fit to lead the Galluzo, I would shoot Carmine on the spot. Working with him these past months, I'd learned to be wary of him. The man thrived on mischief. Even Ange reported a few incidents that would have ended badly for us because of Carmine's commentary. I kept him away from Natalya because my wife was fond of him. Whereas before I welcomed the ammunition Carmine gave me to use against my wife, I'd become more protective of Natalya.

It was time to send him back to Italy.

The dinner was tedious. Whatever spark Natalya gained from six straight hours of sleep had vanished. In her place was an automaton. She ate, and she responded in monotone monosyllabic words. It wasn't exactly how I imagined this gathering would unfold. Among our guests were Chicago politicians I'd invited to show I was a family man and wasn't simply a thug. To show that my father-in-law was a regular guy who'd become a grandfather and not the monster the Italian press had painted him to be. Vincenzo was an excellent diplomat, but I had seen how ruthless he could be, and the monster description wasn't far off. I continued to be baffled by how someone as kind and sweet as Natalya came from such parents. Maybe that was why God hadn't given Vincenzo sons to corrupt, and losing his inner circle had certainly diminished his legend and power.

When the men retired to the study for scotch and cigars, all I could do was brood about my wife and son and give short answers. I was glad Dario had my back. If it wasn't for the license approvals I needed, I had nothing in common with the alderman who had a sleazy private life I'd rather ignore. But I needed him firmly in my pocket before I found a more permanent solution to the Russians.

When all was said and done and our guests were ready to leave, Natalya had disappeared, giving excuses she had a newborn to attend to.

"My wife has contacts in an excellent nanny agency," the alderman said at the door. "Right, sweetheart?"

"I already gave the number to Natalya," she said. "It's usually difficult in the first months."

"I'll keep in touch, Moretti," he said.

Carmine left with the alderman and they chatted on their way to their parked vehicles.

My father-in-law came up beside me. "I appreciate what you've done with Carmine. He seems more confident instead of hanging in the background. He's a smart kid."

"He's smart all right," I muttered. "I'm going to check on Natalya. Dario? You good?"

"I'm going home," my consigliere said. He put a hand on my shoulder and squeezed. "Successful dinner."

I left Vincenzo with Dario. I should have felt exhilarated by the result of the dinner. After months of trying to get the alderman on our side, we had him where we wanted him on the committee, and we could reverse months of losing money.

But what did I lose in the process?

I strode past the kitchen. My mother-in-law was supervising Martha and Nessa. When she saw me, she came up to me with a harried expression. "I am sorry about how my daughter behaved at dinner. She should hire someone other than a mute."

"Stop right there," I cut her off. "My wife is doing an excellent job with Elias and that's all that matters, *capisce*? You damn well don't have the right to criticize my staff. They've been the best support for Natalya when I was too stupid not to be around."

"You can't be around all the time, you're the boss of—"

"Don't make excuses for me." I looked past her to see Martha and Nessa staring at me in surprise. "Do you need my mother-in-law for anything?"

Nessa was already shaking her head vigorously.

Martha was more diplomatic. "We can handle this from here, Mrs. Conte. Please take your rest."

I stared at Elena. I wasn't going to let her reprimand my people when I wasn't around.

She pulled back her shoulders, lifted her chin, and clacked her heels out of the kitchen.

"Thank you," Martha said. "I can tolerate Mrs. Conte, but I don't want Natalya to take the brunt of her displeasure."

Fuck, I didn't think of that. "I'll go to her now."

But when I arrived at the nursery, Natalya wasn't there. Hope rose in my chest and I strode straight into our bedroom, only to deflate when I found it empty.

I texted Tony and Rocco. "Where's my wife?"

Rocco responded. "Attic."

She hadn't been up there since June. I hurried to the opposite wing of the mansion, frustrated that she might have reverted to her aversion of our bedroom. Natalya better not make this an excuse to keep my son from me. The expression on her face in the study struck a deep rooted fear in my heart. That there was no hope of coming back from this. That I'd finally lost her. Since missing our son's birth I'd never again saw the look in her eyes the way I saw it in Paris. My chest grew tight. It was as if she'd stopped loving me.

Rocco met me at the bottom of the stairs leading to the attic. Amusement twitched the corners of his mouth.

"Something funny?" I growled.

"No, boss."

I double-timed it up the steps. I was about to pound on the door when I remembered about Elias. I tried the knob. To my relief, it was unlocked.

Natalya was on her laptop. She gave a start and slammed the lid closed.

Elias was in a portable bassinet beside the coffee table.

"Why are you up here?" she whispered.

"I could ask the same of you," I said. "What were you reading?"

"Baby stuff."

It wasn't, but I let it slide because our son woke up.

"I need to feed him," Natalya said, unbuttoning her pajama top. And when one of her breasts was exposed, I instantly became hard. We hadn't had sex in a month. I wasn't sure if she was receptive anyway. After what I read about postpartum depression, I tried very hard to let her have her way. Case in point—her sleeping in the nursery. I even made an excuse that it bothered my sleep so the onus wouldn't be on her, but on her selfish, manipulative husband.

When she picked up Elias and he latched on to a nipple, an altogether different emotion swamped me.

Intense protectiveness of my wife and child.

These past few weeks, I felt like a stranger around them. It was so much of me on the outside looking in. But in the attic, where the cozy environment was so different from the rest of the house, I felt closer.

I had the overwhelming desire for family. For just the three of us.

"You're still here?" Natalya asked in a tone that was not welcoming at all, but I was overcome with such a possessiveness for them, it didn't incite me to leave her.

"I take pleasure in watching you feed him." My voice came out gruff. The strange emotion I was feeling had worked its way up my throat. "You're beautiful, *tesoro*."

She gave me a strange look before she dropped her gaze to our son.

Elias was staring at his mother, and I had the urge to hug them.

For the first time in a long time, I gave in to the urge.

The self-control I let rule my entire life crumbled.

Up here, I wasn't the boss of the Chicago crime family.

Up here, I was merely a mortal man falling in love with his family.

My real family.

The fear of being weak rattled inside me, but I ignored it to allow me this elation I'd forsaken before.

I sat beside her. She stiffened, even shifted away from me.

"Please don't," I pleaded. I wrapped my arms around her and pulled her against my chest. Something in my voice made her relent and relax her body against mine, but she wouldn't look at me.

I would take that for now. This opportunity to have my family in my arms and look over her shoulder while she fed our son.

I never tried to apologize again for not being there when she gave birth. Like Dario, I couldn't say if I wouldn't have done the same thing, so the apology would have been empty.

"You still have to explain what possessed you to make such a deal with my father," she whispered.

"Arrogance. Ambition."

"Is that why you set expectations? You said you will never love me. Is it because you knew we would be separated when Elias turns eight? Because surely you also know that I'm not willing to let go of my son."

"The expectations have nothing to do with that. More of what I knew I could give," I said. Nothing had changed. I still feared weakness, but I also wanted my family. "I care very deeply, Natalya. You and Elias are very important to me. All I ask is you allow me to show you what could be if you just let me care for you the way I want to."

Elias finished feeding. Natalya pulled away from me, and I was hesitant to release her.

"Let me go."

"Only if you promise we'll talk after this."

"We will, otherwise I'm not sure I won't stab you in your sleep."

Shocked by the viciousness in her voice, my arms slackened and she slipped away. The relaxed vibe in the room vanished. She stood and burped Elias, and when she set him in the bassinet, he promptly fell asleep.

"He's such a good boy," I commented.

She skewered me with a look. "He is, and you would have known if you'd looked in on him more."

"You were upset with me. I didn't want to stress you out more with my presence."

"You mean you took the easy way out. I'm more upset with you now." She walked to the far end of the room and stared out the window, reminding me of the night of the storm when I came up to see her. Tonight was a full moon, and it surrounded her with a glow that made me think of an avenging angel. And she was about to unleash her heavenly punishment on me.

I should go to church more often.

Maybe confess my sins to the priest for being a terrible husband. After all, I set out to manipulate my wife into loving me. I hadn't fulfilled my vow to love and cherish her. Those vows I said with scorn. I wondered if I would ever say them with all my heart.

I walked up behind her to see the moon and the stars cast my estate in such beauty. Beauty I worked so hard to keep, but having Natalya and Elias in this room, I felt a peacefulness I hadn't experienced before. I didn't thrive in peace. I thrived in chaos.

"I deserve your anger."

"You continue to disappoint me, Luca," she said. "Every time I think I've seen the worst of you and think I could survive what little you give to our marriage, fate throws something else our way."

Her words hit me hard, but instead of feeling contrite, I felt offended. I wasn't the worst husband. I didn't beat her. I made sure she had the best care, the best staff to help her around the house. She could spend whatever the fuck she wanted. And I'd fucked her when she wanted, although it pleased me too that she was very sexual. I should get her pregnant more often. Maybe more children would take her focus off my lack of time because apparently, my wife, despite her upbringing, didn't understand what it meant to be the wife of a don. "Survive? I beg your pardon, *tesoro*, but whose cock did you ride when you'd been horny?"

Her head whipped toward me, eyes narrowing. "You throw that back at me now? You know that's the hormones speaking."

I smirked. "You continue to lie to yourself. It's because you love me and I'm the only one who could draw those sexy sounds from the back of your throat."

"We're back to sex. Marriage is more than sex. And if that's your reasoning, then you should be worried because having sex with you is the last thing my body wants right now."

Fuck. I believed her because Rachel did warn me this was a possibility that after women pushed out a baby the size of a bowling ball, the last thing they wanted was to have sex again. That wouldn't do. Sex was the one place we connected. I fought to keep my face neutral.

"I show you affection." I threw my arm at the big-screen TV and the rows of romance books. "You have these impossible stan-dards you set for me. I told you before I'm more villain than hero. You are my wife."

"Am I supposed to be some Cruella de Vil character to match you?" Her eyes flashed in challenge.

"Am I cruel to you?"

"Oh my God, never mind," she muttered something about Dalmatians.

Dammit. I intended to meet her halfway and make peace with her, not make our situation more difficult. If only she would agree to hire a nanny.

"Look," I said quietly. "I'd like to help with Elias. I don't need to leave for Chicago as often."

She looked back at the baby. "You don't seem comfortable holding him."

"It's because of the judgment in your eyes each time I do!" I whispered harshly.

Natalya stared at me incredulously. "Because every time you hold him, it's like you're holding an alien. Have you ever even held a baby before?"

"Of course, I have. I'm godfather to so many." It didn't take someone to head-shrink me to know the reason.

She must have read my mind because Natalya's face turned mocking. "You couldn't look at Elias because of the guilt weighing you down that you decided to give away our firstborn before you even married me."

I wasn't expecting Natalya. I was expecting a malleable mafia wife who would be content to stay at home and bear my children. I wasn't expecting a wife who demanded more from me. Natalya demanded more than all of Emilio's wives combined. My father never let his wives speak to him this way. My brother Junior was different, maybe because he wanted a more loving marriage than our father. But it didn't end well for him. When his wife had a nervous breakdown, it affected his concentration. He became care-less. A carelessness I blamed when he and his wife were killed in a sabotaged car. Our enemies wouldn't have had the chance to tamper with the brakes if Junior had been more vigilant, less distracted, less caught up in his wife's mental problems.

I intended to learn from both of their mistakes.

"We're keeping Elias." I inched closer to her. "I made sure of that. My arrogance caused me to miss my son's birth and guilt had prevented me from being the father he needs." I clasped her elbows to pull her closer. "As his father, I'll make many mistakes, Natalya."

"Are you apologizing before you even try?" she asked. "Your track record with me hasn't been good. You can't blame me for wanting to protect our son from your brand of manipulation."

"As my heir, I intend to teach him everything, but I won't be cruel. Just give me a chance."

Doubt clouded her eyes, and I had no one to blame but myself.

"I'll do better." I kissed the top of her head. "Please." I leaned back and locked our gazes. "He's still a baby. Too young to understand manipulation. Maybe he's the one manipulating us...all that late night crying?"

"Maybe. He *is* a Moretti."

A hint of a smile curved her lips, and I took that as an encouraging sign.

"What chance are you exactly asking for?" she asked. "Are you going to help with the late nights?"

"As much as I can," I promised.

"Because I don't want you to make it a habit to send us out of the room if we are interfering with your sleep like we're a nuisance."

I wanted to defend myself, but I'd just have to prove it.

"I won't. I was an asshole."

"Okay, but this is your last chance."

I nodded. This was the first step to getting back into my wife's good graces and have her look at me with love again.

CHAPTER
Eighteen

NATALYA

Mamma and Papà stayed for a month and left after Elias's baptism. Dario became my son's godfather. While I still insisted on sleeping in the nursery, Luca and I had settled into a new normal. He put a baby monitor in our bedroom, so when the baby cried, sometimes he'd come in and help me. When he didn't have to drive to Chicago for a meeting, he did his part of staying awake when Elias was being fussy.

We hadn't resumed sexual intimacy because even when I was at eight-weeks postnatal, and Dr. Kingsley had already given the go-ahead, my body just wasn't feeling it.

I was too stressed. I wasn't sleeping enough or eating enough, and my breast milk had dwindled to nothing, compounding the stress.

I was stressed because our new normal was a facade, and my double life was catching up with me, blurring the lines between my feelings, the challenges of being a new mother, and my responsibility to Doriana's network.

On the night of the dinner, Carmine had mentioned a deal and a date with the Russians. The date coincided with a job Doriana offered to me, but I turned it down. I didn't even bother looking at the packet. The night Luca came into the attic, I was looking at that information because I got suspicious. As Luca told me how he was going to be a better father and husband to me, he didn't know my heart was breaking. It was breaking because I saw his name listed in Doriana's packet.

My husband had become a human trafficker.

Today was the date of the job and I wasn't surprised Luca was needed in Chicago. I went looking for my husband and found him in the garden with Elias. He was snoozing on the lounger while our baby slept trustingly on his chest.

This was purgatory. I could picture my life with Luca without the threat of something unforgivable hanging over our relationship like a guillotine, about to sever it forever.

He was right.

I loved him despite his villainous, treacherous self.

I was his doormat. Elias gave me the strength to stand up to his father.

But this…

I roused my sleeping husband. He opened his eyes slowly and they warmed when he saw me. My heart flipped. I was stupid. I deserved this. Why couldn't I stop loving him? I wish I could cut out my heart and substitute it with a block of ice.

"You're a beautiful sight to wake up to." He stared at our baby. "You and our baby."

His words continued to wound my heart. I wished I could tell him what I knew. I wanted to save him, but I risked the minors who were going to be sold tonight. "Don't you have to go to Chicago?"

He muttered a curse. "What time is it?"

"Five."

"Yeah, I better get going."

I rolled my lips and bit down on the lower one. I wanted to beg him to stay, but I didn't want to raise suspicions and compromise the hacker named The Friar who was taking on the job. On the other hand, maybe finding the evidence that my husband was a monster just like every human trafficker I despised was what I needed to excise my love for him forever.

He handed me the baby and got out of the lounger. "I'll be in Chicago for the weekend, but I'll try to get back as soon as possible."

He caressed my cheek. "Take care of yourself, okay? You need to eat, *tesoro*. Dr. Kingsley is worried about your weight." His thumb touched the circles under my eyes. "And you're not sleeping."

"It's just the hormones playing havoc with my body."

"If your appetite doesn't improve in the next week, you're going to see Dr. Kingsley, *capisce*?"

"Sometimes it just happens. I'll try to eat better."

We returned to the house, and while he went into our bedroom, I took Elias to the nursery.

I needed a break from all the sweetness he was showing because my emotions were in turmoil and I was about to implode. Doriana confirmed the auction tonight. The location was in a club owned by Vasily Orlov. I'd heard the name mentioned often between Dario and Luca, but it was Carmine who confirmed to me that he was the bane of my husband's existence.

Even so, my eyes demanded proof before I accused my husband of taking part in the sex trafficking of minors. Even if he told me it was a deal he had to make to save our son from being my father's protégé, it was unforgivable. He shouldn't have made the deal with my father in the first place.

I pretended to be asleep when Luca came into the nursery.

I heard him walk to the crib. "Be good for your mamma, *bombolino*. Don't fuss too much. She needs her rest."

A tear rolled down my cheek and I let the pillow soak in my heartache. Happiness was so close, and yet so far. Luca might not accept that he loved me, but all his actions were proving otherwise. He just needed to face them.

I hoped our marriage could survive what I was finding out tonight.

The mattress dipped behind me. I could feel the heat of his body, the warmth of his regard. He leaned over me and kissed my cheek. "I have to go, baby."

I gave a tiny moan.

"Sleep. Take care of yourself and our little one."

When he left the room, I gave in to my tears and sobbed.

"You're not eating again?" Martha asked. She was feeding Elias.

I was pushing around the pot roast. It smelled heavenly, but after a few bites, I lost my appetite. Nerves rioted inside me.

"There's also pie if you want," Yvonne said. She'd been nicer to me ever since I came home from the hospital, even cleaning up the nursery and emptying the Diaper Genie without being asked.

"I just want to sleep," I told them.

"Are you sure you're not depressed?" The older woman took Elias from the bassinet to burp him.

"I wish I knew." I really wish I didn't know many things. My son came first and not being able to provide him with breast milk was making me feel like a failure. "I need to see Doctor Kingsley." This time as a therapist.

"Hmm," Yvonne interjected. "Men in the mob don't like therapists. I guess that's why we have Doctor. Kingsley."

"Luca would be okay with it," Martha said. "He even suggested that to Junior when his wife was having nerve problems. It might have prevented her breakdown."

"What happened? She didn't go?"

"All the men in the family voted against it. Even Junior."

I smiled faintly. "Luca seems to be different."

Martha returned Elias to the bassinet. "That's why everyone's thankful he's the boss. He can be sympathetic to those who deserve it…"

"But get on his wrong side…" Tony said around a mouthful of food.

"Why do you always contradict me?" Martha said sharply.

Everyone laughed when the two started to bicker as usual. Yvonne went around serving pie.

Nessa came up to me and signed. *I can take him if you want to nap for a bit.*

I jumped at the opportunity. "Thanks. Just for a few hours."

After dinner, Rocco was surprised I went in the direction of the attic.

"Back there again?"

"I want to be in my own personal space for a few hours," I told him. Luckily, Mrs. B was trailing me, and I didn't have to look at him. "How about that, Mrs. B? Want to hang out?"

"I thought you wanted personal space," Rocco said.

I picked up the gray cat and hugged her close. "Mrs. B is my therapy cat." It was actually true. She comforted me simply by sitting beside me. I wondered if it was because she reminded me that my husband still had good in him, and I clung to Martha's stories of Luca having a soft spot for cats.

Rocco shook his head. "She gives me allergies."

"Look, I'm lucky to have everyone pitch in, and not every new mother is this lucky, but…you know, I just need this."

"Boss doesn't like it when you hole up in there."

"Then let's not tell him," I said in my brightest voice and smiled as though it was our secret. And because I'd been in a morose state for the past few weeks, Rocco relented.

He grudgingly followed me. Mrs. B meowed. She didn't like being held without initiating. Surprisingly, she didn't struggle when I picked her up.

Half an hour later, I logged in to a chat with The Friar (Th3Fr!#r)

Chimera: Thanks for letting me tag along.

The Friar: Anytime. I'm sharing my screen with you.

He had tapped into the cameras of the club and was following movements into the special auction room. This auction was tricky because the Russians had learned from the last time and cut off all cameras and network feeds from the room.

But apparently, The Friar was more than just a hacker of networks. He was a comms expert, and he had more connections than I had. I always depended on Doriana for any kind of support outside of hacking. The Friar was former military and other things.

Whatever that meant, he was able to get a drone inside the room using one of his contacts at the club, and, right now, it was giving us visibility into the room.

The first to arrive was Orlov and three of his men. Two Middle Eastern men followed, and then three Asians, and another of Scandinavian descent, while three others were of indeterminate ethnicity. I recognized one of the richest men in the world. The men greeted each other and pounded each other's back.

Oh my God. This was worse than the last one.

Chimera: Is this like a society of perverts?

The Friar: Fuckers. We're going to burn them. I'm confirming their identities with facial recognition now.

On the floor, Orlov rubbed his hands. "We're about to start. The Lillies are in the club. They were safely transported by an associate."

My stomach churned. Please, God, not him. I'd give anything for it not to be him.

With each minute that ticked by, the bile in my gut turned more sour. Staff came in and served food and drinks. The stage was behind a glass panel.

The Friar: Confirmed. These are a group of businessmen who belong to the Zavarida Group. We'd been after them for a while.

Chimera: Welcome to America.

The Friar: That's the spirit.

The lights dimmed. After a few minutes, the first girl walked out unsteadily, dressed in a skimpy outfit that barely covered her body. It was obvious they drugged her.

Chimera: I don't know if I can watch this.

I'd never gone this far before. Usually the perverts bid on Lillies from a private room, but it appeared this was a society of men who took pleasure in doing the activity together.

It was over an hour of teeth-grinding, stomach-churning experience. I tried to shut off my feed a few times, but I found the courage to go on.

When the lights came on, the stage had darkened, and once more, Orlov took to the floor. "I hope we've impressed you with our offerings."

A rush of murmurings went around the room.

The door to the room opened, and even when I'd girded myself for the possibility, a strangled sob clawed up my throat when the person walked in.

The Friar: That's Luca Moretti. He transported the Lillies from Vegas to Chicago.

My mind forgot how to form sentences, as if it rebelled at the words my fingers had to type. I had to delete them a couple of times before I typed out one simple sentence.

Chimera: That makes him Orlov's accomplice.

The Friar remained silent.

Chimera: Right?

The Friar: Shit. Someone's tracing us.

"What?" I spoke that aloud instead of typing it.

The Friar: Are you sure you're secure? The signal is coming from your end. I'm disconnecting us now. We're compromised.

Chimera: Wait, let me check.

But he blinked out, and my recording of the auction also ended. But I finally had proof that Luca was involved. The Friar's troubling message muted the ache in my chest.

We're compromised.

Shit. What did he mean? I didn't linger and instead erased the digital trails and backed out of the system before powering off my laptop.

I went to the closet where I had a specially made giant teddy bear. The inside was outfitted with shields to prevent detection and cloning. I put my laptop and my DEC-phone in it.

I paced around the room, wondering what to do next. How would I confront Luca? I paused and stared at Mrs. B who was looking at me with her golden eyes as if absorbing my panic.

"What did he mean?" I asked her.

We're compromised.

The last time I'd been compromised, Santino and Frankie took me hostage. I still had their money. I had most of the money from the auction, which meant I was sitting close to three hundred fifty million dollars. I was still waiting for Doriana to find another way to funnel the money.

The urge to run thrummed through my veins. But where would I go? I brought out a secondary laptop but connected to the regular network to add stuff to my wish list. Things I needed, like baby diapers and formula, just in case I needed to go on the run. Should I confront Luca? What if he didn't take it well that I was nosing into his business? I mean, he wouldn't just execute the mother of his child, right?

Goodness, I was being paranoid. Damn The Friar.

We're compromised.

Dammit. I needed to hold Elias.

"Come on, Mrs. B, let's get out of here."

I left the attic and frowned at the darkness at the bottom of the stairwell. Did we lose electricity?

Reaching the landing, I looked around for Rocco. His room was right at the bottom of the steps, and usually when he heard the attic door open, he was already waiting for me. I felt bad for my bodyguards and—

The hairs on the back of my neck stood on end. Before I could spin around, an arm banded around my chest and yanked me against a soft wall. The stench of leather, stale coffee, and rancid breath assailed my nostrils and almost made me gag.

I struggled against an unknown assailant but stopped when a gun poked at my side and a Russian-accented voice said, "Don't fight."

There was light in the hallway, and three people came into view.

Oh my God. No.

A masked man had a gun pointed at Nessa. She was holding Elias.

Where was Rocco? Tony? Where were all the guards?

"Where's everyone?" I cried.

The masked man holding Nessa hostage said, "They took a little nap."

"How many did you have to shoot?" the Russian man asked.

"Two. Apparently, they didn't like pie."

The pie was laced with drugs. Yvonne. That bitch.

The man holding me kicked the door to Rocco's room and flipped on the lights. I saw my bodyguard hogtied, with a gag over his mouth, still unconscious.

The Russian man spun me around. "You're going to give back all the money you stole from us." He was also wearing a balaclava like his cohort. He gestured to the other man. "I'll watch them." He pointed the gun at Nessa and Elias. "Get her laptop."

"You're making a mistake," I said.

Pain exploded at the side of my jaw. The taste of blood filled my mouth.

"Stop lying!" the Russian man growled. "You've cost our organization millions of dollars. We should just shoot you."

He pinned the barrel to my forehead. "But we need that head of yours. It's surprising how Moretti kept you hidden, but you were careless tonight."

My eyes fell on Elias. I did this. Regret was a crashing wave that threatened to pull me under. I put my baby in danger. I was an unfit mother. He deserved more than having me and Luca as parents.

I spoke through the ache in my jaw, but the pain pulsing in my heart was worst. "Don't hurt them. I'll come with you and undo whatever you think I've done."

The man laughed. "Still denying."

The masked man came back with my backpack and laptop. "I found several hard wallets. If she converted them to crypto, it'll be here."

The Russian man gripped my chin. "Are those all of it?"

"Yes. Those are my things, but why are you—" He squeezed harder.

"Yes," I whimpered.

He let me go and gave instructions to the masked man in Russian.

Nessa and Elias were blurry images through my tears. "I'll do whatever you want," I sobbed. "Just leave my son and Nessa alone."

"They come with us." The Russian man walked toward Elias and I had to control myself from clawing him away from my baby. "He could be leverage. Boss might have some use for him."

Defiance was a scarce commodity when the life of your child was at stake. At this point, I envied Luca with how he could separate what he felt for us and what he needed to do for the family.

Right outside the door that led to the attic, two vehicles were waiting.

Knowing my son was coming with me, I finally took him from Nessa. I looked at the young woman. She was stoic now, but the redness around her eyes indicated she'd been crying at one point.

"Tony and Martha?"

She signed that they were sleeping.

"Thank God." After the initial shock of what had been happening, my mind started thinking back to what I had done that might have given away my identity as an online vigilante. This was bad for many reasons. This might lead back to Doriana and The Friar. Luckily, the laptop that the masked man took was the secondary laptop I brought out. I could still get them what they wanted, but there was less compromising information on it.

The hard wallet the masked man took had around fifty thousand in its ledger. That would buy me time. Elias was too valuable for them to kill, but Nessa was expendable, and she was who I feared for the most.

They loaded us into the vehicle. The house was dark, and I saw a couple of guards slumped on the grounds. I hoped they weren't dead.

As the collateral damage of what I'd done mounted, our convoy exited the estate and turned away from the highway that led to Chicago.

After five minutes on the road, fields of corn surrounded us.

I heard the whistling. Then a boom sounded behind us simultaneously with a flash of light. Our vehicle skidded and swerved. The men were yelling. My body curled around Elias in a protective instinct that I'd give him the best chance of survival.

The SUV slammed into a tree. The seat belt bit into my shoulder, and through some miracle, I found the focus to spring into action. Nessa and I were fumbling with each other. Elias started screaming. The two men were groaning.

I mouthed, "Out."

I wasn't waiting to see if whoever shot at the Russians were our friends either. My first priority was to hide my son. We weren't far from the estate. We could walk back if we had to. Thankfully, the door wasn't jammed. Nessa and I eased out of the vehicle and ran straight into the cornfields.

The Russian man shouted at us to stop. I handed Elias to Nessa and told her to run ahead while I kept to the rear. They were less likely to shoot me.

The moon was bright, and it wasn't lost on me that in movies, bad things happened in cornfields. Nessa paused at a clearing. She was panting hard and not used to running. I wasn't either, and my lungs were about to burst.

I dragged her to a crouch and took Elias from her. He had settled down to cooing. Apparently, he had enjoyed our jog. We crouched and walked to a line of trees.

"I'm going to check what's going on."

Nessa was shaking her head.

"I need you to keep my son safe." I fought back the emotions that wanted to break free. I was going to fix this. Both of them didn't deserve this. My son didn't deserve to have his life threatened.

I removed the locket from my neck. "In case..." The words caught in my throat.

Nessa was shaking her head vigorously. The dam broke, and a river of tears fell from her eyes.

I bit my fist to stop myself from making a loud sob.

"I'll be back, my love," I told Elias. He was staring up at me. I kissed him on the forehead.

Nessa and I stared at each other.

Our mouths pressed into tight lines. We exchanged brief nods.

Then, before I lost the will to leave them, I got up and plunged back into the cornfield.

I was thankful that harvest had come late and the stalks provided cover. I slowed my progress as I approached the road.

Two gunshots rang through the night.

I froze for a microsecond before instinct made me crouch low. The droopy leaves of corn provided cover, but they also made me itchy, like a thousand ants were crawling over my skin. Despite the cool November air, sweat beaded my upper lip.

"They're not here!" someone yelled.

I inched closer, parting the stalks to see who was talking. Two newly arrived black SUVs. Four black-clad men with masks walked between the length of the disabled car Nessa and I rode in. They were armed, and it looked like those two gunshots were for our two Russian abductors.

Friend or foe?

Foe. They wouldn't be wearing masks if they were coming to save us.

Elias's cry split the night.

"There!" One man raised his arm in the direction of the sound while another was already sprinting toward it.

No. No. No.

I ran parallel with him, lungs filled with fear and air that I couldn't exhale, yet I kept on running.

My son was screaming.

Tears streaked down my face, and I kept down the hysteria fighting to break free from my throat. When I reached Nessa and Elias, the man had them cornered. She had moved further from the spot where I'd left them, but she must have realized it was futile to run with my baby crying.

"I found the child and Nessa! Natalya's not with them."

My brain tried to process the familiarity with how he said our names. I'd heard that voice before. I picked up a rock and approached. Nessa spotted me.

I couldn't see her expression, and even as I hoped she wouldn't give me away, I did it on my own.

My son's timing was horrible.

He stopped crying just as I stepped on the proverbial twig.

I was an arm's length away, too far to swing my arm.

The man spun around and pain exploded at my temple.

Blackness came and went, along with voices and the sound of my baby's cry.

CHAPTER
Nineteen

LUCA

"It was a pleasure doing business, gentlemen," Orlov told the Zavarida Group. These men sickened me. I had to grin and shake their hands. They'd been on Carmine's radar for a while. For all my annoyance with the Galluzo underboss, I understood his extreme hatred against human traffickers. His mother had been a victim of one and he was the seed that was born out of such atrocity. I even understood why Natalya had a soft spot for him.

Orlov got his money, but the Zavaridas would be encountering law enforcement when their planes landed. Carmine and I spent weeks planning their downfall, but I wouldn't be relieved until we returned these teenagers, who were no more than children, to their parents.

I thought of Elias. How did I callously think I could give him away to Vincenzo?

When our guests left, Orlov turned to me. "You sure you don't want a cut? You deserve ten percent at least."

"We're done here," I said. "Tell Koshkin I've upheld my end of the deal."

"Aw, come on, Moretti, get off your high horse. Those men could get you into businesses you can't even imagine."

"I'm happy with what I have." I yanked open the door, and it took all of my willpower not to slam it behind me. I used the back exit of the club where my men were waiting for me.

I ran into Dario. He had a phone to his ear and a worried expression on his face. Fuck, did something go wrong with the Zavaridas' flights out of Chicago? We had no control over those, but we gave the details to our contacts in different countries. At least, Carmine did.

"What?" I slipped out the pack of cigarettes and was about to light up when I thought better. I never did it around Elias, but it didn't stop Natalya from looking at me with disapproval whenever I lit up.

"No one's answering their phones at Tralestelle," Dario said.

I stilled. "Maybe there's another storm and cell towers are spotty?"

"The landline keeps going to voicemail," he said.

I had a breakfast meeting with an alderman the next day, but my gut was telling me to go home and check on Natalya and Elias with my own eyes.

Not an hour from now.

Right fucking now.

I strode to the Escalade and got the keys from a soldier—a new recruit who was a distant cousin of Tony who looked like Tony, so I called him Tony-two. "I'm driving. Get in."

Dario and the soldier looked at each other.

"Don't waste my time," I snarled at my consigliere. He got into the passenger side. Tony-two said he would catch a ride with the other guys.

"Why are the men afraid when I drive?" I asked Dario.

"You really want me to answer that?"

"I drive the same speed as all of you," I said in the same beat as, "Try them again."

As Dario tried to get in contact with the mansion, I couldn't help getting antsy. The Escalade pulled into traffic and more than a few cars honked their horns at me.

"That's why," Dario said. "You drive like a maniac and people need to make way for you."

"I'm impatient." I cast him a look that qualified my statement. "No reply?"

"We have a crew that is fifteen minutes from there," Dario said. "I told them to drop everything and go check."

"Good." I'd warned Tony that tonight was going to be an important coup for the Morettis. We could finally break free of Orlov and mind our own business. Carmine had grown more adept in inter-organization negotiations, so he could go back to Italy soon. My rabid appetite for power had quickly dissipated these last few months. It became more trouble and more of a headache than it was worth. I thrived on chaos, but I was getting enough of that from a fussy two-month-old. I smiled faintly, then remembered the alderman.

I slipped out my phone, put it on the dash and told it to call the politician.

My call went to voicemail. "Alan, an emergency came up. I have to miss our tee time tomorrow." I hated golf with a passion anyway. "I'll have Dario make another appointment."

I ended the call.

"He's not going to like that."

"Well, tough shit." It had become harder to stay away from my wife and son. I wasn't sure if it was a comfortable place to be, but I had a compulsion to be with them more often. Maybe it was time to overhaul the mafia code. The nineties had seen a deterioration of the men-of-honor code as many in our ranks turned federal witness. This year, seventy percent of our revenues came from legitimate businesses. We couldn't be fully legitimate. There was a devil in the Morettis, and it needed to be fed.

We were just outside Chicago when Dario received the call from the crew we sent to the mansion.

"Who?" Dario roared.

My blood turned to ice. "Put him on speaker," I barked.

"Three of our men were shot. The rest were drugged, boss."

"My wife and son?"

"They're not here."

My foot rode heavy on the gas. "Tony and Rocco?"

"They were tied up."

"Check surveillance."

"On it, boss."

I weaved through the vehicles and cut too close to some, but it was as though my road home was preordained and that was all I could see. If I saw the slightest opening between cars, I took it.

I rode the gas and honked the horn.

"Stop being tense."

"I can't help it," Dario gritted. "We'll get there sooner if we don't get stopped by cops or end up in a wreck."

"The locket," I said. "We can trace Natalya through it."

"I noticed she started wearing it after she had Elias," Dario said. "Let me see if the tracker on that is working."

And it hadn't run out of battery.

"Holy fuck," Dario said.

"What?" I growled. "Next word out of your mouth better be a location."

My chest was so fucking tight, it felt like it was being compacted in a junkyard car crusher.

"She's a few miles from Tralestelle. In the middle of cornfields."

"We're heading there directly. Don't tell anyone," I said.

"How about Carmine and Ange?"

"Think, Dario. Carmine had a lot riding on this auction and he's not around. Both he and Ange weren't answering my calls earlier tonight."

"Surely not...you think they'd do something to Natalya and your son?"

"At this point, I don't know." And for whatever reason, my brain wouldn't compute. "You're the only one I trust."

The tracker brought us to a deserted stretch of country road. We'd passed one burned-out vehicle. Another one had hit a tree with two men inside strapped to their seat belts, dead, with gunshot wounds to the head. The passenger doors were open. The direction of the footprints was chaotic. I'd have my best human tracker on it.

"Call Salvie," I told one of my men. "And have him figure this out."

"Nothing on the sheriff scanners," another soldier told me. "But with the smoke up ahead, it was only a matter of time."

Dario and I returned to our vehicles. "Has her point moved?"

"Yes. It used to be here when we were on our way, but it has moved four miles ahead and looks to be where that smoke is coming from."

"Dammit, we better get there before the fire department."

"Our men are monitoring."

The minutes it took us to get from one location to the next felt like an eternity. I was caught between a fatalistic existence and one where my life shit unicorns. In my fatalistic one, Natalya and my son were killed by my enemies—and I had more than a few. I'd find out who they were and seek vengeance. But I wanted the life where they lived. I fought against the feeling that I didn't deserve to have a life with them.

"You must prepare, Luca."

"I am," I gritted. "The locket pinging?"

"Yes."

"Then shut up."

"What if they have demands?"

"Then we'll pay them, get my family back, and then hunt them down and slaughter them all." I didn't care anymore if it would be a weakness. I tried to push the dark thoughts from my head about what those fuckers could be doing to my family.

"Tony texted. They've reviewed surveillance, and it appears Natalya and Nessa walked out with them."

"So they weren't drugged?"

"No."

What the fuck? My whole body was thrumming with adrenaline. Did they plan this? Was Natalya so miserable with me she left with my son? "Have they accounted for everyone?"

"Tony and Rocco are checking. It seems Yvonne is missing too."

"Martha?"

Dario exchanged more messages with Tony. "They found her slumped in her room. She didn't make it to the bed and has a concussion.

"Turn here," Dario instructed. I swerved onto a dirt road, but I could see flames licking a structure. I checked behind me to see two more SUVs following us. An alert was sent out to the Moretti crime family to activate lockdown.

"Contact Dom. Tell him what's going on." My niece and sister weren't my concern anymore since they married into the De Lucci crime family, but it was courtesy to let the boss know if our problems could touch any of them.

"Already did."

Still no call from Ange.

The Escalade stopped in front of the blazing house. The last time I'd seen a structure burn like this was two years ago in Vegas.

"Where's Natalya's signal?" I didn't wait for him to answer and stumbled out of the Escalade. The heat of the inferno singed my flesh. Nothing and no one could have survived it. My legs could barely move.

"It's not in the house."

Hope almost choked me as I spun around in the direction of the tree line.

"Natalya!" I roared.

Our men caught up with us and set up a perimeter.

A soldier scowled at me. "You should let us clear the place first, boss."

I glared at him. I knew this, but I was beyond caring. Everything inside me was screaming to find my wife and son. "Natalya."

Dario touched my arm. "Listen."

A baby's cry.

Relief gripped my heart so hard, I was dizzy. I rushed toward the sound.

But before I could take one step into the shadow of trees, Nessa exploded from them.

Confusion and horror hit me.

My arms automatically reached for the bawling Elias, but my eyes refused to accept that my wife wasn't in front of me.

"Where is she?" I shouted at Nessa, but she could only shake her head.

I handed my crying son to Dario, instinctively knowing the

roaring anxiety rampaging inside me would transfer to the baby. I gripped Nessa's shoulders and shook her. "Where. Is. My. Wife?"

She was weeping hysterically, and I could barely fight back the frustration and fury. Fury that someone dared attack my family, frustration that I didn't know what the fuck was going on. Throw in the fear churning in my gut, and I was a mess like she was, except I'd kept it under the veneer of a man who was supposed to be the boss of his crime family.

That veneer was cracking under pressure.

I wondered afterward if it would have been better if we knocked Nessa unconscious. Then maybe I wouldn't go through the pain and torment unlike anything I'd experienced before.

My eyes followed her trembling arm as she slowly pointed toward the burning house.

Without thinking, I charged toward the flames, getting too close before hands forcefully held me back. I threw men off me, but there were too many of them who held me down.

"Natalya," my voice choked, finally drained of any fight. Because if she was in there, she wouldn't have survived.

My eyes swam and turned blurry. I was on my knees, head tilted heavenward and a hideous cry of a wounded animal reverberated around us.

I was holding my son. He was sleeping peacefully, uncaring of the activity going on inside the house. Cops, detectives, and FBI agents walked in and out of the house, asking me endless questions. A few of them weren't sympathetic.

Did I trust them not to do a shitty job? No. But Dario couldn't rip me away from the burning house even when the authorities arrived. My brain wasn't working. My Natalya was inside.

I had failed to protect her.

Nessa told us men who sounded like Russians took them from the house. And then more masked men blew up one of the vehicles and railroaded the second one.

My brave Natalya tried to save them but got hit on the head. I couldn't explain how it consumed me—the thought that someone dared hurt my wife gnawed at my insides like a festering disease and it festered because I didn't know where to unleash my wrath. Who to eviscerate and dismember.

They were all taken to that house that burned afterwards.

The only thing that made sense in what she told us was that Yvonne was a traitor.

Pie.

Who would ruin a good pie and put enough tranquilizers in it that could kill a horse? Martha was still recovering from a head injury. I had no one running my household except a mute who was not making sense.

Nessa said she saw Natalya unconscious on the floor before she and Elias were herded into a separate room. They tried to frighten her. Fired shots into the room but then they let her go and made her run into the fields. They told her not to look back. So that was what she did until the house exploded and then she ran back.

None of this made sense.

Natalya was not dead.

"We refuse to believe, right, sport?" I told Elias.

Finally, close to five p.m., Dario came into the room. "They're gone."

Behind him followed Ange and Carmine.

As my consigliere and lawyer, Dario sent me to the study with Elias so I wouldn't incriminate myself with their leading questions. It was always the husband, wasn't it? Well, fuck them.

"Next time, don't bait them." Dario pinched between his brows. My eyes were probably as bloodshot as his.

Ange and Carmine lingered behind my consigliere like the guilty parties in this. I didn't buy their alibis. They were probably wondering if they were going to survive the day.

"I don't give a shit." I grabbed my whiskey and threw it back, then glared at Ange. "So who betrayed us?"

"Turo."

I gave a snort. "Tell me something new." He was Yvonne's boyfriend.

"None of his crew are answering their phones," Ange said. "I'm having our men go to their homes and their usual haunts. They probably won't be there, but we can ask people who know where they are."

"And these Russians? Any of them look familiar? Orlov's?"

"Our IT is checking into it," Ange said. "The one who held Nessa is a known associate of Orlov, but a low-level one."

My eyes turned to Carmine. "Have you informed Natalya's parents?"

"Not yet."

"Good. The news needs to come from me." My voice cracked. I refused to look at Elias at this point because everything was so overwhelming and I was close to breaking. My son had not lost his mother. My wife was not dead.

The way I was feeling, it was as though wolves were circling, waiting to tear me apart. I cleared my throat. "So where were you, Carmine?"

His gaze dropped to my son before coming back to mine. "It wasn't just Turo. You have another capo regime who was working against you."

"You have proof of this?" Ange growled.

Carmine stepped away from Ange. Dario cast me a brief glance as the tension between the two men pulled taut.

"Yes. I have the recordings. I suspected him and bugged his car. They were communicating with Ilya, the Russian, in the wrecked car."

"Why am I only now hearing about this?" I snapped.

"I thought I had more time." Carmine's voice was a whisper; it was almost as if he was on the verge of tears.

But I was not sympathetic.

Neither was Ange. "If you had come to us sooner, we could have stopped the kidnapping."

My brother's accusations were so laughable, and I would have given him a pass if it wasn't about Natalya. "And you, brother, had let Turo make his play under your nose. You are my underboss. But the buck stops with me. Everyone, and I mean everyone, is going under a security check. Bank accounts and phone messages. I want the mastermind found."

Ange and Carmine gave brief acknowledgments.

I tipped my head for them to go. "Dario. Stay."

I waited for the door to close before I said, "You're the only one I trust. You know that, right?"

He massaged his temple between his fingers. "What a cluster-fuck," he sighed. "Who do you suspect?"

"I don't know. Both? Could they be conspiring against me and this tension between them is fabricated?"

"I thought so too…but…Luca…if you want more answers, we have to listen to Nessa. She's the only witness to this whole shit. Don't you want to hear what she told the cops?"

I couldn't tell my friend that I couldn't stand the sight of her. It was eating me inside that she wasn't Natalya. That my wife was still missing.

I was fucking tired, but maybe it was because my heart was dead. Then my son would make a sound, and it would beat again.

~

The nightmare had barely begun. I hadn't had a decent night of sleep in a week. The cops continued to come and go.

Natalya's parents were back and talking about a funeral, adding to my aggravation. While everyone was buzzing around the house, I locked myself in the study with Elias. He was the only part of Natalya I wanted with me. I slept with my son in the nursery. Martha was back in circulation and helped with my boy when I was too intoxicated to be a proper parent. I told everyone to keep Nessa away from me. I didn't want her around. Somewhere in the back of my raging mind, I knew it wasn't her fault.

But someone needed to pay. One of our crew was found dead on I-55 outside Chicago. Was he running away? Who killed him?

Dario had a wild story from Nessa that the Russians accused Natalya of stealing their money and they took her laptop.

That damned laptop.

What money? My money?

A knock sounded on the door. Dario was my gatekeeper, so it was important. He made sure to keep Vincenzo and Elena away from me.

"Come in," I called out wearily.

My consigliere stuck his head in. "Detective Voss is here."

I could already feel a migraine building. "Hasn't he asked enough questions?"

"They found something in the house."

Bile rose up my throat. Was I ready to hear this?

"Send him in."

Dario gave me a look before he nodded and left to get the detective. I walked over to where my son was sleeping by the window. Since I spent my time locked away, I had a small crib brought in. I caught my reflection in the mirror. I resembled a vampire with my sunken and red eyes and the unhealthy pallor of my skin. Beard grooming became nonexistent and my unruly hair hadn't seen a comb since everything went down. I showered and finger-combed and dressed. Sighing, I tucked my shirt into my trousers and returned behind my desk. I couldn't have the cops call Child Protective Services on me.

The knock sounded again, and Dario walked in with the detective.

"Do you want me to take him?" Dario nodded to Elias.

"He's getting used to the noise and voices," I said. "Let him be. So, Detective, any progress on my wife's case?"

"We'd interviewed Vasily Orlov at length. It's his understanding that you and your wife had an arranged marriage."

"It's not uncommon between Italian families when our businesses benefit."

The detective's brow rose. "Did you love your wife, Mr. Moretti?"

I narrowed my eyes. "You already asked me this last time."

"If we went by the unemotional way you answered the questions last time, then we wouldn't be having this conversation now."

"Are you saying I'm a suspect?"

"It's standard procedure, sir."

"They always suspect the husband."

"You didn't answer the question."

"Natalya and I have an understanding. In time, it's expected we will grow to love each other."

The detective started nodding. "Did you miss your son's birth because you had business elsewhere?"

"Yes." Motherfucking Orlov. What was his game? The Russian called immediately after the news of what happened at Tralestelle got out. He vehemently denied involvement, but I sent the cops his way anyway. This was probably his way of getting back at me.

"What was your wife's reaction?"

"She wasn't happy. Look, if this is to grill me about my marriage, you're wasting time. So, if there's no development on the case, you *should le*ave."

The detective reached into his pocket and slid an evidence bag toward me. "Do you recognize these rings?"

I stared at them, my arms and limbs frozen in horror so I couldn't move and pick them up. "Where did you find them?" My hoarse voice sounded foreign in my ears probably because of the silent roar that had clogged them.

"It was found in the debris of the burnt house. The fire officials declared the property safe to collect evidence, and our CSI found those this morning."

"Natalya's wedding and engagement ring."

My chest grew tight. Was I going to have a heart attack?

"I'm sorry, Mr. Moretti." He took the plastic bag back. "I'll have to keep these longer for evidence."

I could only nod. My whole body felt numb. The walls of the room shrank and curved over me. I didn't even hear the detective leave. Dario came in, and when he saw me, he asked, "What did he want?"

"They…" I staggered to my feet. "Natalya's rings." I hunched over, my hands flat on the desk, unable to find a comfortable position to breathe. "Does it mean…oh God." I stumbled over to my son. Our baby, who could have just lost his mother.

Was it my fault? Did Natalya try to leave me?

I stared at my son with a pain in my chest that I couldn't understand. I sat with my son, trying to make sense of that pain. Was it from the thought that Natalya was forever lost to us? Was it from the guilt eating at me that I spent time in my bullshit instead of making my wife happy? It circled back to that pain mixed with an outrage that she tried to leave me, taking my son from me. Did she think I wouldn't spend every last dime and all my resources to find her?

Dario had left the room. I paced the study, drank more scotch, stewing in a tornado of thoughts and conflicting emotions until I decided I was too smashed to take care of Elias. I handed him to Martha. I needed to be alone in my misery.

Elena seemed to have appointed herself mistress of the house and was busy in the kitchen. Vincenzo stood when he saw me.

"You haven't eaten anything today, Luca." I ignored her, grabbed a bottle of Barolo from the wine rack, and uncorked it.

"What did the detective say?" Vincenzo asked. "Do they have any update on who could be behind this atrocity?"

I opened my mouth to say something, but no words came. Vincenzo grew teary eyed. I did not know why when they were so eager to hold a funeral for their daughter, while this was the first time that I had proof that Natalya might be dead. I blocked my mind to the horror.

No body.

No body to bury.

Not dead.

"They found her wedding ring."

Glass shattered in the kitchen and Elena howled, "Oh, my baby!"

I didn't wait for the aftermath because I didn't have it in me to give comfort. Leaving the crying that detonated behind me, I passed the ever-present guards in the house and went to the attic.

I hadn't been up here since…

No. *Natalya is not dead.*

I pushed the door open. Her fragrance still lingered. Mandarin oranges and jasmine. I took a swig of the wine. It was her favorite one too. I moved to the window. The sun was setting, and the sky was golden. Natalya loved thunderstorms, not this colorful painted sky. At least I knew that much about my wife.

Two chugs of wine.

She loved Paris in the rain. She wanted us to walk in it. Would it have killed me to do it? We would never get a chance again.

"Natalya," I choked. Emotion stung the back of my eyes. "Have I lost you, *tesoro*? I think I would feel it if you're no longer here on this earth." I backed away from the window and dropped on the couch.

I glared at the television that had occupied so much of her time. I guzzled more wine.

Watching all her romance movies, she placed impossible standards on me. I would never have been the hero she wanted me to be, but I'd been trying to be a husband who cared. I'd been giving her more of my time, not because she demanded it, but because I genuinely enjoyed spending time with her. I worried about her. Worried about her descent into depression. The signs were there. But again, I put her second.

I should have put her first instead of trying to get clear of Orlov.

I could have said no and said fuck it to the Galluzo and let them deal with their problems.

Natalya had been drowning. Even Rachel worried because she stopped producing breast milk.

My eyes landed on her romance books.

All these fucking books ruined what could have been a great marriage. I threw the wine bottle at the television. It shattered with the force and burgundy liquid soaked into the carpet.

I rose from the couch and stalked toward the entertainment center and yanked the whole thing from the stand and sent it crashing to the floor.

I looked around to find something to smash it with, then I saw the books. Before I could control myself, I swept a bunch of them to the floor. A voice in my head mocked me for my shortcomings, and I was taking it out on words inked on paper. Words that created worlds for my wife to escape into, worlds away from the one I forced upon her.

Dario appeared at the door, Tony hovering behind him.

"I'm not going to ask if you're okay," Dario said.

"I wasn't the husband she wanted!" My roar reverberated in the attic. I stalked back to the couch. "Fuuuuuuck!" I glowered at the pieces of broken glass on the floor. "Tony, get me another bottle."

"No," Dario said.

I glared at him. "What's your problem?"

"What's my problem?" he sneered. "You made me godfather to Elias. It's my duty to see to that boy's welfare, and right now? You're wallowing in self-pity, or is it pride, Luca?"

"Fuck you!"

"Your son needs you, not this drunk," he said fiercely. "You can't blame a bunch of—"

He cut off, and a puzzled look changed his expression. He walked to the bookshelf. "What the hell…?"

"What are you talking about?"

"Tony, get me a flathead screwdriver," Dario ordered. "There's something behind this." He threw me an impatient look. "Come here."

I dragged myself from the couch and stared at the bookshelf, trying to shake off my alcohol-induced haze. "It's deeper than what it should be."

"Yes." He looked behind it. "And there's a bunch of wiring behind it and enough space…"

Tony came back and handed Dario the tool he requested. This fresh development jarred me out of my despair. "Remember what Nessa was saying about the Russian, Natalya, and the laptop?"

I looked at Tony. "Get Nessa up here."

Tony scowled. "I won't have my niece—"

"Get her up here," I snapped.

When Dario removed part of the back panel of the bookcase, my jaw unhinged.

"Holy fuck," Dario breathed. "What does your wife have going here?"

We cleared out more books until we finally exposed what was behind the panel.

Servers. Network routers. I recognized this equipment as the ones we used in our online gambling site. These were overkill to use at home.

Dario turned to me, his eyes disbelieving. I was sure my expression mirrored his own.

What. The. Fuck.

Weeks later, we still had no answers as to what happened to Natalya.

DNA had come back from the burnt house identifying Turo, Yvonne, and two of his crew.

Vincenzo and Elena admitted they hid Natalya's high IQ and her hacking skills, but swore she'd stopped doing it. I was not surprised they didn't know because my wife had fooled me too. I kicked them out of my house. Carmine went with them. He knew I was on a tear and decided it was best he left the country.

I tasked Dario with finding the best hackers and private investigators to track down the other capo and round up the rest of the missing crew.

In one of our unoccupied buildings, the stench of copper and death surrounded the walls of its basement. Dimly lit with a string of incandescent lights, it had tiled flooring that made cleanup easy.

We interrogated six of our men and one Russian.

None of them knew anything except what Turo had told them, promising a big payday.

Their payday had arrived in the form of mob justice.

I waterboarded them before I gutted every single one of them.

After the last man took a rattling, dying breath, I watched him a bit longer, cocking my head, staring at him intently because I had ceased to feel any emotion. No anger. No frustration. Nothing.

His head lolled to one side before Ange went to him and checked his pulse.

My brother shook his head. With each interrogation, I watched Ange. And I knew him enough that he didn't play a part in Natalya's disappearance. The hackers and investigators validated my instincts and cleared my brother. Ange didn't answer my calls because he was staking out one of Turo's crew. He suspected something big was going down. I still held him accountable for letting two of our capos conspire underneath his nose. I didn't know if I could ever forgive him.

I walked to the sink and washed the blood from my arms and hands. I would do a thorough scrubbing later. "If anything comes up, I'll leave the interrogation up to you, but I want it recorded."

Ange dipped his chin briefly. "You're going back to the mansion?"

I shut off the water and leaned against the sink, my head bowed. "Elias cannot lose another parent to this." My molars ground against each other, unable to say more.

It had been a bloody week, and I was no closer to finding Natalya. But I realized that my rage had slowly morphed into feelings of nothingness.

This had to stop.

My son needed his father.

PART
Two

CHAPTER

Twenty

Two years later

Rayne

The small town of Danvers was buzzing with the oncoming river festival. We were the short stop before the better-known resort city of Grafton near the confluence of the Mississippi and Illinois rivers.

My temperamental pickup chugged through Main Street, a mile-long street of commerce. For a community of less than a thousand, we had fancy shops like Nature Java.

It was my first stop of the day.

After parking my vehicle, I hopped out. I walked the short distance to the glass door of the coffee shop and pushed it open. Bells jingled, drawing the attention of the barista and owner, Brad Bailey. Blond, blue-eyed, lumberjack sexy, and a decent kisser, he glanced away from the espresso machine with a look of relief on his face.

"Thank God you're here. The laptop has locked up."

"Have you been watching too much porn, Bailey?" a customer heckled from the booth.

I grinned and walked past them. Though some faces were familiar, and I knew more than a few by their first names, I was still the geek-squad girl who kept to herself. The one you called when you had a computer problem.

Frequent problems with the coffee shop's laptop were bad for my reputation, except I knew why it was down.

I did a system boot and plugged in my jump drive. Brad walked in with a tall cup of coffee.

"So, how about that date? I want a do-over."

I'd give him brownie points for persistence. "You really should stop visiting all those conspiracy theory sites. They're bogged down with ads and pop-ups. One of these days, I won't be able to recover your computer."

He grinned. "Then I wouldn't see you as often."

I rolled my eyes. "There are plenty of girls in town who are dying for you to ask them out."

Brad leaned in and gave me a dose of those piercing eyes. He was attractive, and he was comfortable, but there was no spark.

"Rayne, since I saw you the first time. I've wanted to put that sparkle back in your eyes."

I winced, remembering the time he meant.

"Can I have some coffee here!" someone called from outside.

Brad made a resigned sigh. "Next time, make me your last call for the day."

Not likely.

I subjected his computer to several scans and added more safeguards. It was usually the harmless stuff, but the last thing he wanted was to get ransomware.

I wouldn't even charge him for this visit. I waved past him and thanked him for the free coffee. Thankfully, a customer had his attention when I walked out. I felt like I was kicking a puppy each time I turned him down.

I was the problem. I wouldn't wish myself on anyone.

Not my nightmares.

Not my panic attacks.

Not my broken pieces.

My next stop was a clothing facility in between here and Grafton. I enjoyed driving out of town. Sometimes Danvers could be claustrophobic with how small it was and how everyone was in everyone's business. Since my tank was low, I stopped at Spiffy's to gas up. Spiffy's was the typical country store with two gas pumps and a convenience store known for its home-cooked meals.

After I gassed up, I pulled into the parking space at the back. My brow rose at the shiny Maserati in the parking lot. Now, we didn't see many of those around. It must be someone from Chicago.

I was a regular at the store, and the staff was used to me.

"Hi, Rayne, we've got chicken and biscuits right out of the oven," Spiffy announced. He was a tall black man with a bald head and a white beard with arms that bulged against the short sleeve of his black tee. He used to be in the Navy. I tried not to dig up too much information about people around me, but it made me feel safe.

"I got a couple of things I need to pick up, but pack me two orders, please." I didn't like going out at night, preferring to eat in.

I was familiar with the store's layout, but people were milling everywhere. They were probably stocking up for a day on the river. It made it hard to move through the displays. I checked my watch, noting I had twenty minutes to make my appointment. I hurriedly scooted between people who felt it was okay to chat in the middle of the aisle. This was a cramped convenience store, not the grocery aisle at Kroger. Finally, I had my gum, power bars, and a couple of packs of beef jerky. I hadn't needed Tylenol lately, but spring was coming, so I picked up a bottle of Benadryl.

In my rush, I spun around too quickly and rammed into somebody. My haul scattered on the floor.

"Oh, I'm so sorry," a deep voice said.

I was already on my haunches, gathering my stuff, but I couldn't help noticing the polished expensive shoes. Then the man crouched in front of me and I looked up.

His eyes reflected shock and so did his mouth, which hung open like he was about to say something, but he forgot the words.

It made me extremely uncomfortable.

"I'm… oh my God," he got out finally. "Nat—"

I laughed, cutting off what he was about to say. "Is that oh my God good or bad?"

He clamped his mouth shut and just stared at me. He was pale beneath his tan.

Extremely uncomfortable had morphed into full-on spooked. It wasn't the first time men had stared at me too long. I was aware I had more than average looks, but this stranger looked like he'd seen a ghost and not a beautiful woman. I quickly dropped my gaze to pick up the rest of the items. Alarm bells trilled loudly, and my fight-or-flight needle sprung to flight. I rose from the floor, and he rose with me, brown eyes still transfixed on my face.

"Well, I better get going," I said, cheeks burning, voice uneasy. "Be sure to grab the chicken and biscuits before they run out."

The urge to escape was overwhelming. I barely heard what Spiffy was saying when he rang me up. I didn't bother with small talk, and I didn't dare glance over my shoulder, but I was sure the stranger in an expensive suit was still staring at me.

He didn't look familiar at all.

Before I drove off, I memorized the Maserati's plates. Shaken by the encounter, I needed to be talked off a ledge.

"Never go back."

Was a repeating threat in my head since I woke up in this town.

I cancelled my appointment at the garment manufacturer and returned to town, to the one person who knew who I was.

Dr. Gleason's clinic was in his house right on the edge of Danvers. He had a part-time nurse who came in, but I didn't see her car. There was no one in the waiting room either, but he must have heard me enter. He opened the double doors to the examination room and asked, "Were you supposed to come in today?"

I was pacing the room, chewing on my nails. "No, but I need to speak to you." The quickening in my breath and pulse signaled an oncoming panic attack. That was a familiar part of my new life, too.

His gaze sharpened behind his spectacles, and he gave a brief nod. "I'm almost done. Give me a few minutes."

The few minutes turned into ten. By that time, I was leaning against the windows and staring off into the distance. I heard the doors and a pregnant woman walked out. She smiled at me and left.

An ache stabbed me in the chest. It happened whenever I saw a pregnant woman or a baby. I didn't know who I was before, but I had a feeling the sadness I felt was in relation to a loss of a child or a miscarriage. My brain was a minefield, and Dr. Gleason warned me about filling the patches of my memories with assumptions.

"What's going on?" Dr. Gleason was the town physician and was looking to sell his practice because he was pushing seventy. He was lanky with a shock of thick salt-and-pepper hair, and he dressed casually in flannel shirts. He loved fishing like most people around here and would sometimes be seen in an angler's hat and coat.

"I had an encounter with a man who seemed…" I was looking for the right term. "Shocked to see me."

"Did you get any flashes of memory?" He invited me into the examination room and had me sit on the table.

"No."

"Headache?"

"Not at all, but I had a panic attack."

"That could be anything."

I blew out a breath. "I know we've been through this over and over. You said the man who dropped me off in the St. Louis shelter said my boyfriend was a bookie. Do you remember if he said mafia or anything?"

"Did this guy look like mafia?"

I laughed nervously. "How do guys in the mafia look? He didn't look like Tony Soprano or anything. He looked good in a suit and appeared to be Italian, but he could also be Middle Eastern or someone from the Mediterranean. Strong features. I have his license plate."

The doctor tapped his mouth. "Do you want to go down that route?" He stood and started tidying his instruments. "You've been doing so well in this town. Don't invite trouble. You have a new identity now."

Besides being the town doctor, Dr. Gleason worked for the shelter for battered women in St. Louis. I was dropped off in their processing center with a broken wrist and bruised face, with retrograde amnesia. I was also unconscious. The doctor was a former neurologist, which was why he was tapped by the St. Louis, Missouri, chapter. Most of the women who came through there had traumatic brain injuries, and he was the closest doctor who could help.

I remembered flashes from childhood, maybe until I was five, but nothing after that. I didn't have an episodic memory, which was how the brain processed past events. I kept my semantic memory, which explained how I retained learned knowledge of facts, words, and objects. This was why I took to the computer easily and identified as a computer nerd. I hated being out in public, but Dr. Gleason attributed my panic attacks and fear to my subconscious.

"Never go back."

I had kept track of the St. Louis gangs and their associates, but I hadn't seen any news about a missing bookie's girlfriend. The man who dropped me off didn't give many details except I interfered with my boyfriend's online racket which matched up with my knowledge of computers. I was tempted to run my fingerprints, but I steered clear of government databases.

"Don't invite trouble" was a mantra Dr. Gleason instilled in me.

"Maybe it's time for me to move to another place?" I said. Maybe I should move to the East Coast. "You've taken care of me for so long."

He smiled briefly. "You've been a special case. I was hoping to witness the return of your memory." He sat behind his desk again and started cleaning his spectacles. "You don't find our resident barista attractive?"

I laughed. "You know, despite my lack of history, I never thought blonds were my type."

CHAPTER

Twenty~One

Luca

"You should visit New York."

"Why?" I replied dryly. "My place is in Chicago."

"You sound bored," Sera said. "When you're bored, that's not a good thing."

"How can I be bored when I have a two-year-old to look after?"

"Aw, I can't imagine you as a doting father."

"You should be the one to fly over with Gio." Gio was Sera's one-year-old son. "Elias could use a playmate."

"I was just there three months ago. I don't think Matteo will let me go so soon again," Sera said. "Please try to visit. Otherwise, it'll be Carlotta pestering you next."

"Good God. You all should leave me and Elias alone. We're fine."

"I don't know, Luca. According to Tony, you hardly leave the mansion."

"Hmm…I'm not sure I want one of my men tattling to you about my movements."

"I'm your concerned niece."

"You're also married to a De Lucci. Besides, I recently had the mansion retrofitted with state-of-the-art technology," I said. "I can run everything from here."

"Okay. But just know we love you."

"Goodbye, niece."

"Love you, Zio."

Ending the call, I threw my phone on the table and left the study to look for my son. I loved and hated talking to my niece. I was happy that she was happy, but I hated when I felt the trace of pity— sympathy—in her voice. She'd always liked Natalya, and I sure as fuck was glad she wasn't one of those women who asked me to look for another wife or tell me that Elias needed a mother. I glanced at the wedding ring on my finger. As far as I was concerned, I was still married. Natalya was presumed dead because of those rings found in the fire, but that proved nothing, especially after Dario and I discovered her double life.

It made me reevaluate all my interactions with her, especially that night of the storm when she disappeared. Milkshake and fries. She'd been five months pregnant. How dare she risk herself? I didn't know if I admired or hated my wife for it. There wasn't a day I had not thought of her. In the beginning days of her disappearance and the discovery in the attic, I would alternate between rage and grief.

Because I missed her.

Because I hated myself for wasting my time trying not to fall in love with her when it was inevitable.

Because in between saying our vows and her disappearance, I *did* fall in love with her. Why else would there be an immense phys- ical pain in the center of my chest that at one point I went to the emergency room thinking I was about to have a heart attack? How some nights, missing her brought me to my knees, and I would roar and rage, drunk or sober, because I needed an outlet for the agony of barbed wires squeezing my rib cage tighter and tighter in an attempt to expel the vacuum of emptiness. Like a black hole, it sucked me in, and if it wasn't for my son, I would have surrendered to it.

And that was why sometimes I hated Natalya. Because she won in the end. She had become my weakness.

I passed the kitchen, and it was empty. Elias was a wild child. Poor Martha couldn't keep up with him, but there was Tony and Rocco, as usual. They'd become attached to the boy. My own guilt was reflected in theirs that they had failed to protect Natalya.

I ran into Nessa. I'd been able to tolerate her now, but I forbade her to be the primary caregiver for Elias because one time I heard my son call her Mamma.

It punched me in the gut, and I screamed at the poor woman. It wasn't her fault. I apologized later, but that was when I made Martha my son's nanny. It didn't feel weird when he called her Nonna because at one point, she was a mother figure to me too.

"Where are they?"

Nessa pointed toward the pool. Then she gestured for me to wait and grabbed her notepad and scribbled on it. *I'm going to make snacks. Do you want any?*

I shook my head. "What's for dinner?" I didn't like snacking and preferred to eat full meals.

She smiled widely and wrote on her notepad. *Beef Wellington.*

I raised a brow. "Really? I guess Martha gave up her secret. Well, carry on."

When I reached the pool area, my son saw me immediately and toddled over. "Dadda, Papà." He alternated between the two. It was amusing. I scooped him up, and he piped, "Cookies!"

"I see that, sport."

I glanced over at Martha who was sitting on the lounge chair, exhausted. "Yes. I gave him cookies. What do you expect? I'm too old to run after him."

"And yet you gave him cookies when it's almost close to dinner?"

Ignoring me, she asked, "Has Dario found a nanny yet?"

"Not yet." I whooped him up one more time, thrilled to hear his laughter, and then an ache would set in because I imagined Natalya beside me. To feel joy was to feel the sadness that followed. It was the endless cycle that had become my life.

"It's kind of hard to find a good one connected to the family when you insist on an applicant who is fifty or older. Who would want to take care of a two-year-old when they are fifty?"

"Why, Martha, are you complaining so much?"

Rocco came out to the pool. "Dario wants to talk to you."

"Okay, yeah...thanks." It was my time with Elias. I sent Dario to look over our real estate acquisition in Grafton. Chicago had expanded its legitimate business. The alderman connected to us was a shoo-in to become mayor of Chicago and possibly a senate run in a few years, but I'd found out he was playing me against Orlov. Hedging his bets. It pissed me off.

Rocco was still staring at me.

"What?"

"He said it was important he talk to you immediately."

I handed Elias to him. "Here. Take care of him and give Martha a break."

I walked back into the house, but not before hearing Martha calling out, "You still need to hire a new nanny."

I smiled inwardly. The old woman could handle Elias. It would keep her young. Returning to my study, I already spotted two missed calls from Dario. Hell, I hoped there was no screwup with the Grafton deal. I threw myself on the chair and called him back.

He answered on the first ring. "Where were you?" He sounded breathless.

"It's four p.m., asshole. It's my time with Elias."

"I think I found her," he said.

He didn't need to explain the *her* he was talking about because our search for Natalya never ended. It might have stopped occasionally when the trail had gone cold, but we never stopped looking. Now and then we'd have hits on traffic cams. I was using my wife's own weapon of technology and had hired a group of hackers to find her.

The south end of Illinois had yielded the most hits. That was why Chicago did business there in the guise of real estate deals. No one would question our presence. The last facial recognition sighting was three months ago. I didn't expect Dario to call me himself.

"Luca?"

"Where?" I gripped the phone and slowly rose from the chair.

"A town called Danvers. I caught her license plate before her car drove out of the parking lot."

"She ran from you?"

"I might have scared her. I think I looked at her as if I'd seen a ghost. It would have creeped out any woman. I have her information. Sending it to you now."

I held my breath. An image popped on our messaging. An Illinois driver's license.

Rayne Parish.

It couldn't have been a coincidence. I traced an unsteady finger on the image. My chest tightened with the potent mixture of grief and rage that had hit me in the early days of her disappearance.

Even with the atrocious driver's license picture, the face was clearly Natalya's. But instead of blonde, she was brunette. Instead of straight long hair, it was shoulder length. She even had bangs.

Rayne Parish.

Paris Rain.

"Luca? What do you think?"

A knife twisted in my chest. "It's her."

CHAPTER
Twenty~Two

RAYNE

I couldn't sleep. My anxiety was at an all-time high. For the first time, I was glad I lived in town, renting the studio on top of a pizzeria. I decided against living in seclusion because I needed reliable internet access. The lure of the Dark Web was there. I'd logged on a few times and took part in chat rooms. I'd even gotten invitations by a few to hack into some companies or politicians' websites known for their unethical practices, but in my two years, I'd never taken the plunge.

I took out my phone and stared at the license plate of the Maserati. Fear. I was afraid of what it would unlock. Dr. Gleason told me to let myself remember things naturally because force-feeding information would make the brain confabulate and produce false memories.

Dawn cast purple light into the lone window of my room. In the summer, it could get really hot on top of a pizzeria. Now that it was spring, it was just right, except my allergies were terrible.

I rolled out of bed and stared at my meager belongings, yet remembering how far I'd come. I was Jane Doe before I was Rayne Parish. When I woke up from my coma, I told them my name was Rayne. I felt like I was a Rayne. When it was time to give me a new identity, I told the man I wanted to be Rayne Parish.

I was already a patient of Doc Gleason when I woke up from my coma. I had lived on the second floor of his house while I recovered use of my wrist and I earned my stay by organizing his records.

It was funny how my first paid job came about. I found the poor doc cursing at his laptop because he needed to computerize his medical records. I told him to give me a chance.

He was reluctant and a curmudgeon about it at first. After all, I'd already been known to mess up my boyfriend's business. But eventually he trusted me. I earned money for new clothes instead of donated ones. I bought a cheap laptop. And when word spread in town that there was a geek-squad girl in residence, I made this town my home.

I stood up and walked to the window. Diagonally across was Brad's coffee shop. He lived in an apartment on top of the business. It seemed to be a standard for this small town where buildings were multi-use and convenient. He opened at six thirty, but he started his day earlier to accept the deliveries. Someone else made the pies and cakes, cookies and sandwiches. But he was really known for his coffee and roasted the beans right in a back room that functioned as a kitchen and a coffee roasting area.

Would it really be so bad to try to make it work with him? Would I come to love him? But the other problem was this town never really felt like home. I was missing a part of myself, a part locked deep inside my head.

Later that morning, after I finished my job at the garment

factory, I paid Brad a visit and maybe to have second breakfast. I smiled at the *Lord of the Rings* reference. I liked fantasy movies and had devoured them when I had time to watch movies for entertainment. Like my missing memories, I wouldn't be surprised if I'd watched them before. A few of them were weirdly familiar. Like the memory was right there, but a thin film was blocking it.

Brad was surprised to see me when I walked in. The hopeful look on his face nearly made me double back and leave, but I needed to give a good man a fair chance before the desire to pack up and leave took hold. Maybe the reason Danvers didn't feel like home was because I refused to put down roots. I didn't have best friends, more like acquaintances, and my closest friend was a hacker who I didn't know in real life.

"Rayne!" he said, coming behind the counter and giving me an overly enthusiastic hug that almost squeezed the breath out of me. "Sorry." He pulled back and smiled sheepishly. "Just happy to see you." He searched my eyes. "I thought I scared you off yesterday."

"Well, you didn't," I said lightly and slid my butt on a barstool. "At least not enough to keep me from wanting a piece of Miss Mabel's strawberry pie. And a cappuccino, please."

He gave me a salute. "Coming right up."

While he attended to my order, I gave him a once-over. The tee he was wearing stretched across his muscular back. He had a nice ass that filled out those worn-out jeans. He kept fit, just as I knew he kept a bench press in his apartment despite going to the gym regularly.

"Your laptop working okay today?" I asked.

He glanced over his shoulder. "Yeah. For now." He winked at me.

I shook my head and laughed.

The door to the coffee shop tinkled and a couple in their sixties walked in. I recognized my clients when I started out. I helped them sort their Wi-Fi and phone problems so they could FaceTime with their grandchildren.

They walked up to the counter. We exchanged greetings and talked about their grandchildren. They also wondered if I could drop by tomorrow to check their Wi-Fi. And this was usually how I got work around this town. Someone would see me and say, "Hey... I got a problem with this, could you..."

After Brad placed the cappuccino and the strawberry pie in front of me, he attended to the newcomers.

The coffee shop had a good crowd—people reading books, scrolling through their phones. A few were actually having conversations.

I was about to take my first sip from my cup when I spotted two men through the front window display. They checked the menu before coming in.

I was sure one of them was Maserati Man—who I'd labeled MM—from yesterday. I didn't get a good look at his companion before I instinctively shifted in my seat and faced away from the door.

I heard them come in and I prayed they'd get their coffee and leave.

Picking up my fork, I shoveled a bite of pie in my mouth.

I could barely taste it.

"What's good here?" The voice was MM's companion. I was sure of it. It was a low bass and slightly deeper than MM's. It knotted my insides and made me want to throw up.

Brad told them the specials.

"No self-respecting Italian would drink that fancy coffee shit."

My hackles rose. The arrogance. I wanted to say something.

"I'm sorry, sir, but you asked what our specialty was. We have espresso, but it might not live up to your self-respecting Italian standards."

Bravo, Brad. I might have just fallen in-crush with him.

"How about pie?" MM asked. "Miss…which one are you having?"

"She's having the strawberry," Brad answered.

"My friend was asking *her*."

That arrogant prick. All thoughts of self-preservation flew out the window and I swiveled on the stool and faced them.

And got punched in the gut.

The most beautiful man stood beside MM and I thought the latter was gorgeous. Still, I was offended for my friend and couldn't stop myself from saying, "It's very good, but I don't think you city folks would appreciate our small-town offerings."

"My apologies," the arrogant one said. "It was a long drive from Chicago. I will have a double espresso and the pie the lady is having."

"Is that to go?" Brad asked.

Please say yes, please say yes.

The man was staring right at me when he said, "We're dining in."

Luca

It's her.

I was still getting used to her shorter hair and its color. I had a feeling it was the natural one, and I thought it made her look more mature. More beautiful.

Every part inside me roared to throw her over my shoulder, pack her into the Escalade, and bring her home.

This prick in front of me was in love with Natalya. There was no fucking doubt. It was not a mere protectiveness for a friend. There was too much hostility in the way he rang us up. It bled from him. It made me second-guess drinking or eating what he served. It also made me want to take out my gun and shoot the asshole between his eyes.

"Please take a seat," the guy named Brad said. At least that was on his nametag. So generic. "I'll take it out to you."

"We'll be fine at the counter." I wasn't going to have him mess with my espresso.

"The table here is fine." Dario clasped my elbow and dragged me to the far corner of the coffee shop, away from Natalya.

"What are you doing?" I whisper-snarled at him.

"What did I say?" he snapped in my ear. "Don't come on too strong."

"The asshole is in love with her."

"So?"

"What if…what if…" I couldn't say it. It made me see red.

"*Cazzo*, calm down. Get over there." Dario nudged me to the chair that was close to the window and sat beside me. "We'll sit here and observe the interaction."

"I don't know if I'm going to trust anything he serves me," I voiced my concerns.

"Well, don't drink or eat anything," Dario sighed. "You were the one who came out swinging like a dick."

"Are you on my side or not?" I was still seething. I seethed even more when Brad and Natalya exchanged a private joke and laughed.

Dario sighed a heavier sigh this time. "Why do I get a feeling we're going to leave this joint in handcuffs?"

"There's not a cop around. They use the county sheriff." I wasn't even kidding. I'd done my research. She lived on top of a pizzeria close to here. Why was my wife living like this? But what was shocking, she didn't recognize me at all. She was irritated, yes, and a tad anxious, because Dario spooked her yesterday. But other than that, she looked at us like we were strangers.

A blonde woman rushed in. "I'm sorry. I'm sorry, I'm late."

Brad shook his head. "Second time this week, Hazel. Here, take this to the gentlemen at table eight."

More people came in. The coffee shop was doing brisk business. This man who was interested in my wife wasn't a jobless punk. He probably was a law-abiding citizen with a clean criminal record, paid his taxes on time, and didn't murder people who pissed him off. He was the epitome of a small-town America utopian, down to his golden-blond head.

I despised him on principle.

Hazel came by and handed us our espressos and slices of pie. "What brings you to Danvers? Passing through?"

"Cozy town," Dario commented. "What's there to do?"

While the blonde server chatted up my friend, I stared at my espresso, wondering if I would find something unsavory at the bottom of the cup. I decided not to touch it and looked out the window. My men were around. I didn't want them to look too conspicuous, but I had them casing the area. On the surface, it was just a gateway to the city of Grafton. Population one thousand and change. Perfect for hiding. Or not. Because if I were running from someone, I'd take my chances in a big city.

Hazel and Dario finished their conversation and our server went to the counter to pick up other orders to serve.

Brad the prick had leaned over the counter and flirted with my wife.

Flirted!

Something was very wrong. It was like a doppelgänger existed, doing everything the opposite of what my wife would do. Her voice sounded like Natalya's but had gained a hick drawl to it. I was starting to have my doubts, but from what Dario had dug up, her business was computer maintenance. The first known record of a Rayne Parish was around the time Natalya had disappeared and her first known address was with Dr. Jacob Gleason, who ran the only clinic in town.

I recognized the sparseness in her private records. It screamed a fake identity. Fill in the date and place of birth. Orphan. Raised in a group home. All bullshit.

I continued to brood and watch the interaction between my wife and Brad. Hazel returned to our table and stared at my untouched espresso and pie.

Dario had enthusiastically finished his.

"Anything wrong with your order?"

"It's fine," Dario answered for me and grabbed my plate and started digging into it. "My friend's acid reflux suddenly hit him."

Our server looked sympathetic. "Oh, I'm sorry. We do have the best espresso in town."

I forced a smile. "So I've heard."

"Well, if you need anything else."

My wife in my car, on the way back to Chicago. "We're good. We'll just hang here a bit." And find out what exactly was the relationship between that *stronzo* and my wife.

"Hazel? You got the shop a minute? Rayne and I are heading to the office."

I surged up from my chair. Dario sat me down. "*Madone*! Keep it together. What. Did. I. Fucking. Tell. You?"

"This. Is. Bullshit."

"Stop acting like a twelve-year-old or I'm going to haul you out of here. I knew you weren't ready."

Fuck, I wasn't ready. I was ready yesterday.

Dario and I were whispering harshly, quietly, but it seemed we were attracting attention. How long had Natalya been in there with that fucker? My expensive suit suddenly felt like an ill-fitting cheaply made Armani knock-off. I imagined this was how the Hulk felt like when he exploded out of his clothes. Thinking of the Hulk reminded me of Elias.

My son loved that temperamental green giant. It probably reminded him of me.

When Natalya came into view again, Brad was following closely behind her. Too closely. My fingers curled over the fork that was on the table. He cast Dario a smug look before he transferred his attention to my wife.

"We are not stabbing anyone with a fork today," Dario sighed. "I thought this was going to be fun, but I'm regretting this now."

"How could this be fun?" I growled.

"You're making me tense as fuck," Dario hissed.

And then something almost made me flip the table.

The bastard leaned in and gave Natalya a kiss.

Brad whatever-his-last-name was a dead man.

"I can't wait for tonight," he said. "I'll pick you up at seven."

He was making a date with my fucking wife? Right in front of me?

Death was too good for him. I was going to pull out all his fingernails and teeth, and cut off his balls and make him choke on them.

Dario was staring at his plate before he surreptitiously stole a glance at me. He frowned. I was grinning. I was grinning because I hadn't had the thought of having this much fun in a long time.

He knew exactly where my humor was coming from.

Natalya passed by our table without even looking at us.

Until tonight, tesoro. I'm going to find out what game you're playing.

CHAPTER
Twenty~Three

We were supposed to play it by ear. If MM and his arrogant friend left Danvers, we wouldn't go through with the date. But after I did my jobs that day, Brad texted me that shady characters were in the town. A group of ten, including MM and his friend, were spotted having a late lunch at the Danvers diner.

According to Brad, a couple of the waitresses swooned over their table. I didn't know why that irritated me. Brad had no clue where they were staying. None of his friends had information.

"They paid in cash at the coffee shop," Brad said. Twirling the pad thai around his fork before taking a bite. "So I didn't get their names. They also paid cash at the diner. That bothers me. You're right to be wary of them. Are you sure you hadn't seen the Maserati guy until yesterday?"

"He doesn't look familiar at all." I wasn't totally honest. Physically, they didn't ring a bell, but I couldn't trust my feelings of doom either, especially with what little history I had with my past. I dug into my own spicy noodle dish. We were at a trendy Thai restaurant in a strip mall near Grafton.

"Well, I'm glad I pressed you on what's going on," my date said. He was out of his usual tee or flannel, and he was wearing a checkered button-down shirt. I was in a sleeveless gossamer blouse, cream pants, and heels. It was my only decent date outfit.

"I don't want to get you involved."

"I'm already involved," he said. "I remember the first time I saw you come into the coffee shop. You tried to hide the bruising on your face and you had a wrist splint. I wanted to hunt down the bastard who did that to you."

It wasn't a secret that I left an abusive relationship. It wasn't a secret that I might be hiding from an ex-boyfriend. What was a secret was I had amnesia. I hadn't slipped so far. It was so easy not to answer questions about parents or siblings or where I grew up because people shut up when they found out I grew up in foster care.

"You know," he said, smiling. "I wouldn't be surprised if they were mesmerized by your stunning face. I sure was."

I was used to flattery from Brad, but I still blushed, especially when we were on a date. Well, this time it was a fake date. We'd gone out three times until I finally decided it wasn't working.

"So you bumped into him the other day, and today he walks into my coffee shop with his wingman." Brad refilled my wineglass.

"His obnoxious wingman, jeez." I sipped my wine. "I'm sorry you have to deal with that."

"You defended me, sweetheart. I'm sorry you had to deal with that too."

"But it was my fault."

"Hey—I'm here. No one's going to get to you. Now let's forget about these assholes and enjoy our dinner. Fake or not, I'm running with it."

He gave me a boyish grin that should have made any woman's heart flutter. Why couldn't I fall in love with this man? He was the all-American boy next door. Blond, blue eyed, tanned. A golden god. No wonder the women in Danvers hated me.

But maybe…my heart was in a deep freeze and all it needed was a patient man. A patient man like Brad.

It was almost six months ago when I shut him down cold because I felt nothing, but maybe…

There were times our conversations were awkward, but it was because I was hiding so many things. But judging how he was willing to take on my problems, maybe Doc Gleason was right. I should give him a chance.

After dinner, Brad drove past our town on I-90. It was a beautiful night, but I had a feeling it was because he didn't want it to end.

"How about you make me your coffee glace?"

He glanced briefly at me, but I saw the flash of white teeth. "I see why you turned down dessert at the restaurant."

"They didn't have the sticky rice." I pouted. "And I didn't want to waste calories on fried ice cream."

"You can afford it."

"And you're so diplomatic."

"Seriously, Rayne, you don't have to worry about calories."

"Says the man who runs every night."

"My body is used to it." We talked about sports and how he got a football scholarship for college. "But really, I just wanted to live in a small town and open a coffee shop."

It might have been my imagination, but the car sped up and we got into town in no time. Well, I hope he wasn't expecting sex, but maybe the coffee ice cream would be enough foreplay. I didn't know if the twisting in the pit of my stomach was anxiety or excitement.

He parked in the back alley of Nature Java. It was dimly lit. My anxiety skyrocketed. Again, I wasn't sure if it was from what I was about to do with Brad, or from MM and his cohorts. Were they lurking in the shadows? I'd been listening to too many true crime podcasts.

Brad came around to my side and opened the door. I hopped out, but before I could take another step, I was pinned to the vehicle and his mouth was on mine. His tongue teased the seam of my mouth, and I let him in. He groaned and crushed my body against the vehicle.

I tried to feel something.

It was...nice.

My hands pushed against his chest.

He was panting hard. "Sorry, but I thought if they were watching, they'd get the message."

I shook my head and breathed a brief laugh. "I couldn't fault you for going above and beyond."

"Honestly, I've been dying to do that for a while. Have I lost my chance of offering you dessert?"

I sidestepped him and tugged at his hand, leading him to the back entrance of the coffee shop. "No way am I letting you deny me dessert."

Thirty minutes later, I was buzzed from sugar and caffeine. "I don't know how I'm going to sleep tonight."

"How about we stream a movie at my place?" he asked.

He raised both hands. "Just friends. We sit on the couch. Unless you make the first move, I'm not touching you."

I regarded him.

He raised an open palm in a swear. "Scout's honor. And I was really a Boy Scout."

I had to laugh at that. "Well, lead the way, and oh, one thing. I'm choosing the movie."

"Anything you say, sweetheart."

I'd known Brad for two years, and never did I doubt that he was going to do anything I didn't want. That eased my anxiety a little. He wasn't expecting any fooling around to happen. And he was sober, too. He had wine at the restaurant and that was it.

The stairs leading to his apartment were in the kitchen. They made creaking noises that were typical of the buildings in this town.

At the top of the stairs, his whole body froze, and he mumbled *fuck*.

"What's wrong?" And that was when I saw it. The door was open.

"Let's go."

We turned to hurry down the stairs but stopped when MM and another person stood there.

"Oh my God," I croaked.

The door to Brad's apartment creaked open, making us spin around.

The asshole from the coffee shop emerged. "Nice of you to join us."

He had a gun pointed at us.

Luca

I had learned self-control over the years. They had crucified me as a wildcard for one incident.

One.

Okay, maybe several.

The blond oaf shielded Natalya. My index finger stroked the barrel. It would be so easy to slip and pull the trigger.

"Get inside." I waved the gun and stepped aside. "Don't try anything."

Brad scowled at me. I'd give him credit for not pissing in his pants. Seeing how Natalya clung to his arm tested my composure. Earlier, all I wanted to do was kidnap my wife from her apartment and take off with her, but there would be too many unanswered questions, questions that could only be answered by patience and witnessing their interaction. However, Dario felt I might forget all self-control and cause a scene in public like I almost did at the coffee shop. Scenes all crime families wanted to avoid in the age of smartphones. So I had a man follow them and send me updates of their date. While I seethed and simmered with the images being reported back from the restaurant, I rifled through Natalya's and Brad's apartments to find clues of her life in this small town and evidence of their relationship.

Watching him kiss her made me want to set this prick on fire. I listened at the top of the stairs like a pathetic stalker to their laughter and conversation while they ate dessert but I finally had confirmation that they were just friends.

Brad wanted them to be more.

I could kill him for touching her and not lose sleep over it, but something still wasn't adding up. Natalya looked at me like I was an annoying ant she wanted to squash under her shoe. I knew my wife's every expression, every mannerism, and every tell, but this woman in front of me showed very little of what was familiar.

Dario and Tony walked in and closed the door.

Dario whispered in my ear, "Rocco found the doctor. He's taking him to another location."

"What do you want from us?" Natalya asked.

There was defiance in her voice, but also fear. And I hated that she was afraid of me.

"You," I told her.

"Please tell me this isn't about the pie," Brad groaned.

"What you've done is far worse than fucking pie." My voice was steady, my insides were not. My blood was on a simmer. "Tie him to the chair. Let's see how—"

"You're so brave with your thugs and gun," Brad spat. "If you want Rayne, why don't we fight it out like real men, huh?"

"Brad…" Natalya grabbed his arm. "Don't—"

"I will not let them tie me up," he told her. "And let them do what they please with you? Fuck that."

"I don't like what you're insinuating," I growled at him.

"No? Then shoot me. I'm not going to let you tie me up."

Guilt and unworthiness stabbed me in the chest. I recognized chivalry, and I didn't know what to do with this realization. Was he so in love with my wife that he was willing to die for her? Was this the romance hero she was forever looking for in me?

I handed my gun to Tony. "Hold it. Don't interfere."

"Boss, I don't think—" Tony said when he didn't lift his hand to take it.

"Did. I. Stutter?"

Reluctantly, he accepted the weapon. I shed my suit and rolled up my sleeves.

Natalya's eyes were darting between me and her blond companion. He was grinning at me like he couldn't wait to turn me into mincemeat.

He was two inches shorter, but he clearly fed on protein shakes along with his coffee and outweighed me by twenty, thirty pounds.

I cocked my elbows and called him over with my hands.

Without warning, he launched his shoulder into my gut. We

crashed to the floor and he immediately punched me across my face.

Motherfucker.

"That all you got?" I grinned even when I tasted copper.

He slugged me again. I was the idiot who welcomed the pain of wanting him to fuel my fury. Before he could get a third hit, I locked my hands between us and shoved them against his torso. He rose on his knees and I had him against my thighs. I lifted my hips, threw him over, and sprang to my feet.

He rolled quickly to his knees, but I spun and back-kicked him across his cheek.

"Brad!" Natalya cried, coming forward.

"Hold her back!" I ordered.

Brad staggered to his feet and shook his head. He took on a boxing stance. More alert. He was bleeding from his mouth.

We came at each other and exchanged blows. I was mostly dodging his jabs, and getting in mine and wearing him out.

He kissed my fucking wife. I hit him again and again until he was lumbering like a drunk.

"Enough, please," Natalya cried.

I glared at Natalya. "This is for you."

I grabbed Brad's arm and used my hip to flip him over, sending him crashing onto his coffee table.

I was sweaty, still riled up, and pissed that I messed up my pristine dress shirt with blood that wasn't mine.

"Sit his ass in that chair."

Brad's face was showing signs of swelling. He'd be lucky to see through both eyes tomorrow. I grabbed a fistful of his blond hair and leaned in. "It's not your bulk, you prick. May I suggest jujitsu lessons?"

"Fuck you." He spat in my face. He just signed his death sentence.

I straightened. Tony scrambled to hand me a paper towel. I wiped the gunk off my face without taking my eyes off the blond.

"That was a bad idea. I was going to let you live." I admired his chivalry, but he had no self-preservation.

I looked at Dario. His face told the entire story that was streaming through my head.

Kill the idiot, burn down the coffee shop.

"Give me the gun."

Tony handed me the nine-millimeter and suppressor.

"No!" Natalya cried. Her face was several shades of red from all her crying. Her lips were swollen and they reminded me that the bastard kissed her.

"Brad is innocent. He doesn't know…"

"That he kissed a married woman?" I spun on them both while I screwed on the silencer. She was on her knees in front of Brad and I toyed with the idea of shooting them both. But no, I couldn't kill the mother of my son in cold blood even if she cheated on me.

"What?" Natalya's expression was one I remembered now. One of guilt and incredulity.

"What?" Brad echoed. "What's he saying, Rayne?"

"You're a good actress. I'll give you that. You fooled even me. But these tears…I remember them."

"I wasn't married to the bastard," she continued sobbing. "Who-ever sent you to kill me? I wasn't married to him."

Dario stepped forward and touched my arm that held the gun. "What are you talking about?" he voiced the question in my head. I felt something other than fury.

Confusion.

"She's talking about the asshole who beat her up and broke her wrist!" Brad tried to get up, but my reflexes weren't connected to my head and my gun lifted over Rayne's head pointing at him. He must had seen something in my eyes because he dropped back to his seat.

She put herself in front of my gun.

And that brought about another round of damned emotions that excavated the organ that was in my chest. *Take my black heart and stomp it under your shoes, will you, Natalya?* "You would die for him?" Dark thoughts vomited from my head.

Shoot him.

Shoot her.

Turn the gun on myself.

No. What about Elias?

Reclaim my wife.

Throw her over my shoulder and ask questions later.

Wait.

Who beat her?

Who broke her wrist?

I'll kill them.

"Brad's innocent." Her voice was as ragged as the million questions trying to form in my head. "He doesn't know I have amnesia."

Her last statement was a physical blow to my solar plexus. I staggered back, gun lowering to my side. Blood pounded in my ears, and yet I was feeling light-headed, like I'd been drained of every last drop.

"That explains a lot." Dario's voice came to me from afar.

The surprised expression on Brad's face was comical, if not believable. "Rayne?"

"You're lying." There was no conviction in my voice. It didn't even sound like me. My mind grappled for logic. "You remember your way around the computer."

"Semantic memory. Doc Gleason—"

"Enough!" I snapped. I turned to Tony. "We need answers from the doctor."

"There appears to be many things I don't know." I dragged her toward me and away from Brad. I inhaled sharply at the contact, closing my eyes briefly. The first time in two years since I held her this close. I wouldn't be letting her go again. Tralestelle would be her prison and she would live there with me and Elias for the rest of her life. "If I find out you're lying to me, *tesoro*, I'm going to burn down this entire town for hiding you from me."

"From you? I thought…"

"Yes…from me."

"You don't look like an online bookie."

Despite the tense situation, Dario breathed a short laugh. I didn't find it amusing. Because if what she said was true, someone took great pains to hide Natalya from me.

I stared at her, still baffled by the whole situation, but amnesia explained a lot. If it wasn't a convenient excuse not to kill Lover-boy. I could use him to keep her in line. "No, I don't."

"Who are you?" she whispered. Her eyes still expressed fear, but there was also curiosity and something else.

I decided to play the game a while longer. "You'll find out soon enough." I glanced at Tony. "Tie him up. I'll call. And then we can decide whether to kill him or burn this whole place down, or both."

"You're a monster," Natalya sobbed.

But I'm your monster, tesoro. I grabbed her arm and hauled her beside me. Time to visit the doctor.

CHAPTER
Twenty~Four

RAYNE

I sat beside the man who seemed to be the boss of everyone. Another one of their crew was driving while MM was beside the driver of the blacked-out Escalade. All throughout the craziness, none of them had revealed each other's name.

"Stop chewing your nails," the boss said. "You never used to do that."

"You seem to know me well." I clasped my hands between my knees. "Why don't you tell me why you're going through so much trouble to get me back?"

In the Escalade's darkness, his eyes scorched my cheeks. He was studying my features intently. Back in Brad's apartment, when this man hauled me against him, my body reacted. Not sexual or emotional, but something visceral I couldn't quite put my finger on. "I think you know me. I think you're the clue to my past."

"No shit." He chuckled without humor.

"So why taunt me when you can put me out of my misery?" I was hooking my star to a stranger, desperate to end two years of missing memories. "I don't even know how old I really am." My voice cracked into a broken whisper. "I don't—"

"Twenty-five."

"And how—"

"I won't say any more until I've talked to the doctor." He turned his attention to his phone for a while. It didn't take a genius to know what he was reading.

But I was getting antsy. The Escalade went on the interstate and it felt like we'd been driving for a while in the opposite direction from Grafton. "What's your name?"

"That's enough." He slipped his phone into his pocket before leaning against the window and resting his jaw on his fist as though he was contemplating something troubling. "Don't ask me any more…Na…Rayne. I don't want to force-feed you information. It's not good."

"You shouldn't believe everything you read on the internet."

"Better safe than sorry," he clipped. "If you really have amnesia, then we'll talk to this Doctor Gleason."

"Seems he used to be the chief attending for neurology at Chicago Medical," MM said. "Interesting he decided to retire in this small town and switch to family practice."

"We could retire him sooner," the boss said without missing a beat.

"Please don't hurt him. He helped me when I had no one."

I heard the growl before I was yanked into his arms and his mouth came crashing down on mine. His kiss was fire, his tongue demanding, and I opened beneath him. My body responded to the familiarity of his embrace. I was desperate to seek more. Each pull of his mouth and plundering of his tongue was going to unlock the shadows of my past. But at the first sign of arousal between my legs, my mind recoiled, and I blanched.

I struggled.

He broke the kiss, but not the embrace. "Since the first time I saw you, I wanted to do that." His breath made me shiver. It was as if his presence awakened that sensation that was missing since my amnesia.

"I know you," I said with certainty. I wedged my arms between us and pushed. "I know you, but inside me…" My words caught in my throat. "I don't want to remember." As desperate as I was for a trigger to my memories, the kiss only unearthed a heartache I couldn't understand.

He cursed and let me go. "Don't say that."

"Because what if the reason my mind refused to remember was because you've hurt me terribly, the pain was more than I could bear and I blanked it out." What if it wasn't retrograde amnesia I had but dissociative? Doc Gleason considered that possibility.

He looked out the window again. "I never hit you. It wasn't me."

He couldn't look at me, and I couldn't look away from him. "What if it wasn't physical?" My voice was monotone. "When I kissed you, it felt…I don't know how to describe it. It was as if you breathed heartache into me. You've hurt me somehow."

"Don't jump to conclusions."

He didn't deny it.

He fixed his collar and settled back in the leather seats, giving the abandoned structures outside his attention. "Stop speculating before you paint me as a mass murderer."

Interesting choice of words, but I'd already known for a fact that the man beside me was dangerous. My head pounded. I recognized the beginnings of a migraine I hadn't had in a long time.

"Does your head hurt?" MM asked. "Your memory might be coming back."

"Oh my God, stop getting your information from the internet. No, I don't suddenly have a headache and a flash of memory."

We turned from the state route and exited to one that was surrounded by barren land. Like it'd been an industrial place at one time. "How do you even know this place?"

No one answered me.

"If you're going to kill me here," I said quietly. "Please don't hurt Brad or his business."

"It's not good to beg for the life of a man who kissed what's mine."

I jerked in his direction. "You're saying you own me?" I swallowed. "Are you a pimp? A human trafficker. Oh my God, oh my God." I hunched over. I was going to throw up. "Pull over."

"Are you..."

"Pull over!" I shrieked.

The Escalade screeched to a shoulder. I stumbled out and retched on the side of a road. Did I escape traffickers? My mind raced with all possibilities. But he said I was a married woman. My head pounded. Too much processing. I was rejecting what my mind was trying to piece together. This was exactly what Dr. Gleason said I shouldn't do. But deep down inside, I know this man held the answers to all my questions.

"Here." A bottle of water appeared beside me and I gulped it down.

"You okay?" MM asked.

The boss was outside the vehicle, watching. His stance wasn't unconcerned. I would even say it was wary. Even without seeing the expression on his face, I could tell that he was a coiled spring about to pounce.

No doubt we had a connection. Even MM treated me with familiarity.

We got back on the road and no one spoke as if a single word would spark an explosion in the charged atmosphere of the interior. Every single one of us was waiting for answers.

After five more minutes, we reached an abandoned warehouse. The boss got out first and then helped me down.

It was dark when we entered the structure, but a light shone in a corner. We came upon two men, leaning against a wall and Dr. Gleason sitting on the floor. Rechargeable lamps illuminated the area.

"Doc," I cried and ran to his side.

"Are you all right?" he asked.

I nodded vigorously. "You?" I checked him for injuries.

"I'm fine."

MM, the boss, and more of their goons surrounded us. I counted seven people total against Doc and me.

The boss asked his man, "Anything?"

"He said he's bound by doctor-patient confidentiality," the goon replied.

"Your man seems hesitant to torture old men like me," Doc said. "I wonder if you have fewer scruples."

The boss stared at Doc. "I wouldn't test that theory."

"He beat up Brad," I shared.

"It was a fair fight." The boss raised an arrogant brow at me, a hint of mockery lifted the corners of his mouth.

MM whispered in his ear, and he nodded, checking his watch. "We're on the clock. I want everything on Rayne Parish that would help me care for her—"

"Care?" I laughed incredulously. "If punching me in the face is care, then I'd rather fight you on this."

"I did not do those things to you!" He glared at Doc. "Speak."

Doc Gleason glanced at me. "Rayne?"

I nodded. "He knows me. I'm sure."

Doc's mouth tightened before lifting his chin at the boss. "Rayne was dropped off at a St. Louis shelter for abused women and human trafficking…"

I watched MM's and the boss's faces closely for their reactions as the Doc detailed how he brought me back to this town. I was in a coma for a week before I woke up not knowing my name. Their expressions went from skeptical to downright scary, and the boss's face simply shut off. It was hard to tell what he was thinking, but I was sure it was going in different directions.

After Doc finished talking, the boss's eyes fell on me. "And you simply found your way around computers again?"

"Yes."

"Interesting. So this man said that you were interfering with your boyfriend's work as a bookie and that it was illegal."

"You say it as if it isn't true," I said. "So why don't you tell me the truth?"

"You're not ready for the truth."

"Oh, is this some kind of Colonel Jessup's way of saying I can't handle the truth?"

The boss laughed. A real laugh. And it amazed me how it changed his features into a man who I could be attracted to. Oh my God, no wonder Brad did nothing for me. It was because I was attracted to dark-haired men who were morally corrupt. The lure of the Dark Web made more sense.

"I've watched that one," he said. "I didn't think it was your type of film."

"You know I like movies?"

He lost the amusement in his eyes. "I couldn't live up to your expectations of romance heroes."

"Romance heroes? I like fantasy, not necessarily romance, but I do like heroic behavior."

"Oh, *tesoro*, I don't know if that bump on your head changed your taste in movies." He looked at Doc. "It could happen, right?"

"Personality changes? Yes, but her scans didn't show any permanent damage to the frontal lobe."

"You've done extensive scans on her brain?"

Doc didn't say anything.

"How about the truth?" I said. "At least tell me my real name. Maybe that might trigger my memories." That was a long shot. "I'm just tired of this limbo."

"Natalya." His roughened voice caught in his throat, like it was agony to say it. I approached him slowly. Intensity glittered in his dark eyes as if he was waiting for me to suddenly remember everything.

There was nothing. But my mind didn't reject the name. "Natalya? I like it…it fits."

MM asked beside me, "Anything?"

"It doesn't work that way," Doc Gleason scoffed. "Believe me, I've done extensive research on this. The mind and memories are a complicated network. They're unpredictable. You can't force someone to remember."

"So you told us." The boss's words were like gravel. And his whole body was a powder keg. There seemed to be much more he wanted to say. I stepped to within an inch of him. Our bodies almost touching. The tip of my shoes meeting his. The room was just reduced to him and me.

"Tell me," I said softly.

His throat showed rapid movement, like he was trying to swallow. "You weren't a bookie's girlfriend."

Somehow, my mind had already accepted that I'd been living a lie. My whole body was lighting up with the first and significant truth that would clue me in to who I was before Rayne Parish.

His jaw clenched with determination.

"You're my wife, Natalya."

I saw the truth in his eyes, but an excruciating pain blasted through the chambers of my heart, a pitiful cry escaping my lips.

I will never love you.

The edges of my vision darkened, and then there was no more.

Luca

"Natalya!"

I caught her in my arms when her knees gave way. Then her eyes rolled back but not before slaying me with the anguish that flashed through them. The wounded sound that escaped her lips clawed at my chest. Did she remember something? What was it?

My questions stampeded on each other. Dario spread his jacket on the dusty cement flooring. I laid Natalya on top of it and leaned over her, glaring at the doctor. "What happened?"

"Obviously, the shock was too much for her." The doctor winced, going to his knees. "I'm getting too old for this."

He put his fingers on her pulse. "Her heartbeat is fine. See? She's already coming around."

Natalya's lids fluttered. "What…?" Then, as if remembering something, she whispered, "Oh my God."

She leaned on one side to get up.

"Is she okay to sit up?" I barked.

"I'm fine," she responded too quickly for my liking.

"Does this happen often?" It was an exercise in patience not to be apprised of everything about her condition. I was worried. I was angry. I was everything I shouldn't be feeling, because Natalya needed my reassurance.

"Once or twice?" She angled away from me toward the doctor, and I resisted the urge to pull her back. She should be turning to me.

"Did you remember something?"

She puffed a breath and shook her head but averted her gaze. Instead, she said, "I think I need to lie down."

"Stubborn as ever." I scooped her up, ignoring her protests, rose to my feet, and walked toward the exit.

"I live in—"

Impatience slowed my strides. "I know where you live, but you're coming home with me."

She started to struggle. "You can't simply kidnap me!"

I lowered her to her feet but grabbed her biceps. "You are my wife. You are not spending another second away from me and—" I caught myself. I was about to say Elias.

"And? And what? Your arrogant ass?" she cried.

"Is she always this difficult?" I asked Dr. Gleason.

"Well, she is persistent."

That was a rhetorical question, but whatever. "You're coming with us too."

The doc chuckled like I'd lost my mind. "I don't think so."

"I'm not giving you a choice either."

He glanced at Natalya. "He is an arrogant ass."

"I'm picking you up again. I'd prefer if you don't struggle because the last thing I want is to drop you on your head, but then again, maybe that might jar your memory."

"Asshole," she muttered before putting her fingers against her temple.

"Is your head hurting?"

"If it's hurting, it's because you're a steamrolling asshole who is forcing me into doing things I don't want."

My fists clenched at my sides. "Do you need a sedative for this trip?"

"Unbelievable." She turned away from me and staggered to the entrance of the warehouse.

I followed closely, but when she nearly stumbled, I swooped her up in my arms again.

"You're making me dizzy."

"Stop fighting it. Close your eyes."

It was as though the fight went out of her. "I'm so tired."

"She's having information overload," the doctor said.

"You think telling her she's my wife triggered something?" I had a feeling it did, but I was a coward to press her because she didn't react favorably. She was hiding something.

Gleason didn't immediately respond, but when he did, he said, "The brain is processing. Give her time."

We came up on the Escalade. The doctor asked, "Who are you people?"

Before I could think of an answer, one of my men came to me. "Boss, Tony called. He had to jet from Bailey's apartment."

"Why?"

Natalya's eyes popped open. "I'm never going to forgive you if you hurt Brad."

"Seems the cops came around. He got out using a window."

The woman in my arms gave a brief laugh. "Brad sent them the Maserati's license plate."

I tipped my chin for my soldier to open the door. "One thing we need to get squared away is your loyalties, *tesoro*."

My eyes met Dario's over the doctor's shoulder. He gave a tight nod, which meant he took precautions and switched license plates.

We did this whenever we went out of town. The plates would come up stolen.

"Doctor, you'll ride with my friend."

The old man seemed conflicted, but I bet he didn't want to be separated from his most interesting patient.

"This is a small town, but I have patients."

"You've taken vacations to Europe and gone to conferences. What do you do then?"

Dr. Gleason split a look between Dario and me, then stared at Natalya. She had her eyes closed, but I was sure she was still conscious to the surrounding conversation.

The doctor exhaled a resigned sigh. "I'll make arrangements."

"You shouldn't let him trample over you too," Natalya groaned.

The soldier, who informed me of Tony's flight from the coffee house, came back and said, "Tony is behind the diner from lunch today. We sent a car for him. There's an ambulance in front of the coffeeshop."

"They're going to check out Gleason's house next." That was the next logical choice. "We're leaving."

The Maserati followed the Escalade into our private airstrip near Grafton. The Cessna jet I used to fly down here sat in the hangar. Our pilot already had the plane warmed up and ready to go. The license plate would register to a stolen vehicle in Chicago that made it to one of our chop shops. Dario was monitoring local police channels and there was an APB for a dark blue Maserati with stolen plates. It would be stupid for Dario to drive back to Chicago with the doctor in it.

"Seriously, who are you people?" Gleason repeated his earlier question as he stared at the plane.

Natalya resisted my help to get out of the vehicle. In fact, she

flat-out refused to get out of the SUV. "You can't do this. Doc"—
she looked remorsefully at Gleason—"I'm sorry my crap is
affecting you." Then back at me, she flung more accusations.
"You're destroying his practice."

The doctor regarded me thoughtfully before returning his gaze
to Natalya. "Somehow I think this isn't new for these guys." Then
he asked me, "Where are we going? You should tell us that at least."

"Chicago."

"Fuck," Gleason said. "No wonder you look familiar."

"Familiar? Well, he still doesn't look familiar to me," Natalya
retorted.

"Are you coming on your own, or do I have to sedate you?" I
asked her.

She looked at the doc again. "Who is he?"

"You can call me Luca." Fuck if I let someone else introduce
me.

Natalya was trying to think too hard again. I could feel her eyes
panicking when her gaze flew back to the doctor.

"Luca Moretti," Doc Gleason said incredulously. "The Chicago
mob."

"Wh-what?" Even from her stubborn position inside the vehicle,
she seemed to sway.

"Come on, Natalya." That declaration of who I was seemed to
have drained the fight out of her and I easily gathered her into my
arms.

"I can't get away, can I?" Her words walloped me with a guilt I
tried to ignore.

I wanted her surrender, not her defeat. "I'm afraid not."

"The don of the Chicago mob." Gleason, for his part, seemed
excited with the discovery. He turned to Dario. "And you are?"

I left my friend to explain.

Once we were in the air, the doctor seemed more cooperative.

Even drank scotch with us. The configuration of the seating allowed for a face-to-face among four people. Natalya kept a protective arm around her body as she stuck to the window, staring into the darkness and ignoring the men. She shut down after she found out who I was. I didn't think her memory had come back. She thought she was a bookie's girlfriend. A far cry from a man in my position.

I quizzed Gleason on what to expect and how to care for my wife.

"I want fresh X-rays," I told the doctor. "I have connections at a hospital."

"To be honest, I've never dealt with long-term memory loss from trauma. Most of the time, my patients got their memories back in a few days. One patient lasted a few weeks. But the bulk of the memories came back all at once."

"Will exposure to familiar surroundings help?"

"Oh, definitely..." Then the doctor punted. "Still unpredictable."

I looked at Dario. "Have you informed the mansion's staff?"

"Yes. Rocco said they've activated lockdown."

"Lockdown?" Natalya finally gave us her attention. "Doc and I are going to be your prisoners?"

"I don't know who did this to you," I said. "It's for your protection."

"How sure are you I didn't leave you on purpose?"

The fingers of my right hand dug into the seat's leather arm. She just struck at the theory that brought me rage in the past two years. "You wouldn't leave me because you were in love with me." Plus, you wouldn't leave Elias. How do I tell her we have a son?

She laughed derisively. "Right now, I hate you. I don't want to go back with you."

I blanched. She delivered those words with venom and they left no doubt her past feelings for me were gone. Yet here I was, still in love with her and not willing to let her go again. I chased the pain that punched in my chest with two fingers of scotch.

Dario stared at me like he didn't know whether to laugh or be concerned for Natalya. Did he think I would hurt her? It was a miracle I managed to smile through all the fucked-up emotions she wrenched out of me. They were uncomfortable and unwelcome.

Even if I deserved them.

"You'll realize you love me," I told her. When her eyes narrowed at my confidence, I added, "And you'll wonder what the fuss is all about."

I waited with bated breath for her reply.

She was still staring at me and studying my face, after which she said, "Please tell me I wasn't stupid enough to fall for your looks."

"That was part of it, I presume." I leaned into her conspiratorially. "You were infatuated. You were a virgin, and I was the first man who gave you the orgasms you deserved."

She blushed and glanced away.

Ahh...there was my Natalya.

Dr. Gleason also found the window interesting, while Dario was choking on his drink.

"You're impossible," she muttered.

"I'm merely stating the facts. Why, in the last—" I cut myself off. I nearly said the last months of her pregnancy. "That's why I wouldn't believe that you would leave me willingly."

"Why?" Her head swiveled back in my direction, face full of indignation. "Because I couldn't get enough of your cock?"

I grinned. "Don't forget my mouth."

"Aaaallll right," Dario interrupted. "Could we save the sexual history for later? That's TMI."

I stared at the doc. "What do you say, Gleason? You think sex would jolt her memory?"

She sputtered. "You're the last man—"

"Don't finish that sentence," I cut in sharply. "Brad Bailey is lucky to escape with his life. I would have burned that cute little coffee shop of his to the ground."

"You really would have shot him? Burned down his business?"

"He touched what's mine," I gritted.

"Get over yourself."

Dario kicked my foot to remind me I had to tread carefully. It was unfair to level my self-righteousness at Natalya.

I had no qualms when it came to killing men who did the same illegal shit that I did, but I drew the line at killing innocent people unless I had no choice but to defend myself. If they tried to kill me, they ceased to be innocent. I had a very fine line. If Brad drew a gun on me, I would have shot him without question and had no problems sleeping at night. I always welcomed an alternative unless a person is beyond redemption and there was no choice but to put him down.

Realizing Natalya had amnesia reduced the acid that ate at my insides when I saw her kiss another man.

But the image was forever seared into my memory. My rage competed with an overwhelming urge to reclaim her. I'd caged the possessive beast inside me, but it was rattling the bars that were keeping me sane.

I clamped my mouth shut before I said anything stupid that would make her resist me.

CHAPTER
Twenty~Five

I will never love you.

I woke up in the dark on a bed that wasn't mine, and in clothes I didn't recognize. I thought I was still in that nightmare. A room of gold. A long table that stretched from end to end. A faceless man sitting at its head, and I was on the opposite end. I was being punished for something. A distance stretched between us that felt more than physical. The walls of the room were endless, and he seemed unreachable.

I woke up with an ache in my head and a loss in my heart.

"Natalya, are you okay?" A voice spoke in the darkness and I saw movement on the couch.

Luca. It was the voice from my dream, which felt more like a nightmare.

Natalya was my name, but I still couldn't respond to it. It was as if there was an impermeable membrane between my old memories and who I was now. On the plane, my brain struggled, and it gave me an almighty migraine. I asked for a painkiller, but it seemed the bastard gave me a sedative.

I sat up on the bed. "You drugged me."

The figure rose from the couch and approached the bed. "It was for your own good."

"You've known me less than a day and you're making decisions for me."

"Gleason saw what I gave you."

I looked around me. "So where am I? Is this room my new prison?"

He sat on the bed. "It's not. I didn't want to overwhelm you when we came home. It's best to start with this room."

"Am I to be locked up here?"

"No."

He reached out a hand, but I flinched. "I need to pee." My bladder was so full, it was a surprise I didn't wet myself.

He assisted me without asking and I let him, but after a couple of steps when I was sure I wouldn't fall over, I said, "I got this."

He exhaled a frustrated breath. "I only want your comfort, Natalya."

I lumbered into the bathroom and shut the door on him.

"I will stand out here, and if I hear nothing in two minutes, I'm breaking down this door."

"God! Would you let a woman pee in peace?" I grumbled as I sat down on the toilet and let the pressure go. I looked around the bathroom, taking in the luxurious space of gold and white marble. There was an elegant soaking tub, and a glass-enclosed shower with one of those rainfall showerheads.

After I finished, I flushed the toilet to let Luca know I was still alive. There was no doubt which side of the double sink was his and hers. I inspected the lotions, cleansers, and moisturizers on one side.

They were high-end ones and nothing compared to the drugstore variety I used on my face. I grabbed the toothbrush and scrubbed out the cotton from my mouth. Even the toothpaste tasted expensive.

"Can you please open this door?"

Arguing wasn't worth it, so while brushing my teeth, I unlocked the door. The light from the bathroom revealed a disheveled Luca. Far from the commanding mafia boss of earlier, he had bloodshot eyes with bags under them that weren't there before, and his trim beard needed grooming. When I met him this morning—yesterday morning—he was obviously meticulous about his facial hair.

I gave him an unimpressed once-over and resumed my place in front of the mirror.

"It would make me feel better about your care if you are less argumentative," he told me.

I almost choked on the toothpaste. I quickly gargled and pinned his image in the mirror with my stare. "Let's get one thing straight. While I figure out who I am in your life, it is not my responsibility to make you feel better."

"But it is mine."

"I don't care if you make me feel better. All I want is the truth."

"We have to be careful."

"Don't baby me."

"The doctor—"

"We will run it by the doc, but I don't want you hovering around me. Clearly, I survived without you these past two years. I'm not delicate."

His eyes flashed and he stalked inside. Alarmed, I spun around and he caged me against the sink.

"No. You're selfish."

"Excuse me?"

"You're not the one who lives with the memory that I had failed to protect my wife," he gritted. "You're not the one who has to live with the torment of not knowing if you were alive or dead. Of what happened to you. If you had left me on purpose."

The torment in his eyes clogged the words I wanted to say. "You said I loved you. Why would you think I left you?"

He leaned away slightly, jaw hardening, before he took a full step back. "There's much to unpack here. I might know, and then I might not." He caught his lower lip between his teeth as if giving himself more time to frame his words.

"You're speaking in riddles and it's making me nervous. You think I could sleep after you leave me with something like this?"

"Do you need another sedative?"

I huffed an irritated breath. "Is that your answer to everything?"

"I'm doing it for your own good."

"Again with the high-handedness."

"You'll get used to it." He extended his arms as though he couldn't help it. I understood he was used to giving orders, but did I sympathize? No.

"How long were we married?"

He gave a start, as if surprised by my question. "Less than a year."

"I was barely twenty-three when I disappeared?"

"You were."

"Luca." He knew me when I was younger, but I think I'd changed in the last two years. "I don't think I'm the same girl anymore."

He was quiet for what felt like a minute. It lasted seconds. Finally, he said, "No. You're not."

"How can you say you love me the same?" He was quiet again, and this time it did last longer. The refreshing taste of the toothpaste turned more acidic the longer he didn't respond.

He was struggling to say something. The rise and fall of his chest and the clenching of his jaw gave him away.

"You're not sure, are you?"

"This is not conversation for now," he clipped. He held out his hand. "Come."

"I don't think it's a good idea that we sleep in the same room." My indignation at the sleeping situation was delayed, but I needed to voice it.

When I didn't take his hand, he simply grabbed mine and tugged, and I stumbled into him. I glared up at his amused face. That face came closer. "Since I'm the person who would most likely trigger your memory, I'd say it's a good idea. But your concern is noted. For now, we'll sleep in the same room. I'm on the couch anyway. We can decide later what is appropriate."

"Why can't—"

"Sleep. You'll need it." I sensed foreboding in his words, but for the first time since I met Luca, his touch gave me reassurance, and I clung to his hand as he led me to the bed.

He tucked me in like he would a child.

I blinked up at him, his features hidden in the backlit window. I felt rather than saw the tenderness in his eyes.

"Good night, *tesoro*." He stroked my face lightly like I was the most precious thing. "I'll be right here if you need anything."

He bent further and kissed my forehead lightly.

I thought I wouldn't be able to sleep, but I was wrong, because next I blinked, an arrow of sunlight peeked through the drawn drapes of the darkened room. Luca must have pulled them closed because I remembered moonlight bathing the room through its tall windows.

My gaze followed the lines of the room. If this was our bedroom before, I had poor taste in interior design. The curtains were beige, and save for the expensive Persian rugs on the floor, the room was basic. The walls needed a repaint and I couldn't even identify the shade. Taupe? Green? The closet took over an entire wall. It was a stark contrast to my life in Danvers.

I sat up carefully, glad that my brain was sharper and the fog from the sedative had lifted.

Natalya. The name didn't grate. I didn't have any nightmares or dreams either, or if I did, I had no recollection. My eyes fell on the sleeping form on the sofa. That couldn't be comfortable. Luca was a big guy. The sofa wasn't long enough to fit his entire frame, and he had a foot resting on the floor, while the other one was cocked on the couch. He had a pillow underneath his head and an arm thrown across his forehead.

During our earlier conversation in the bathroom, I tried very hard not to look past his face. He'd been wearing a white undershirt and drawstring pajamas, but I couldn't help but wonder if he slept in the nude.

Heat rose to my cheeks, reminding me of his filthy words on the plane. In front of Dr. Gleason no less. It was not said in a medical way either. "Yes, we did have sexual intercourse, and I gave you cunnilingus." And despite the sedative, how my body reacted to him was appalling.

Gingerly, I left the bed and padded barefoot toward the sleeping Luca. I couldn't help staring at his crotch. With the position of his legs, his morning wood was clearly outlined, and it was impressive. I gulped. That thing had been inside me. Wetness pulsed between my legs and a force propelled my feet to move closer.

I stared at his face. So beautiful in his sleep. Even with the roughness of his beard, it couldn't hide the chiseled proportions of his jaw, the proud nose. His mouth was firm yet also held a hint of a pout. Dark brows, thick lashes.

Next, my gaze strayed down his white shirt. It wasn't one of those skintight ones I saw Brad wear, but the way it clung to him, the bulges and the dips, hinted of a man who kept in shape. My eyes couldn't help looking at his erection again.

"Like what you see?"

I sprang back with a yelp, my heart leaping to my throat.

Luca's eyes were slightly more open. It was hard to tell he wasn't sleeping, save for the sly tilt to the corners of his mouth.

"There's much to do. Get up." I escaped into the bathroom and slammed the door. I did my business and brushed my teeth.

The door swung open and Luca walked in. "Are you always going to run to the bathroom when the conversation becomes uncomfortable?"

"I…" I spat the toothpaste. He was standing with his back to me and was going to piss. "Couldn't you wait until I'm done?" I hurriedly rinsed my mouth.

He chuckled, unperturbed. "I need to take a leak."

I rushed out from the room and he called, "I'll be more mindful next time."

While Luca did his morning routine, I investigated the closet. A row of suits in blue, gray, and black and white dress shirts were arranged in an orderly fashion. Underneath them were several pairs of shoes. Tucked in another corner was more casual wear.

I felt him before he spoke in my ear. "Your clothes are over there. Martha has laundered a few."

I bent forward so I could look behind me. The clean, woodsy scent of his aftershave assailed my nostrils and stirred a longing inside me to lean closer. His hair was wet, his chest bare, and I dared not look lower.

A mischievous glint entered his eyes. "Normally, you'd appreciate me walking around naked, but I considered your recent puritanical sensibilities."

Of course, my eyes lowered and was relieved and maybe a tad disappointed he had a towel slung around his hips.

I wanted to inhale all of him and my body felt like it was coming down with a fever. Why couldn't I have reacted this way to other men? Was my DNA drawn to his? At this point, my logic was appalling, and my body's reaction infuriated me.

Luca Moretti was too potent for my senses. I needed some kind of armor against him. I was ill-prepared to handle a man like him. "When don't you wear suits?"

"I like wearing them."

"Obviously."

His mouth quirked. "But I dressed more casual for you when I stayed here."

"Stayed here? Oh, you mean we also lived in Chicago?"

His gaze dropped. "Do you want to shower now, or after breakfast?" He moved away from me to rifle through the more casual section of his clothes.

I stared at his back for a long time, baffled for an instant with his retreat, but maybe there was something "shocking" with that as well.

He pulled on a worn-out tee, before casting me a brief glance. "There's more to it, and I don't want to get into it right now."

Fair enough. He gave me no choice but to turn away when he whipped off the towel. I caught a glimpse of cock nestled against dark hair in between muscular thighs. I ran out of the closet and heard Luca's laughter.

Asshole.

In my rush to get out of the closet, I forgot to bring clothes, and I was too chicken to return to the closet to pick them out. I locked the bathroom door, but it was the kind of lock that could easily be rigged, and I wouldn't put it past Luca to barge in if he really wanted to. I was getting the idea that he was a man who did as he pleased.

I found a terrycloth robe in the bathroom closet and decided that would do. The rainfall shower did a lot to improve my mood. All those dopamine receptors were welcome. After I dried my hair, I returned to the bedroom to see Luca back on the couch, bare feet propped on a leather cube, and texting.

Clothes were laid out on the bed.

"You picked out my clothes?"

He glanced up briefly from the screen. "Don't get too excited." His eyes gave me a head-to-toe appraisal before he shook his head, grinned mysteriously, and shifted in his seat. "That's what you typically wear around the house." He told me without looking at me and resumed typing into the phone.

Expensive threads, tailored linen pants, and printed orange flowers on a silk blouse. Lacy panties sat folded beside it.

"You're a bit thinner." He finally put the phone away and leaned back to watch me lazily. It made me wish I had on more than a robe, but I wasn't giving him the satisfaction of letting him know he flustered me. "We'll put some meat back on you soon enough."

My chin tilted up. "You're confident that I'll accept being your wife again."

That seemed to annoy him. Good. Payback was sweet.

"No divorce." He stood and stalked toward me, invading my space, he lowered his head. "We won't throw away our marriage."

"What if I never get my memory back?"

"Then we'll start from scratch."

"What if I changed too much and we're no longer compatible?"

"Why all the negativity?" he shot back. A slight sneer touched his mouth. "You truly think I couldn't make you love me again? We're compatible in bed." His gaze didn't even move down my body, but just the heat in them made my skin sensitive to the fabric of the robe.

"Marriage is more than sex."

"Don't challenge me, *tesoro,*" he whispered, but the tone left no question what the challenge was. "I'm trying to be less of a villain here. I already have too many points against me."

"And you're the type to keep score?"

"I'm not heartless, you know." For a moment, our gazes locked and the flash of anguish in his eyes pulled the same emotion from my heart. It reminded me of what he told me about being the one left behind and not knowing.

"I know this is too much to take in." He cleared his throat. "A husband. This house. The challenge is only beginning." He turned away and walked back to the couch. "Get dressed. After Gleason looks you over, there's someone I want you to meet."

CHAPTER
Twenty-Six

RAYNE

"Your vitals are good." Doc Gleason folded away the blood pressure monitor. We were in Luca's study. I was actually starving and wanted breakfast first, but the doc wanted to draw blood. When Luca and I walked in, I was surprised to see him unwrapping diagnostic instruments, and he already had a stethoscope around his neck.

"You sleep okay?" Doc asked.

"I did," I replied from my position on the recliner. "And you? Did they treat you well?"

"You expect me to answer anything but yes?" He chuckled, glancing at Luca, who was leaning against his desk, observing us. He was still in a tee and sweatpants and dark sneakers. Somehow I got the impression those weren't his usual attire.

"I assure you, *tesoro*, we did not keep the doc locked up in the basement." He cast an amused glance at the doctor. "Please tell her you were in a room with amenities that could rival a five-star hotel."

The doc shrugged. "Five-star living is pushing it, but it wasn't bad. Good mattress, and Martha said if I didn't give her any headaches, she'd give me a good breakfast."

"Do I know her?" I asked Luca.

"Doesn't ring any bells?"

"No."

He exchanged a look with the doctor. "Are you done with her?"

"As much as I can do given the tools available." He transferred the samples into a medical cooler.

"Kingsley would have been here if she didn't have appointments this morning. She'll pick those up this afternoon."

"She and I had an interesting conversation this morning."

I crossed my arms over my chest and split a look between the two. "And this Kingsley. I assume she's a doctor too. Was she my doctor?"

Luca straightened and walked toward me. A guarded expression shuttered his face, and I wondered if this checkup was to make sure I could withstand the revelations of the day. Was he going to tell me I took part in the family business? Most of what I'd learned about organized crime was when I researched St. Louis gangs and from binge-watching *The Sopranos*. For the mafia, the women remained oblivious to the husband's business and played up their social standing in charities and churches. Also, I woke up realizing I spoke Italian. It was part of my semantic memory. That would explain why I had a light foreign accent in the beginning. I wondered if I'd been in America illegally and why I was afraid to dig deeper about who I was and worked hard to give myself a Midwestern accent.

I straightened in my recliner while Luca crouched in front of me. "You know Martha and Rachel Kingsley very well. Martha has been the housekeeper here for thirty years. She was like a mother figure to me, and I believe to you too. Rachel was your doctor when you were pregnant."

My heart pounded in my ears. "Were?" My throat constricted. I dragged the question out. "Did I lose the baby?"

Luca braced my knees and shook his head. "No. We have a son." He smiled in a way that was both heartbreak and joy.

A son!

"Is he okay?" I croaked.

"He's fine, Natalya." For the first time since I'd met Luca, his eyes gleamed with tears. "He's two." His voice was ragged and full of an emotion I was waiting to come to me.

I waited to feel something other than shock and heartbreak over the lost years, but there was a feeling I couldn't identify. Not sadness or joy. But something else.

The smile on Luca's face faded and his eyes dimmed. "Say something." The words cracked with desperation.

"I always wondered why I was sad whenever I saw children and pregnant women." I glanced at my clenched fingers on my lap. "Was I a bad mother?" I looked up suddenly. "Please be honest. Because…" I beat on my chest with a fist, finally identifying the feeling inside me. "I feel undeserving."

Shock met my eyes. "Natalya, you were a fantastic mother." Luca slid his hands up my thighs to move closer. Then he lifted my chin with a finger. I didn't realize I had lowered my eyes again. "You were going through postpartum difficulties, but never doubt that you were an excellent mother."

"You're not telling me that to make me feel better?" I asked. "Because if my memory comes back, and I find out you've been sparing my feelings, that's going to be worse."

"You were a wonderful mother to Elias." The warmth in his eyes and tone eased the self-doubt, but something was still not adding up.

"He couldn't be more than a few months old when I disappeared."

"Eight weeks."

"Did I breastfeed?" I didn't know why my mind went to my breasts. "Because shouldn't I be like…" I cupped my hands like I was holding melons in front of my chest.

"You did complain about breast tenderness," Doc Gleason said. "I attributed it to hormonal changes from the trauma you experienced, but Doctor Kingsley and I talked about your health right before you disappeared and—"

Luca glanced sharply at the doctor. "I thought we weren't overloading her?"

"She needs to see the big picture," Doc told him before continuing. "She was sure you were heading into a state of postpartum depression and were feeling inadequate because you stopped producing breast milk."

The doctor leaned against the overhang of the window. One arm wrapped around his torso. The other arm was cocked and resting on it. He was tapping a finger on his mouth and scrutinizing me like a specimen under a microscope.

Luca and I waited for him to say something until the man in front of me lost patience. "Is there something else you want to say before I introduce Natalya to our son? Is it the right time to do so?"

"You think after dropping that bombshell I can just forget you mentioned him?" I fired at him.

"I don't want our son to be forced to acknowledge his mother either."

I opened my mouth, but a searing pain in my heart caused me to clamp it shut. I didn't know what Luca saw on my face, but I recognized remorse when I saw it.

"Natalya, I didn't mean…" he started, but it was too late.

"Forget it," I snapped. "Talk about the big picture. I'm seeing the state of our marriage."

"That's not fair," he growled. "I just want what's best for our son and for you."

Pushing my bruised feelings aside because he was right, and acknowledging that his lack of sensitivity was part of his personality, I wondered who I was then. I angled my head toward the doc. "Any ideas? Are you seeing the bigger picture now? Why I still can't remember who I was before I lost my memory because I sure as hell don't think I like the person I was then."

"Don't say that." Luca's voice was hoarse. "You were perfect, very giving. I was the problem. I didn't take care of you the way I should have."

"So you're admitting you could have caused me to run away?"

"I don't think so," he insisted. "But you were hiding things from me."

"I'm so confused," I said. "Did you think I left you on purpose or not?"

"Before I lose track of my deductions," the doc interjected. "I'm thinking the amnesia is both physical and psychological. Doctor Kingsley indicated you had feelings of inadequacy as Elias's mom. What could have happened that night must have worked with your feelings of inadequacy. Your mental state wasn't at its best, and your mind disassociated from your current reality."

"Being married to Luca and being a mother?" I clarified.

"Correct."

"Will she be ready to meet Elias?" Luca asked.

"I met the kid. Cute boy." Doc grinned in a way that, for the first time, excitement rather than dread took hold of me. "Go for it. It's better than speculating on what did or didn't happen in your marriage." He looked pointedly at me while Luca typed something on his phone. "Your mind is in a vulnerable but open state right now. The right stimulus might trigger an avalanche of memories."

Luca put the phone away. "Martha is bringing Elias." He paced a figure eight before he smacked his forehead with his palm. "Fuck. We didn't talk about how to introduce you."

"I think it's best if you just introduce me as a friend first?" I said. "That way less pressure on both of us."

Luca scrubbed his face. "I didn't think this through."

"I'm not a child psychologist, but Martha and I discussed this briefly when I saw the boy," Doc said.

"Martha is not a psychologist either," Luca pointed out.

"Look, I'm just a doctor in a small town, but I've encountered situations like this regarding kids meeting new people. It's nothing new. And since we're not introducing Rayne as his mother, just behave like you would introducing other people. Elias, I presume, has strong attachments to you and Martha as his primary caregivers. The toughest part for kids that age is insecurity. As long as one of you is in the room, he'll be fine."

"Don't force him to interact with me," I said.

Luca wasn't able to respond before the light knock came on the door. While holding my eyes, he called out, "Come in."

The door opened. I held my breath. A toddler came barreling through and said in a lilting voice, "Dadda! Papà."

The boy didn't even notice me and went straight to Luca. He was beautiful, with a head of dark, bouncy curls. Luca caught him in his arms and lifted him. "How's my *bombolino*?" He turned to face us. "Say hi to Papà's friend."

"Hi." Elias stared at me for two seconds before cupping Luca's face. "Waffles."

"You hungry, sport?"

"Yas!"

Then Elias found Doc Gleason more interesting over Luca's shoulders.

"He's beautiful," I breathed. I was still wrapping my mind

around having a son. My arms itched to wrap around the wiggly bundle in Luca's arms. Luca was staring at me while his son tried to reach over to grab the stethoscope around Doc's neck.

"Give him time," Luca said in a quiet voice.

"It's totally fine. I just can't believe…this." No words would come.

"Natalya…" a tremulous voice said beside me.

I turned to see a woman in her late fifties or early sixties. I was so transfixed on Elias, I totally forgot there was another person in the room. A hopeful expression crossed her face and her eyes were bright with unshed tears.

"I don't know you." My voice cracked as I rose to my feet. "But I guess, you're Martha?"

She nodded vigorously and her mouth twisted, attempting to hold back a sob while forming words.

"Thank you for taking care of Elias." I made a move toward her, unsure of myself, but Martha closed the distance and hugged me tight. Then she started sobbing.

"Nonna is crying," Elias said in the garbled language of a toddler, but I had no trouble deciphering.

"She is because she's happy," Luca told him

I turned toward Elias. "Your nonna is my friend, too."

The boy puckered his brows, and even if I wasn't versed in toddler death glares, that laser suspicion was aimed at me.

"Martha," Luca said, his tone firm, lowering our son. "Take Elias to the breakfast room."

The older woman let go, dabbed at her eyes and sniffed. She went to Elias to guide him out.

It didn't take a child expert to see that Elias had a different attachment to his dad.

The boy pouted. "Papà…eat?"

"Yes." He smiled reassuringly. "We'll follow."

"K."

Before leaving, Elias turned his little body my way and said, "Bye."

"Bye, Elias. See you at breakfast." He nodded like an adult before allowing himself to be led from the room.

Collective exhales signified how a toddler could cause so much tension.

"First hurdle over," Doc commented.

"I pictured that encounter differently." Luca scratched his brow, his shoulders sagging with the weight of disappointment.

"I think it went well," I said. "I'd be worried if he took to a stranger quickly."

Luca gave a shake of his head and the corner of his mouth lifted in a smile that was more self-mockery than cheer. His gaze fell to the desk, and he started to fiddle with the stacks of paper there. "He likes Tony and Rocco."

I did not know why I felt the need to reassure him. "He is too young to remember me."

"You don't seem put out," he said in a disgruntled tone that amused me rather than irritated me. "If my son treated me like chopped liver, I'd be very hurt."

"Luca, goodness. This is new even for me. I can't invent emotions that are not there."

My reply didn't appease him, and he continued to find the desk more interesting than the people around him. It gave me another perspective into Elias. He was interested in me, but he was uncertain about the situation, like his father was right now. I didn't want to point it out because it was just my conclusion to what happened. "Come on. I'm hungry."

"Baby steps," the doctor punned, unhooking the stethoscope from his neck and putting it in the case. "And yes, where's breakfast?"

CHAPTER
Twenty~Seven

LUCA

To say this entire morning had become a shitshow was putting it mildly. It wasn't what I was picturing at all. First in my study, it was Elias who was avoiding his mother. Fine. I could deal with that. But I'd been looking forward to us finally sitting down and having breakfast as a family.

I was sitting at the head of the table. Natalya was on my left with the doctor beside her. On my right, Martha was feeding Elias.

This time, it was Natalya who was the one unreceptive with our son. I wondered if Elias's rejection earlier in the study was having a delayed reaction.

My boy had been trying to get her attention, and all she did was brush him off.

"Natya…wafs," my son asked his mother. Elias rarely offered his food to anyone, including me.

"I'm good," she said with a smile I had hoped to never see

again. It was the smile she gave me the day I took her home after giving birth to Elias. A smile that was resigned and one that was frozen in place when I wished she would get angry at me instead.

The flesh of my fingers dug into the stem of the fork. I leaned into her. "What's wrong with your food?"

"It's fine." She wouldn't look at me. It wasn't fine. I glanced at the doctor. He was giving Natalya a speculative gaze too.

"Good. Fine," I said. "Are you sure?"

She didn't answer.

I sliced the waffle with more vigor than was necessary and popped a piece into my mouth. While I chewed, my gaze wandered around the table, falling upon Elias first. He was bubbly when we came in. He usually was when food was within reach, but now my son had turned sullen.

The day was going downhill fast.

I chewed the waffle with precision, swallowed it, and put another bite in my mouth. My jaw started to hurt with the chewing, but it also could be from the tension that had fallen over the room.

So much so that I got irritated when Natalya picked up a piece of bacon and took a minuscule bite. The only ones at the table who were truly eating were the doctor and me.

Natalya, realizing what she had done, pasted a smile on her face so wide I'd be surprised if she didn't pull a cheek muscle. "Are you full, Elias?"

He nodded.

"Then can I have your waffle?"

He nodded again.

Natalya pushed her plate across the table and my son picked up the piece with his hand and transferred it to her plate.

"Thank you."

"Yo welcome."

"Papà…canna go?" Insecurity filled the expression on my son's face. He wasn't comfortable at the table and wanted to play with his trucks.

Fuck. I was raging inside, but my rage was directed at myself. In my eagerness to get my family back, I might have caused more problems.

"Go ahead, sport, but no running." I tipped my chin to Martha, who looked concerned.

When they left, I put down my fork and knife and steepled my fingers. "Do you want something else to eat?"

Natalya's head was bowed in defeat, and a jolt of fear pushed out my anger. Static raised the hair on the back of my neck.

When her gaze lifted to mine, my lungs expanded with that fear.

"I can't do this." The chair scraped back. She stood and ran out of the dining room.

"What the fuck?" I surged out of my own and went after her.

I spotted her retreating figure running into the gardens.

I lengthened my strides and followed her. I found her at the edge of the patio, bent over and sobbing.

I touched her shoulder. She spun around and batted my hand away.

The poison-soaked glare she shot my way had me flinching.

Her cheeks were wet with tears. "You don't love me!"

I never told her. Telling her now would sound lame. "Natalya, I—"

She stabbed her finger in the direction of the mansion, her eyes accusatory. "Don't. It was in that room where you told me of your expectations. You said…I will never love you."

I stilled. "Your memory is back?"

"No!" She was still yelling, stepping left, stepping right, swaying as if she would fall, but I was afraid to touch her again. "I wasn't sure if it was a fake memory. Since I met you, I had this voice in my head—your voice telling me this."

"I've changed," I said.

"Do you love me now?"

"Of course!"

"I don't believe you." Fury mixed with her tears. "It doesn't feel true!" She pounded a fist on her chest. "In here. I feel it's a lie."

I pinched my temples between an index finger and thumb before gesturing toward her. "I've never told you—"

"See!"

"When you disappeared, I realized what a stubborn fool I'd been." I took a wary step toward her. It was then I caught sight of Doc Gleason in the background. "I missed you. I missed you because I loved you."

She looked up at the sky, still continuing to cry. "The thought that I would leave you is now making sense. Did you set those expectations when I was pregnant? It felt like I was pregnant, but that would mean you've been cruel to me for months and I just took it."

"I was never cruel."

"Telling me you'll never love me isn't cruel?"

"Love is not a requirement in an arranged marriage!" I said. "You were young, Natalya. You had romantic notions that I was your hero. You had delusions of making me one." Fuck, I was gaslighting her. I made her fall in love with me. "I admit." I exhaled heavily. "During our honeymoon, I manipulated you into falling in love with me."

"Arranged marriage?" she asked. "I…I'm *someone*?"

This was getting complicated. I shot the doctor an I'm-fucking-this-up-so-badly look.

She stopped crying, but her gaze was shooting in all directions. I couldn't tell if she was in full-blown panic or a mental spiral of information overload. And she was continuing to sway.

Fuck it.

I reached for her. And was relieved when she didn't fight me when I made her sit on the stone benches that circled the patio.

I crouched in front of her. "You're the daughter of one of the most powerful men in Italy." Or used to be. The Galluzo was in a debatable position with Carmine at the helm. Despite his year of learning the ropes from my half brother and me, I doubted he was fit to lead for long. He just wasn't forceful enough and the clans would eat him alive.

She looked at Doc Gleason. "You knew this?"

"I googled it on the plane while you slept."

Her attention returned to me. "What else? What is this manipulation?"

"Natalya…"

"I don't trust you right now. And if you don't tell me the truth, if my memories come back and I find out you lied to me, I'll find a way to leave again."

"You'll leave Elias?"

"No. I'm taking my son with me."

I stood, fighting the sneer that threatened to form on my face, reminding me that the mental state of Natalya was more important than my ego. "Right now, Elias isn't comfortable around you."

"I'm going to work on that." Tears brimmed her eyes again, but instead of despair, determination glinted behind those tears. "Because that boy inside needs to know that I would have never left him."

"You didn't. You wouldn't."

"What happened that night?" she asked.

"Good question." I went down on my haunches again. "I don't know for sure. You and Elias were kidnapped by Russian thugs, but Orlov—he's the head of the Russian mafia in Chicago—swore he had nothing to do with it."

"How did you get Elias back? And why wasn't I with him? I

wouldn't have abandoned him."

Fringes of hysteria crept into her tone. I got up from my crouch and sat beside her, enclosed her with my arms, and rested her head on my chest. She was too overwhelmed to resist, but she needed to hear this.

"You didn't. They took you and Nessa...she's the nanny. You left your locket with them." I cleared my throat. "There was a tracker on it. You didn't know that."

She had stopped crying, and after a long indrawn breath, she pushed away and stared up at me. "Is Nessa still here?"

"Yes."

"Was I close to her?"

Her eyes searched mine. I caught my bottom lip with my teeth and contemplated what to say.

"Why can't you answer me?"

"She's not my biggest fan."

The doc choked on a laugh.

"What did you do to her?" Her tone was accusatory and all the angst of those days came crashing back.

I let go of her and sprang to my feet. "She wasn't you!" I jutted my arm in her direction and repeated. "She wasn't you. I traced the tracker and when she came out from the forest line, I resented her for not being you! I hated her that day."

"That's not fair," she whispered. Eyes wide in a way that was wonder.

I faced her squarely. Every vein in my body popped with anger and fury at this whole damned situation. "You think I didn't know that? I do."

"Is that why she's no longer Elias's nanny?"

My shoulders slumped and the way the rage leaked out of me to be replaced by despair had enough force to make me take a step back as I said in a choked whisper, "Our son called her Mamma."

Natalya's mouth twitched in despair. Twisting one direction, flattening, twisting again, and turning down while tears continued to roll down her cheeks. Finally, on a ragged sob, she only said one word, "Luca…"

～

Rayne

"Luca…"

For the first time since I met him, the anguish he experienced with my disappearance sunk into my lungs and pulled the world from under me. The enormity of the emotion I was feeling for him was more than the sympathy I would have had for a stranger in the same situation. Because if I wasn't sitting down, I would have fallen to my knees.

In front of me was the broken man he was trying to hide from his family and our son. In front of me was the husband who had lost his wife and had to live with the not knowing whether she was alive or dead.

Whether she left him on purpose or his enemies took her.

For me, not knowing who I was had its challenges, but I built a life and moved on.

I was seeing a man who never moved on.

Was it because he missed me and loved me? Or was it because of the guilt that he didn't show me that love before it was too late?

Rising unsteadily, I went to him.

I reached out, but he recoiled.

"Don't give me your pity," he said roughly. "I deserve your scorn."

I believed him. I crossed my arms and glanced at Doc Gleason.

"If it wasn't too early, I'd say we all need a drink," he said. "And to think we're still missing all the pieces."

"I want to talk to Nessa," I told Luca.

His mouth compressed into a thin line, and a muscle pulsed at his jaw. He slipped out his phone and texted someone. "She works in the kitchen. Is she ready for this?" His question was directed at Doc Gleason.

"If she was the last person who saw me before I disappeared, don't you think it's important that I talk to her?"

"She's right. Information could be lost in translation," the doc said.

"You've eaten very little," Luca said. Either he was really concerned for my health or he was trying to stall my meeting with Nessa. I hated that I didn't completely trust him, but as the blanks were starting to fit into my memory, my reactions to him were making more sense. He might have regretted how he treated me during our marriage, but I was a different person now. I could feel it deep in the core of me.

"We can talk in the dining room."

On our way there, we met several people in the big foyer. I recognized Tony. Beside him was a dark-haired woman with bangs and straight, short hair in a staff uniform. I hadn't seen Tony since Brad...Oh my God. Brad.

I turned to Doc. "Have you spoken to Brad?"

"No." He looked at Luca.

Luca was glaring at both of us. "No."

"What do you mean, no?" I flared. "We need to check on him. You body-slammed him on the coffee table."

His mouth twisted in a sneer. "He deserved it."

"You even pointed a gun—"

A series of images flowed in a reel through my mind.

Luca with a gun pointed at someone. But it wasn't Brad.

My gaze swung toward Tony.

It was Tony, but he was beaten up and bloody and on his knees. We were surrounded by mafia soldiers. In this very hall.

"Natalya?" Luca's voice came to me from far away.

My lungs couldn't keep up with my heartbeat, or was it the other way around?

The room spun.

"You're under a strange assumption that I'm giving you a choice."

Two of his soldiers hauled a bloody Tony to the center of the foyer. They shoved him to a kneeling position.

"Tony…" My voice cracked, then I turned pleading eyes to my husband. "I'll do anything."

He drew out his gun and pointed it at Tony.

"No!"

"No!" I screamed.

Fingers gripped my shoulders, and Luca's wild eyes searched mine.

I shoved at him and backed away. "You're a monster."

"What the hell are you talking about?"

"Here in this very foyer." I pointed at Tony. "You were going to execute him."

Luca's face contorted in what could only be frustration. He scrubbed his face with his hand and twisted away from me.

"Fuck!" His roar bounced around the grand foyer. Then he spun back on me. "Is this a fucking joke?"

My chin tilted up, fury lighting me up from the inside. "Are you denying it happened?"

"I'm not!" he snarled, reminding me of a frothing, rabid dog. "But why the fucking fuck do you remember only the bad parts of our marriage?"

"Maybe because there weren't enough of the good!" I yelled

back. I retreated to the woman beside Tony. She was in my flashes, too. "Are you Nessa?"

She nodded.

"She doesn't speak." Tony kept his eyes trained on Luca whose daggered looks in our direction only fueled my need to pump the girl for more information.

Nessa grinned and brought out her notepad while casting a defiant look at her boss. If Luca was a cartoon character, I imagined he would have smoke coming out of his ears and breathing fire like a dragon.

As if sensing the tense situation, Doc moved in front of Luca while Tony also used his body to shield us against the man who looked ready for a second explosion.

"Can we talk somewhere?" I asked Nessa.

"The dining room," Luca gritted. "You've barely eaten."

Nessa scribbled on her notepad. "Attic."

"She wants us to talk in the attic," I informed everyone.

Luca's mouth tightened, and his nostrils flared. He sidestepped Doc, who gripped his arm, but he shook it off. "I'm fine."

He walked toward us. "You're going to keep my wife away from me, Tony?"

"That depends, boss," he said in an uncannily calm tone given Luca's threatening approach. "You assigned me as her bodyguard before. I'd like to be assigned to her again."

The men locked eyes for a while. Finally, Luca said, "Your niece is a pain in the ass."

"But she's loyal, more to Natalya than to you," Tony said. "You're fair. I think you would want someone on Natalya's side."

This was interesting information. I wondered if that was why Luca didn't want me talking to her.

Luca cocked his chin to the side, muttering about people not knowing where their loyalties should be. He squared against us again and pointed a finger at Nessa. "The truth. You and I don't see eye to eye, but Natalya needs the truth." Then he told Tony, "Since you're eager to be her bodyguard, why don't you bring up the food?"

My husband seemed to have a preoccupation with my diet.

"What do you want to eat, *tesoro*?" He seemed to have recovered from his outburst. "I can have Martha make you something."

"I thought she was taking care of Elias."

"I'm capable of watching over our boy."

"Something easy. I'm not picky."

"Have Martha make a quiche," he said to no one in particular.

"I said something easy," I retorted.

"Well, I don't feel like making it easy for anyone today," Luca said, striding away from us. "Come on, Doc, we can have that drink in my study."

If Tony hadn't said that Nessa was more loyal to me than Luca, I probably would have reservations following her to the attic. An attic to me was musty and old and where people hid their secrets and, in Luca's case, maybe the literal skeletons of a dead body or two.

I was following Nessa past the kitchen when a loud screech gave me goose bumps. I spun around, thinking I was under attack. A gray cat was running full tilt toward me, her pitiful meows, loud and heart-rending, reminded me of a mother cat looking for her kittens.

It stopped two feet from where I stood and made what could only be described as a loud, scolding meowing sound.

"Uh…" I glanced at Nessa. She had a hand over her mouth like she was trying not to cry. Martha joined us and shook her head, her face equally devastated and bittersweet. "She remembers you," she choked.

I knelt in front of the cat and put the back of my hand against her nose so she could sniff me, the action so familiar.

"Her name is Mrs. B," Martha said. "I forgot about her. She missed you. For days after you disappeared, she haunted the halls with her cries, looking for you."

"I can tell." Any doubt that I had about being collectively lied to dissipated. I always trusted an animal's instinct. Mrs. B sniffed me a bit more. I wasn't ready to pick her up, and the cat was hesitant as well. She was standoffish. It was as though I needed to grovel at her paws before she allowed me the honor of carrying her. Mrs. B did, however, rub her face against my leg.

I stood and made an elaborate gesture for Nessa to proceed. Mrs. B trotted behind us, then ran crisscross in front of me. I had to watch where I stepped before I tripped all over her.

When we arrived in the attic, contrary to my earlier reservations, what greeted me was a space filled with morning light, a widescreen TV that made me giddy, and rows of books I couldn't help running my fingers through. Romance books, some with broken spines, a couple of special editions, and more than a few belonging to the same series with how their spines beautifully aligned. As I picked one out, I weighed its heft in my hand, but my eyes became critical toward the bookshelf. An instinct that I'd seen this one before.

"There's something behind this." I turned around to face Nessa. "This space is mine."

She signed *Yes,* and I understood it.

ASL worked in my brain. New skill unlocked. "I know how to sign."

Nessa replied. *You learned it to communicate with me.*

I laughed. "No wonder your loyalty is to me."

I took down a few more books. "There's equipment behind this." I glanced over my shoulder. Nessa was sitting on the couch and she signed. *Yes. Boss found it.*

"He didn't know?"

She shook her head. *He was in Chicago most of the time.*

I abandoned the books and sat beside her. My gaze noted the shelf above the TV. A row of photographs were arranged there. A close up of me as a blonde, and one where I was holding a baby Elias, but my mind rejected the idea to approach and inspect those frames. There was fear. There were too many questions, and I wasn't sure what to ask her first. "He left me here often?"

She nodded.

"What did I do? Am I a hacker?" I wondered if that was why I was tempted by the Dark Web. Oh my God, then that was what he meant by a second life.

No one is sure. She grabbed her notepad. *No one knew you were that good with computers.* She underlined *that.*

I laughed. "For almost a year?"

She nodded vigorously and grinned like a proud mother.

"Did you suspect?" I asked.

She averted her gaze.

"Did you?"

Maybe a little, she signed. *The memory you remembered? You were the reason Zio Tony was beaten up. You left Tralestelle without telling anyone. No one knew you had a backpack except me, and I saw the computer inside.*

"You didn't tell anyone?"

She shook her head.

"Why?"

Not sure. I felt sorry for the way the boss was treating you. And then she suddenly signed. *Erase. Erase.*

My mouth pulled into a smile. "He told you not to lie, remember?"

He confuses me. I think he reacts more than acts when it comes to you.

"I know it's subjective, but do you think he loved me?"

Nessa gave me a long look before she expunged a big exhale while surging to her feet. She walked to the window.

"Nessa? I can take it. It's okay if he didn't love me. He said as much."

She bent over and clutched her stomach and started shaking. I thought she was having a seizure.

Worried, I rushed to her side. "Are you all right?"

Boss, she started signing, while still keeled over in what appeared to be laughter. *Is the king of denial.*

Hope rose in my heart. It would be easier to contemplate learning about my relationship with Luca if I wasn't a pathetic doormat.

She pointed below us. I came closer to the window to see where she was pointing at. Luca was in the garden following a toddling Elias. Doc Gleason was trailing behind them on a phone. A phone! I sure as hell hoped he was talking to Brad.

My gaze returned to father and son and a tenderness for them expanded in my heart of whatever they both went through, especially Luca. Elias had been an infant, but surely he felt something viscerally wrong when he stopped hearing my voice, the rocking of my arms, and the smell of my skin. Tears formed at the corners of my eyes. My heart was opening up to the idea of Elias being my son.

Nessa tugged my arm. *I'm still not sure what he feels for you. He's a very contradictory man.*

Amusement tinged my voice. "I'm getting that."

A knock sounded on the door and Martha peeked through. "How are you two up here?"

"Nessa is filling me in on my contradictory husband."

The older woman came in carrying a tray. Nessa walked over to help her.

"I'm sorry Luca made you do this. I would have been happy with a peanut butter sandwich."

Martha clucked. "That wouldn't do. The boss is adamant about not taking the abundance of food for granted."

"Where do you want this?" Tony came into view, holding a carafe of coffee.

"Are we having a breakfast brunch up here?"

Tony chuckled and put the coffee and the mugs on the coffee table as Martha instructed. "I would love to, but I'm on a thin line with the boss. I'm gonna head back downstairs."

Tony retreated from the attic.

I was starving. I sliced a piece of quiche, transferred it to a plate, and took a bite.

"What have you told Natalya about that night?" Martha asked.

"Nothing yet," I answered around a mouthful of quiche. "I was impressed with the space up here and had to explore."

"You loved it up here."

"I can see why."

"You fooled every one of us thinking you were reading your romance books and watching romance movies."

"Wow," I said. "You all must think I'm such a lady of leisure."

Martha gave a light laugh. "Not at all. Everyone was happy you updated the appliances in the mansion and you were a genius, keeping the household budget straight."

"Seems I had a boring existence."

Nessa was shaking with laughter again and decided to join me for breakfast.

After the first few bites and sips of coffee, I came back to the purpose of holing up here. "So what happened that night I was abducted?"

Fifteen minutes later, I was processing.

CHAPTER
Twenty-Eight

Luca

"I don't appreciate being let into the house like I'm your mistress."

I looked up from the pool table at Rachel. She walked into the mansion's game room with an amused look on her face. I returned my attention to the game, sank my shot, and circled the table, chalking my cue stick.

"Damn, that didn't distract you one bit?" Dario grumbled. My consigliere arrived an hour ago. It had gotten too hot in the garden and I brought my boy back inside. He was sleeping on the couch beside Gleason.

"Not when I need this distraction. Hi, Rachel. Corner pocket." I positioned to sink the eight ball and finished the game.

Doc, who was nodding off, startled awake. He got up and met Rachel. "We talked on the phone."

The two doctors exchanged handshakes.

"Glad to meet you," Rachel said. "But I actually have to see Natalya to believe she's back."

"Not right now," I countered.

"Why not now? When we talked earlier, you were excited." Rachel grabbed a cue stick from the wall.

"Another game?" Dario asked.

"Unless you're going to use your stick on Luca's head," Rachel said. Her eyes fell on my son, then on Gleason. "Did he make you a babysitter? Where's Martha?"

"I'm babysitting," I corrected. "My wife commandeered my staff." She, Nessa, and Martha had been in the attic for the past two hours. I threw an irritated glance at Dario. "What are you waiting for? Rack 'em."

"The game isn't improving your mood," he observed.

What I really wanted was a cigarette, but I wasn't smoking while my son was in the room. I'd become more of a social smoker now, and I didn't want the sudden appearance of my wife to drive me into the habit again. "You're pissing me off right now and making my mood worse."

Dario didn't seem perturbed with my short temper. The bastard's twitchy mouth spoke volumes of his amusement.

"What's up with him?" Rachel asked. "And why did you have Rocco sneak me in? Is she vulnerable right now? She met Elias, right?"

"*Him* is pissed." I kept my focus on the green woven fabric. Green was calming, right? "Rocco snuck you in because I didn't want Natalya to see you. I changed my mind. Vulnerable? That's debatable. She's met Elias. They're still making up their minds about each other. She seems to be doing just fine and is currently in the attic with Martha and Nessa."

"Nessa? Oh dear." Rachel snorted a brief laugh.

My friend was aware Nessa didn't particularly like me, and I honestly wasn't sure why I didn't get rid of her. She was a superb cook. She didn't even talk back, but her condemning gaze irritated the fuck out of me.

I made a break of the balls Dario just set but failed to sink any or rail the required number, ending on a foul.

"*Cazzo*!" I growled.

"Ooh, I think I might have upset your balance." Rachel moved around the table and took aim at a ball. "I'll take solid."

"Guess I'm sidelined." Dario took his seat beside Gleason.

"Is someone going to explain why Luca is in a bad mood when he was fine this morning?" Rachel asked.

"Stop talking about me like I'm not here." My eyes focused on the balls she seemed to be sinking with no issue. Rachel was a pool shark. I should have known better than to let her push Dario out of the game. I preferred playing against Dario. He was less likely to psychoanalyze me while we played, which was usually how Rachel gave me therapy because I couldn't sit still on a couch.

"Well?" She continued potting her balls. Those might as well be mine.

Still staring at the rolling spheres, I said, "She only remembers the bad shit that happened between us so far."

"And so far, it's the *really bad* shit," Dario chortled.

"Like what?"

"The time I told her I will never love her."

Rachel had already heard my confession about that and had called me a moron. Not very psychologically worded, and I wondered if the Morettis wasted money sending her to psych school.

"What else?" she clipped.

"The time I pulled the gun on Tony."

"Typical. You never told me if you were really going to shoot Tony."

"I was pissed, but I'd probably shoot him where it hurt, but not kill him, and no, I don't want to discuss the time I chopped off his finger."

"You were only seventeen."

"He deserved it, according to Emilio."

"Should I be in this room to hear this?" Gleason spoke up and the doctor's eyes darted between us.

"Are you asking if I'm thinking of shooting you, too?" I asked mildly.

"Shame on you, Luca, trying to frighten an old man." Rachel missed her shot.

"I don't think he's frightened," I remarked sardonically. Rounding the table to sink my balls, I knocked my first one into the corner pocket and called another. "I've had zero body count since he made my acquaintance."

"Luca has this weird sense of justice," Rachel told Gleason. "But it's a very thin line."

"Just don't try to kill me or hurt my family." I winked at the doctor, who'd turned a tad pale. "And if your heart is as criminally black as mine, all bets are off."

"Understood." The word was strangled.

Dario laughed and squeezed the doc's shoulder. "You're a friend of the family."

"I see."

"We'll make it worth your while." Gleason was smart. He knew he'd seen too much. There was only one way to keep him quiet, and that was to bring him in. I needed him here in the mansion until Natalya regained her memory and be on call when there were setbacks. Having a neuro on payroll would ensure the care my wife needed.

"I guess I don't have a choice," Gleason said. "It would have been nice to have one."

I sunk three more balls but missed the fifth one. I leaned against the wall to let Rachel have her turn.

I balanced the cue stick on my shoulders and twisted from side to side. I missed my workout this morning and had been stiff as hell. "You'll have a comfortable retirement."

My eyes met Dario's across the pool table. My adviser had done a deep dive into the doc's background. He was selling his practice anyway, and from his reaction when he found out I was the Chicago mob boss, I didn't think he would balk too much.

Rachel missed the eight ball. I had two more to sink.

I chalked my cue stick and prepared to take my shot.

"You don't want Natalya to see me because she'll remember you missed Elias's birth."

Something snapped inside me. I flung the stick on the table. "Bitch."

Rachel merely raised a brow. "That's what you're afraid she'll remember."

"Wow," Gleason said.

"I don't need input from you, old man."

Gleason did a zipper gesture against his mouth. Dario was biting his fist, probably trying to avoid making commentary.

I hated people right now.

"Ziarach!"

Shit. Elias was awake. He rolled off the couch and toddled toward Rachel. Elias combined "Zia" and "Rachel." It was cute. But what was not so cute was the way they all seemed to be ganging up against me.

Elias always looked for me first when he woke up.

"Hi, little man." My friend lowered the stick and scooped up my son, who erupted in toddler chatter that made little sense.

I was unreasonably agitated, but for this part, I didn't need an audience who wasn't in my inner circle.

I opened the door. "Rocco!"

My soldier came forward. "Escort Doctor Gleason to his room."

"Oh, shouldn't I be hearing this too?"

"You've heard enough."

I nudged the old man out of the game room and into Rocco's care and slammed the door before facing the two people who knew me the most.

Two people who appeared to be finding amusement in my predicament.

My eyes were looking elsewhere when I gritted, "Both of you should be on my side."

Rachel was rocking Elias. "I'm on the winning side. It looks like Natalya is finally winning."

"Damn, where's that scotch?" Dario added. "We need to toast to it."

"This is ridiculous. I wasn't such a terrible husband." That sounded lame to my ears.

At this, Rachel's eyes softened. "You're a good father, but a terrible husband."

"I am not a nine-to-five husband. The Chicago family is like a corporation and I'm its CEO. Why couldn't she be happy with everything I could give her? This house. The money. I wasn't a bad husband. When she was pregnant, I went to most of her appointments. I ran her baths, massaged her feet. Made sure she had the best nutrition."

"Except you told her you'll never love her." Rachel lowered my boy, who seemed to have had enough of grown-ups and went to the corner of the room where he played with his trucks. He had them in almost every room in the house. "You're able to do those things because you never made yourself vulnerable to her. Granted, the night of Elias's birth, you had an excuse."

When I stayed silent, she pressed. "How badly do you want

your wife back? That's the hard question you should ask yourself. Not for Elias, but for your marriage. Because from what I've witnessed of your marriage, you and your wife have different expectations of love."

"Did you know?" I gritted. "There was this man who is in love with my wife and was willing to die for her?"

"Whoa." Rachel reared back and sat beside Dario. "Were you there?"

"I was," he said. "I thought Luca was going to shoot the man right there except Natalya went in front of the gun."

I needed a drink. I went behind the bar of the game room and grabbed a beer. "You guys want one?"

"He's in avoidance," Rachel said.

I took out three beers and went to them. "I'm not avoiding. I need alcohol for this conversation and so do both of you."

"I haven't had lunch yet," Rachel said. "What's on the menu?"

I exhaled a sigh. "My cook is with Natalya. We're going to starve or order pizza. Can we talk about my issue?"

"I came here for Natalya, but it seems you're the one who needs therapy."

I leaned against the pool table in front of them and guzzled down a beer. "You should be happy. Luca Moretti is finally ready to listen."

Rachel laughed and leaned against the armrest of the couch in a move to get comfortable. "All right. I'm not a neurologist, but I don't think Gleason can give you a definitive answer either. But before anything else, I find it interesting she remembers her hacker personality. Though most of it is semantic memory, I think that's part of her personality that she was the most comfortable with and where she feels she has power in her life. From what you told me, her parents suppressed her intelligence because they feared she'd get exploited. That's really hard on someone with a high IQ. So she created this double life."

They should be shot. "I don't know how parents wouldn't be proud of a child genius."

"I bet Elena has something to do with it," Dario said. "In her eyes, that's not a marketable aspect. I mean, you married her and stashed her in this mansion." His chest started shaking with amusement. "Not knowing she installed a ghost bridge in your house."

"Shut up," I growled, but my mouth twitched. My wife was brilliant. "I would have been thrilled with her. She might overhaul our gaming websites."

Dario snapped his finger. "Right?"

"So you're not intimidated at all by her IQ and her computer abilities?"

"If I had known this, I would have been prepared for it..." I paused. "Once I've gained her loyalty, of course. I assumed I was getting a wife who would run my household and give me heirs."

"That right there." Rachel pointed her bottle at me. "Lose that assumption."

"I already did. I wish Natalya had been honest with me. I was honest with her."

"About said expectations?"

I scowled at her. "Can we move past that? I was wrong, all right? To set expectations and crush my wife's—ah fuck." Crush Natalya's heart and spirit. I couldn't say the words aloud, but they wrapped my chest in a vise of shame and guilt. I needed to fix this. All this time I was seeing her as a weakness, but she wasn't. She made me want things. I wanted to build a future with her.

Another thought occurred to me.

"But it's not a split personality, right? This Rayne person never existed?"

"Doc Gleason doesn't think so. It's simply amnesia. Natalya and Rayne are the same person. Do they feel different?"

"Other than she hates me right now? I don't think so."

"She appears more confident," Dario said. "And there's that slight change in her speech pattern."

"That could be from building a life for herself and adapting. Her IQ doesn't disappear simply because she has amnesia. The skill to shape an identity and what it needs to survive is still there." Rachel pointed out. "She was twenty-two when she married you, twenty-three when she became a mother. She spent two years alone and built self-reliance. You're just dealing with a more mature version of your wife, independent from the influence of the mafia and its constraints."

I didn't like the sound of Natalya building a life for herself away from me. "Have I..." I blew out a breath. "Gleason said she's remembering the bad stuff because that might be related to how her amnesia formed."

"He did mention dissociation might have something to do with it. Psychology is not an exact science and the way the brain handles memory isn't either. But remember, when Natalya went missing, she was on the brink or was already in postpartum depression."

"Perfect storm," Dario said.

"Exactly," Rachel said.

"I want to fix this," I said in a resolute voice, because I couldn't imagine being without her again. I had so many regrets after she disappeared. I played many scenarios where I treated her with the love she deserved. This was our second chance. "Whatever it takes. I don't want to wait until she recovers her memory to prove how much..."

My breath hitched, and the two stared at me.

"How much she means to me." I wasn't going to declare the words for the first time to them. But Rachel and Dario must have seen something on my face because I saw approval on theirs, even relief, especially on my consigliere's face.

"Are you going to confess that you manipulated her?" Rachel asked.

I spread my hands helplessly. "I don't know how. I tried to earlier, but I got sidetracked." The more I thought about how I fucked up, the more I realized the mountain I had to climb to win my wife back—with or without the amnesia.

"Are you ready to declare her alive to the family and associates?" Dario asked.

"Not yet. I need to figure out how to woo back my wife first."

And this time without the intent of manipulation, but with the intent of showing her that I was in love with her. That she was a priority, and yes, my love for her was my weakness, but it was also an emotion that was giving me strength. And with clarity that I hadn't seen in my thirty-seven years, love was something worth dying for.

Take that, Brad Bailey.

CHAPTER
Twenty~Nine

LUCA

It was late in the afternoon, and Natalya hadn't emerged from the attic. Gleason had been up to see her. Rachel was itching to meet her but agreed that it was best if we didn't overwhelm her.

Everyone in my household seemed to be working against me, though, even Martha. My housekeeper had looked in on me and Elias, but mostly I'd been taking care of my son all day. Not that I minded. My amnesiac wife seemed to hold everyone's interest. I wondered if it was because they couldn't wait for her to remember everything including my being a shitty husband.

I was alone with my boy. He wanted to see the ducks in the pond. The pond was at the end of the gardens where we had quite a menagerie. Our ducks and cats seemed to get along. Elias giggled when one of the cats—I was thinking one of Mrs. B's kittens—walked alongside a Muscovy duck. Mrs. B was nowhere around. I got a text from Martha that she and my wife had a grand reunion. I guessed her favorite person was back.

I had a bag of corn and oats with me and let Elias scatter them on the ground. I sat back and watched my son giggle and chatter in happiness while the ducks surrounded him. I had an incessant need for my boy to connect to what was good and innocent before the life that awaited him tested his humanity. Though Emilio didn't force the mafia life on his children, the ones who followed his footsteps won his approval and support, while those who didn't became outcasts.

"Papà...duck." Elias ran toward me, eyes shining with glee. I stared into his innocence and prayed for it to last longer. Men grew up fast in the family. It was necessary for survival, and I couldn't see a way out of it. I would love my son no matter what path he chose because I didn't want him to live with regrets. I just had to look at what happened to my brothers from Emilio's first wife.

Junior was stressed before he was ready and ended up dead.

Ange went to jail, and unlike me, money couldn't buy his freedom and he spent ten years incarcerated. As the underworld underwent a shift, the one to lead the family had to be strategic.

No one questioned Emilio when he named me his successor. No one questioned it to his face, but it didn't mean there weren't grumblings. That I didn't have enough street cred. It was mostly the old-school mobsters who couldn't get behind that the money wasn't on the streets unless your business was drugs. Everything was online and international and in real-estate construction.

After Elias had fallen asleep on my lap, I carried him back to the house. It was five p.m. There was finally activity in the kitchen. Nessa was chopping vegetables and had two stock pots simmering. The flour was out and chicken pieces were in restaurant-sized plastic containers.

The pizza boxes from lunch were stacked on the dining table.

I shifted my son to one arm and flipped one of them open to grab a slice.

Nessa glanced up, narrowed her eyes, and jerked her head at the pots. She was telling me it was almost dinner and to stop snacking.

"What? I'm hungry," I said. "And by the looks of it, it'll be an hour or two anyway."

She pursed her lips and went back to chopping. I had my ways of annoying her too. She knew I didn't like snacking before dinner, but today was a special case.

I glanced at the chalkboard beside the stovetop. Chicken and dumplings.

"That's the first thing you cooked for Natalya when she arrived."

She glanced up again and grinned.

"Did she remember anything else?"

She shook her head.

"Oh, you're back." Martha walked into the kitchen and saw me with Elias.

"Where's my wife?"

"She's in the attic."

"Still?" She better not use it to hide again or I'd wreck that damned place.

"It's familiar to her, and she likes it up there. She did come down to look for Elias."

I glanced at my son drooling on my shoulder. "There won't be much interaction. And he might end up cranky if we force him awake."

"She doesn't have to interact with him," Martha said softly. "Why don't you go up there and spend time with her. It's a beautiful time of the day up there."

She didn't have to tell me twice. With Elias in my arms, I

walked past Rocco who was on a bench at the bottom of the steps. He was talking to another soldier.

"Where's Tony?"

"He's with the doctor in the living room. Making sure he won't snoop."

Good idea. I took the steps to the attic, two at a time. I rapped lightly.

At Natalya's answer to come in, I opened the door and couldn't say that I wasn't surprised that my wife had removed the paneling from the back of the bookcases. She stacked her books on a separate shelf. She was sitting on the couch in front of the entertainment center.

"You're not surprised to see me?" I asked.

"I'm surprised you hadn't come up sooner," she said. A warm look came over her face when her eyes fell on Elias. "Martha said he would be pooped when it's you taking care of him."

"He can be a handful."

"She also said you never wanted to hire a nanny under the age of forty."

Fifty if truth be told.

She averted her eyes. "Is that because you don't want Elias to call anyone Mamma?"

"It doesn't sound right when it's not you." I took another step into the room, but I didn't want to discuss my craziness, so I tipped my chin toward the network of computers.

"My network engineers redid your configuration." That was all Natalya needed to know at the moment. I wasn't stupid. I had a genius hacker in my house who could wreak havoc on our online business and I wasn't about to tell her I had servers in the basement. I walked to the crib by the window and lowered my sleeping son into it.

She must have sensed the lack of information. "Can I have a

laptop? I promise not to hack you. I'm only half-kidding." She winked. "Nessa told me you came up here often with Elias." A smile touched the corners of her mouth as she flung a look at the picture frames on the shelves. "This is almost like a—"

"A shrine?" The corners of my mouth hitched up. I walked to her side and sat beside her. "That's what Dario calls it. He must have heard it from Tony or Martha."

"Yes." Then the gaze she cast me was full of questioning wonder that pierced my chest with something uncomfortable. I wasn't used to explaining the crazy things I did when Natalya disappeared. "Nessa told me you wrecked the TV and other furniture that used to be here. Why rebuild it if you hated that I used this place to get away and hide things from you?"

I focused my gaze on the dotted lights of the router. I deserved to be laid open like this, right? It was a struggle to find the right answer. How could I find the words to explain what I did when I couldn't explain it to myself? Wait. I could. But that would expose my fear, my weakness.

"Do you really wanna know?" I still wasn't looking at her.

"Yes."

"Would it change how you look at me?" I couldn't stop myself from asking. I turned to her and could have kicked myself when the wonder faded into sadness in her eyes.

Be vulnerable, asshole.

"I wouldn't know, Luca," she said in a flat voice.

"I'm sorry." I raked my teeth over my bottom lip before I let out a big exhale and this time embarrassment with myself made me look elsewhere because I couldn't bear it if I saw pity. "I can't explain it other than I missed you with an ache that I couldn't get out of my chest, and it eased a little when I was up here with Elias." Raggedness serrated my next breath. "Because somehow…I felt that you were out there, alive, and even if you were far away, Elias and I…I felt closer to you when I was up here."

A suppressed sob came from her, and my eyes snapped to hers.

They were filled with tears, and her mouth compressed until a choked cry burst from her lips. "That's the most heartfelt thing you've said to me."

"Natalya." My voice was full of leashed longing. "I must kiss you, *tesoro*."

She gave a brief nod.

I scooted closer, and I thought I would grab her face and plunder her mouth, but instead, my own touched hers tentatively and another fractured sob rose in her throat. I gently kissed her, and I tasted her tears and doubts and fears, or maybe they were my own. Our tongues mingled in slow exploration, and I schooled my own urges, the urge to take control and dominate. An alarm in my head told me this Natalya wasn't the girl who had fallen in love with me in Paris. I wasn't even sure if I destroyed her love before she disappeared.

I sensed a new beginning and hope.

But hope deflated when she gave a pained noise at the back of her throat and pulled away.

"It hurts," she whispered, and I believed her. For I saw the anguish in her eyes and I wanted to roar.

I did this to her.

Rayne

"It hurts, Luca, and I don't know why."

He reluctantly let me go. It also hurt to look at him because I saw his torment, and I was sure he was taking all the blame. I hated this amnesia. It made me sorry for the Natalya I couldn't remember. And therein lay the problem.

"Don't you regret this."

I gave a brief scornful laugh. "The kiss? We probably shouldn't have."

"Why? We both felt the pull. Don't deny it."

"I'm one confused woman and mixing in this pull, as you call it, only makes things murkier."

"It could make you remember faster."

"What is from my past and what is from the now?"

"You can't separate them."

"I don't know if the pain I'm feeling is for the Natalya you claim you love or for myself."

He reared back and slid toward the opposite armrest. "You mean you see yourself as two people?"

I rolled my eyes. "Don't look so horrified. I doubt I have a split personality."

A crease appeared between his brows. "I've cleared that with Gleason. He said that's not the case."

My mouth curved into a grin. "So you guys discussed it."

He found the corner of the room interesting. "Yes."

"You're not telling me the whole truth."

He jumped to his feet and walked to the window again, looking down at our son. He didn't say anything for a while, running a hand across his face several times before he said, "The doctor who delivered Elias was here today."

"Why didn't I meet her?"

"Because it might trigger more memories and there's a fifty percent chance it'll be the bad ones again."

"Were you an ass to me while I was pregnant?"

"Do you want me to answer that?"

Luca was like a petulant child who was sorry for what he'd done, but wouldn't confess to the worst of his sins, and hoped for blanket forgiveness. "No wonder you thought there might have been a possibility that I had left you."

"A slim possibility. I'd been trying to be a better husband and father by then."

"If you say so."

He scowled at me, and I didn't know whether to laugh or get exasperated. Even if it was only two distinct memories that came back to me, they had tremendous impact. If I tried to piece those fragments together, my head would explode. "So, you're keeping the doctor away from me, but you're also telling me this because you want to warn me of bad behavior that I might remember in the future?"

His mouth thinned.

"You're warning me in advance?"

"I'm just putting it in perspective. All marriages have good and bad days, and my position as boss has interfered. Although I would admit I hid behind the position because of the way you affected me," he explained in a way that told me he didn't feel like explaining.

"Papà." Our boy had woken up. An expression of relief crossed Luca's face, and he immediately went to check on him. "Hey, sport. You need a change." He carried Elias under his armpits and strode to the bathroom.

This I had to see. "Need help? Not sure if I remember how to change a diaper."

He laid Elias on the changing table and grabbed a diaper and wipes.

"I usually do this on the floor since I can lock him down with my leg so he doesn't interfere." Luca gave a slight smile. "But he's usually calm when he wakes up."

"Ungry," Elias chattered.

"Soon, kid," Luca mumbled. "Talk to him while I make a quick change here."

"Hey, Elias…remember me?"

"Wafles?"

"Hahah, that's not my name, but yes. It's…what do I tell him?"

Luca had paused in his diaper-changing duties, and the intensity in his eyes made my heart pound. Something as basic as diaper changing in this tiny bathroom, and despite the god-awful smell of Elias's soiled diaper, made this moment strangely familiar.

"Mamma," Luca said. "Might as well start with the truth, and he hasn't called anyone that in a long time."

How could one word cause havoc inside me? Elias smiled at me, and I absorbed that smile to the bottom of my heart.

Without thinking, I extended a hand toward my son. I cupped his cheek, and he turned his mouth toward it as if inhaling.

"Mamma," I repeated. The word still sounded foreign to my tongue.

"Now we take care of this shit." Luca tossed the dirty diaper into a diaper trash bin and washed his hands. "We need to get this boy fed."

I laughed. "That's all they do at this age, huh?"

"Sleep, eat, shit. Play, watch cartoons." Luca sighed. "I'm not sure our son and I are giving you a strong incentive to regain your memory."

Elias, freed from his father's ministrations rolled to his feet and he was staring down at me. "Catch."

Oh shit. And the boy leapt.

I caught him, but I must have swallowed my heart. I glared at Luca. "Is this something you do with him?"

He was scratching the back of his head. "Yeah. Sorry, forgot to warn you. I wasn't expecting it. He only does it when I'm around."

Then Luca shot me a tender look that gave me more extra heart-beats. "Our son looks good on you."

We spent the rest of the evening in the attic. Elias demanded I feed him his chicken and dumplings. Luca said our boy was testing my boundaries, and it was up to me to show him how much he could get away with. But when we watched cartoons, Elias sandwiched himself between his dad and the armrest, and that was how he fell asleep. Meanwhile, I was aware of the heat from Luca's body, of his powerful legs confined by the fabric of his sweatpants. I had an eyeful of them this morning and then some.

"I'm going to ask Martha to get him." Luca whipped out his phone.

I put my hand on his arm. "We need to figure out the sleeping arrangements between us."

"Same as this morning."

I shot him a look that said he was crazy.

A slow smile curved his mouth. "You think you can't resist me?"

Exasperated, I threw up a hand. "Have you always been this cocky?"

He cupped my cheek in an intimate gesture like he was going to kiss me. I had no room to move unless I got up. "*Tesoro*, why deny us the pleasure while you regain your memory?"

I grabbed his hand and removed it from my face. "And why muddle up my memory with sex?"

He chuckled deep in his throat, not in the least embarrassed. "Did I say sex?"

"You know that's what's going to happen."

"I agree that I have powers of persuasion, although in the last months of your pregnancy, you demanded sex from me."

"If that were true, that was the hormones speaking."

His eyes heated. "I should get you pregnant more often."

"Luca!" I didn't know whether my irritation was at him or at myself because my skin became too tight, too hot, and heat pulsed between my legs so unexpectedly, I thought he heard it. Not even with our son sleeping right beside him could we contain the flames of our attraction. I wondered if we burned too hot, our relationship turned to ashes. "Be serious."

"I am." His mouth twitched. "But I think you'll remember me sooner if…" His teeth raked his lower lip and he thumbed his chin as if wiping away drool. "You will remember me sooner if I'm buried deep inside you."

"You're impossible." The words came out in a croaked whisper.

"And yet you don't move away," he rasped, his hand clasping my thigh.

"Do not kiss me," I warned.

He regarded me for long beats before he sighed, leaned away, and stared at the TV screen. "I can move to Elias's room."

"If he was used to me, I would offer. Unless you want me to sleep up here."

A strange look crossed his face. "No."

"You can have our bedroom. I'm sure there are plenty of other rooms—"

"You sleep in our bed." His tone was terse. I didn't even need to pretend why he was being bullheaded about this. He was possessive. And the marriage bed was a symbol of that possessiveness. It didn't matter if he was in it. It was where he had taken me over and over.

"I'll tell Martha to give Elias a bath," he said.

"Why bother her? We could do it. Tell her to have the rest of the night off."

"You always spoil our household staff. You're bad for my reputation. People will say the boss has gone soft."

"For taking care of your son? I would think they'll say you're very much a family man. Isn't that what the mafia is all about?"

"And now my wife has kicked me out of our bedroom."

The drama. Somehow, I expected it from Luca. There was a flair around him that suited him. People underestimated him for being petty and petulant, but I'd seen the deadly look in his eyes. He was a dangerous man who lulled you to lower your guard before he struck.

He picked up my hand and kissed the back of it. "I'm going to woo you again."

A determined gleam entered his eyes. And I was the target of that determination. Elation fluttered inside me. What girl wouldn't want to be wooed by a man like Luca? At face value, he was a good catch. He was attractive and if I didn't witness him almost shoot Brad, the way my body responded to his kiss spoke of the sheer chemistry between us. If he were a stranger, he'd be the best candidate for a fling...maybe a one-night stand?

Where was this wildness coming from?

I was having trouble breathing normally. Everything inside me felt more constricted.

He searched my face. "You're tired."

"Or overwhelmed."

"That won't do."

"It hasn't even been twenty-four hours." I cupped my feverish cheeks. "The memories are lurking...I just need to unlock some more." I couldn't believe I'd made significant headway in such a short period compared to the two years where I hadn't. My memories seemed to be triggered by surroundings more than people. The dining room. The foyer.

"Have you been to the nursery?" he asked.

"Yes."

"I think that's enough for you today."

I agreed.

CHAPTER
Thirty

RAYNE

When Luca said he was going to woo me, he wasn't kidding. The second morning of living in the mansion, an elaborate floral arrangement of white flowers greeted me. It was before breakfast and Martha told me to check it out in the grand foyer where it sat on the round marble center table.

The card on it said…

Here's to future memories.

Love, Luca and Elias

I put it in the living room. I appreciated them, but it was a neutral feeling. Past Natalya might have liked them, but I appreciated the spring blooms in their natural setting.

On the third day, it was a box of chocolates. I never thought I liked chocolates. I tried the ones from the convenience store and my tongue didn't like the chalky texture. While Luca was ensconced in a meeting with Dario, I walked around the house and started handing them out.

Apparently word got back to my husband, and he walked into the kitchen and saw me handing the last of the pieces to Martha, Nessa, and a couple of the guards who happened to come by. Probably after they found out I was handing out chocolates.

"What are you doing?" he barked.

"I don't like chocolate." I smiled at him sheepishly and nodded to the other people in the kitchen. "But they do."

He calmly crossed his arms, and like he was explaining to a child, he said, "You do. You like these. Have you tried even one?"

I shook my head. There were only two left in the box of twenty-four.

He emitted an extended exhale. "*Tesoro*, please try one. If you don't like it, you can spit it out. It won't hurt my feelings."

I doubted he wouldn't be hurt. He already jumped down my throat for passing the chocolate around. It was just that I had an unpleasant experience, plus the chocolate protein bars were the worst. I preferred the fruity ones.

Picking up a piece, I put it in my mouth. It melted. The cocoa flavor enrobed my tongue, then exploded in decadence. Still disbelieving, I rolled around the remnants of the flavorful chocolate, waiting for chalkiness to follow the addictive bittersweet, but it didn't.

I put a hand on my mouth. "Oh my God."

Luca's eyes twinkled with satisfaction. He picked up the last piece of chocolate and popped it into his mouth. My eyes widened, and I wanted to snatch it back from him, but I was still processing and processing.

"This taste…" I finally said. "I know it."

Luca took a step toward me, taking the box away, and said,

"Yes, you do." And oblivious to the people around us, he fused our chocolate-flavored mouths and gave me a languid kiss. When he pulled back, there was a smear on his mouth. And apparently on mine too, because we both reached out to wipe it from our faces.

He seemed satisfied that he'd made his point and left the kitchen.

I turned to look at Martha and Nessa, who were both wearing identical silly grins.

Nessa signed, *He's a ten*.

I laughed lightly. Luca appeared to be charming the person who liked him the least.

This morning, I'd been lounging with Doc on the patio. It was day four of living in the mansion and I was getting bored. I wasn't allowed on any computer, and I didn't even have a phone and had to borrow Luca's to cancel appointments I already had. I imagined Doc Gleason was bored too, although he and Dario went fishing yesterday in a lake not too far from here. Elias was getting more comfortable being left alone with me. My son preferred Doc, maybe because he was used to kids and babies in his practice. Right now, Elias was ignoring us and was busy with his trucks on the mat.

Luca had chocolates brought in again this morning. I found out he was having them flown in from Paris. I kept them in the room and had become very stingy about sharing them even with Elias, who I maintained shouldn't be eating sugar anyway. Besides, he was too young to appreciate fine chocolate, or so I told myself.

Selfish, selfish mom.

Oddly, I didn't feel any guilt.

Doc was sipping on a fruity drink and wearing a Hawaiian shirt and shorts, complete with a straw fedora.

"Are you enjoying your vacation?" I teased. It was a warm spring day, and it seemed we had a heat wave which had ebbed in the past few days but had returned full force. I was not a fan of heat, and I was glad for the covered patio, and that Elias didn't want to go into the pool.

"I am."

"Have you talked to Brad again? I hope he hasn't reported us missing."

"I convinced him not to, but he was giving us a week before he reports it to the sheriff." Gleason gave me a pained look. "It's a small town and our disappearance hasn't gone unnoticed, not to mention the bruises on his face."

"Yes," I groaned. "I checked my voicemail, and it was full. I just changed the recording to say I was on vacation."

Gleason laughed. "I did the same. I hope they don't think we're carrying on a May-December affair."

"May-December is so old fashioned," I said. "The right term is age gap." Hmm…that was interesting how that word just came up.

"Then it'll be a triple age gap. Let's not talk about it. I'm old enough to be your father twice over." Gleason looked comically appalled.

"Now Luca and I, there's the age gap," I mused.

"So, don't you have any more of that chocolate?" Doc asked. "I heard more were delivered this morning."

"I'm not in a sharing mood."

"How's the memory coming along?" Doc settled back in the lounger.

"Not much development after the first day." I tipped my chin at Elias. "I'm getting more fond of him."

Doc guffawed. "I certainly hope so. He's your son."

"I wished he'd stop calling me Waf-waf."

"It's not uncommon at that age to have their own language." Doc removed his glasses and wiped at his eyes. "The chocolate. Did it trigger anything?"

"Except that I can be protective of my stash? No. Luca said we had our honeymoon in Paris."

The man beside me gave a non-committal response. "Hmm."

I angled my eyes at him. "I think he's losing patience."

"I think he should acquire more of it. He's not too pushy, is he?"

"Well, if forcing us to come with him at gunpoint is not pushy, then of course not."

Gleason rolled his eyes. "I wondered if you were always a smartass. From what Martha has told me, you were a very sweet girl."

I snorted. "Maybe the knock on the head altered my brain chemistry. I told Luca he better not expect the same wife because I'm getting the feeling I'm not."

"Or maybe you're just a more mature version of her."

"I realize you guys have been discussing me behind my back."

"You're a very interesting subject."

"I'm glad I provide stimulating conversation," I said dryly.

"We just want to help you." Doc showered me with a fatherly look.

Footfalls approached and Tony appeared in our line of vision. "Boss wants you in the study."

"Uhm." I looked at Elias.

"I'll watch him," Tony and Doc announced in unison.

Elias looked up from his trucks and said, "'re you goin', Waf-waf?"

Tony gave me a look. "He still calls you that?"

"It's been only four days, but I hope he hasn't imprinted that name on me." I went down on my haunches and rolled one of his trucks. "Your papà wants to see me."

"Canna go?" he asked.

"Nope," Tony was the one who answered. "Your papà has something to discuss with her."

Elias shrugged and returned his attention to his toys. "Okay."

"He's such a good boy."

"He has his moments," Tony said fondly.

Well, I thought Luca and I were very lucky to have a son like Elias. Even if I didn't remember giving birth to him, with each passing day, a visceral attachment was emerging. It was hard to explain. Touch and smell. I loved the smell of his skin even when he was sweaty from running around. I wondered if he remembered my voice in a way. Doc told me babies started hearing their mother's voice in the womb. I hoped the months in my womb cemented a bond between us that the separation couldn't erase. I hoped I'd sung him lullabies. He'd had one or two tantrums I'd witnessed, but he was very introspective, and in my mind, he was a well-behaved two-year-old. He behaved better than some adults I knew. I couldn't fault Luca as a father. Elias loved him.

Tony nudged me, reminding me I was needed inside. I got up and entered the house and was taken aback by the number of people milling around, some dressed in suits, others wearing more casual wear like jeans and leather jackets. I spotted Dario among the men, so my rising panic abated. It appeared to be a large meeting of some sort. I wanted to slink away, more so when all eyes zeroed in on me.

When Dario spotted me, he immediately looked apologetic and started for me. We met halfway and his hand went to the small of my back. I angled my head toward him and spoke out of the corner of my mouth.

"What's going on?"

"Cat's out of the bag. Luca is doing damage control," the consigliere said.

"As in I'm the cat?"

"Yes. Don't worry. They know better than to cause trouble."

"Is Luca going to introduce me because I would have dressed up for this." I was in casual linen pants and a halter top.

"Later, but he has something for you."

"More chocolates," I snarked because I hated being the center of attention.

Dario chuckled. "No."

Dario rapped on the door of the study before opening it.

A stocky man, also dressed in a suit, turned our way. He had a head of salt-and-pepper hair. His face bore a slight resemblance to Luca but was harsher. I sensed this was his brother the underboss.

Luca was behind his desk. He rose and rounded it to greet me. The man stood.

Luca didn't make any introductions.

The man and I stared at each other.

"Natalya, I'm Ange." The forced smile on his face only increased my desire to retreat. He opened his arms, but all my limbs were paralyzed. "I'm glad you're okay."

"Natalya, what's wrong?" Luca asked gruffly. "Do you remember anything?" That was when I noticed the other soldiers in the room. All of Luca's trusted soldiers besides Dario were alert around me.

I could feel the tension pull tight between Luca and Ange.

"I don't know you," I admitted. "I only suspected you were Luca's brother with the family resemblance."

Ange's expression didn't change except for the minor relief I saw in his eyes, the slight slackening of his jaw.

"This is an insult, brother." He turned to Luca. "I'm your underboss and Natalya is my sister-in-law. Don't tell me you still suspect me of being involved in her kidnapping?"

"We've had our differences." That wasn't exactly a direct answer.

"You think I would do that to family?" Ange growled. "And you don't know yet if she—"

"Careful with your next words, brother," Luca warned.

"Okay, guys, I'm getting thrown into the mob drama here and I'm not used to it. So, can we dial down the aggression, because you're both making me nervous."

"No one is in danger here," Ange told me. "Least of all from me."

"Good to know," I said.

"Actually, Ange was kind enough to bring by your laptop," Luca said.

That was when I noticed the box on the desk.

"Finally." The chains of antsiness loosened slightly. I would have been lighter if it wasn't for the tension building in the room.

"It's all configured for security. The connection information is in the box," Ange said, looking at Luca. "I made sure the guys got that right because when I got it for Sandra—that's my daughter—it was all screwed up."

"Natalya will figure it out," Luca said. He grinned at me. "My brother's nervous because there's a big game in a few days and he wants assurance you won't hack it."

I rolled my eyes. "I don't even know what you're talking about. Can I have it now?" My hands were itching to grab the device and disappear into the attic.

Luca picked up the box and handed it to me. "It's top of the line. Let me know if you're happy with it. Just a reminder, baby, dinner will be at seven." That was four hours away. Four hours to play with my new toy. Would that be enough time?

I received the box with grabby hands, my mouth curved impishly in response to Luca's own indulgent smile. "Thank you!" I couldn't help myself when I rose on tiptoe to give him a quick kiss and hurried to the door. I wasn't sure if it was from excitement or desire to escape the charged testosterone in the room. When I made it to the door though, I said, "Don't bother taxing your network people in tracking the data packets with a sniffer. I'm not doing any hacking today."

With that, I winked, left, and snickered to myself. Luca's and Dario's expressions were amused.

Ange's was horrified.

Priceless.

CHAPTER
Thirty~One

LUCA

"Whoa. Are you sure we didn't bring home a doppelgänger?" Dario asked. All pairs of eyes focused on my wife's departure. I jerked my head at Rocco and my soldiers to accompany her to the attic where I was sure she was heading.

My mouth curved with humor and bemusement. "I always wondered when Natalya slipped and said something out of character and it's turning out it was very much in character."

When the door closed, Ange collapsed into the seat in front of my desk while I returned to my chair. Dario sat opposite Ange. The boss, the consigliere, and the underboss. We had business to discuss. The business of Natalya was at the forefront.

"You should have informed me immediately, so the family could prepare for all consequences," Ange said. "What if you were caught in Danvers? You abducted a woman and a doctor. We don't want scrutiny so close to our online poker games."

"In case I hadn't made it clear, my wife is a priority over every-thing else. And don't turn it back on me. The family owes me this. That night my wife was giving birth, everything I did was for family. The night my wife disappeared, where was I again? Making sure the family would be clear from the Russians. So don't tell me I've done nothing for the family, including brokering deals with everyone—things you have no interest in doing. Our real estate business is thriving, and we're trying not to grow too fast because you're not pulling in enough money for us to clean. So don't put this back on me."

"How are you going to bring her back from the dead?"

"I'm assuming you're talking about it figuratively, because there never was a death certificate."

"Her parents held a funeral for her in Palermo. There's even a gravestone. They said it was insulting that you didn't attend." The hairs on the back of my neck stood on end when I remembered the time Vincenzo told me they were going ahead with the funeral. He said it was the right thing to do because we didn't know what happened to Natalya, and it had been two months. They said, what if her soul was languishing in purgatory because she didn't get the blessing from the church?

"What? So they would have an opportunity to kill me?"

"You still think that?"

"Ange, in the mafia's history, how many double- and triple-crossings had led to a mob boss's demise? *Une Famiglia* doesn't exist anymore. At that time of the funeral, I had the Galluzo under scrutiny." It was also the time I thought Natalya had betrayed me when I'd found out how her parents erased the school hacking from her records. "Regarding Natalya's reintroduction as my wife, I hope to give her more time in case her memory comes back, but I don't see how I could keep this news from leaking out. I, for one, would hate to give our enemies enough time to plan their move."

"You're going to risk your wife?"

"I won't coerce her if she doesn't want to." But I could tell she was as desperate as I was in finding out what happened to her. Who our enemies were.

"You have to tell her parents. And Carmine."

My mouth wanted to curl into a snarl. I hated that motherfucker. If I had solid proof that he was involved, I'd fly over to Italy and kill him myself.

"We keep a lid on this for now and see how much control you have over your men."

"Then why did you parade Natalya in front of them?"

"You did surprise me with this visit."

"You expected me not to question why you have one of my capos specifically deliver a fully tricked-out laptop to your house? Why you've been avoiding my calls, and why I find out you were not where you said you were four days ago?"

"I'm glad you came down here to find out yourself."

"Was this a test?" Ange surged from his chair and homed in on me like a rabid Rottweiler. "If you think I'm not capable of leading under you, then why keep me?"

"Sit down," I enunciated. Dario sat forward, ready to intervene, but I leaned back and clasped my hands over my torso. "A test? Maybe. You're my underboss, Ange. The capos are your responsibility. The last time you ignored two of them, they were making deals under you with the Russians that cost me two years with Natalya. And you wonder why I don't hold you responsible for my wife's disappearance?" The more I thought about his role in this or his lack of oversight, the more I wanted to murder my own blood. "If you weren't my brother, if we didn't share so much together, you would have been in that basement with those *stronzos*. That's why I tapped one of your newer capos to deliver Natalya's laptop. To see if you're paying attention."

"And did I pass your test, then, almighty brother?" Ange asked sarcastically.

"I'm satisfied."

I could tell he was still fuming. I could see it in his darkened gaze. I missed the days when we settled our differences by beating each other senseless on the mat. Ange used to be my sparring partner in mixed martial arts, but after Emilio declared me boss, we drifted apart. Now we just stared at each other until one of us gave in. It was always Ange. Because I was still the boss and he'd have to kill me before I wavered. My brother took his seat again. "What do you want me to do?"

"Do damage control as much as possible. Can you handle that?"

"Exactly what is it you want me to handle?"

"I'm going to ignore Vincenzo and Carmine until I figure out what Natalya wants to do. They will have heard rumors by now."

He nodded.

"Ignore all inquiries from Orlov. We don't owe him anything."

"Good," Ange muttered. "But he's been calling me about the Game of Bosses."

"He's been blowing up my phone about that stupid game too."

"You sure you don't want a rematch?" Ange grumbled. "Maybe he'd be less of a pain in our asses."

Inwardly, I was amused. The Russian just stole a shipment of vodka from Ange. No money off the family because it was Ange and his capo in charge of it who were paying it back.

"I don't have time for that shit." Not to mention, I didn't feel like training for it, but it seemed I hadn't lost the skill and instincts, judging from how I handled Brad Bailey.

"Koshkin, if he calls me, will be hard to ignore, so I'm handling him," I told Ange. "Eventually the Chicago PD will hear about it. Detective Voss is in charge, but it's become a cold case in the last year."

"You want me to handle him too?" His tone was brusque.

"No. That's going to be trickier."

"Because you kidnapped a doctor."

I woke up my computer and turned my screen to Ange to show Gleason on the patio reclining on a lounger, sipping a drink. "Does it look like I kidnapped him? His voicemail says he had a family emergency. That should clear us for now."

I made the mistake of looking at Dario. We both had our poker faces on, but Ange had been around us too long not to know we had more information. "There's a catch…"

Dario tried to keep his mouth straight in the ensuing twitchy silence, but a chuckle escaped his lips. "There might be someone out of our control with knowledge of the abduction."

"I'm not finding it funny," I snapped. I didn't want a reminder of that fucker's mouth on Natalya. "We'll handle him. Do nothing."

"Why?" Ange persisted. "I can send a couple of men down there and—"

"Brad Bailey is not to be touched," I told my brother. "Do we have an understanding?"

Ange grinned and sat back. "Understood."

"As your consigliere, I don't approve of you giving Ange Brad Bailey's name." It was the first time Dario got me alone and away from my brother. It was an afternoon of meetings and catching up on business. Ange was clearly unhappy that Natalya was the focus of my attention just when we had big games lined up. It was the first time since Natalya's disappearance that I'd given him so much control over them. He'd been hoping I'd be in Chicago, but I reminded him I'd monitored the last ones while I was in the mansion.

"Didn't you hear what I said?" I rocked back on my heels while sipping the thirty-year-old scotch Ange brought with him. It was part of our last shipment from a cult distillery that recently closed. "I told him he's not to be touched."

I wanted Brad Bailey dead, but not by my hands. His heart wasn't black enough for me to kill him without guilt.

"You said nothing about not burning down his coffee shop with him in it."

"I gave Ange simple instructions. I don't want to micromanage."

Dario gave me one of his disapproving looks. "You're better than this, Luca. You think this won't get back to Natalya? Even if you said you didn't give the direct order, the buck stops with you."

I exhaled a heavy sigh. "You're no fun. If you must, be specific with Ange and tell him to leave Brad Bailey and everything that belongs to him alone."

Dario squeezed my shoulder. "Good call."

"*Vaffanculo*," I muttered.

Dario barked a laugh and left my side in search of my brother. It had become more crowded. I was sure Nessa and Martha were cursing me, but they should lay the blame on Ange for this gathering. I caught Gleason's gaze. He was in a conversation with one of the capos, but he raised his glass to me. I gave him one bottle of the expensive scotch. It should fetch at least 8k a bottle and we had two hundred cases. We could make twenty million easy. More if we auctioned them.

And that was why I was the boss. Ange's default was to force liquor stores to carry them or sell them to the many high-brow restaurants in the area. Why make distribution harder when the world was our market?

In my peripheral vision, a figure appeared at the top of the grand staircase and demanded my attention. I turned to it, to them, and my whole world became clear.

Natalya was in a slim-fitting navy-blue dress I remembered her wearing in Paris. At her side was Elias in sailor's clothes. The pull of my wife and son was irresistible. I lowered my scotch on the side table, and my strides headed in their direction. I ascended the steps, eyes unwavering with Natalya's. She stood unsure at the top of the grand staircase. Then our wiggle-some boy drew my attention. He was urging his mother to join the party.

Yes, I was as excited as my son.

"It isn't quite seven." Her voice was breathless. "I wasn't sure if I should mingle with all the men. I don't see their wives. And I googled…"

I reached her at the top of the steps. "I'll send them all home if I have to. I want to spend dinner with my wife and not stare at their ugly faces."

"I'm not intruding?"

I gave her a reassuring smile. "Not at all."

"Papà…up." Elias made a wanting-to-be-carried gesture. I plucked him from Natalya's side and settled him on my left arm while offering my right one to Natalya. She hesitated for a brief second, and then she clasped my elbow.

Together, we descended the steps. Why had we never done this? When Vincenzo and Elena had been here, I was already with the men, leaving the women to their own activities. I cursed my idiocy. My wife had become an afterthought. Someone to beget with heirs.

"I'm feeling very self-conscious," she whispered.

All eyes were on us. It was like a spotlight was following us down.

"Get used to it," I told her. "We should entertain more."

She cast me a look that was a cross between incredulity and irritation. "Luca, these past few days…"

"I don't want to discuss them. I'm not asking for a performance rating. Just let me do what I feel I should have done as your husband." I lowered Elias to the floor, and he immediately spotted Ange.

"Ziiiooo!" he yelled and stumble-walked toward my brother. Ange high-fived him. Tony was in the crowd and made his way to my son.

"Elias is more at home in this crowd than I am," Natalya said.

"Let's loosen you up." I guided her to the kitchen where the impromptu bar was set up.

"I could strangle Ange," was the first sentence Martha uttered when she saw us. "I was ready to order pizza."

"Why didn't you?" I didn't care what my brother thought. My house wasn't a restaurant and this unscheduled visit, even when I half expected it, didn't mean my staff should drop everything and cater to their needs.

"Really?" the housekeeper said, looking doubtful. "You would have been okay with that?"

"Why are you looking at me?" Natalya asked. "I'm not sure I'm in a position to make decisions in this house."

Failure and confusion etched her panic-stricken face.

Fuck, I didn't want her pressured at all. "You're not. Calm down." I poured her a glass of Barolo. "Drink this."

She accepted the wine without hesitation, took a guzzle, and in her haste, the liquid sloshed over her fingers.

Christ.

"Natalya." I infused my tone with the calm she should be feeling. The uncertainty in her eyes killed me. "This isn't on you." Martha realized her error and moved away.

"Are you hungry?" I asked.

"No." She made a face. "You always seem preoccupied with what I eat."

She mentioned this in the past, but this last time gave me pause to ponder why I did that. "Let's go outside—"

"But your guests—"

"They're not guests, they're family—"

"Elias…"

Shit. I looked at Martha. "Can you check on Elias? He's with Tony and Ange."

Martha waved us off, and I didn't wait for anyone else to stop me. Business had been concluded.

We left through the kitchen side door that led to the gardens where there was a fountain with an angel. We had several of these scattered around the property. But since we had more effective ways to scan for wiretappings and bugs nowadays, we found less and less use for these garden ornaments.

Right now, the falling water provided a soothing sound, which I hoped would alleviate my wife's nerves.

"How do you like your laptop?" I asked.

Her face brightened against the moonlight filtering through the clouds. Her eyes came alive. A distinctive gleam of confidence shuttered the doubt in them moments ago. "Impressive bells and whistles. I approve of the processor and the memory. The graphic card is nice."

"Nice," I repeated dryly. "It was all top-of-the-line."

"I don't need top-of-the-line for what I do."

"And what is it that you do?" I found myself asking a question that wasn't for small talk. I genuinely wanted to find out everything about my wife I never had the chance to explore. It also explained in a roundabout way why I kept asking whether she or Elias had eaten.

"I'm not sure yet," she mused, staring off into the distance. "To be honest, even when you gave me the laptop, I felt something missing."

"I'm not sure what programs you want to download. I'll leave that up to you."

"It's just so much work to redo what I had on the laptop we left in Danvers."

"You have all the time to do it here. The connection is very secure."

"Give my kudos to your IT team. I did surface-level hacking…"

My expression must have changed because she laughed.

"Let's call it ethical hacking, and that was one thing I did back in Danvers and the surrounding towns."

"You've acquired quite a list of clients."

"I'm the cheapest," she returned, looking away.

"You could have charged more, but you didn't want to draw attention to yourself."

I sat on the edge of the fountain, encouraging her to sit beside me. She glanced back at the house.

"They'll manage," I interjected before she could say anything.

"But dinner…I heard Nessa was making spaghetti and meatballs."

"She knows those guys are sick of spag and meatballs."

Her burst of laughter surprised me. It was the laugh I'd often heard from her when we were in Paris—open and uninhibited—which became more and more scarce further into our marriage because I killed it. When Elias had been a month old, I peeked into the nursery one day and that was the last time I'd heard it. My unworthiness only grew stronger, but I refused to give up. If only I could find out how to make her laugh like this often.

She took a sip of wine, but her cheeks were round with her smile. "Nessa is the quiet one, but she's full of surprises."

"And vindictiveness," I muttered.

"Luca!" she admonished.

"It's true," I sighed. "I'm not saying I don't deserve it from her."

We sat in silence for a few minutes, just the sound of the fountain keeping us company. A rumble of thunder indicated an impending storm. The chatter inside the house and random roar of laughter provided background noise.

"They might be looking for us."

"Martha knows where we are."

"Well, Nessa surely doesn't want us to miss dinner." She stood and moved to go inside.

I remained seated and said, "My preoccupation with whether or not you've eaten is born of expectations."

Her back was to me, but I could feel rather than see the stiffening of her spine. She slowly turned around.

"I don't think I truly apologized, Natalya, but I'm sorry for being a shitty husband. If you get your memory back and you remember every single time I let you down, every time I returned to Chicago and made it feel like I abandoned you, I'm truly fucking sorry."

"What does this have to do with—"

"With food? Because that was the expectation I had of myself as a provider. As long as I gave you and Elias the basic necessities—food, clothing, shelter—I'd done my duty." I pushed up from my seat and walked toward her.

Staring into her upturned face, I noted how her mouth was slightly parted, and her eyes sparked with curiosity. Because here I was, Luca Moretti, confessing his boundaries and the secrets of what made him tick. Or used to tick.

"I considered love a weakness. But I had no problem receiving it. To me, better for people to love me and give me their loyalty than for me to love them and become my weakness." It was like an expulsion of my sins. Of the selfish protection around my heart.

"Oh, Luca…"

"I manipulated you to love me. I did it with all knowledge and calculation. Don't look at me with pity."

"I'm not. I'm just wondering how I fell for that. I didn't think I was so gullible."

"You love romance movies and books. I used Paris as a backdrop." I regarded her intently. "But I wonder now if that was a front."

"I like science fiction and fantasy movies. I do love it when there's romance with action." She drained her wine. "I might try reading a few of those books in the attic. They looked like I bought them from a thrift shop. Maybe they were my mother's?"

Her question was beyond hilarious. I threw back my head and laughed. It took almost a minute before I could say anything without choking on laughter. There were tears in my eyes. "Elena Conte...would never read that. I doubt if there's a romantic bone in her."

"Was my relationship with my mother that bad?"

I ran the back of my hand down her cheek. Her eyes widened, but she didn't shy away. That was progress. "Don't worry about that right now."

Her shoulders rose, and her whole person deflated on an exhale. "When I was in Danvers, I was content and had moved on, thinking I was lucky to escape with my life. But now, there are so many possibilities. Things are not clear between us. I'm not sure if I should trust you, but deep down, I can tell, you're not a bad person. Your morals are questionable." She puffed a laugh as if it was an inside joke. "But I've seen you with Elias. There's good in you. You're shaped by your environment, the family." Her mouth twitched. "I finished *The Godfather one*, *two*, and *three*. And I googled you."

"Heaven forbid."

"We should go back in or people will notice."

As if on cue, Nessa appeared. Of course, she ignored me and signed to Natalya.

"She said if we want any spaghetti and meatballs, we better go inside."

"We'll follow soon.

"Natalya." Her attention returned to me. She'd been responding more and more to her name and I refused to use Rayne because she was never Rayne to me. The thunder sounded closer, and it reminded me of another time I let her down.

"You don't have to mingle with the family if you're not comfortable," I said.

"Luca." The way she said my name was uncompromising. It was a tone I'd never heard her use before and it made me pay attention, like I was about to be pushed off a cliff. "I'm tired of babying this amnesia, and Doc Gleason might not agree, but I want to find those assholes who did this to us. If you think exposing my return to the public would facilitate our enemies making a move, then do it."

She nailed me right in the eyes and continued with steel in her voice, "I can sense it. You want to use me, but you're afraid of what it would do to my recovery. Since I met you, I had this feeling that the other shoe is about to drop, and I'm tired of waiting for it to do so. It's not the way I want to live. The rest of my memory is there. I just need that one trigger. I can feel it."

Natalya and I were on the same wavelength. "The trigger might not be in there." I nodded at the house.

"Where?"

"After this circus, I want you to come with me somewhere."

CHAPTER
Thirty-Two

RAYNE

"I'm glad to finally meet you."

The woman in front of me was Rachel Kingsley. Luca had planned a field trip and wanted all the support he could get for what we were about to do. Ange and most of the Chicago mafia didn't leave until after midnight, and even then, it was because Luca had to send them away.

We assembled in the grand foyer. Elias was already in bed, and Nessa was staying with him in the nursery. With us was Doc Gleason, Tony, and Dario who decided to spend the night.

"I'm not gonna ask if there is a jolt of familiarity," Luca said dryly. "Clearly there isn't."

I stared at the woman a while longer and cocked my head at him. "No. There isn't. But I'm curious what you've done that you're afraid I'll remember."

"It seems his sins are already stacked against him. He didn't want to add to them," Rachel said.

"He's apologized in advance though," I said.

"Can we get this party moving?" Luca grumbled. "Rachel, ride with me and Natalya. Gleason, you can go with Dario."

As we piled into our SUVs, I noticed that we formed a convoy of three. Luca was driving and Tony was beside him. Rachel and I were in the second row. Dario drove the lead vehicle while another group of mafia soldiers brought up the rear. I thought most of the men had left, but I saw them scattered around the estate, and more than a few had rifles slung on their shoulders.

"You're already expecting trouble?" I leaned between the console and asked Luca as the guard at the gate waved us through.

"We can't keep your reappearance a secret even if I tell Ange to keep quiet about it. He brought a slew of men with him." Luca seemed irritated at this. "I'm just preparing for the worst. I haven't heard from the Galluzo or your parents yet but word will reach them. It's only a matter of time."

I leaned back. "I guess it's too much to expect CIA-level security."

Rachel laughed beside me. "I see what you mean by Natalya being different."

"Am I that different?" I was finding this fascinating about who I was before.

"Let me put it this way," Rachel said. "You're more blunt and more self-assured."

"I'm feeling far from self-assured."

"Not about the amnesia, but I don't think you'll let Luca get away with things as much."

"I brought you here for support just in case Natalya had a break-through memory," Luca said. "And not to massacre my reputation." Glancing briefly in the rearview mirror, he continued, "We're not sure if anyone was keeping tabs on you in Danvers. If there was, your disappearance would trip alarms."

"So you're thinking they're only waiting me out?"

"We have no records of who dropped you off in St. Louis."

"I could have told you that," I said. "And we've already established my whole background is bullshit."

Rachel gave another puff of laughter. "I see Luca is going to have his hands full whether you get your memory back or not."

I didn't say anything. I'd already mentioned it to Luca several times.

"They've taken great pains to either hide you from me or from the people who are after you. If the ones who did this to you are responsible for your kidnapping, they would have kept you prisoner until your memory returned."

Luca turned from the main road into a narrower one that had cornfields on both sides. He didn't tell me where we were going. I thought he was taking me to the hospital where I'd given birth and have those X-rays of my brain he wanted me to have.

He'd been surreptitiously casting me glances in the rearview mirror. It took little deduction that this area was supposed to trigger something. "Was this where the Russians took me?" I asked.

"Is it familiar or is that your theory?"

His question made me think. And this was the reason why Gleason didn't want to force information on me because my mind might start filling the empty spots in my memory to produce false ones. On the other hand, there wasn't enough to formulate a complete scene. A pit of anxiety started forming in my gut that I'd taken my memories only so far and I would never get them back.

"Are you feeling okay?" Rachel asked. "Is this exercise confusing for you?"

"I'm okay. Physically, I'm fine. No flashes or anything, but this place is making me anxious, and I'm not sure if it's the pressure of having me remember things."

"Should I turn back?" Luca asked.

"No!" I said, the agitation growing. "Keep going. We've come this far."

A crack of thunder reverberated and shook the car.

"Shit," Tony said. "It's going to rain."

"Was it raining the night I was taken?"

"No," Luca clipped.

"But you love—" Tony started.

"Shut up, Tony," Luca snapped.

"Everyone calm down," I said. "I don't want people to be on pins and needles around me and watching everything they say or do. That's just adding to the pressure. I think this little field trip is necessary because this is where I lost my memory. So, I'm all for going through with it."

The silence that followed my statement was loud and only heightened the rumblings of thunder which in turn escalated the tension in the car. I checked the weather earlier, and it called for rain. A cold front would be rolling in, bringing cooler temperatures.

Trees loomed over the road and the moon had long disappeared behind the clouds. The headlights of our convoy led the way, but it was pitch black further out.

We'd been on a narrow road for twelve minutes when the vehicle in front of us slowed and made a turn onto a gravel drive-way. The first large drop of rain hit my window. The SUV rocked and creaked and the overgrowth on the side of the road hinted of an abandoned property.

There were lights up ahead and I was surprised to see two vehicles already there.

"I sent an advanced party to sweep the place," Luca said.

"Who owns it?"

"Used to own," Luca corrected. "One of the Russians who abducted you. The bank has repossessed the property."

"So we're trespassing."

"There's nothing to steal. It's just a piece of land now."

I found out what he meant when we reached what only could have been the house and what was left of it—charred frame of a wall with a broken window.

When Luca parked the SUV, I immediately got out. I walked up to the structure's rubble. Opposite of the wall was a chimney. What I could see was as far as the headlights illuminated. Years of greenery had sprouted from the ruins.

Drops of rain splattered on my face. Lightning streaked across the sky.

Luca walked to my side.

"You thought I was in there," I said, still riveted on the burned-out house.

He didn't answer. When I glanced at him, his jaw was clenched, and his throat was working like he was swallowing repeatedly.

"It was on fire when we arrived." His voice was low and guttural. His Adam's apple bobbed again. "I thought you were in there." He got the words out quickly before inhaling a ragged breath.

"Luca…"

He turned to me and I was sucker-punched by the torment etched on his entire face. His eyes gleamed. His mouth moved and twisted but no further words came. His expression contorted into one final twist of agony before he crushed against him and buried his face into my shoulder.

"I thought I lost you," he choked.

Tears stung my eyes. His anguish was so raw, it swept me away. His body shook, and I wasn't sure if he was crying or not. Instinct made me cling to him. He was like a proud lion punctured with a deep wound seeking comfort from me, the one person who could take his pain away.

I didn't even realize it started to rain until we were soaked. Luca had shielded me with his body, and I didn't feel cold. We stood in front of the ruins. The ruins that held the answers to the night I disappeared.

～

My body rapidly chilled when Luca let me go. It was pouring rain by the time we returned to the SUV.

Luca got a mylar blanket from the Escalade's cargo area. I was just wearing a T-shirt, and I didn't think twice about stripping when he handed me the blanket. I caught a weird expression on his face just before he closed the door. That gave me pause and I wondered how taking off my clothes in front of Luca seemed so natural. Warmth suffused my cheeks, but the rest of my body was still cold.

Rachel didn't stay out of the SUV for long, so she was dry. She tapped my knee. "The two of you out there…" She clutched her hands over her chest.

"Are you crying?" I asked.

"What? No!"

She totally was.

Luca got into the SUV. "I'm sorry if I wasted your time."

"Hmm…" Rachel said.

"What?" Luca looked at us.

"I don't think it was a waste of time. It's closure," Rachel said. "You're erasing what you experienced that day of the fire with a better memory. Natalya has returned to you."

Have I returned though?

Unlike his vulnerability in the rain, Luca scoffed, "Don't

psychoanalyze me. What's next?" He gunned the engine. The rain was abating.

Rachel leaned over to me. "He's the king of avoidance."

My teeth were chattering, but I managed, "Nessa said he's the king of denial."

"I'm right fucking here," he growled.

Tony was the only one who had no comment, but when Luca was checking his side-view mirror, the other man glanced at me and shook his head with a grin on his face.

Luca blasted the heat in the cabin, and I warmed up fast. I begged him to turn it off because I was sweating.

"Take a shower when you get home," he told me. "I don't want you getting sick."

"That's a myth," Rachel said.

"No, it's not."

The two bickered all the way home. I was disappointed the burned-out house didn't trigger a memory, but like Rachel said, that exercise had done more for Luca. But something happened between us in the rain. Whereas before I felt disconnected from his grief, like he was grieving for another person and I empathized with him, this time it was as if he was grieving directly to me.

It was intense, and I couldn't describe the pain I felt as he clutched me to him. The words in my ear were muffled in the deluge of the rain, but whatever they meant, they transmitted directly into my heart like a live wire.

The trip home seemed faster, or it was because I was so lost in my thoughts, soaking in these new emotions. I wanted to check on Elias before I turned in, but Luca was a tyrant about me taking a warm shower.

So that was what I did. Somehow, even when the surface of my skin was warm and my cheeks seemed to be running a fever, there was a marrow-deep chill in my bones. Once I got under the shower,

I stayed under it longer than normal. And when I stepped out, I was so impatient that I had to dry my hair when all I wanted to do was hug my son.

After quickly drying my hair and putting on pajamas, I stepped out of the room, surprised to see Mrs. B sitting on my bed.

I padded into the room. "You don't like thunderstorms either, and they let you up here?"

I could hear the cat purring like a chatterbox. "I'm going to go see Elias, and I'll be right back. You can snuggle with me."

But the cat jumped off the bed and ran ahead of me. She seemed to know where I was going.

The door to the nursery was ajar, and Luca was already inside. He was pulling a shirt over his head when he heard me.

"No, Mrs. B, you can't come in here," Luca muttered.

"She was in my bedroom," I said.

"Thunderstorm."

"Yes, Martha told me." I walked over to the twin bed where Elias was sleeping.

At the edge of the mattress, I leaned over to kiss my son. He was on his back, oblivious to his parents. "Bet he didn't even wake up when you came in."

Luca shook his head. "I'm going for a shot of whiskey. Do you want to join me in the study?"

"No, I'm..." My eyes fell on Mrs. B, sitting on a gigantic teddy bear that was on its side. The cat was staring at me with intent golden eyes. My whole body went cold. It was like I was in a trance, mesmerized by the giant stuffed toy.

"What's wrong?" Luca's voice was sharp.

The words, when they came, sounded alien. It was like I'd disconnected from myself. "Where did that teddy bear come from?"

"It was in the closet. Elias probably wanted to ride on it."

I walked to it and dropped to my knees. Mrs. B jumped off and rubbed her body against mine.

Swallowing hard, I turned the stuff toy, so the zipper was facing me. A zipper I knew that was expertly hidden in a seam. Luca came up behind me. I was breathing hard now because images flashed in my head like an endless reel, but I fought against the oncoming migraine.

I pulled down the zipper, and my hand went in. The action was so instinctive, I closed my eyes when my fingers touched what it expected to touch. The bumps and indentations of the stickers on the surface of my old laptop, the familiar width of it between my index finger and thumb, and the heft when I lifted it out.

A cry snagged in my throat with the avalanche of memories that crashed through my head.

I remembered everything.

CHAPTER
Thirty-Three

NATALYA

I awoke to the glare of incandescent lights and angry voices. I was lying on the floor with my brain about to pound out of my skull.

"You nearly killed our meal ticket! Are you stupid or what?" a man yelled. He was taller and wider than the first man I saw. Both of them still had their masks on.

"She was going to hit me with a rock." The statement sounded like the whine of a rottweiler beaten by a chihuahua.

The other man scoffed, "She's what? A hundred pounds?"

My thoughts were fuzzy as hell. I must have made a sound because I felt, rather than saw, two pairs of eyes pin me down with the weight of their stares.

"Elias," I whispered, forcing my elbows to prop me up on my side. "Where's my son?"

"He's with the nanny." The first man who spoke crouched in front of me. A tattoo of a knife through a skull was inked on the back

of his hand. I'd seen that tattoo before. But it was as though cotton had replaced the network in my brain and my neurons refused to fire. Tattoo Man dragged me to a chair. My laptop was waiting for my password.

He put a piece of paper in front of me.

"Transfer the money you stole to these accounts."

He wasn't making sense. All I could do was stare at the numbers on the paper, then at the screen, and then back at the paper again. He slapped the back of my chair, jolting me. "Are you stupid or what?"

"I can't think…" I mumbled. "Concussion."

"She's just faking it," Whiner said. I heard the click of a gun and then the cold barrel touched my temple. My fingers went numb.

I typed in the password thrice. My fingers moved like limbs that had been left in the same position for so long that they forgot how to bend.

"I'm so sorry," I sobbed, my body shuddering. "I just don't know…"

Confusion seized me. That was when I realized it was the wrong computer. "I can't get you all the money. Where are the ledgers?"

"The what?" Whiner asked.

"She meant these…hard wallets, right?" Tattoo Man asked.

I nodded. "I have fifty thousand—"

"Bullshit. I was told you have three hundred fifty million total."

"I don't have them here. I just can't right now…" They were going to kill me. "I'd give you the money if I could."

"Well, we can't shoot you, but you know what? We can start with Nessa," the man said. I caught the sadistic tone in his voice.

He whipped out his phone and turned away from me. "We don't have it yet. She got feisty, and uh, our guy hit her…yeah…yeah…she said she was concussed. Yeah…that's what I thought." Long pause.

"Fuck. And if that doesn't work?" Another long pause. "Okay...okay."

When he ended the call. He turned to me. "One last chance, Natalya."

Even if I wanted to, my concentration was toast, and I wasn't sure if it was from my blurry vision either. Besides my brain being hazy, it was panicking at the intricate hoops I needed to go through to get at the money from this laptop.

"We need to go back to the mansion. The things I need are there," I told them.

Tattoo Man glared at me, then flicked his eyes to Whiner. "Kill the nanny."

"No!" I jumped to my feet and started after Whiner, but the other guy grabbed my arm and twisted it behind me.

A shot rang out.

"No. Nessa!" I screamed. I went wild with fury and stomped on Tattoo Man's foot. He cursed and let me go, but when I scrambled in the direction where Whiner disappeared, fingers yanked my hair and a stinging slap spun me around. I didn't know where the pain was coming from. My scalp, my jaw, or my heart. "You asshole!"

I couldn't see through the blur of tears. "Nessa..."

"One last chance."

Whiner appeared. "That was a waste."

Tattoo Man jerked me again and shoved me back in the chair. I could only sob in front of the laptop.

"Your son is next."

"I can't..." My ragged breath caught on a sob. They wouldn't do it, right? But I wasn't sure, and I wasn't going to risk it. My son was all alone. I could hear him crying. My mother's heart ached to go to him, but I had consigned him to death. I didn't deserve him. "They didn't bring what I need."

"You should have told them," Tattoo Man said. "Kill the son."

"No! Luca will give you what you want. Whatever you need. He can match it."

"That's not what we want."

I shot out of my chair despite the pounding in my head and went after Whiner when he headed back to the room.

Bang!

Nooooo!!!

"Nooooo." I woke up to hands pushing against my shoulders. Weighing me down. I punched, clawed, and kicked. I tried to bite an arm trying to pin me down.

Someone cursed and then, "Natalya!"

"You killed Elias. You killed him!"

"Our son is fine!"

The hands that were restraining me disappeared, and I was engulfed in a familiar embrace. I struggled some more until Luca's reassuring voice finally cleared the dark haze of the nightmare of memories. "He's fine. It was a dream."

I couldn't stop shaking. I was not cold. Warmth surrounded me, but the shudder rippling through me was uncontrollable, and so were the tears that wouldn't stop.

At one point Luca talked to someone else in the room, but mostly, he was murmuring words of comfort. That he was with me. That Elias was fine. That I was safe with him now. He said those words over and over until the meaning of them sunk in and quelled the terror and despair in my heart. Finally, I was able to focus on what was real and my crying subsided.

I noticed I wasn't in the nursery, but in the bedroom and it was daytime.

He was rubbing my back. The action comforted me. I exhaled a deep breath and pulled away.

"I'm better."

Luca studied my face. "You gave us a fright, baby."

My mouth tipped up at one corner. "I passed out, I guess?"

"Yes. You were unconscious for hours and wouldn't wake up." His jaw clenched. "I never want to hear the sound that came from your lips again."

I gave him a puzzled look.

"A sound like a wounded animal." His voice pitched low. "Do you remember that night?"

"Part of it replayed in a dream...a nightmare. I must have slipped from unconsciousness to sleep." I probed the memories of that night. "I remember everything until the second time they knocked me out."

Luca's face turned murderous. "So it was more than that one time Nessa told us about?"

"I think the second time was when my amnesia took hold and they broke my wrist." My voice cracked, and I felt tears coming on again. "When I thought they killed Elias."

Luca's eyes slid shut, his mouth tightened as if he was trying to keep from asking me more questions. When his eyes opened, they were calm, but I wondered what passed through him in those few seconds as he processed my words. "I don't want to push you. Gleason is on his way. When you're ready, you can tell me."

Doc checked me over and told me to take it easy, but I needed to get everything off my chest. It was nine in the morning anyway. I felt like death warmed over, my pounding headache wouldn't go away, and there was that phantom twitchiness from my previously broken right wrist, so I relented when he offered painkillers.

After breakfast, I met with Luca and Dario in the study.

My husband eyed me warily. "We can leave this for a few days."

"No, we can't because I want to move on from this." I brought the laptop with me. Before I connected to their network, I quarantined and neutralized the Trojan they installed on my laptop. If anyone had messed with my laptop, it would have been that time I gave birth to Elias. I learned from Martha they found oral Miso-prostol in Yvonne's room, a drug used to induce labor. That would mean they had access to my DEC-phone and knew how to use it. My stomach soured at the thought that Doriana was involved. And The Friar? To think I admired that hacker. Many things made little sense. Doriana could have asked me to transfer the money to her accounts.

Luca gave a brief nod and rounded the desk and took his seat. Dario and I sat in front of it. I had the computer on my lap. My fingers were flying over the keyboard as I lined up all the screens I wanted to share with them. I glanced at Luca and then at Dario. "I work for a hacking network involved in stopping human trafficking. Santino and Frankie didn't kidnap me because I was Vincenzo's daughter…"

"Holy fuck," Luca whispered. I could see the cogs turning in his brain, and he'd already come to the right conclusion. "You have Orlov's money."

I rolled my lips. "Yes."

Dario was also staring at me with narrowed, semi-accusing eyes. "That night of the power outage. One of his lieutenants had an auction that got hit by hackers."

My head sunk between my shoulders. "Yes."

"Son of a bitch." Luca's chair scraped back, and he walked to the window. He didn't say anything for a few seconds. "Three hundred fifty million dollars."

"I haven't checked yet."

"Where are they?"

"Swiss banks and cryptocurrency."

"I don't understand," Dario said. "Why is the money with you? You said a hacking network. Didn't they demand the money be turned over? Why leave it with you?"

"I don't know. I wasn't the only one who nearly got in trouble. My handler did too, and she was uneasy about receiving the money."

"That's a lot of money. She could have disappeared," Luca said, face grim. "Are you going to contact her?"

"I will."

Luca moved away from the window, but instead of returning to his chair, he walked to me and turned my chair slightly. Then he got into a crouch. His whole body was locked tight, jaw clenched hard. I could feel the aggression thrumming through him. He voiced it in measured words. "We could have avoided a lot of heartache if you trusted me with this."

I inhaled a ragged sob. "You didn't give me enough reasons to trust you." This was it. The moment of truth I'd waited years to find out. I turned my screen toward him and played the video. Luca's brows furrowed, then he recognized what was playing on the screen. Dario got up from his seat and went behind Luca.

"*Madone*," Dario muttered. "How? There were no cameras in that room."

"We had a drone planted in it."

"We?" Luca stood, glaring down at me. "We?" he repeated. "Your handler?"

"No. Someone I tag-teamed with."

"This was the night you got abducted." Luca wasn't asking a question. He sounded like a lawyer entering evidence in court. "The footage got cut off. What happened?"

"The hacker discovered we'd been compromised."

Luca sneered. "Convenient, don't you think? To leave the video out of context."

My spine stiffened. "Are you denying you were involved in the sex trafficking of minors?"

Luca stared at me for a charged, furious minute. Even if he was motionless, the earlier aggression morphed into rage. It was pulsing at his temple, in the clenching muscle at his jaw, at the tensed cords of his neck. His hands at his sides barely moved. A minute expired, and he wordlessly stepped up to his desk and picked up his phone. Soundlessly scrolling through it before handing it to me.

My attention fell on the headline of a news article that was two years old. "Zavarida Group members exposed." It went on to say that law enforcement groups around the world apprehended several high-profile businessmen and politicians belonging to a sex cult linked to human trafficking.

"You…"

"Carmine and I coordinated that operation for months. If you and your partner screwed up the transactions, that would have alerted those men and it would have risked those kids."

I inhaled sharply. "None of the Lillies were over eighteen."

"You should have trusted me, Natalya."

I was shaking my head because I wasn't sure now if I did the right thing. The memories were too new, but they were still memories from two years ago and not every detail was clear. I returned his phone. He tossed it on the desk and crouched in front of me again. "That night, Carmine was not there for the auction. He didn't respond until that morning when the cops came to the house."

"You suspected him of my disappearance?"

"Did he know you were doing these things?"

"No." I gave a brief snort of derision. "But come to think of it. He'd been asking me if I've been hacking again, but he wouldn't put those kids in danger. There was nothing Carmine despised more than human traffickers. He hated Santino for working with the Russians."

"So he knew about Santino's arrangement with Orlov before your father found out?"

"I don't know."

Luca walked back to his desk, leaning back until his chair creaked. Dario returned to his seat.

"You know what I think?" Luca linked his fingers across his torso, drumming them in the way I'd seen him do when he was analyzing information. "I've long suspected your cousin was trying to drive a wedge between us. We never figured out the drive-by shooting incident in front of the club. I bet Carmine set it up, and he thought I would remain in Chicago and miss your first checkup. I'm beginning to see what his endgame is." Luca looked at his consigliere. "What do you think, Dario?"

"I agree."

"Surely you don't think…" I started but trailed off. It was like I was hit by a freight train. "Oh my God…"

He nodded. "He wants to control the Galluzo and Chicago. I wouldn't be surprised if he manipulated Santino to overthrow Vincenzo and gave him a list of his inner circle to get rid of. He told Santino to kidnap you. *He* was the one who told me you were with Frankie Rossi, and made sure Vincenzo knew the information came from him to curry favor."

"And we brought that snake into our midst where he gathered supporters from both our organization and Orlov's," Dario added. "Planted seeds of discontent to empower them to overthrow Luca and Orlov. The money they planned to get from Natalya was to finance their coup."

"I can confirm one of the men in that burnt house was Turo—Yvonne's boyfriend," I said. "Although they wore masks, I recognized the knife through a skull inked on the back of his right hand. The voice also matches." I was too concussed to make the connections that night, but it seemed clear as day after my dream. Luca and Dario didn't look surprised. "But…you already know this."

"Two of our capos were involved including a group of Russians from Orlov's organization. The Russians were the ones who abducted you from the house. Nessa also confirmed that she thought she heard Yvonne."

"The night I gave birth was the only time I could think of that someone could have messed with my laptop. Yvonne was left to mind the mansion. I didn't have the teddy bear then. My laptop was in a backpack. She could have let anyone in to install the Trojan or she could have done it with simple instructions. Once I logged in to the auction, I was compromised."

"They didn't count on you getting amnesia. No money meant no funding. My bet is still on Carmine. He panicked and erased all evidence of the conspiracy. That's why he turned on Turo and burned the house down. I couldn't believe he had the audacity to show up at the mansion." Luca's jaw worked reflexively and he stared at me directly before saying, "He gave me ammunition to manipulate you."

A phantom pain speared my womb and an involuntary cry escaped my lips, my hand instinctively lowering to the area where I'd felt Elias move frequently as a baby.

"Are you all right?" Luca rose from his seat, his eyes widening in panic. "Should I call Gleason?"

I closed my eyes and shook my head. My brain and my heart were in survival mode while I exhumed the layers of events in the hierarchy of pain. The pain that changed my feelings for Luca forever. The night he missed our son's birth.

When I peeled my eyes open, Luca's eyes were focused on my hand that was splayed on my abdomen and his throat bobbed. "So now you know."

"Now I know why you kept me from meeting Rachel."

"And?" He speared Dario a look before returning it to me. His consigliere mumbled his excuse and left the study.

"Are you asking me if I forgive you for that night you missed Elias's birth? Because I'm not sure if it was a matter for forgiveness. I don't understand the pain I'm feeling because you were simply doing your duty to family."

He nodded briefly, his gaze watchful. "I understand."

"Do you?" I shook my head. "But that's not the end of it, is it? I don't know if your worst transgression was promising our firstborn to Papà."

Luca dropped his gaze, his shoulder slumping in defeat. He moved away from the desk and I thought he was rounding it so he could plead his case in front of me, but instead he moved to the window and looked outside. "I don't want to make excuses anymore. Ambition blinded me, but please know these past two years without you, our son has taught me so much about what mattered the most, what was important." He raised his arm and sliced it in the air in a careless wave. "To see what's bullshit." He turned around. "I can only promise that I have changed, Natalya." He swallowed hard. "I love you. I'll always love you. Time hasn't change that and I promise to make it up to you for being a shitty husband." He erased the distance between us and crouched in front of me. "Let me prove it to you, *tesoro*." He searched my face. "Give me this chance, please?"

There was humility and sincerity in his plea, but the return of my memories was an avalanche of jumbled thoughts and emotions. Now that I'd eliminated Luca's role in the sex trafficking of minors I could concentrate on the conflicts of our relationship. Knowing who I was now, could I live with this man who had caused me so much pain? "I need to sort through my feelings, so I'll be needing some space."

A muscle twitched at his jaw. "Of course."

"I hope you can be patient with me."

"However long you need," He pressed a kiss to my forehead, and when he leaned away, a wry smile tipped his mouth. "As long as it doesn't take another two years."

∿

Luca

It had been a week since Natalya regained her memory. In that week, there was no progress in our relationship.

Patience was easier declared than done. Patience was definitely not my strong suit when Brad Bailey was staring at my wife with longing eyes and indulging my son with a fatherly smile that should belong exclusively to me.

Gleason told me the coffee shop owner was threatening to go to the cops unless he saw Natalya and the doctor with his own eyes. The doctor also said there was nothing more he could do for my wife, and it was time for him to go home.

I questioned my sanity for allowing Bailey to pick up Gleason, but I had a masochistic desire to see how my wife reacted to him. I didn't know whether I was relieved or disappointed that Natalya gave me no reason to go homicidal over Bailey.

"You're surprisingly calm," Rachel said beside me as both of us watched Gleason, Bailey, my wife, and Elias linger in front of the barista's Ford Expedition. Rachel came by to say goodbye to the doctor.

"Did Natalya ask you here to stage an intervention in case I went gonzo?" My wife had daily sessions with Rachel, and it annoyed me they invoked doctor-client-privilege bullshit and kept me in the dark about their discussions. I asked if I should be part of Natalya's therapy, but Rachel thought I would only hinder my wife from opening up if I were present.

I was offended, even if I agreed with that assessment. I hated feeling helpless, and I wanted to understand why my wife was avoiding me. Was there something else she wasn't telling me?

Bailey and Natalya hugged one more time. The man shot me daggered looks past her shoulder. I awarded him with a slow smug grin, even when it hurt my jaw to maintain that smile when his hug went on a bit too long.

I cleared my throat and stepped forward. "Bailey, you should get going."

Natalya stepped back from the barista and glared at me for my rudeness. "Luca."

"No, it's all right. I get where the man is coming from."

"You mean you get where *her husband* is coming from?"

Bailey, for all his wisecracks, extended his hand. "No hard feelings."

I raised a brow and shook his hand.

"Just make her happy."

Oh, for the love of God. Despite his martyr-like declaration, the extra squeeze in our handshake didn't go unnoticed. We locked gazes for a while longer, and I was sure the expression in mine reflected the veiled threat in his.

"Well, this was an interesting vacation." Gleason came to our side, angling his arm between us, his purpose clear. Bailey and I broke our stalemate so I could shake the old man's hand.

But a shake wasn't enough for Gleason. I pulled him in for a hug. "Take care of yourself, Doc. Come visit us sometime."

I felt him stiffen, and I wanted to laugh. When we broke apart, I said, "Or we can drop by for a visit on our way to Grafton. We have business there."

"That would be nice," he responded feebly.

"Maybe Dario and you can go fishing." While the doc and I made small talk, my eyes followed Bailey as he made his way to the driver's side. Natalya stepped back with Elias and stood beside Rachel.

"Maybe. I wish you all the best, Moretti."

"There's always a spot for you in my organization."

"I'm an old man. I don't need the excitement."

I clapped him one more time on the back and squeezed his shoulder before I sent him on his way. I'd grown fond of the old bugger and I didn't mind having him around.

"I'm going to miss him," Natalya said as the taillights of the SUV blinked some distance down the driveway.

"I'm sure you meant Doc Gleason, right?" I gritted.

Natalya glared at me, and without answering me, she picked up Elias and marched back into the mansion.

My eyes followed them. I realized Natalya and Elias had grown closer. My boy didn't even bother with me this week and was all about his mother. A seed of anxiety started to grow in my gut.

"Don't say a word," I growled at Rachel.

"I wasn't," my friend remarked dryly. "I enjoy seeing you dig your hole deeper."

I cast her an irritated glance before I started after Natalya. "Do you have a session with her today?"

"No. She doesn't need therapy, really." Rachel matched my strides.

"If you're thinking I do, think again."

"No, but your idiocy is tiring."

I paused right in front of the door and veered toward the gardens at the back of the mansion. Rachel sighed and followed me.

When we were in front of the Botticelli angel fountain, I faced her. "What am I doing wrong?"

"The question is, what are you doing right now?"

"I give her flowers every day. Different ones each time because she has to remember by now that she loves them, yet I've seen her give them away to my men to give to their wives or girlfriends—" I paused when Rachel burst out laughing. "It's not funny. I'm trying here. She kept the peonies from yesterday. She seems to like those. Hates the white roses."

Rachel raised a brow. "Those were her *wedding* flowers."

Her innuendo was so strong, I smacked my forehead in realization. "Her mother."

My friend shrugged. "Yes. And those chocolates are good, by the way."

I scowled at her. "I'm going to ask her out to dinner tonight."

"What, like a date?"

I prayed for patience. "Of. Course. Like. A. Date."

"Well, good luck with that."

I started to pace. "Then what the hell do you think I should do?"

Rachel gave a long-suffering sigh. "All right. I'll clue you in."

I made an elaborate, if not a derisive wave with my arm. "Please do. Because I'm out of fucking ideas."

"You're waiting for Natalya to remember she loves you."

Confused, I looked at her. "She already knows she loves me. She remembers everything."

"Memories evoke emotions, but those emotions are different from the ones people experience when they fall in love."

"I'm not following."

"At the risk of sounding unromantic...what is falling in love if not brain chemistry? How did she fall in love with you?"

I sighed heavily. "Paris."

"Where you manipulated her..." At my scathing look, she quickly added, "But she *did* fall in love with you."

"If you're suggesting we take off to Paris, I don't think she'd be willing to leave Elias. And she's in a vulnerable situation right now." I had horrific nightmares that Natalya had amnesia again and was running barefoot through the cornfields, with Turo and his crew chasing her.

"But you have to bring back that rush for her. Falling in love is broken down into chemicals and hormones in the body. Adrenaline and dopamine among them. There's attraction definitely, and that's an altogether different set of hormones. You just need to bring in the swoons, Luca. For her, she knows in her head she loves you, but the heart needs to catch up because she's been without those feelings for two years. And she's been obsessing about the bad parts of your marriage because those memories came back first. Her mind at the time of amnesia was protecting her from the heartbreak. And that's why it's harder for the emotion of love to manifest."

"In a weird way, you're making sense," I muttered. "Should I kidnap my wife somewhere? Maybe to an island?"

Rachel rolled her eyes. "You need to make her feel secure that Elias would be fine, but both of you need alone time to reconnect."

"I have an idea."

CHAPTER
Thirty-Four

NATALYA

"Why did we leave so early again?" We were on a private jet to an undisclosed location. Luca woke me up at four in the morning and rushed me to pack. I was barely coherent without coffee, but he seemed to be in a chipper mood at a god-awful hour, which irked me. I barely said anything to him as he bundled me and Elias into the Escalade. Martha and Tony were with us.

"I heard from your parents and they want to visit."

"And you didn't tell me this?" Though I was annoyed that Luca was playing gatekeeper to my family in Italy, a part of me was relieved. I was still trying to merge who I was before to who I was now. It wasn't easy, especially the part about what I should be feeling.

"They just called last night. I told them we already had plans." His gaze softened. "What we're building here is more important."

Sadness came at the heels of that statement. One of the first genuine feelings since my memories returned. "You said that to me in Paris. Little did I realize it wasn't about our relationship." I turned to the window. The glare of the rising sun bothered my eyes, so I pulled the shield down. I leaned back against the headrest. Bittersweet emotions and memories were all I could attach to our time in Paris. It was as though I judged that time through the events that followed. It was confusing because the weeks leading to my disappearance, Luca had been trying to make up for being a shitty husband, including the part he played in the deal with my father. I *knew* I was in love with him. I'd seen the love in his eyes for me and Elias, and the only barrier to our true happiness was my suspicion that he'd been involved in human trafficking. After Luca revealed the truth, I waited for my love to return.

I didn't want to confuse lust and love. He still slept with our son in the nursery. It was the only time he spent with Elias since my memory returned. I used my son to be the new barrier between my husband and me. During one of our sessions, I asked Rachel why I was doing this. She told me it could be because I needed Luca to prove something to me. She advised me to be honest. To let Luca know my likes and dislikes, because my husband was struggling to get to know this blended person of my past and present.

I was ruthless about the flowers. A smile touched my lips.

"Finally, she smiles."

My eyes popped open, and I turned my head to look at him. "Were you watching me this whole time?"

"Yes." He said it in a challenging tone, like he dared me to deny him the right to stare at me.

"It's creepy."

"What made you smile?"

"I don't think you're going to like it."

"Try me."

I gave a brief laugh. "Okay. If you insist. It was the pleasure I took in getting rid of those damned flowers I didn't like."

Instead of the frustrated expression I'd gotten so accustomed to seeing on his face, Luca smiled broadly.

My brain did a stutter. "You're not mad I did that?"

He gathered my left hand in both of his, cupping it like it was so precious to even hold my hand. "No. Because now I know peonies are your favorite." He brought my hand to his chest. I could feel his heartbeat, and I wondered if it matched the sudden quickening of mine. Heat crept up my cheeks, and my eyes lowered to stare at where my hand was on his chest, but I couldn't help the impish grin that curved my lips, shy and teasing.

Still with an averted gaze, I said, "I do love the chocolates. You can continue with that."

I could feel him branding me with his eyes, so I slowly lifted my head to look, and my breath caught at the expression of tenderness reflected in them.

With a secret smile, he let go of my hand and got out of the seat. He walked to the back of the plane, and when he returned, he carried with him a box of chocolates with the signature packaging.

"Did you think I would forget to bring them?"

It was all I could do not to grab the box. Who said you couldn't have chocolate early in the morning? I quickly unraveled the bow and opened the lid to see my favorite selection, and it triggered the same glee I remembered when he did the same thing in Paris. A flutter in my heart.

"I wasn't expecting it." I picked the chocolate dusted with cocoa powder and popped it into my mouth.

He gave a deep-chested chuckle. "I'd buy the entire damned store if I could get you a lifetime supply of them."

"You would?" Surprisingly, I wouldn't put it past Luca.

"Yeah, but these French are so protective of their craft, they don't do franchises. There isn't even a store in the U.S."

"Probably because your taste buds don't deserve it."

"Baby, I hate to tell you this, but you're as American as I am now."

True, probably more since I'd spent two years in small-town America, but Danvers never felt like home to me.

"So you're going to fly them in from Paris for me?" I offered Luca a chocolate with an accompanying coquettishness I hadn't experienced in a long time. The old Natalya was still in there. Did I want to be that hopeful new bride again?

"I have my connections." He grinned and took one.

And as the chocolate melted in my mouth, it dissolved the sadness I felt earlier. "Where are we going?"

"I told you, baby, it's a surprise."

Luca

"I can't believe we left our son to go away for a vacation."

We—or rather I—didn't waste any time. Sera and Carlotta were waiting for us when our jet landed in the De Luccis' private hangar. My niece had her one-year-old son, Gio, with her, and he distracted Elias. As expected, she and my sister bombarded Natalya with questions. They were annoyed at me for not wanting to stay overnight in one of their residences, but I'd rather face a firing squad than have Carlotta corner my wife and ask her all kinds of uncomfortable questions. I loved my half sister, but she could be overwhelming. As her brother, I could only take her in small doses, and my wife was overwhelmed by her situation as it was.

"Think of it as a honeymoon-redo," I told her. The Morettis kept losing our women to the De Luccis. Might as well take advantage of our familial ties and use everything in their arsenal to win back my wife. They built their crime family on a strong nuclear one. I envied that.

Sometimes.

Natalya was quiet for a few seconds. We had just merged onto the Long Island Expressway on our way to Montauk. It was off-season this time of the year, and for someone like me who hated tourist spots, it was the perfect time.

"Is it just going to be the two of us?" she asked.

"It's like a honeymoon, so of course."

"No guards?"

"No guards. No housekeepers. We can either cook or go to restaurants."

Glancing over at Natalya, the pensive look on her face troubled me. "Are you worried it's just the two of us?"

She gave a brief laugh, momentarily lightening her expression. "It's more than that. Wasn't the reason we kind of sped up my memories' return was so we can find out who did this to us? It seems like we're running away from what should be done."

I reached over to take her hand, brought the back of it to press a kiss, and kept our joined hands on my lap. It was instinctive. It felt right. "Remember what I told you on the plane?"

"That what we're building is more important?"

"Yes. We have enemies. They managed to tear us apart. The reason they managed to tear us apart was because we kept secrets from each other." I shot her a quick glance again. "No, don't do that." Her head dropped in what only could look like guilt. "We move on from our mistakes, Natalya."

When she glanced up at me, her eyes were glinting with tears. "I'm afraid to trust you with my heart again," she whispered. "I've been going over this in my mind. At that time, right before I disappeared, I was in love with you. I was thankful for the breadcrumbs you were finally showing. I was your doormat."

If I weren't driving, I would have closed my eyes at the pain her words invoked. "Don't say that." My own words came out hoarse. "I was trying to make it right. Do you remember? I asked you in the attic…the night of the dinner party. The night when you found out my deal with your father."

She withdrew her hand from mine, and I let her. She hugged her biceps. "How can I forget?" She turned her head to stare out the window.

I decided to wait until we got to Montauk before I reminded her of all the things that were going right before she disappeared. It gave me time to brood. I was impatient, but strategic. I was glad I had that chat with Rachel so I could put my wife's present emotions into perspective. I'd fallen in love with Natalya in Paris. I realized the exact moment. It was that time I paid attention to her favorite chocolate flavors. I could have just bought an assorted box instead of a carefully curated one. I saw Natalya take a picture of the selection with her phone. When she wasn't looking, I forwarded that image to my phone. I deceived myself into thinking I was manipulating her emotions when in fact, I was fighting against the exhilaration that I was about to put a smile on her face. When I thought about that memory, I didn't feel the same rush. It had been too long ago, and many things had happened between then and now. What transcended the passing of time was tragedy. Because two years down the road, every time I thought I'd lost Natalya in that fire, I still felt the twisting of the dagger in my chest. It could still trigger my nightmares.

Love faded unless one nurtured it, but pain didn't, and whoever said time healed all wounds was a liar.

"Ohh…" Natalya breathed beside me. Her face was almost plastered to the side of the window. "This is a cute little town."

"Sera never took you here?"

"No. I guess because that time I was with them, it was winter."

I checked the phone mounted on the dash. "We'll be at the house in ten minutes."

Dom, my nephew, had forwarded me several properties. He grumbled it had been such a short notice. I gave him less than twenty-four hours. Now that made me smug. He may be the boss of one of the most powerful crime families in New York, but he was still my nephew, and I could make demands like this.

Our SUV made the turn off the highway into a narrower road. It passed a couple of smaller houses before the bigger and more secluded ones started. That was as far as the GPS would go. Dom sent me instructions on how to get there because the address didn't show up correctly on the map app. After a few more miles, we ended in a roundabout intersecting a gravel road. I took the graveled lane.

Dense trees flanked the beginning of the driveway, their limbs hanging over us like a canopy. When they cleared, I could see the ocean.

"Oh my God," Natalya breathed. "Oh my God," she repeated.

I exhaled slowly and prayed we were heading for the right property because, glancing at my wife's face, I'd hate it if we had to turn around. It would also affect the momentum of my plans.

Full-court press. She was going to fall in love with me again, even if it killed me.

Because love was worth dying for.

Her love was there. I saw flashes of it in her eyes before doubt would replace them. And that whole shit was on me.

When the house came into view, I wanted to do a fist pump. It was the one I selected from the properties Dom showed me. Set high on the Montauk bluffs, it was a modern take on the Chinese teahouse. Floor-to-ceiling windows gave an unobstructed view of the ocean. Even I felt a lift in my spirits as the house drew closer.

"We're staying here?" Natalya gushed.

"You like it?"

"I didn't think I was a beach person, but I can't wait to get to the oceanfront."

"Four hundred eighty-five feet of private beach."

"Wow, how much did this cost you?"

I punched the app for the garage door opener. The gates lifted as our SUV continued to roll down the driveway. "That's between Dom and me."

"I'm still feeling guilty we left Elias."

"Say that to me again when you get a full view of the ocean."

My wife turned toward me, and the smile on her face was the smile when I gave her chocolates that first time.

CHAPTER
Thirty~Five

NATALYA

Luca told me to explore while he brought in our things. It took little convincing. The second the vehicle cleared the trees, unveiling a wide-open space, my spirits soared.

I wondered if I'd been claustrophobic, and I needed a change of scenery away from the mansion that had caused me more heartache than happiness. I circled the living room. The view was a lifelike panoramic painting of the Atlantic Ocean. I'd never seen anything like it. I opened the side door and stepped onto the patio.

How was it possible that I felt powerful and insignificant at the same time? I breathed in the saltwater air. It would be too cold for swimsuits in April. I checked the weather earlier, and the forecast said it was going to be in the fifties this week.

I felt Luca's warmth behind me, but I waited for him to speak.

"You approve?" he rumbled.

A smile played on my lips. I turned to face him. "This is a strange first date."

He chuckled and took a step closer, closer in a way that made me back up a step until the small of my back hit the railing. Closer in a way that had him caging me in with each arm on either side of me, making me tilt my chin up. Closer in a way that made my breath hitch and my heart pound faster.

His body was scant centimeters away. He didn't press me against the railing, but his restraint was palpable.

"Ahh, but it's not a first date. It's our honeymoon."

I worried he could hear the pounding in my chest. "I don't think I'm ready for a honeymoon."

"Relax," he said softly, and the way he said it made me replay all our sexual escapades in Paris. The first time he took me from behind, the first time I took him in my mouth. The many times and places where he ate me out. Heat and wetness pooled between my legs.

A satisfied gleam entered his eyes, as though he sensed my reaction to that single word. "I put our things in opposite bedrooms."

My brows furrowed. "What do you mean, opposite?"

He turned away from me and pointed to one corner and then the other. "Opposite sides of the house. There are four bedrooms on the property. Two on each side." He turned back to face me with a rueful curve to his mouth. "I'm afraid I'll forget my good intentions if I'm near you."

I didn't know what to say to that. On our wedding day, I couldn't wait for him to own my sensuality. When I saw him again after two years, I pegged him as a man who could be my one-night stand. I was willing to risk having sex with him. But finding out we were bound by marriage gave me pause. Our relationship was complicated before, made more complex by my amnesia.

His gaze was intent on my face. "Honestly, I'm not sure how

long I can keep my hands off you." He had caged me in again, and I glanced at his hand on my right, gripping the railing.

"Maybe you shouldn't be standing this close." I swallowed and tried to get saliva back on my tongue. "I'm thirsty."

He stared at me for a beat before he stood back. I walked past him, straight into the kitchen. Since we were both new to this property, it was no use asking him where things were. I opened the refrigerator, and it was empty. I searched the pantry for a glass and pressed it against the water dispenser. Luca prowled into the kitchen, spread his arms, and gripped the counter, leaning into it.

Tension pinged between us.

"I'm attracted to you." It annoyed me that my words were part squeak, part breathless.

His face had one of those patient expressions, but his eyes grew more alert at my admission. When he didn't comment, I continued, "I think physically, I'll always be attracted to you."

"That's a relief," he said dryly. "We could work with that."

There was another thing that bothered me when I had googled him recently. Before I got my memories back, it didn't bother me, but now that I'd remembered, it had caused me a lot of misery during our marriage and I had to know. "I saw pictures of you and Jessica after I disappeared."

"I never cheated on you, if that's your question. I already told you we moved in the same circles. She's an heiress who loves hanging out with morally gray men. She has daddy issues, and it's her form of rebellion. Her father used to be an alderman on the city council and had been a pain in our asses because he blocked our licenses, so I enjoyed flaunting Jessica in his face. When he retired, so had my interest in Jessica. I kept her around because she was convenient."

I stared at his throat. "Has she met Elias?"

His jaw fell open, and I recognized the self-righteousness that stiffened every line in his body. "No. I still considered myself married when you disappeared. When I said my vows, even if I scorned them, I meant them. I don't care that mafia laws allow me a mistress." He released his death grip on the counter and rounded it to get to me, reminding me of a predator. He stepped right up to me, but he didn't cage me in like he did on the porch. He lowered his head. "I was desperate for you and you alone. My cock ached to be buried inside you, *tesoro*, and my hand was a poor substitute, but it got me through those endless miserable nights when I missed you."

Oh my God, those filthy words still did it for me, but that he'd stayed celibate for two years because of his commitment to our marriage made my whole body come alive. Devotion and fidelity were an aphrodisiac to me apparently, and I wanted to jump his bones right there, but there was still so much to unpack between us and I managed, "Don't…"

"Don't…?" he said against my mouth. "Does it make you feel guilty? After having you, no other woman could replace you. I wondered…have you given yourself to another man?"

The accusation sounded so absurd, I snapped, "No."

"Why not?" The way he asked that question was enough for me to deny his accusation because his face had morphed to murderous. I kept forgetting how Luca was such a mercurial man.

Honesty, Rachel's voice said in my head. Even though it was going to make him a smug bastard, he deserved to know that I inadvertently stayed celibate because my body craved only his. "Because no other man seemed to do it for me."

Yep. Smug. His brow arched at the same time a corner of his mouth curved.

"If you must know, that time you showed up at Danvers with Dario was the first time I was willing to consider having a one-night stand if it was you."

I was expecting more smugness, but a pained expression crossed his face. The suddenness of how he grabbed me made me yelp. He plastered our bodies together, and I gasped at the hardness that was pressing against my belly.

His tortured voice said in my ear, "I want to savor this. You back in my arms again. I want to fuck you so badly, kiss you so badly, but if I start kissing you, I won't be able to stop and I don't want it to be reduced to a quick fuck on the kitchen counter."

Luca let me go suddenly and strode away, calling over his shoulder, "Be ready in fifteen minutes. We'll have to do groceries."

That one-eighty had my head spinning and every single cell in my body aching with frustration.

Luca

I started the water, switching it to the coldest temperature. I yelled when it hit me with unforgiving needles. But my body was one rip-roaring fever. I nearly threw Natalya on the counter so I could bury my face in her pussy. The craving was so strong, I had to get away from her. No way were we having sex for the first time in the kitchen and have me last two seconds.

The water cooled my skin, but not the fire raging in my veins. I relented and twisted the dial to a reasonable temp. I fisted my cock and closed my eyes.

As the water swished over me, I imagined what I would have done. I wouldn't have stopped at eating her out. I'd remove her pants, drag her panties down with them, and lift her legs over my shoulders. I would slip my hands under her ass and lift her hips sky high and devour her with my mouth. It wouldn't be comfortable for her, but with the way I was feeling right now, I wanted to punish her for two years of suffering. I wanted her to scream my name over and over and beg me to stop.

My fist stroked my erection faster. I was about to explode. I would pull out my cock and shove into her, pumping her fast and hard. Was she on birth control? I didn't care. All I wanted was to claim her again. Fill her with my cum and have it drip down her legs.

I groaned when I started coming. My hand slapped the tile and darkness edged my vision. After a few seconds, I switched off the water. I was still breathing hard, but partly relieved that I had taken the edge off.

For now.

Ten minutes later, I returned to the living room dressed for a casual day. I'd gotten used to wearing clothes other than suits ever since Elias was born. The boy had an uncanny ability to throw up when I had changed into one.

Natalya appeared five minutes later. Her dark hair was in a ponytail. Sometimes, it still jarred me that she was no longer blonde. For two years, that was the image I had of her.

"What?" She looked down at her khaki pants and dark sweater and white sneakers.

"Still getting used to you not being blonde."

She self-consciously patted her hair. "Did you prefer me as a blonde?"

"I prefer whatever you're comfortable with."

Her mouth twitched. "Are you being diplomatic?"

"Not at all." I cleared my throat, tilting my head to scratch my right brow to buy myself more time, but I felt I had to apologize for earlier. "I'm sorry for running out."

"I wondered about that. It was like I suddenly caught a disease."

"I had to get out of the kitchen before I made you my lunch."

She was giving me a strange look. One with narrowed eyes and puckered brows, like she wasn't sure she understood me.

"I wanted to bury my face between your legs," I stated, inhaling sharply. Fuck, saying that wasn't helping. "I had to beat one out in the shower."

Her cheeks pinkened.

I gave a shake of my head. "Are you ready to go?" I was behaving like a schoolboy who was taking his crush on a first date. I was the fucking boss of the Chicago mob. But the stakes of my marriage were too high to fuck up by hiding my emotions. That was what caused problems in our marriage.

"Where are we going?" Her voice came out a whisper.

The air between us became awkward as fuck. Maybe it was better to just fuck and get it out of our system.

"I thought we could have lunch first and then go grocery shopping."

The strange look on her face returned. "Have you ever gone grocery shopping?"

"Sure, I have," I said. "When I was in Chicago, I didn't have a Martha."

She crossed her arms. "You had a wife who could have done that for you."

I bit back a curse and gritted, "That's why I suggested it."

"What are we doing here, Luca?" she asked. "You know, we could just have it delivered."

Something in what she said triggered a sadness inside me of something lost. "I took our marriage for granted." Closing the distance between us, I continued, "I want us to experience this domestic bliss…"

She raised a brow, arms still folded over her chest. "Or torture."

I chuckled. "That too." I put my hands on her shoulders. "What

I'm saying, baby, is I want you to show me how you lived away from me these past two years."

"And as usual, you start with the basics."

I shrugged. "Of course."

So we started with lunch at a sushi place. That much had not changed. Before our marriage, we defaulted to Japanese food when we couldn't think of anything else. My shortcomings as a husband were becoming more stark. I could only remember a handful of times we went out on a date after we returned from Paris. I wouldn't even call them dates because they were usually after her checkups. When I realized I wanted more from Natalya, Elias made it impossible to go out on romantic dinners because we'd been sleep-deprived. Her more so than me. In my attempt to make her feel better with her decisions, I'd become the selfish husband in retrospect.

Now I was pushing the cart around in the grocery store while she inspected the cereal selections. When she saw my frown, she laughed, "Don't tell Martha and Nessa I've grown addicted to Cap'n Crunch."

I checked the sugar content on the box. "It isn't good for you, baby."

"Just while we're here." She pouted. "I want it for dinner. I'll leave breakfast up to you."

"You want cereal for dinner?"

"You woke me at four this morning. I don't think I want to cook or eat anything heavy."

We passed by the dairy section, and while she picked up milk, I grabbed eggs and yogurt. "I was thinking we could walk on the beach this evening."

"I'm fading." She gave me exaggerated droopy eyes that made me chuckle. I gave her a quick hug. "Okay, *tesoro*." I was glad I hadn't made solid plans tonight.

When we returned to the house and put the groceries away, we immediately set out for the beach. The wind was brisk. Natalya had to put on an extra jacket. We took off our shoes and walked parallel to the shore. It was five in the afternoon. Sunset wouldn't be happening until seven, but from the way Natalya kept on yawning, I didn't think she was going to last.

The surf of the Atlantic Ocean crashed near our feet. "So what was it like? Living on your own, not knowing what you liked?"

She watched a swooping seagull for a beat before answering. "By trial and error. Some things were instinctive. Naturally, I used Doc Gleason as my benchmark. I ate what he ate, drank what he drank, and struck out on my own to explore later. It felt like a reset of sorts."

"I'm surprised you liked cereal. Your body has changed from feminine to athletic."

She glanced up at me warily. "Brad. He was my physical therapist. I caught the gym bug from him. After my wrist healed, I lived in the gym for almost six months."

At the mention of the coffee shop owner, my shoulders tensed. I moved closer to Natalya. I brushed her hand closest to mine. Slowly, but deliberately, I linked our fingers. She didn't pull away.

"It didn't last, but I went to the gym occasionally and I also started running," she said. "I think it was a way of reclaiming my life. Something I could control."

"We have a gym at the mansion. It's in the basement."

"I know. Danvers didn't feel like home, but I made something for myself there. I don't know how it fits in my life now."

"We'll figure it out."

Natalya stopped walking. "Can we sit here?"

"Sure."

We dropped our asses on the sand. I had never done this before. Why hadn't I done this before? My life was the concrete jungles of

Chicago and Vegas and other metropolitan areas. The only isolated place I loved spending time in was Tralestelle. Here, with the ocean and its vastness and depths of unknown secrets, I should be itching to get back to the city, but I wasn't.

I dislodged the block of apprehension in my throat. "This is the first time...in...in my life I've sat on the beach with someone." For fuck's sake, I was stammering and I couldn't meet Natalya's eyes. It was as if I'd confessed to an embarrassing disease.

I could feel her regard burning down the side of my face.

"How come?" she asked.

This time, I glanced at her and shot her a brief smile. "Maybe for the same reasons you haven't."

"Mamma didn't like the sun because she said it ruins the complexion," she said, her voice a raspy whisper in the wind. "She also worried I would mess up my hair color."

"Did you change your hair color because you were hiding?"

"That"—she thought for a few beats, digging her toes in the sand. Her pretty little toes—"and it was high maintenance."

"Do you miss being high maintenance?"

She jerked back and cast me a horrified look. "No! I mean, nerds like me are pretty low maintenance. We like a lot of sugary snacks, as I found out. But I promise to do better for Elias."

"You should. That's where we will clash, *tesoro*. What we feed our child."

She rolled her eyes. "You and your preoccupation with food. Waffles aren't exactly the best to feed a child, especially when you drown them in maple syrup."

I fought back a smile to wear a serious face as I said, "Then when we return, we should pay attention to what we feed Elias. Martha caves in easily when it comes to sweets."

"The poor woman. Elias is too active for her."

"But you're there now."

My last statement was met with silence and a pained smile. I was never going to let her go, but I didn't want to come on too strong when her mind was in a fragile state of discovering who she was. But waiting for her to make up her mind whether she loved me the same or not was excruciating. For two years, the what-ifs tormented me the most. I should have loved her the way she loved me. Regretted the work I could have delegated to someone else and spent those times making Natalya happy instead. Had it only been two weeks since I found her again? Fate had given me a second chance, but fate had a sick sense of humor by giving her the worst memories of me to come back first.

"I need to ask you for something," I said gruffly. Natalya visibly stiffened, even edged slightly away from me. "I've asked you to trust me before. I'm asking you again now. Not just for Elias, but because I'm in love with you. And I believe…" I paused. "You still love me."

Natalya inhaled sharply, then looked away.

"I was an idiot," I admitted. "I was so careless with your heart."

"You trampled on it," she said viciously, her eyes glassy with tears and condemnation. "Why did you do it, Luca? Why make me fall in love with you and then not want it?"

I'd contemplated that question myself. "It's a combination of things. I saw what love had done to Junior. I didn't want his weakness, but I needed to gain your loyalty by making you love me. I hid behind the men-of-honor code to put the Chicago family first."

"Loving someone isn't a weakness," she said. "If that's how you feel, then we were over before we started. You didn't have to forsake your duty to family by forsaking me. If I'd felt more secure in your love, I think I would have understood you when you missed Elias's birth."

"I get that now," I said fiercely. I got up from her side and sank to my knees in front of her. "I've loved you since Paris."

She made a derisive sound. "You don't have to lie—"

"I'm not. It started when I gave you the chocolates. I convinced myself it was part of the master plan to make you fall in love with me. I have this vicious cycle of when I start feeling something for you, I back the hell away. When you asked me to walk in the rain…"

"You were fighting it."

I nodded grimly. "And justified it to the others by belittling it."

"You were an asshole."

I still was. "There'll always be that asshole in me. You need to call me on my bullshit."

She looked past my shoulder at the ocean. The silence was loud against the crashing of the waves. When her eyes returned to me, she said, "It also happened during the first checkup."

My shoulders drooped, and I wanted to hug her, afraid she'd run away while I confessed one of my first monumental failures as a supportive husband to his pregnant wife. "Hearing the fetal heartbeat—with you in my arms, I choked with fear, because my mind skipped ahead that I would lose both of you."

"That's crazy."

"And then when you left the mansion during that rainstorm, I lost it in front of my men. I had to do damage control."

"That's why you made an example of Tony."

"To show my men that I was not ruled by my emotions for my wife."

"After that, you set expectations."

The litany of my sins continued. "I had to, Natalya. I wanted to show you how much I care for you, but I didn't want you to get the wrong idea because that would also make me vulnerable to that weakness."

"So what changed? How can I trust you not to be a coward again about love?"

Fuck it, I needed to touch her. She flinched when my hand tried to brush her face, so I settled by putting them on her knees. "What changed? The second I saw you and Elias, I started to change."

Her mouth curved into a sneer. "You sent me to sleep in the nursery."

"No, Natalya. *That* was what you wanted. I didn't want to put the onus on you, so I behaved like an ass. And no, I'm not gaslighting you. I'd been after you to hire a nanny. You were stressed, baby. I didn't know it was because you suspected me of sex trafficking."

Remorse tinged her eyes. "Sometimes I wondered if we could have avoided all these tragedies if I were honest with you from the start. I couldn't demand you tell me everything when I was hiding so many secrets of my own."

"We can't regret that now," I told her with conviction. "What happened, happened. This was more my fault than yours, Natalya. I was the manipulative bastard. You couldn't trust me because I didn't give you enough reason to do so. But now I have you back. I just want to move forward."

She dropped her gaze. "I have the Russians' money. What do we do? Doriana isn't responding anymore."

I crawled back to her side and faced the ocean. The *we* in her statement gave me hope. I'd take any crumbs she could give me and run with it. "We'll figure that out too." I put an arm around her and drew her close. There were a few seconds of resistance and those few seconds felt like minutes in which I held my breath, waiting for her to reject me.

She slumped into me in a way that hinted of surrender. The hope had turned into full-blown elation but there was a cloud still hovering, an Orlov-sized cloud.

"I'm so tired," she murmured.

I wasn't sure if she meant she was exhausted from our trip today or about the whole Russian thing.

"I've got you." I kissed the top of her head while she burrowed further into my chest. "I want you to relax. You're not alone in this anymore, all right?"

She didn't say the word but nodded in affirmation.

That was enough for me.

CHAPTER
Thirty-Six

NATALYA

"Something smells good. Is that garlic?"

Luca glanced away from the ingredients he was tossing in the skillet like he was a master chef on some cooking show. "Help yourself to coffee and take a seat. This is almost ready."

I slid onto a barstool behind the kitchen island, admiring his fine ass in gray sweatpants and his broad back in a white undershirt. A week had passed since we arrived in Montauk. Despite the good insulation in the house, I woke up to the smell of garlic. That was because I left the French doors to my room slightly open. I wanted the sound of the ocean to lull me to sleep and wake me up slowly. My sleep had been dreamless save for a few erotic ones starring Luca, my waking-up moments peaceful. There was something healing about this place and this isolation.

"What are you cooking? That looks like a lot for breakfast."

"Sausage fried rice."

My mouth watered. I told Luca how I discovered my love of eating leftover Chinese food at midnight during one of our beach walks.

"No wonder you had me cook a lot of rice yesterday," I said. Our discussion also included what type of rice made the best fried rice. All Asian cookbooks would tell you that cold leftover rice made the best. We mimicked the same activities we did when we were on our honeymoon. We ate at restaurants, watched movies on the wide-screen TV, we ate at home—I prepared dinner while breakfast was Luca's domain, or we simply ordered takeout. The exception was Luca didn't disappear for secret meetings and I didn't secretly get on my laptop.

And the sex? So far, there was no sex.

Luca turned around and set the giant platter of fried rice in front of me.

"That's a lot," I repeated.

"Eat what you can." He parked his ass beside me. "You'll need it for tonight."

I shook my head and laughed briefly. "We're really going to do this?"

"No backing out now."

On our second night in Montauk, Luca took me to an Argentinian restaurant. What was special about that night was it was usually closed on Thursdays during the off-season. We had the restaurant all to ourselves with our own string quartet playing romantic music. We also found out there was going to be a tango festival today.

Luca apparently knew how to dance the tango. Jealousy stabbed me in the chest when I wondered who he had danced with.

"It's hard to back out when I've already bought a new dress and new shoes." I laughed into my coffee even when the wings of nerves fluttered madly in my stomach. Of course I had to look up the tango scenes in *True Lies* and *Scent of a Woman*. Those were iconic, and they looked easy, sexy.

They were not easy.

I must have groaned, because Luca nudged my shoulder. "We won't have to do anything fancy. Just float around. I'll guide you."

I started digging into my breakfast and cocked my head in his direction. He was giving me those panty-melting gazes that further turned the flutter of butterflies in my stomach into a riot. I was feeling the no-sex strain in our interactions, and there was nothing more torturous than dancing the tango. It wasn't only the proximity, but the music itself. We practiced a bare minimum, because every time we did, an inferno overcame my body while drenching my panties at the same time. It could be sweat, but who was I kidding? I knew it affected Luca too.

Whoever said tango was a sensual dance wasn't lying.

"What do you want to do today?" he asked.

"We explored most of Montauk. I'm not sure if my body is aching from the dance practices or all the walking."

He grinned devilishly and shot me a look full of promise. "We can't have that now."

He'd been doing that from day one, but he never followed through. We always said good night in the middle of the kitchen before we headed into our own rooms.

Did he want me to make the first move? He was not unaffected. He was never ashamed of his boner when one of our dance rehearsals got too heated. I remembered when he asked me to swing my leg over his thigh and my pussy rubbed against those hard muscles, Luca's groan was reminiscent of those times he came inside me. And I think I left a wet spot on his pants.

"You're blushing," Luca observed. "You're too young to have hot flashes."

"Fuck you, Luca," I mumbled.

Before he took a sip of coffee, he muttered, "Soon."

And I could've just spontaneously combusted in my chair.

After breakfast and as was our routine, we walked on the beach. Our most meaningful conversations occurred here. I wondered if it was because we felt free to share our thoughts and feelings that were too big to contain within four walls. Here we trusted the ocean to cleanse our sins and shortcomings while also carrying away our heartaches we whispered to each other. I was ready to face another one.

"Did you bring your phone with you?" I asked.

Luca glanced at me with a puzzled look. "Yeah, why?"

"I was never ready," I told him. "But I think I am now."

He stopped walking. "Ready for what, baby?"

"You offered for me to look at pictures and videos of Elias you took in the past two years. At first it was because we didn't want to affect the way my memory returned." I inhaled sharply as if drawing strength from the ocean. I let out a slow exhale. "When all my memories returned?" Tears stung my eyes. "All I wanted was to hug my boy, but I was a coward not to witness all those years he'd spent without me."

"I get that." He pulled me down to the sand, angled one way to slip his phone out. "You were back in that mindset where you didn't feel worthy."

"Yes." That one word came out as a ragged syllable. "I feel better…about us."

Luca rolled his lips and nodded. "That's…good."

"We're not suddenly fixed, but I remember feeling hope when you started trying. I could feel that now in the past week as you continue to try. You're an open book. Honest." I put a hand over my heart. "It doesn't feel like heartache anymore."

He tapped the phone on his lips. "This might make you sad. I don't want you sad."

"I have to see them sometime," I said. "I want to see them now."

Luca nodded and swiped his phone. He handed it to me and I almost laughed when it was mostly pictures of Elias. I was sure he had a burner for the mafia stuff. I fortified my emotions, buckled down, and started scrolling. The first image of Elias was way older than what I expected.

A lump formed in my throat. "How old was he here?"

Luca looked at the picture for a while. "Seven months. I... Martha and Nessa might have more pictures before that age."

Our eyes met. There was pain reflected there.

"I was just..." A muscle twitched at his jawline. I imagined him grinding his molars. His mouth flattened and no words would come. The seagulls squawked above us. They weren't flapping their wings, but the wind beneath them kept them suspended. I reached for Luca's hand and squeezed.

He snatched me in his arms and hugged me tight. "I was just lost without you, baby. Our son...he was my lifeline. Without him, I don't think this man in front of you would exist." His voice sounded so broken, the walls around my heart cracked. The emotions that I'd once felt for him filtered through.

And when he pulled back, the anguish reflected in his eyes, of a man who'd lost his entire world, drew out the remnants of the love I used to feel for him.

The love before I found out about his deal with Papà.

The love before the time he missed Elias's birth.

The love before he stomped on my heart and told me of his expectations.

I forgive him, and it's liberating.

He swallowed hard. "Our son kept me tethered to this world. To what was right. Without him, I would have gone down the path that would have burned the family to ashes. Without Elias, I would have lost everything."

I cupped his jaw. "I'm glad you had him." Tears rolled down my cheeks, bringing with it the pain of missing them for two years, but also the love, a fabric with jagged edges defining the girl I once was, and the woman I was now.

"You and he are my world, *tesoro*," he enunciated. "Don't leave me again."

"I won't."

We stared at each other for a while, our lips a hairsbreadth away. I was afraid to close the distance because every time he kissed me, it only gave me heartache. Was that why he hesitated too?

He gave voice to my thoughts. "I'm afraid to kiss you."

"Why?"

"Because I might not be able to stop and I'll fuck you right here."

I laughed lightly because apparently, we had different reasons. "Yes, I don't think getting sand everywhere will be very comfortable." We leaned away at almost the same time.

My eyes returned to the phone, and I clicked play on the video. Elias was crawling. The tears returned, but this time it wasn't because of loss. It was of something else.

Luca cleared his throat. "This one." He pressed the triangle on another video. "I captured him at the right moment."

Elias crawled to the couch and used it to stand up. He looked over his shoulder right at the phone's camera.

"Come on, sport, you can do it." It was Luca's voice.

Elias made a cheery sound and toddled a few steps forward.

Luca said on the video, "Holy fuck."

I burst into tears. My baby's first steps.

CHAPTER
Thirty-Seven

NATALYA

I'd never taken so much care with my appearance since Paris. Makeup and hair on point. I took a curling iron to my hair and it gave me bouncy and sassy waves. My lashes were thick enough, but I extended them with mascara. Cat eyeliner and shimmery metallic green shadow. Very red lipstick.

My dress was made of black jersey with a plunging back and exposed my bare arms. The skirt hit right at mid-calf but was asymmetrical. I was so thankful to have packed sexy underwear because with all that twirling around, there was no doubt my panties were going to do a peekaboo.

The four-inch heels sexified the shape of my legs. I'd worn nothing but sneakers for the past two years, but before I disappeared, I was used to wearing heels at Mamma's insistence. Wearing them while practicing the dance with Luca, I was thankful for all those years of ballet that made me flexible because even though Luca said we were going to keep to the simple moves, many times we got carried away. He'd pull my leg over his thigh and drag me along.

It was so damned erotic.

Giving myself one last twirl in front of the mirror, I grabbed my sequined bag and left the room.

My heels clacked on the wooden floor. I came to the kitchen, but movement near the windows drew my attention. Luca was on the phone, but when he saw me, he immediately ended the call and stalked toward me.

He was wearing a tux that left no doubt it was custom made to fit his wide shoulders, the sharp lines crisp and tapered, accentuated his trim torso without being too tight.

"God, Natalya," he breathed, stopping a foot from me. "I don't think we'll make it out of the house." His eyes were nothing but raw, feral hunger. And they were eating me alive from head to toe. Speaking of which, my toes curled inside my shoes. With the four inches, it brought me almost to the top of Luca's chin.

The dress became too clingy and my nipples became sensitive to the jersey material.

"I don't know if I should bring a purse, but can I keep my lipstick in your pocket?"

"Sure, baby." His gaze was still busy devouring every inch of my body.

"So, shall we?" I was getting self-conscious.

He drew me close. "Are you sure you wanna leave?"

His hooded eyes stoked my awareness that very little encouragement was needed to just change plans and go at it.

"I—" I started.

The ringtone of a phone blasted between us.

It was Luca. He shook his head. "Sera wants to FaceTime."

"Oh, I had my phone on silent," I said. "I promised to show her my dress."

We talked to Sera and Elias every morning and before bedtime.

"You caught us at a bad time," Luca told his niece.

I grabbed his phone. "Don't believe him."

Sera was laughing, but she had Elias on her lap. Our boy tried to grab Sera's phone for himself.

"Look at Mamma," Sera said. "Oh my God, I didn't recognize you. I'm still getting used to you not being blonde. Show me."

I handed the phone back to Luca. "Here, hold it while I model."

Luca rolled his eyes but did as he was told. "You don't want to see how I look?"

"Eh," Sera said. "I've seen you enough times in a tux."

I laughed. Luca held the phone toward me while I backed up a couple of steps and did a couple of tango steps, including a twirl.

Sera squealed. "I looooove it!"

I walked back to Luca, and he hauled me against him. "The things I want to do to you."

"Yeah, yeah, you've been threatening for a week."

"Oh my, I can just feel the tension between you two. Say bye, Elias."

"Wait..." I choked on my amusement that was reflected on Sera's face. The impatience of the man beside me was as palpable as the throbbing between my legs.

"No more waiting," Luca grumbled. "Bye, sport."

"Bye, Papà..." Elias looked at me, then at Sera, then back at me again. "Bye, Waf-waf."

Sera laughed. "You guys need to fix that."

"For real." I stared at Luca. "Next time we're here, it'll be the three of us."

"Sounds good to me." Luca didn't wait a second longer and ended the call.

Pocketing the phone, he ushered me to the exit without another word.

"Are we in a rush?"

He glared at me as though his impatience was my fault. "I'm just doing the right thing here." I detected the strain in his voice. "After the tango..." His eyes glittered with possessive intent. "You're all mine."

I could orgasm to those words and the rawness with how he said them.

The Audi SUV was already parked at the entrance. Luca helped me into the seat and closed the door. But he braced his hands on the roof and stared at me through the tinted window. He just stood there looking at me and making me nervous. He straightened and rapped my window lightly with the side of his fist before he prowled around the front of the vehicle, his eyes on the ground, hands in his pockets as though he was still deep in thought.

When he slid into the driver's side, I asked, "What was that all about?"

He didn't look at me and started the engine. "I'll give you three guesses."

I wasn't really as dense as I sounded, but I was suddenly feeling all powerful. "You're having second thoughts of doing the tango in front of everyone?"

He used the heel of one hand to steer the vehicle around. Points for making that look sexy.

"It's related." The Audi started up the driveway.

"You'd rather stay at home and cuddle and watch movies?" I tongue-in-cheeked.

Still staring straight ahead, he emitted a brief chuckle. It was a few seconds before he stole a glance at me, then he returned his attention to the road. "Oh, *tesoro*, you're really asking for it."

I'd been asking for it since day three. We had more self-restraint than a dating couple with a three-date rule. But given everything that had happened between us, I thought we were handling things just fine. Reconnecting was harder than falling in love for the first time because of all the baggage that came with it.

Forget fine, I was damned proud of how far we'd come. Until tonight, I didn't know how much I'd missed the girl who had the confidence to flirt with her husband.

Husband. I finally could refer to Luca as my husband and my own possessiveness had been sharpening its claws. Much to my relief, he'd stopped walking on eggshells around me. He didn't rein in his dirty talk. He didn't disguise his desire for me. It went a long way to restoring the confidence I'd lost. I still had to work on deserving Elias, but with Luca at my side, I didn't feel that it was insurmountable.

Luca glanced at me again when I didn't respond. I merely shot him a flirtatious smile. The SUV had turned onto Montauk Highway and it was a brief five minutes to the festival. Whether he could see it in the dim light of the interior or not, I didn't really care. I thought how our talks on the beach had been so liberating and cleansing. This final one where I allowed myself to enjoy Elias's first two years was cathartic. All emotions. All at once. The anger was less. The sadness was there and the bittersweet, but it ended with joy and hope and forgiveness. And hope was what propelled me the whole day because I'd finally reached the point of allowing my heart to fall in love with my husband again.

How could I hold back and let myself doubt when Luca never moved on?

He searched for me.

He fought another man for me and almost killed him.

He built a shrine for me.

I wasn't even appalled the first time I saw it. It was quite endearing. But my emotions then were for a man grieving for a woman that wasn't me. The day when we visited the burnt house was the day I felt all that grief directed at me. As I thought back to it now, that must have triggered how I remembered my laptop from the teddy bear.

The brain and heart worked in mysterious ways.

"You're deep in thought," he said. "Care to share?"

"I'm thinking about the shrine you made for me."

Another rumble of laughter shook his chest. It suited Luca as much as his brooding did. We shared so much unfettered joy in the past few days, of shared laughter over silly things like burnt toast to how sneaky the gulls were in dropping bread in the freshwater pond to lure the fish to the surface.

"And you're not afraid of how obsessed I am with you?" he asked.

"It seemed obsessive, especially since you weren't sure if I was alive or dead."

"I stopped lying to myself a long time ago," he said, turning into the parking lot of the festival. "I've always been obsessed. I just didn't know it…"

He left those words hanging, and I mulled them over while he looked for a space to park. Nessa said he was the king of denial. I bit my inner cheek to keep from laughing. Luca really was.

"*Vaffanculo*," he cursed at the car in front of us with the matching gesture. "Make up your mind."

"There's a lot of parking over on that end. You don't have to squeeze in beside that car."

"I don't want you walking a long way in those heels," Luca said shortly.

"Aw," I said. "That's sweet, but you can carry me, *caro*."

Luca smiled at me. "Of course I can and I will."

The tango festival was at a recreation center that had an outdoor space. I wasn't sure if the organizers were going to hold it outside, though, unless they had a wooden platform for the dancers. I cringed at the idea of dancing on concrete and grass.

Plus, the weather called for rain later that night.

Festivalgoers crowded the parking lot. They were not confined to the people who arrived in cars, but also those who walked in from nearby hotels and establishments.

Luca finally parked the Audi. "Don't get down. I'll come get you."

"You don't have to carry me. I was kidding."

I clasped my fingers together. I couldn't believe the giddiness and excitement I was feeling. Luca rounded the vehicle, adjusting his bow tie. When he opened my door, he held out his hand. I put mine in his and gingerly slid to the ground.

His eyes darkened when I looked up at him. I was taken aback by the naked hunger I saw there. Oh boy. "Don't carry me, okay? It's a short distance, and I probably should get used to these shoes."

He tucked my hand on his elbow and whispered in my ear, "Just remember, I'm at your service."

The way he said *service* scattered my thoughts, and I had an image of his face between my legs while I was flat on my back with my legs spread and cocked frog-style. I was looking at myself from above and I realized it had been from a dream. Thankfully, my motor skills were in order as I put one foot ahead of the other. The sounds of the orchestra drifted into the parking lot and it added to the energy of the night.

As we entered the facility, someone checked our tickets and wrapped our event tags around our wrists. Past the check-in table, there were groups of people already practicing. The festival had offered private lessons throughout the week, but Luca said I didn't need them since he taught me himself.

They held the competition outdoors. Festival lights reminiscent of fiestas surrounded the raised platform in the middle of the lawn.

An orchestra was playing on a separate raised stage with dominant melodies from violins and cellos.

We got our drinks. Mine was a strawberry margarita while Luca had the Malbec. Then we walked around to check the vast array of Argentinian finger foods. I think I'd eaten three empanadas, but I was careful not to eat too much. Luca and I had our caricature drawn by an artist. There were other activities to pass the time and in between we watched the competition. The dance moves were awe-inspiring, but I couldn't envision myself doing all the fancy leg flicking.

Luca was behind me, hugging me close. I glanced up at him. "I'd like to continue our dancing when we go home, but I don't think I want to do all that leg-flicking stuff. I don't want to end up with a dislocated kneecap."

He gave a hearty chuckle and sipped his wine. "Not a fan of that either. I prefer the leg wrap."

I rolled my eyes. "I bet you do."

When the emcee started announcing the winners, Luca put our things in the vehicle and returned in time for the opening of the main dance floor to the public. However, reminiscent of the street tango of Buenos Aires, several platforms were also set up in different spots around the center. Soon, it was a jumble of music, punching up the craziness of the night.

To prevent a crowded dance floor, each couple was assigned sets, but we got on the first one.

I breathed a sigh of relief when the orchestra started with "Por Una Cabeza." It was the quintessential tango music of the movies, a melody people were familiar with and one Luca and I loved rehearsing to.

Picking up my right hand, Luca led me to the dance floor. My feet were like lead and wobbled on my heels, but I kept my chin up. When we claimed our space, we made a quarter turn to face each other. Luca stepped into me and caressed my face like he was touching the most precious jewel in the world. Our gazes locked, the intensity in his eyes trapping the oxygen in my lungs. His hand trailed down my side before he picked up my right hand once more and I put my left one on his shoulder.

We started to move.

At first I was too busy remembering the steps—when to walk, when to do the figure of eight, and its reverse.

Luca's hand on my back straightened my spine, and he said in a commanding voice, "Eyes on me, *tesoro*."

I felt those words all the way between my legs and I saw all the passion and smolder in Luca's eyes.

"Just watch me, baby," he murmured.

His tone and the crescendo of the music sunk all the way into my veins and set my skin on fire. Soon, the dance floor receded to just us. Even when Luca moved behind me and we walked diagonally one way, and then back, I flowed with him seamlessly. We spun around, fluid like water, and when he lifted me up and then lowered me into a dip, I trusted him not to let me fall.

He pulled me back into an embrace and we continued to spin, our gazes locked on each other, while we traced the floor with our steps. My confidence grew, and when I hooked my leg over his thigh and he back-stepped, dragging me along with my legs spread, the dance became a sensual expression between lovers. An ode to our passion. When the music faded and stopped, we stood there, breathless for a few beats.

His head lowered to meet mine, nose to nose. "You were magnificent, *tesoro*."

"So were you."

"You want to try the others?" he asked.

"Sure."

He grinned, knowing as much as I did we were testing our

limits. We flitted from one dance platform to another. Each dance was foreplay that tuned our awareness for each other to a peak.

It was close to midnight when I fell into Luca's arms in surrender. "I can't feel my feet."

"I'll massage them for you when we get home."

His hair was unkempt, and it made him look less like a polished Lucifer in a tuxedo, more like a mortal man.

A big fat drop of rain fell on my cheek. "Uh-oh," I said. "Party's over."

And true to my words, the big fat drops turned into a downpour. "Come on." Luca hurriedly shed his jacket and put it over me while we zigzagged through the crowd, rounding the rec center, and then raced for our SUV. We were laughing and soaked by the time we reached the Audi. He lifted me in, then hurried around to slide into the driver's side.

The moment he closed his door, the laughter died on our lips and tension pulled our gazes together.

We crashed into each other, our lips locking and devouring. His fingers dug into my hair as he angled my head so he could go deeper. He made an impatient sound and broke the kiss.

I was dazed and wet and aroused.

"This is a bad place to do this," he growled, firing the engine. "Now it's a madhouse to get out."

My hand went between my legs. My pussy was pulsing with need and my whole body was in a weird state of shivering because I was wet but fevered because I very much wanted to fuck.

"Do not make yourself come," he warned.

CHAPTER
Thirty-Eight

Luca

"Every one of your orgasms is mine, *capisce*?"

I'd been hard all night. But I had masochistic tendencies when it came to Natalya. It had been a torturous week and I couldn't count the times I used my hand to get relief. But no more. I was going to sink into her tight, wet pussy and pound into her until I had my fill.

She exhaled a ragged breath with a shiver.

"You cold?" Frowning, I pulled out of the parking space, mindful of people, and then turned on the heat in the SUV.

"I don't know whether I'm cold or hot," she responded. "I did like the heat of your body, though. You're steaming."

"You're not helping, *tesoro*." I finally got the SUV back on the road. Thank fuck, the house wasn't too far away. The windshield wipers were going at top speed as the crowd scattered and vehicles honked.

The traffic was slow going, and I managed a glance at her. "You have no idea how much I want to taste that sweet pussy. You were hot all over my thigh tonight."

She gave a secretive smile. "I was."

"If only the people around us knew how much I wanted to toss up those skirts and push my tongue inside your wet cunt."

"Not helping, Luca," she whined, her hand going back between her thighs. "I love your crude mouth."

"You're going to love it some more." I grabbed her wrist. "Stop that."

"I'm about to explode," she breathed.

"You," I gritted. "Will explode on my mouth." I let go of her wrist and gripped the steering wheel with both hands. The urge to thrust my fingers into her was so strong, that was the only restraint I could think of. Fortunately, the cars started moving. The rain lessened to a steady drum around us.

"What a perfect ending with the rain," Natalya said when we got clear of the clusterfuck after the festival. Most of the vehicles were heading the opposite direction. Thank fuck.

It was dark on our way back and I couldn't see her expression, but I could imagine a happy gleam in her eyes from her voice.

"It's only going to get more perfect."

"How so, sir?"

My dick twitched at the sass. I was hard as a rock and I couldn't wait to lay her bare to my eyes. It was a need two years in the making. When I saw the gravel driveway, I almost wept with relief. My foot rode the gas and the back tires kicked up pebbles. We bounced on the uneven road and that didn't help the images of bouncing in my mind.

"The last time I fucked you was when you were pregnant." My voice was strained.

"God, that would mean that was also the last time I had a cock inside me," she whispered, her tone bemused.

"And my cock is all you're going to have," I told her. If the thought of Bailey's mouth on her made me want to kill the man, I couldn't imagine if they had fucked.

The Audi screeched in front of the garage.

"You're not parking it inside?"

I switched off the engine and glanced at her. "No one is around for miles, and I've had this fantasy of you all night."

Her throat bobbed. "What fantasy?"

I flashed her a grin and exited the vehicle. I looked down at my shoes. I flicked a finger on my nose and cast Natalya a quick glance. I could feel her eyes on me, apprehensive. Meanwhile, every molecule in my body was roaring for release.

Soon, cocksuckers.

I would be balls deep inside my wife.

Fuck, the thought almost made me come. I should have beat one out earlier tonight.

I stared at Natalya through the windshield.

Her eyes were so wary, it almost made me laugh. But that would defeat the whole purpose and destroy the mood.

I opened the door, but before she could get down. I stopped her.

"What…?"

"Brace, baby."

My fingers grabbed her outside thighs and quickly spun her in her seat so both legs were facing me.

"Luca…" she whimpered.

"My tongue aches to lick that pretty pussy, baby." My fingers went beneath her skirt and sought the heat that had been driving me crazy all night. When I touched her molten center, she made a sound at the back of her throat, almost like a suppressed sob.

I leaned my head closer as my fingers circled her clit. It felt swollen, and I could almost feel its throbbing. But was it the blood pounding in my ears? "Are you aching here?"

"Yes," she gasped.

My control snapped. I yanked her ass forward, and she fell against the seat. Spreading her thighs apart, I dove in and the smell of her drove me feral. I pushed the thin scrap of fabric aside and thrust my tongue into her hole, scooping all her wetness before dragging my tongue up her pink flesh, fastening around her swollen clit, and sucked.

She screamed and clawed at my hair.

I poured two years of need in the way I attacked her pussy with my mouth. Lick, flick, suck. I added my fingers, feeling those muscles inside her clench around me. Checking on her, I saw she was panting hard, but when she noticed I had stopped, she looked at me.

"Why did you stop?"

While my fingers continued to finger-fuck her, I leaned over her to give her a taste of herself in a deep, searing kiss, then I resumed eating her out.

Fuck, I needed this. She squirmed in the seat, and I had only noticed how those fucking pointy heels were digging into my sides, probably making me bleed. But did I care? No. It wasn't the first time I fucked her and bled all over her.

My mouth was exactly where it wanted to be. On her pussy with my tongue inside it. After the initial attack, I licked her more slowly, up and down her wet slit, and then nibbled at the tender flesh between the juncture of her thigh.

My cock pulsed behind my pants.

I dragged her to a sitting position like she was a rag doll.

"Luca...I want more."

"I know, baby. Wrap your arms around my neck." She did as she was told. I bumped the car door closed. I marched with her wrapped around me and went to the garage keypad and entered the code.

The gates opened.

The second we entered the house, Natalya gripped my face and kissed me. Her need shouted for mine. I spun us around so she was against the wall. But we kissed and kissed. We kissed away the years and the heartache, the sorrow and the grief. We kissed away the time we would never get back, but as my tongue devoured hers, I could only taste hope.

When we broke apart, I went for her panties while she went for my buckle.

"*Tesoro*," I gritted, flicking her hands away. "Let me do this."

I stripped away her panties and got them off one foot, but I was already surging up and lifting her against the wall. "Inside. I need inside you. Right now."

Once my cock was out, I wasted no time thrusting inside her. We both yelled at the same time, from the emotion, from the intensity, from the significance of the moment. We kept still, joined, and stared at each other.

"Are you going to move?" she gasped.

"I'm afraid it's going to be over too fast." My voice was ragged with the mix of yearning and lust. I dropped my forehead to hers. "I'm afraid this isn't real and you're still gone. I don't want it to be over too fast because I've waited so long for this moment."

I withdrew slightly, and the pleasure almost blinded me. "My God. I haven't tasted this pussy in years, haven't been inside you for two fucking years." Madness rampaged inside me with those thoughts. She must have felt it too, because she stiffened.

"I'm here now, Luca." She cupped my jaw as if to tame a wild beast. "I'm real and here to stay."

I thrust back inside her and ground against her clit, making her cry out again. "You promise?" I growled against her lips.

"Yes, yes," she chanted. "That feels so good, ahhhh."

Unleashing all, I pounded into her in brutal upthrusts. With one hand, I ripped the dress's neckline off and exposed her tits right at my mouth level. I sucked and bit and grazed her nipple. Her inner muscles continued to clench around me. Somewhere in the back of my mind, I thought about consequences, but at that moment, I didn't care.

I needed more inside her and snatched her from the wall. With my hands supporting her ass and still connected, I walked to the bedroom and crashed on the mattress. My cock went deeper and Natalya moaned loudly. Her pussy had my dick in a death grip, my balls were drawn up. One more...I had to...

"Natalya." Her name was three syllables of choked emotions. "I love you so much, *tesoro*. Please say you still love me." I felt every word of my tortured whisper. I had never begged anyone to love me. But I would beg her until the end of time and I had my wife's love again. One I hoped to deserve with this second chance.

Her eyes glazed with tears. "*Car*o, I still love you...so so much."

Relief and exhilaration merged into one joy-filled exhale. Since Natalya returned, I'd been living my life with a death sentence, waiting for my heart to be ripped out in punishment for my sins during our marriage. My mouth crashed on hers for one last kiss.

I pounded deep this time and didn't stop. Tingles shot up my spine, heat gripped my balls and I emptied inside her in one final thrust. I continued moving and shuddering at the same time. The edges of my vision dimmed with the intense pleasure ratcheting inside me. One explosive moment and I was putty in her hands. I collapsed on top of her. At her distressed sound, I rolled over, trying to catch my breath.

Natalya rolled into me and put her hand over my heart.

"We need to get out of these wet clothes." I managed a rough chuckle.

"You feel so warm," she protested.

"I don't want you to get sick, baby." The top of the blankets was damp. I removed the dress I'd torn and put her under the comforter. "I promised you a foot massage."

"I'm going to fall asleep," she mumbled.

"Be right back."

Natalya

When Luca returned, I didn't want to get out from under the blankets.

"Come on, baby, time to get you into the bath."

"Do I have to?" I whined.

"You don't have to do anything." His voice came to me in the darkness. Strong arms scooped and lifted my body. If there was one thing I couldn't fault with Luca, he took care of me toward the end of my pregnancy. I'd been a cynic too, thinking that it was all because he wanted me to have a healthy baby, and didn't equate it as caring toward a wife. In retrospect, his actions made sense. I didn't hallucinate the love in his eyes during those unguarded moments. He'd just been fighting it. He felt safe to show his caring behind the walls of his expectations. Did that erase what he had done? No. But I loved him enough to give him a second chance.

And after seeing what he had in store for me in the bathroom, tears of happiness pricked my eyes.

"Oh, Luca." My voice warbled as emotions fought against the words.

In the dim light and against the white marble and gold accents, candles of different sizes were lit. Bouquets of peonies scattered around the bathroom, with petals scattered around the tiles and on the water.

"I was lucky that besides rose petals, peonies worked too," he said, voice soft, but its effect was loud and clear where it mattered. My heart was bursting with love for this man who considered himself a villain, but he had journeyed to become my hero. He walked us to the bathtub and lowered me into the warm water. I sighed when my feet touched the therapeutic bath.

"I can't believe you did all this." My voice came out gushy and I didn't care.

He smiled wryly, getting into the opposite end of the tub and immediately picked up my foot and massaged its sole. My eyes rolled back at the pleasure and I moaned. "Oh my God, that's almost like an orgasm."

The massage stopped. "I'm offended, *tesoro*."

A languid smile of surrender curved my mouth. "Don't be. This has been one of the best nights of my life."

He looked thoughtful. "I have to confess I had help from my sister and niece. These were delivered when you were taking a nap."

"I enjoy subterfuge in case you forgot."

He continued massaging my foot, sliding those powerful hands along my calf muscles. If I were Mrs. B, I would be purring right now.

"About that. No more secrets, *capisce*?"

"Okay," I mumbled.

"We have more to discuss, but let's enjoy tonight."

He picked up my other foot.

"I'm all yours, *caro*," I murmured happily.

I must have fallen asleep in the bathtub because when I woke up it was to the shrill ring of Luca's phone.

He was wrapped around me, and my back was sweaty when he moved away. The mattress shifted under his weight.

"Moretti. This better—" He cut off.

My spine stiffened.

"When?" His growl was grittier, having just woken up.

I was wide awake now.

I sat up and looked at him. "What is it?" My thoughts went to Elias. My heart pounded erratically. Even though my son was protected by what could be deemed as Fort Knox, I felt antsy that we were not there. There was no guilt though because Luca and I needed this trip to sort out our relationship so we could become better parents.

"Okay, talk to you in a few hours."

Luca ended the call and switched on the night lamp, turning to me.

"That was Dario," he said, his voice grim. "Orlov knows about the money."

I bit my lower lip. "The money I took?"

"Yeah. And he wants it back."

CHAPTER
Thirty-Nine

Luca

"I don't appreciate being blindsided again, Luca," Ange said on our video conference call with Dario.

"I told you Natalya got her memory back." My brother was still annoyed I took off for New York without telling him. Admittedly, hierarchy-wise, I should have told Ange because he was the under-boss, but it wasn't as if I left no one in charge. Dom told me Ange had complained to him. I would have put a stop to that shit, but Dom said it was more like an uncle-nephew conversation. I called bullshit.

"But not that she had Orlov's money all along!" Ange snapped. "We've been negotiating with this prick's demands for almost a year, and your wife could have saved us all that trouble."

"What are his demands now?" I asked.

"Either we give him the money or Natalya works for him on a few jobs," Ange said.

"I'll talk to Natalya about the former, but fuck working for him." The thought of Orlov having any conversation with my wife made me want to smash something. For the first time, I understood Vincenzo's act of suppressing Natalya's genius. If the wrong organization got hold of Natalya, they could exploit her skills against her will. Well, good thing she married me. I would die to protect her. "I don't want him to have any control over my wife."

"I told him as much," Dario said. "He gave another option."

"Really?" I quirked a brow. "What?"

"The Game of Bosses."

I didn't answer for a while. I wasn't in top shape. The last one I competed in, I had to prepare for months. Orlov's skill level was unknown, and I was also four years older than him.

"That's an option."

"No," Ange growled. "He'll use that as an excuse to kill you."

"Didn't you suggest it the last time we talked?"

"I was joking. I didn't think you'd do it. And there was an extra week to prepare if you did."

"You have no faith in me, brother?" Ange was probably right. But what was the other option? I doubt Natalya wanted to give the money back. Come to think of it, I didn't want her to give it back because that would mean all we'd gone through for the past two years would have been for nothing.

"Ask Natalya for the money. If she really loves you, she'll return it."

"Love doesn't work that way." I spoke the words easily, and I surprised myself, and apparently, my brother and Dario too, judging from the way their brows shot to their hairlines.

"Oh, you're an expert now?" Ange scoffed.

"Love doesn't work that way because you don't ask the person you love to give up her integrity."

"She's a daughter of the Galluzo. She should know better."

"She's a Moretti. We never make money off that shit."

"This conversation is going nowhere. We'll talk when you get back to Chicago." Ange cut off his feed, leaving Dario and me on the call.

"What do you think?" I asked him.

"Ange underestimates you," Dario said. "Didn't you just kick Bailey's ass? That was with no practice."

"I doubt that man ever stepped into a cage," I said quietly, thoughtfully. "How many weeks is it to the fight?"

"Three."

Fuck.

That was cutting it close. And I wasn't sure what shape I was in. Double fuck.

"Absolutely not, Luca. You're not going to fight in a death match."

My wife's eyes flashed at me in fury. She was magnificent. She'd also been pissed at me since we returned from Montauk. Dom and a convoy of De Lucci soldiers escorted us back to Manhattan. My nephew raised the alert just in case a faction of the Russian mafia in New York thought that ambushing us or snatching my wife to curry favor with Orlov was a good idea.

We were at Sera and Matteo's apartment on Fifth Avenue where we were staying overnight before our flight back to Chicago.

Dom called a family meeting and not the mafia family. In the living room were Sera, Carlotta, and Natalya. Elias was at her feet playing toy trucks with Gio, both kids oblivious to the uproar in the Moretti family. Dom was standing beside his dad, Paulie.

"It's not a death match." I was sitting on a lone couch with an ankle crossed over a knee in a very nonchalant posture. I didn't want my wife to worry. I'd worry about it later.

"I'll return the money," Natalya said.

I raised a brow. "You'd do that for me?"

"Of course! You're my husband and I love you."

She said that too quickly. My eyes narrowed. "There's a catch."

My wife waved a hand. "I'll just steal it again and not get caught."

Paulie, Dom, and Sera laughed. Carlotta made the sign of the cross and said, "My dear sister-in-law, what you're doing is admirable, but that's not going to appease my brother."

"Nor the Russians," I said. "Orlov's going to make you swear to stop stealing from him, and you'll have to comply."

"Honor among thieves," Paulie muttered.

"Yes."

"Then I'll return it and that'll be that," she said, but by the mutinous set of her jaw, I didn't trust her. She'd probably do it and tell me later.

"There's still a catch."

All through our exchange our spectators' eyes bounced from my wife to me, and everyone except Carlotta seemed to find it amusing. That sister of mine had the least sense of humor. It was odd that she married the light-hearted Paulie, whose brother, Cesar, was the broody De Lucci and Sera's father-in-law. Both men had been my mentors when Chicago branched out heavily into real estate. We were one big happy fucking family in more ways than one. But now, more than ever, I was glad they had our backs while things in Chicago were brewing.

"Not really. As long as you don't tell me to stop hacking human traffickers."

"You're upsetting the balance in the underworld, baby."

Dom and Paulie were nodding vigorously. "You tell him, Natalya."

"What's the matter with you two?" Carlotta snapped at her son and husband. "We're supposed to be discouraging Luca from getting his ass kicked."

"You and Ange," I tsked. "Always thinking that I have no chance against the Russian."

"They're known for their stringent training," my sister pointed out.

That was true. Dario kept me updated on the movements of our key opponents and allies. Orlov was a gym rat and had put on stacks of muscles in recent years. That could work to my advantage because that meant he wasn't as quick.

"Yet I beat Orlov ten years ago."

"You trained for three months," Sera said. "And you were younger."

"Age and training aside, the more I think about it, the more I want to get this over and done with. Orlov is going to bring up the rematch every time we have to negotiate a deal. It would get Koshkin off my back too since I'm sure he'll be whining to Koshkin that my wife stole his money."

"I talked to Koshkin," Dom said. "He's finding it amusing that Natalya was the one who stole the money, but as head of the Moscow Cadre, Koshkin has to go with what Orlov decides. Human trafficking is still a part of their business."

"And Koshkin and I have an understanding," I countered. "I do not tell them how to run their business as long as their shit doesn't touch Chicago." I speared a look at my wife. "But if they target you, all bets are off. It's going to be war. I don't care if it's against Koshkin."

"You can use the Game of Bosses to make your demands," Dom said. "So far the chatter on the Dark Web is that Chicago was responsible for thwarting Orlov's human trafficking business, but there are no details that it was Natalya." Dom looked at my wife. "Orlov himself wouldn't want to make it known that his operations were easily infiltrated by hackers. How old were you then?"

"I just turned twenty-two when I interfered in his arrangement with Santino," Natalya said. "But there's more to it." She clamped her mouth in a thin line and I knew she was uncomfortable talking about her associates.

Dom flicked his gaze to me, and I gave a shake of my head. He didn't know that Natalya belonged to a network of hackers who targeted human traffickers. Natalya also hadn't been able to contact Doriana. The encrypted channel she shared with her had been deactivated. There was also this other hacker who she'd been online with the night she was taken. She was hesitant to dig deeper, and I didn't press her. Her self-confidence had taken a beating, knowing that she'd been careless and compromised her partners.

"Orlov has yet to contact me directly, but I'm not a fan of waiting around." I glanced at Natalya. "You might as well accompany me to Chicago."

CHAPTER
Forty

NATALYA

"Doriana is dead."

I stared at the private message from The Friar who now had a new code name Dead Poet. I wasn't sure if I was communicating with the same hacker, just as he wasn't sure I was the same Chimera from two years ago. I'd taken all precautions when I'd logged back into the Dark Web, this time with a foolproof infrastructure that Luca's formidable IT department had vetted.

Dead_Poet: The compromise came from her end. She'd never recovered from the Santino leak.

Mrs_B's revenge: Yet she continued to hand us jobs.

Dead_Poet: I suspect one of her sources had been playing her. Using her. I thought at first it was you.

Mrs_B's revenge: You still don't trust me, do you?

Dead_Poet: No.

Mrs_B's revenge: Fair enough. So it's on me to decide where to distribute the money.

Dead_Poet: Yeah. I already unloaded mine.

I didn't answer him. And our cursors sat blinking for a while. I didn't know if I was going to join another vigilante network on the Dark Web. Organized crime was getting way too savvy with their own army of hackers. I wasn't invincible as I had thought before. Oh, the hubris of youth.

Mrs_B's revenge: I guess this is it.

Dead_Poet: Yeah. Good luck.

I backed out of the chatroom before he did and unplugged the extra appliance to quarantine any attempts to introduce malware. We hadn't exposed our true enemy, but Luca and I had our suspicions. For Luca, it had been since I disappeared, while I'd only drawn mine from the last week since I regained my memory.

Carmine.

It broke my heart. He'd been my confidant since I'd been a teenager.

Luca confessed he used Carmine to find out how to manipulate me, and I admitted how Carmine had played mind games with me. It was all about control. Everyone underestimated him, thinking he was weak when he was a master chess player.

He had also gone missing.

Which was why Papà and Mamma couldn't come over. It was another blow to the leadership of the Galluzo mafia and it was about to fall apart, which could mean a bloody war.

This was what Luca was trying to avoid on top of talking to Orlov.

My husband was in meetings, and my son was sleeping peacefully beside me. We returned to Chicago this morning. It was the first time I'd been to Luca's penthouse. It took up an entire floor of the M condominium in Lincoln Park. It was one of the many properties of the Chicago crime family and the security was top-notch. Ange and Dario had apartments below us.

Gingerly, I left the bed because it took Elias a while to fall asleep since he kept looking for Gio. Sera and Matteo and the rest of the De Luccis would be in Chicago for the match if Luca accepted Orlov's challenge.

I stared at the Chicago skyline and wondered if Luca was right all along that Tralestelle was where it was better to raise a family. That would depend on how solid his relationship was going to be with Ange. Now, more than ever, Luca needed a strong underboss.

I checked the time on the clock by the nightstand. It was half past midnight. Luca had been gone for three hours and I could only pray that cooler heads would prevail.

Luca

"You're a grandstander as much as I am, Moretti." Orlov smirked at me from his seat in the conference room. "Gladiators originated in Rome."

"A slight correction," Dario said. "It originated from the Etruscans, which make them still Italian. They held fights at funerals of noblemen."

"Whose funeral are we talking about?" I asked dryly.

"Your father-in-law's, perhaps?" Orlov taunted me before turning to Umberto "Berto" Pirelli, who Vincenzo tapped to take over after Carmine flew the coop. The Galluzo mafia experienced a series of bad luck that unfortunately started when Sera turned down the arranged marriage with Santino. It put me in a difficult position, but I wouldn't have met Natalya. I wouldn't have Elias. Fate worked in mysterious ways, but I hated to leave things to fate when the future of my family was at stake. I wanted to ensure their safety.

"Vincenzo and I have an understanding. We will put our misunderstanding behind us. He was ill-advised by his inner circle and Carmine." Berto looked at me. He was too scholarly looking to be the boss of his clan, but I underestimated my wife, and the deadliest enforcers I knew were low-key. "And I hope you will back my bid for underboss, Moretti."

"We will discuss after this." I looked at Dario, who nodded tightly. My consigliere had more personal stakes in this.

In the room with us was Orlov, two of his brigadiers—the equivalent of our capos, and his adviser. Berto made the trip with two of his soldiers who were not allowed in the room. As my guest, I extended him the protection of Chicago. Dario was on my right and Ange was on my left.

This was an unprecedented sit-down with complicated issues because it involved the daughter of the Galluzo who was my wife. The power shift of the Galluzo affected their relationship with both Orlov and my organization.

"Natalya is not returning your money," I told Orlov in measured tones that left no doubt there was no negotiation. "We will be turning it over to organizations that help human trafficking victims."

Orlov gave a bitter laugh. "You're such a Boy Scout. You get married and surrender your balls to your wife?"

I shrugged. "She takes good care of them. You should take a

wife sometime and maybe you wouldn't need to spend two hours a day in the gym."

Orlov's eyes narrowed into malicious slits. "You're having me watched."

"As if you're not doing the same."

"Is that why you hide in your mansion? You're afraid I will spy on you?"

"Not at all. I'm tired of the city."

"Or you're enjoying fatherhood too much," one of Orlov's brigadiers said.

My hand automatically sought the place on my body where a gun would have been. Fortunately for the fucker, we agreed to check our weapons at the door because tempers were bound to fray and killing each other was not in everyone's best interest.

"Refrain from any reference to my son," I spoke evenly. "You might not make it home tonight."

"He threatens me, Orlov," the man sputtered.

"Then stop acting like an idiot," Orlov said sharply. "That is why I offer the Game of Bosses. Natalya Conte Moretti threatened my organization first."

"We do this, my wife is a clean slate to you. You will also tell us who gave her up."

"I'm rethinking this," the Russian muttered. "What do I really get out of this deal? I lose my leverage over you."

"I don't like people having leverage over me. My wife and son's safety are my priority. If I do not extract this promise from you to leave her alone, we go to war." I looked at Berto. "You will back me on this if you want my influence for underboss. Your organization is at a critical point. If it falls, then ruthless clans will take over. You need to restore the balance and I could help you." I turned my attention back to Orlov. "I'll meet you in a rematch."

Orlov stroked his blond goatee and didn't respond immediately, but I was used to his methods. He was trying to keep me on edge, but what he didn't know was I had already made up my mind. Protect Natalya at all costs. The Russian knew I had the support of New York. Koshkin was neutral because the Game of Bosses was his baby, and Moscow made the most money.

Finally, he said, "You know, with your wife's skills we can make a lot of money…cryptocurrency—"

"Find your own hacker—"

"And marry her?" Orlov raised a brow.

"Do we have a deal, Orlov?" I enunciated each word.

"Fine."

I stood up immediately to signal the end of the meeting. There was one other issue I needed to clear up within my organization without the Russians in the room.

Orlov and his brigadiers walked over to me, and we shook hands.

When the Russians left, Ange closed the door. My brother wasn't happy. Despite the grudge he held when he expected to be named boss, politics still wasn't his domain and he preferred the streets.

The immediate problem was between Dario and Berto.

Right now, they were eyeing each other like opponents in a coliseum.

The reason I manipulated Vincenzo to reject Berto's bid for underboss in favor of Carmine was because his father was responsible for the death of Dario's own. That was twenty years ago when there was bad blood between Chicago and the Galluzo.

I didn't have a chance to discuss this with Dario before Berto showed up.

Just as well. I hated repeating myself.

"Gentlemen." I gestured for them to sit. Ange kept his position at the door to keep an eye on the two. Sometimes I felt guilty for doubting my brother's loyalty. His loyalty would always be for the good of the Chicago crime family. Now that I had Natalya back in my arms, I could see past my resentment. Ange and I balanced each other out.

Dario's jaw was clenched. He was feeling murderous to be in the same room as his sworn enemy.

"My apologies, Dario, for not discussing with you sooner. There was not enough time," I said.

"My apologies, too," Berto said. "Vincenzo also extends his. We realize my appearance here was sudden."

"You shouldn't have kept Carmine's disappearance a secret for three days," Dario gritted. "My sources say he'd been acting panicked since the news of Natalya's return reached them."

"That won't happen again."

"Before you promise that." I looked at my consigliere. "Do we have a problem with this new leadership, Dario?"

"I don't have a choice, do I?" Dario said sarcastically. "We should have followed our instincts before and let the Galluzo self-destruct in their problems." He let out a sigh. "But I've grown fond of Natalya and do not wish to see her legacy destroyed." He looked at me. "You have my support." And then at Berto. "Let's not let the sins of the father be visited upon the sons." He stood and extended his arm.

Berto also stood, and both men shook hands.

Ange and I looked at each other, our faces barely changing expressions, but the atmosphere of relief cleared the air in the room.

Now to get ready for the games.

Fuck me.

CHAPTER
Forty-One

My husband was fucking hot.

Sweaty, muscles bunched, eyes glinting with killer instinct.

He was sparring with Ange on the mat. Apparently, they grew up doing this. This was a familiar scene from what I'd witnessed from my father's men back home. Most of them thought they would be a Don Corleone one day and the *The Godfather* movies became their creed, but for the mafiosi interested in mixed martial arts and the allure of underground fighting, Bruce Lee was their idol.

Ange was built more powerfully, but Luca was faster. They'd been trading hits and kicks for the past half hour until Luca executed a spinning back kick. It struck Ange's jaw so hard I heard a cringe-inducing thwack. The blow sent Ange to his knees, and his mouthguard went flying.

"*Madone!*" Dario called a break. "Enough!"

Luca smiled, his lips more puffy than usual with the mouthguard. When he held out a hand to Ange, his brother swatted it away.

Uh-oh.

Luca made a "what the hell" gesture and said something to his brother before he held out his hand again. This time Ange accepted the help. I couldn't see his expression, but his body language indicated he'd accepted the hand-up grudgingly. When Luca hauled his brother to his feet, they exchanged quick hugs, but the way my husband clasped Ange's neck with an equally swift neck squeeze made my heart clench.

Dario told me they hadn't sparred in years since Luca took over as boss. Both kept in shape separately.

It was week two of Luca's training, and what a revelation. Because I'd seen Luca mostly in elegant threads, no way did I picture him as this brutal fighter. What happened with Brad was a mere blip of what Luca could do, especially when up against an opponent like Ange. Since they'd fought before, they were familiar with each other's strengths and weaknesses.

Luca came off the mat and stalked toward me. From the gleam in his eyes, I was his new prey, and my lady parts pulsed with excitement. I was already wet from all his grunting during practice. Another benefit of fighting was the adrenaline and being the recipient of the excess aggression. Sadly, we had to pick up my parents from the airport and that was why Elias was with me. Besides, Luca was at the beginning of his two-week sex moratorium.

He stepped straight into me and gave me a kiss. Heat radiated off him.

"Papà, up!" Elias chirped.

"Later, sport." He ruffled his hair. "I need to shower."

While waiting for Luca, I chatted with Dario. Around five minutes into our conversation, Tony walked into the gym and headed straight for Dario to whisper something into his ear.

They excused themselves and left me and Elias standing there.

"We go?" my son asked, pouting.

I led him to the dumbbell area so he would have something to occupy his mind, but I was getting impatient. Good thing Luca appeared.

"You're by yourself?" he asked. There were employees and mafia soldiers working out around the gym but my husband didn't seem pleased. "Where's Dario?"

Before I could answer him, the man in question returned with Tony.

The expression on their faces made me uneasy.

"Detective Voss is in the lobby," Dario said. "Ange had been giving him the runaround for the past week, but he refused to leave this time. He must have followed you to this building."

"Who's Detective Voss?" I asked.

"He's the detective on your case." Luca checked his watch. "We're going to be late if we chat with him."

"We can leave through the basement," Tony suggested.

"Do you want to show your face to the detective?" Luca asked me. "We can decide when to bring him up to speed."

"Will I get in trouble for the hacking?"

"I doubt it, baby. The money was illegal, but seeing you will give the detective a bone to chew on," Luca said with derision. "Make him feel like he's making progress."

"He's just doing his job," I told my husband.

Luca gave me a long look. "We need to talk about your allegiances, *tesoro*. That detective wants nothing more than to put me away."

Dario said, "Should we rethink letting Natalya meet the detective?"

Annoyed at the men, I went over to Elias and picked up his

hand. "Come on. The sooner we get this over with, the better. Tony, you can bring the vehicle to the entrance of the building."

Startled that I made the call, Tony's eyes darted to Luca. "Boss?"

"You heard her." Luca put his hand on the small of my back and led me into the elevator. I watched our reflections on the stainless-steel doors. Luca would steal glances at me, but I compressed my lips to keep from speaking. He'd just have to trust me how to handle the detective and I was glad he didn't countermand what I told Tony. If we were going to work as a couple, he should trust me to do the right thing as his wife.

I heard more than a few exhales in the elevator. Particularly, Dario's. Because he was Luca's adviser and this was a significant moment where my husband didn't defer to his suggestion.

When the elevator reached the lobby and we stepped out, I imme-diately clocked the detective. He reminded me of the hard-boiled investigators of noir films. Sort of like Humphrey Bogart with a craggy face that couldn't be described as handsome or attractive, but he still had presence. He rose from the couched seating in front of the recep-tion. Mafia soldiers patrolled the lobby along with security contractors.

His rough face softened with a smile directed at me. "Mrs. Moretti." He approached us and we stopped a foot from each other. "Detective Terry Voss. I'm so glad to see you're all right. I heard about your amnesia."

Ange had already briefed the LEOs about the reason for my long absence. We shook hands, and before Luca could cut in, I said, "As you can see, I'm perfectly fine, but you caught us at a bad time. I'm sure we can arrange a meeting later?" I gave the practiced smile that Mamma always insisted I use in public. Not too wide and no teeth.

The detective scratched his jaw. "I have new information."

"You know who took my wife?" Luca asked.

"We've established that outliers of both Orlov's and your organization had planned it," Detective Voss said. "All those men disappeared." The detective's eyes bore into Luca, and I feared Dario was correct and that we should have prepared better and had gotten our stories straight. "We've found remains that could be one of them."

Luca tensed. "Who?"

"I can't talk about an ongoing investigation."

Dario cut in, "We're done here. I know you have to take Mrs. Moretti's statement at some point. We'll contact you."

"Wanna go." Elias rubbed his eyes and was making a fuss. There was no better time for him to be on the brink of a tantrum.

Luca picked up our son. "We're going, sport."

"I'm sorry, but we really have to go," I told the detective.

"That's fine." Voss smiled in a way that put me on edge. He handed me a card. "Give me a call anytime."

We headed for the door. And it could be my imagination that my husband's strides quickened more than usual, like he couldn't get us away fast enough from the detective.

Detective Voss called behind us. "By the way…"

Luca stopped right before the doors of the building, but he didn't turn around, and merely cocked his head to the left, waiting for Voss to say something.

"Have you heard anything interesting about that abandoned building at Bromley Industrial Park?"

My husband turned and shrugged. "There are several in that area."

The detective walked up to us. Luca was relaxed, but tension pinged between the two, reminding me of gunslingers at high noon.

He stopped in front of us, the same distance as before, and that was when I realized he wanted to be far enough to see everything and everyone around him. "Just wondering if you heard anything unusual. Vehicles that belonged to some of your associates have been seen in that area." The detective tipped an imaginary fedora. "Thanks for your time."

He left the building ahead of us.

Luca lost his relaxed demeanor and cursed, "Fuck!"

CHAPTER
Forty~Two

Luca

"*Porca puttana!*"

Natalya glanced at me sharply. She'd already scolded me about cussing so much in front of our son, especially when Elias just repeated the word *fuck* after me.

"He could be bluffing," Dario said.

He could be right. The body they had found couldn't be from our handiwork.

We were in the three-vehicle Escalade convoy on the way to pick up Natalya's parents. Dario was supposed to ride in the other SUV, but we needed to discuss this.

"Would someone please explain to me what this is all about?" my wife asked.

"We do our interrogations in one of those buildings' basements." I ground my molars. Interrogation was a euphemism, but my meaning was not lost on Natalya. The building in question was under a shell company that no way in hell a Chicago PD detective could trace back to us.

"Oh my God," she breathed. "Have you used it recently?"

"No, and neither has Ange. It was heavily used immediately after your disappearance." I had blocked what I had done to protect my son's innocence, but the darkness was lurking at the edges of consciousness. "We did things, Natalya, I don't care to repeat to you, but it was necessary to eliminate the rats in our organization."

"Could be a relative who squealed to the police," Tony, who was our driver, said.

"Text Ange. Make sure he hasn't used that basement in the last six months." After each interrogation, the basement was thoroughly bleached. But forensics could use reagents like luminol to revive the DNA in blood. Still, the efficacy faded with time. Two years was a lot of time. My lungs loosened with relief, but not enough because I was worried for my brother.

"But why bring it up now?" Natalya asked. "And they said they discovered a body."

"Could be one of Orlov's," I told her. "There's no way it would be one of ours." Because we used an incinerator, but I didn't have to give my wife that detail either.

"I'm sorry if I messed up," Natalya whispered.

My gaze whipped to her, and I gathered her left hand in mine. "No, *tesoro*. You did great. And it's good we're aware that the detective has this information. We have our own informants in the Chicago PD."

"I texted one of them just now," Dario said. "He can meet me after his shift. That would be after we pick up Vincenzo and Elena."

"I don't want you to worry," I told Natalya gently. "Just focus on your parents, *capisce*?"

. . .

When we met Vincenzo and Elena at the Moretti hangar, I wished I could send them back to Italy. Or maybe I could tell the immigration agent who met us there to tell them that their passports were denied entry. I nearly yanked Natalya behind me when the excitement on Elena's face turned to horror.

Her first words to her daughter were, "*Cara mia*, your hair!"

But if there was one thing I'd learned about Natalya, she'd gained a lot of confidence since her time away from me. I hated that I wasn't the one who helped her grow, but took pride that she outwitted us all with her intelligence.

I couldn't see my wife's expression, but at least Vincenzo engulfed his daughter in a hug that spoke of the lost years and the depth of grief that we experienced. There were tears in her father's eyes, and I took solace in them. Elena followed her husband's lead and filled her eyes with the requisite tears, and it made me despise her more.

~

Natalya

"Oh, *bambolina*," my father cried as he swept me into those arms that comforted me as a child. The familiar scent of his cigar, and that spicy cologne, was a memory that existed during my amnesia. My reaction to my mother troubled me. There was something akin to hatred. I despised her for suppressing my growth through guilt.

My father pulled away and gripped both my cheeks, giving it an emotional squeeze. "I thought you were dead, and we had a funeral for you."

A ghost walked over my grave.

Mamma made the sign of the cross. "We didn't want your soul to rot in purgatory."

Fuck you, Mamma.

I concentrated on Papà's round face. His hair had grown whiter, and it pained me to see all the stress catch up with him. But I wasn't his innocent daughter anymore. I'd been on the other side of the law, even Luca temporarily questioned whose side I was on. I was a vigilante, and with my self-revelations today, I had to make sure I could live in the world where the two men I loved existed. On my terms.

"That's such a flattering welcome from you, Elena." The icy tone of my husband wasn't lost on anyone.

Luckily, Elias was done being ignored and pulled away from Luca's hand. "Nonno! Nonno!"

"Here's my *bombolino*." Papà proudly lifted my son. "You are so big already."

"Strong too!" My son showed his biceps and looked at Luca. "Like Papà."

A familiar fear gripped my heart, but my husband put his arm around me, giving my shoulder a squeeze. Reminding me that my father was not going to take our son away anymore. It was like reprocessing all these emotions again, and I was glad Luca was at my side while I did this. I was feeling more secure in his love.

When we returned to the M building, we put our parents in a unit three floors down from the penthouse. As usual, my mother complained. My father had pulled Luca away to discuss his new underboss, leaving me with Mamma.

"This is not the way to treat your parents." Mamma sniffed, looking around the apartment that had an amazing view of the Chicago skyline. "We should be staying with you in the penthouse."

"Luca and I want privacy."

"For what?"

Lord, please give me patience. "We just found each other again."

"Didn't you two go away to the Hamptons?"

I didn't correct her on the exact location. It wouldn't have mattered to Mamma, and she would have waved her hand in an impatient gesture. "After spending over two years apart, we're just only becoming a family. I'm a different person."

She looked me up and down. "And is this different person going to wear jeans and a T-shirt to dinner, or is this your way to spite me?"

"Mamma, what is really wrong with you?" I snapped. "You can't be happy that your daughter is alive? Or are you blaming me for the constant hiding you and Papà had to go through because of the turmoil the Galluzo keeps going through?"

"I don't believe your amnesia is real." Her proclamation caught me off guard. "I think you just wanted to escape your life with Luca."

"You think I would leave my son?" I whispered, my voice hoarse, because a pain in my chest that had planted itself since childhood grew so big, I thought I would throw up.

"You've always been selfish."

"Are we referring to that time you had your heart attack?"

"What else?" she flared. "Do you know how depressed I've been? How I lived in fear that I was going to get another one."

"And you still blame me…"

"It was always your fault." With a huff, she yanked out the last of her clothes to hang in the closet.

Meanwhile, I stood frozen. I'd always been her punching bag. My heart cried for the girl who had never experienced a mother's love. Elias's whole life flashed before me and I knew deep in my heart with a mother's instinct that I would never speak such venom to my son. Standing there as I took in Mamma's petulance, I understood that not all people were meant to be parents, and especially not Elena Conte.

With that last thought, the last thread of my mother's control over me frayed and snapped.

"I need to check on dinner." I didn't. Martha had it under control, but I wasn't going to be Mamma's punching bag anymore. "I'll send Tony to get you or just get on the elevator. You can't miss the button for the penthouse."

"Why I never…"

I didn't wait for Mamma's tirade about why I was the worst daughter ever born and left the room, running into Papà and Luca.

Luca saw my face and his own grew scary.

"What did Elena say now?" Papà sighed. It was just words, and he wasn't going to say anything to my mother. I understood his stance because if he defended me, then Mamma would bring up a litany of his shortcomings as a husband and Papà was allergic to that conversation.

"The usual." I kissed his cheek and didn't explain any further and he seemed okay with the response, but not my husband.

Luca stopped me from leaving. "Are you okay?"

"Yes." I stared at the entrance to the room where Papà had disappeared before lifting my gaze to his. "I'm finally freaking okay with all this. Since you're here, I won't send Tony down to escort them."

"I'll take care of it."

I nodded briefly. Though I didn't want Luca fighting my battles, I couldn't deny him the satisfaction. It didn't escape my notice that he was hanging on by his own thread. And I might have a tiny bit of satisfaction about what was about to happen.

CHAPTER
Forty-Three

Luca

"What did my daughter complain about now?"

My shoe barely stepped into the room before this poor excuse of a mother went on a tirade.

"Elena." Vincenzo's face was red. "Enough. We just got Natalya back. Can't we just be thankful for that?"

Her mother put a hand over her chest, panting. "I'm having a hard time breathing. Can you get my blood pressure monitor, Vincenzo?"

This manipulative bitch. "Stop, Vincenzo."

Horrified, Elena looked at me, but Natalya's father did as I ordered. He knew his wife was faking it. If there was something Carmine had hinted at, it was Elena's tendency to use her health to manipulate the people around her. I'd checked on their medical records recently and Elena was healthier than her husband with acceptable blood pressure levels. I wouldn't even care if she dropped dead at my feet. It might save us a bunch of headaches. Vincenzo, in the meantime, was more at risk, and knowing Natalya had genuine love for her father, I felt the need to protect him more.

I advanced on her. Her eyes widened. Even Vincenzo held out an arm. "Now look here, Moretti."

I pointed a finger at Conte to silence him. I owned his balls, what with Berto and me on better terms than he was with his under-boss. Vincenzo was a mere figurehead.

"Listen up, Elena. Be thankful you're here and not hiding in some shithole in Italy because Berto and I negotiated your travel," I gritted. "But I will not tolerate you insulting or belittling my wife, *capisce*? While you're under *our* roof, and *our* guests, I do not want to see a single frown line on my wife's face because of you. I would prefer if you not talk to her. But if you can act like a mother who actually cares that her daughter is alive, care that you have a daughter who fights for what's right and uses her God-given talent to do so, then start groveling now. God knows she deserves a better mother." Vincenzo did not escape my anger. "A better father. I still don't understand how you're not proud of what she has done and accomplished."

"It was for her protection," Vincenzo said. "We panicked when she hacked into her school. My advisers said it was not good to have a daughter with that skill because our enemies might exploit her, and we couldn't find a suitable match for her. You know how most of these bosses have egos."

"Can't say I don't have an ego, but I would be proud to have a wife who can outwit me."

"You're of the new breed of bosses, Moretti."

"I did tell Natalya we need more women in our ranks because men are idiots. But that's not the point I'm making. I don't want Natalya to feel insecure in her own home." My ire at Elena rose again. "If I hear a single word criticizing my wife of anything—and

I mean *anything*—I'm sending both of you packing for Italy and leaving Berto to deal with you."

"How dare you—"

"Shut up, Elena," Vincenzo snapped. "You've done enough."

Natalya's father walked up to me with a solemn expression. He gripped my jaw and gave me a kiss on both cheeks. His eyes were suspiciously glassy. "Thank you for being a good husband to Natalya. I may not have been the best father, but"—he pounded his chest—"it feels good here, knowing if I die, she is in good hands."

Vincenzo had the inclination for theatrics, but I could see the sincerity in his eyes.

"We'll see you upstairs." I cleared my throat and turned around. I proceeded down the hallway, clenching and unclenching my fists, not realizing how if Elena continued to run her mouth, the desire to strangle her would be there.

When the elevator doors slid open, Ange was about to step out. He moved aside to let me in and punched the button for the penthouse.

"Natalya sent me to rescue Elena from you."

A grin touched my mouth. "She did, did she?"

"Elena is a piece of work."

"Being married to a man with too much power will do that to you," I said. When we reached the penthouse, I saw Natalya with Martha. They finished setting the table. Tony was the one watching over Elias. They were in front of the television watching cartoons of a certain type I believed were meant more for the likes of Tony.

My wife gave me a brief glance, and I gave her a reassuring one that communicated I hadn't murdered her mother yet.

"Come on, sport, you shouldn't be watching that."

"Stewie!" My son chortled. I glanced at Tony. "No evening cartoons."

"Elias likes Stewie."

"I heard him swear in the last episode," I muttered.

Tony laughed. "Elias already said the F word in the car."

"I still need to get on you about that, Luca," Natalya called from the kitchen.

"Thanks for reminding my wife."

"Don't worry, boss, they cut out the good stuff on this channel."

It was apparent, curbing the cursing with Elias was a losing battle given Tony was his constant companion. He had genuine affection for my son, which went a long way in my trust. Swear words aside.

When I went into the kitchen, I told Natalya, "All the cursing out of Elias's mouth is Tony's fault."

She and Martha exchanged glances and shook their heads in what I could only describe as resignation.

The study was at the end of the west hallway. When I first married Natalya and when I was in Chicago, I only used the penthouse for crashing. Most of our meetings were in the evenings at clubs or restaurants. I wasn't lying to Natalya that it was useless to play house with me and she was already pregnant then. I'd since changed my routine. I left Ange to handle the street business, and I rarely entered clubs anymore.

We were doing less and earning more, taking advantage of technology. That was the smart shift in our operations.

"Where's Dario?" I asked.

"He's meeting his contact with the Chicago PD right now," Ange said. "I'd say Voss is bluffing. I sent one of the capos and his crew to go over every surface with luminol. We can change the flooring and paint the walls if you want, but it would be weirder if we have construction vans over there with no permits."

"Does it need any cosmetic repairs?"

"Nah, we just changed that shit five years ago. We were able to sneak things in."

"And we don't want to do it now when there are eyes on us." I walked to the end of the study, where I had the corner view of Lincoln Park. "Voss wants to rattle us. I bet he paid a visit to Orlov too."

"Speaking of our Russian friend, he's taking this tournament seriously."

I turned away from the window and took a seat behind my desk. Opening the drawer, I pulled out the bottle of special whiskey. I tipped my chin to where the glasses were. "What's Orlov up to? Living in the gym?"

Ange slid a glass to me. I filled his and then mine. "*Salute.*"

My brother took a measured sip before saying, "No, he's trying to trim down."

I quirked a brow. "Really?" I swirled the amber liquid in my glass.

"He knows you're faster." Ange chuckled, fished out his phone, and swiped it to the photo app. "Forgot to send these to you. This is from our guy watching him."

"What the hell?" I had a good chuckle. It was several pics and videos of Orlov with an entourage of trainers running alongside him like he was competing for a world-boxing heavyweight title.

"What are the odds now?" I asked.

"He's still the underdog, three to one."

"Hmm...that's a lot of pressure."

"That came from Koshkin's camp," Ange said. "You know how the Russians are. They'll swing the odds in their favor."

"Maybe we should bet on Orlov, then."

Ange grinned. He knew members of the administration of both camps were forbidden to bet on the Orlov-Moretti matchup. The soldiers could, though.

"You're evenly matched. It could go either way. Your southpaw was a well-kept secret ten years ago. No one knew how powerful your left hook was back then, but I see you've developed quite a back kick." My brother leaned forward. "We still have to work on your ground game. If Orlov pins you to the mat, you're in trouble. He still outweighs you by thirty pounds. And if those biceps wrap around your neck."

"Game over."

"Not exactly." Ange's grin grew wider. "We can work on that too."

"In other words, you're going to enjoy knocking me out in the next two weeks," I said dryly.

My brother's face took on an evil expression that had me rethinking our training sessions.

CHAPTER
Forty~Four

LUCA

It was fight day, and I hated everyone. Which was ironic as fuck because the penthouse was full of people. Sera and Matteo flew in this morning with Dom and Carlotta. The rest of the De Luccis were staying in New York because of a big fight that would determine the leadership of the Rossi crime family.

The Game of Bosses was one of the biggest underworld events in recent history ever since the pay-per-view matches became popular. Europe had more matches than the U.S. where the games were only supposed to be in Las Vegas and New York. With my acceptance of Orlov's challenge, the basement of Skyland Towers had been converted into an underground fighting arena.

I was relieved we weren't fighting over concrete flooring which was the norm in illegal matches. Egotistical and high-maintenance bosses had its perks. The day before, Ange and I had stopped training and visited the site. Our crew and my IT team had monitored the installation. Orlov had sent his own men as well.

A rap on the door drew my attention. Dom stepped in. "What are you doing holed up in here?"

"Do you think I enjoy hearing how people are betting that Orlov will win?" I snapped.

Dom laughed. The fucker.

He closed the door and walked up to the oak desk. "You shouldn't take it personally. The odds are against him. They make more money that way."

"If. He. Wins," I said. "I have no intention of losing, so why even risk it?" When Dom couldn't stop laughing, I asked, "Who did you bet on?"

My nephew laughed harder and I could only sit and stew and glare at him. When he finally stopped to say something, there were tears in his eyes. "Do you really want me to answer that? I'm rooting for you to win, Zio, but it's much more fun to bet on the underdog."

"You have no loyalty."

"It's a bet. Nothing personal."

"It's feeling very personal."

"If it makes you feel better, Sera put her money on you. She also made Matteo promise to bet on you."

"See, now there's loyalty."

"Aw, come on, Zio. It's just a game."

I did see the humor in this. It didn't mean I had to make him feel good about betting against his own blood.

I rose from my chair and walked over to my nephew. He eyed me warily, but his mouth was twitching.

I leaned into him. "Watch me hold a grudge."

He patted my back. "But you love me. Come on. Join the fun."

· · ·

The smell in the kitchen of toasting garlic bread made my mouth water. If I hadn't been on a regimented diet in the past three weeks, the craving wouldn't be this bad. Carlotta's recipe of beef lasagna had always been my favorite and I made fucking sure Natalya saved me a piece or two for after the fight.

"The secret is in the béchamel," Carlotta said. She was teaching Natalya how to make it. "And use fresh sausages."

"She knows that, Lottie." I walked into the kitchen.

"Hey, Zio." Sera had both elbows on the counter.

"You're learning too?" I asked my niece.

"No. Matteo knows how to make it. I just eat."

"She's waiting for the first bite," Carlotta said.

Martha came over with bread. "You hungry?"

I shrugged. "I could eat, but you know, no bread until after the fight."

Natalya moved to my side and clasped my hand, lifting her mouth for a kiss. I gave her a quick one. It was all I could do not to haul her into our bedroom and fuck her.

"I'll get your meal number three," she said with all sweetness.

"I can do it myself."

"Talk to your sister and niece," she said. "You haven't spent enough time together. And we transferred your food to the utility room after our groceries this morning." Her voice faded as she left the kitchen.

"So." Carlotta put the lasagna in the oven. "I noticed Elena isn't that chatty."

"What was that?" I cupped my ear mockingly. "Did you say catty?"

Martha shook her head with a hidden smile and returned to her spot of chopping vegetables.

"Ah, Luca, *fratello mio*." My sister made a soundless laugh. Her chest shook with it. "She's your mother-in-law. Make nice."

"You don't know what you're talking about. You haven't met one like Elena." I looked over my shoulder at the living room, where most of the men were watching a UFC fight. My mother-in-law was looking after Elias and seemed to be content enough.

"I'm so lucky with mine," Sera said dreamily.

"Hey, I would make a good mother-in-law," Carlotta said. "If my children ever get their act together and—"

"He's too busy being boss and Lucia is too busy breaking hearts," I said. "Look at me. I wouldn't be married if Sera didn't jilt—"

"There was no jilting done," my niece snapped at me.

We continued arguing. It was much like the old times and I realized how much I missed this part of the family. Lottie didn't get along with Emilio's third wife and rarely visited. Our age gap was twenty years, and she'd been more mothering than a typical sibling. Sera was more like a sister to me than a niece. Hell, I was only four years older than Dom.

"What's the holdup with the food?" Ange came into the kitchen.

Martha approached our group bearing a platter. "These wings are fresh out of the air fryer."

My brother made a face. "Eh, what happened to frying it in real oil?"

"So Luca can also eat," Martha said.

"Here, caro." Natalya returned with my lunch of sweet potato and grilled chicken. I'd leaned up and packed on muscle in the past three weeks. Ange was of the opinion I should have put on more fat for padding, but hell, I wasn't a wrestler and I preferred staying lean for the fight, so I depended on Dom for meal plan advice since the De Luccis owned a boxing gym.

"What's with all this babying of Luca?" Ange scoffed.

"He is our baby brother." Carlotta stood beside me and ruffled my hair. "And it's his big day."

"Eat it up, Zio." Dom laughed, coming up beside my brother. I wasn't sure if he meant all the mothering or the food.

"Are you going to help warm me up later?" I asked my nephew.

"Matteo and I are coming." Dom picked up a wing and did fancy footwork shit.

"We're going to meet you at the venue," Sera said. "The girls are going to have their hair and makeup done. Dom's crew will be with us."

"It's a basement fight," I reminded them.

"A high-class basement fight..." Dom said. "Just like the movies."

Hours later, I was sick of warming up.

"Remind me never to sign up for one of these again."

Dom left the gym to take a call and left Matteo to keep me moving.

"It's not working." Sera's husband was holding the warm-up mitts. He was talking to Ange who was sitting on the bench watching us. The chicken wings gave my brother acid-reflux, so it had been left to Dom and Matteo to get me through the drills. "He's still thinking about the fight."

"Of course I'm thinking about the fight. It's in an hour," I muttered.

"Give me rapid punches," Matteo ordered.

"You're supposed to warm me up, not wear me out." I lowered my arms. "I'm done."

Ange laughed. "Maybe you should meditate."

I glared at my brother. "Does it look like I fucking meditate?"

"Bruce Lee did." Matteo joined Ange on the bench. "And he's the father of mixed martial arts."

"I bet you Orlov does it," Ange mused. "We should have kept track of things he's been doing other than training."

"What? Check for his aura?" I scoffed.

"Yeah, your chakras don't seem aligned," Matteo said.

"Fuck you, De Lucci. What the fuck do you know about fucking chakras?"

He and Ange burst out laughing and high-fived. "Yep, his aggression is peaking."

I blew out a breath and shook my head. "You're supposed to keep me aggressive, not give me a stroke by annoying me to death."

The door slammed open and a grim-looking Dom walked into the room, followed by soldiers from both our families, including my two capos.

He stopped before me. "We have a problem."

Ange and Matteo got up slowly from their seats.

"What? Don't tell me Orlov is backing out?"

"No. Someone took Natalya."

CHAPTER
Forty~Five

LUCA

"How the fuck did this happen?" I snarled, grabbing Dom's collar. "They were your soldiers."

"Let's calm down." His face shut down into a stoic mask.

I let him go and turned to Ange. "Where's Dario?"

The name of my consigliere barely left my mouth when he entered the facility and hustled across the gym. He had my phone and had been screening my calls, so I could concentrate on the fight.

"You have a message."

It was from an unknown number that asked me to call back. "Can you track Natalya?" I asked.

"She's not wearing any trackers right now," Dario said.

"Have you asked for the footage from the salon the girls went to?" Ange asked Dom.

"The camera is broken."

"All right." My head spun with possibilities. "Everyone out

except Dom and Ange and Dario." I looked at Matteo. "You can stay."

My whole body surged with adrenaline. I was so pumped, it was a wonder the phone didn't crack when Dario handed it to me. My fingers were rubbery when I handled the device and I was all thumbs when I clicked the return call.

The phone rang twice before a familiar voice answered.

"Moretti."

Carmine. "What the fuck did you do to Natalya?"

"She's fine. She just needs to help me win some money."

"I want to talk to her."

"In a moment. I need some things to be clear to you first."

"You want me to throw the fight?" That was the first thing that came to me because Ange and I discussed this. Natalya was already free from Orlov when I agreed to the fight. There was no stopping us from using another entity to bet on the underdog and make us a lot of money.

"The odds are now five to one," Carmine said. "News has spread how much you and your brother have been training and you are going to kick Orlov's ass, so it's important that Natalya's kidnapping should be kept a secret."

I glanced at Dom, and he nodded. "Everyone's on gag order."

Dario said he also issued that directive.

"And if I throw the fight? How will I know you won't hurt Natalya out of spite?"

"You won't."

"I want to see her or I'm not doing this. Call me back with video."

I ended the call. The urge to hurl the phone against the wall was overwhelming. Rage was running a heated circuit through my body. I wasn't sure if I could control it and not kill Orlov by accident.

"Whose suggestion was it to go to the salon?" I asked.

The men looked at each other.

Matteo stepped forward. "I only heard Sera mention it. She said Natalya was feeling sorry for her mother and wanted to do something nice for her."

"Dario, confiscate Elena's phone and check all her messages." When my consigliere hadn't moved a single muscle, I snarled, "Now!"

He bowed his head and excused himself from the huddle. I checked my phone, willing it to ring. I was about to punch the number again, thinking that Carmine's pride was getting the better of him because I ended the call abruptly when it rang with an incoming video call.

Carmine's face filled the screen.

"Where the fuck is Natalya?"

"Luca!" a voice cried.

"Natalya."

"Never. Hang up. On me. Again," Carmine said coldly.

It took tremendous effort not to spew every derogative name at him. I thought my jaw would crack when I spoke in a calm and respectful tone. "Natalya, *per favore.*"

"Much better."

When my wife's face filled the screen, my knees nearly buckled with relief. It was enough that she was alive for now. "Baby, are you okay?"

"I'm fine." She sniffed. "I can't believe my cousin would do this."

"He's not your cousin."

"I'm sorry you have to throw the fight for me."

I froze. I hadn't agreed to it. And this was not the fierce Natalya I knew. I swallowed. "I'll do anything for you, *tesoro.* You know this, right?"

"I know," she whispered. "I'm so sorry, Luca."

Carmine's face filled the screen again. "There. You have proof of life. Now win me my money. And don't do it too quickly. It needs to look real. End it in the fourth round."

"What if Orlov kicks my ass and does it in the first round?"

"You're stronger than that. Otherwise, they'll know you threw the fight."

"One more thing, Carmine. Hurt her and I will make it my mission to hunt you down and make sure your death is slow. There's no place on this earth you can hide, *capisce*?"

His smile was full of mockery, and this time, I let him end the call.

~

Natalya

"I want you to transfer half the money to these and divide the rest between these bets." Carmine pointed to the screen in front of me.

My stomach knotted in anxiety, not sure if we could pull this off, but I had enough proof that we could. Carmine had changed in the past two years. Physically, his face had acquired lines of ruthlessness I had not seen before, or maybe it was a mask the whole time. I saw him now as a weasel hell-bent on his long con and plan for revenge. No trace remained of the young man who'd been sympathetic to an introverted fourteen-year-old girl. He was a man who had a terrible start in life, and Papà, who believed in him, gave him the opportunity to lead the Galluzo as underboss. The betrayal hurt deeper than I first expected, but I had two weeks to get used to it. To build my hatred for what he had done and feel no remorse for what I was about to do.

"Did you hear me?" He tapped impatiently at the back of my chair.

"I heard you," I replied tonelessly. "Hundred fifty million spread equally between these numbered accounts. How do you want to place the bets?"

"Put a hundred on Orlov, and fifty that Luca will lose by the fourth round." He chuckled with villainous glee. "Your husband is going to receive the humiliation of his life."

Tears pricked my eyes. *Hang on, Luca. Just hang on, caro. I will fix this.* I couldn't remember how many times I tried to talk myself out of this. The fight and training occupied Luca's mind, and he didn't notice my anxiety. It also helped that Mamma and Papà were here.

As I worked on his money, Carmine continued to rant. "You had to go and have amnesia and ruin my plans."

My fingers quit typing on the keyboard. "You cost me two years of my life I can never get back." The screen blurred as I remembered Elias's first step, of Luca starting to make the turn into putting us first. The image of baby Elias sleeping on Luca's chest was imprinted on my mind forever. I would never get that time back. And that was why I needed to do this.

Carmine spun my chair around. "And it was thirty years of mine. I deserved everything the Galluzo had to offer, and I almost got it all, but your husband had to go fall in love with you and fight to keep your son."

At my blank stare, he sneered. "You were supposed to end up hating him when you found out that he was giving up Elias to Vincenzo. You were going to go with your son, divorce his ass, and I would make you my queen."

I recoiled from Carmine.

"Oh, don't give me that look." He straightened and stepped away from me in disgust. "You don't turn me on sexually at all. I would have allowed you lovers and I would have mine. We would have kept Vincenzo's legacy alive. Now the Pirellis are taking over and it's the end of the Conte line."

The door opened and a red-haired mercenary walked in. Carmine didn't have any mafia soldiers on his payroll. He depended on private military contractors. They were the ones who took me from the salon.

"The game is about to start. Are all the bets in?" Red asked.

"Yes, they're in," I answered. Carmine was going to ask me anyway. I angled the screen in his direction, detailing the clear placements of bets.

"Do you mind if I watch in here, sir?" Red asked.

"Sure, why not? You set up the feed." Carmine took the chair beside me. "We should have popcorn and champagne, don't you think?"

By this time, my stomach was a wasteland of bubbling acid, and I didn't think I could eat anything, least of all popcorn. Even the water tasted sour and only aggravated the bile backing up my throat.

With all eyes riveted on the wide screen on the wall, Red pumped up the volume just as the crowd dressed in suits and cocktail dresses gathered around the twenty-foot octagon. Composed of associates of the Russian and Italian mafia, low crisscross fences surrounded the area preventing them from spilling over. The match was livestreamed globally through a server controlled by Koshkin and he was predicted to make ten billion dollars from the Game of Bosses.

Orlov and Luca were the game openers at six p.m., the only slot available because it was a last-minute addition to the schedule. This served me well because I couldn't stand the suspense.

"There will be no introduction of the fighters," the announcer spoke on the loudspeaker. "You all know who they are." Illegal distribution of the video would be under threat of being hunted down by the Russian mafia, and since the inception of the games in the nineties, not one fight had been leaked. At one point, I wondered why they didn't wear masks, but the participants were not regular fighters who did this as a living and found the face cover cumbersome and claustrophobic. The tattoos were a dead giveaway anyway.

I identified Luca immediately, and my heart skipped, or rather leapt, extra beats. The filter of the television couldn't mask the rage on his face. For those who didn't know his expressions like I did, that wasn't stoicism. When the camera did a close-up, I could see the fire in his eyes. A muscle was pulsing at his jaw. In his corner were Dom and Ange.

The Russian was more flamboyant, and he was spewing challenges at Luca.

"This is fun. And to think Orlov didn't know I was doing him a favor," Carmine made commentary.

Interesting that the referees were the ones wearing masks although it made sense in a way since vendettas were embedded into the DNA of the two men meeting on the mat. The fighters met in the center and listened to the rules. Luca said the rules were just guidelines and kidney punches, eye gouging, and below-the-belt hits were a matter of honor.

When the players moved away from each other to begin the fight, I was close to throwing up.

Red glanced back at me, then over at Carmine, before returning his attention to the screen.

I swallowed, not knowing where to concentrate, but my hand crawled slowly under the desk where a knife was taped to its underside.

On the screen, the fighters stalked each other and all we could hear was cheering and yelling.

The Russian struck first. Luca blocked. They started exchanging blows. Luca was taller and had a longer reach. Orlov looked shorter because he stacked muscles from the way his neck disappeared. He lunged at Luca, sending them crashing to the mat.

They grappled around the mat, and Luca threw Orlov off his back and sprang to his feet.

I kept my eyes on the clock.

When it crossed the three-minute mark, Red pivoted with his gun raised at Carmine.

Goose bumps erupted all over my skin. Gunfire erupted from outside.

"It's over, Carmine," Red said. "We've locked your accounts."

"Who the fuck are you?"

"A friend of Doriana's."

The Friar, aka Dead Poet.

"That bitch." Carmine stood slowly. I scooted my chair away from him, stood, and walked to Red's side.

"She begged for her life in the end," Carmine jeered. "If she knew who you guys were, she would have given you up." Then he changed tactics. "We can talk about this. We stand to make half a billion from the games. Imagine what you can do with it."

Carmine was a hypocrite. He said he hated human traffickers, and it was enough we rescued the victims, but he had no problem profiting from the money that came from it. For him, he felt that was owed to him after what happened to his mother.

"Luca will not be humiliated because of you," I snapped.

The door crashed open. A force knocked me over, and I instinctively crawled away from the source. Fists and grunts and cursing exploded behind me. Pain in my scalp made me cry out as I was yanked to my feet and the cold barrel of a gun poked at my temple.

"I'll kill her," Carmine shouted. He backed away with me. Red had neutralized the mercenary who broke into the room. Another mercenary named Trevor appeared. He and Red worked together.

"Take it easy," Red said. "We're lowering our weapons...see?" He and Trevor slowly crouched to the floor, but Red's eyes were level with the knife I had in my hand. A knife Carmine in his panic didn't realize I possessed.

At the minuscule nod from Red, I went limp in Carmine's arms. My pulse pounded in my ears, muffling my captor's shout, I raised my arm and stabbed his thigh and yanked it upward. No remorse. It was him or me.

"Bitch!" Carmine screamed. We both fell to the floor, but before I could gather my wits, Red was already hauling me up and into his arms.

"You're okay, you're okay." He was holding my shaking form. More mercenaries spilled into the room and there were brief status updates. They were on our side, thank God.

I pushed away from Red. "Luca."

He grinned. "Let's get you to your husband."

CHAPTER
Forty~Six

LUCA

I blocked a blow aimed for my head. My brow was already bleeding. The asshole also tried a series of kidney punches which I deflected. Orlov dove in with rapid jabs, but I held my arms cocked and protected my head. I wasn't going down yet. At the end of the second round, Dom assured me they'd found Natalya, and he was just waiting for confirmation, but I wasn't willing to risk her. Carmine asked for a show. I wasn't giving it to him.

"What's the matter with you?" The Russian was getting frustrated. I was hanging on, letting him stalk me while I danced around the octagon, hardly going on offense. The crowd was booing me, but I didn't give a fuck. Our match wasn't a judged fight and it depended who got knocked out or pinned down first. And by the way it was looking, I was the underdog.

"You gone stupid or something?" Orlov snarled, coming at me like a rabid bulldog.

I absorbed all the insults and the attacks. The effort to hold back was killing me, but Natalya's life was the most important because I was afraid if I let loose on Orlov, I wouldn't be able to hold back. Even when a second of doubt entered my head that she was in league with Carmine, I hung on to my love for her. Love was not a weakness. Love was something I would die for. I had no pride left. I was willing to be ridiculed because of love.

The referee called the end of round three. When my back was turned, Orlov lunged at me, spun me around, and punched me across the jaw.

A roar rose in the crowd.

The blow sent me to the floor, and the side of my head exploded in pain as it bounced off the mat.

"There," he spat. "Some excitement, *mudak*."

Blood and sweat blurred my vision. Dom and Ange jumped over the fence into the octagon. I rolled on my back and Dom's troubled face appeared above me while Ange confronted Orlov. Shouting ensued, while more men piled inside the fighting area.

"You okay, Zio?"

"Natalya?" I grunted.

Dom's face swam in front of me but he appeared to be grinning. "Why don't you look?"

I pushed myself up to a sitting position and twisted to my corner. There, fighting through the crowd, was Natalya. I scampered to my feet.

"You can't leave the mat!" Dom hauled me back.

"Fuck that." I shoved him away.

Four arms held me back, including Ange's. "Don't forfeit, asshole. Look. She's fine."

"I'm good. Let me go!" When they released me, I rushed to the corner just as my wife reached the fencing. I hauled her over the barrier and hugged her fiercely, uncaring if my sweat bled into her, not wanting to let her go, wanting to leave the fight and just say fuck it to everything. The fight. The crime family. The prestige and power. I wanted to just take Natalya and Elias and fucking go.

I gave her a quick, grinding kiss and searched her face. "Are you all right?"

"Yes!" she shouted. The noise of the crowd became deafening from the turn of events. "Now go win the fight."

A different kind of adrenaline mainlined my veins. Killer instinct erased anxiety, and with it, a future with Natalya was within reach.

Dom clapped my shoulder. "Get back in the fight before they call forfeit."

"Fuck that." I gave Natalya another quick kiss and lifted her over the barrier, then I turned to meet my opponent head-on.

My skull was throbbing, but I cracked my neck from side to side. When the referee gave the go-ahead, I stalked toward Orlov.

He came at me swinging. I leaned away from his jab and landed a left hook. The Russian fell on his ass.

I could have knocked him out with a roundhouse kick, but I had a spring in my step, and I owed the crowd a show.

"What the fuck, Luca?" Ange yelled. "Stop horsing around. Finish him off."

I did the boxer shuffle and waited for Orlov to get up. His mouth was bleeding, but I saw the deadly gleam in his eyes. He knew I was back in the game and he loved it. He faked another jab, then went low, tackling my torso, lifting me up over his shoulder and slamming me onto the mat. Blood thundered in my ears, and in slow motion, we grappled for control. He tried to weigh my thighs down under a massive bicep, and while blocking a blow to my head, I freed one leg and pinned his neck in a leg lock. That temporarily gave me control, and I broke free. I rolled to my knees about to scramble to my feet when he lunged at me, taking me back down to the mat.

He was under me, and with my back to his chest, his legs scissored my torso as he fought to get his arms around my neck.

The crowd roared. Ange screamed.

And through the pounding in my ears, it was my brother's voice I heard in my head.

Respect the choke!

Orlov's forearm pressed across my throat attempting to cut off my breath. His other hand was on top of my head, trying to slip it behind my neck to complete the blood choke. I clawed at that hand and failed. Orlov's arms locked my neck between them.

Three seconds to blackout.

"Luca!" Natalya's scream reached me.

Two seconds. My vision dimmed around the edges. Must not fail.

With oxygen and blood competing in its race for scarcity, my strength sputtered.

I concentrated all my remaining power to my hands, shoving, dislodging Orlov's foot off my torso. Freeing myself from the leg lock, I shifted my body on instinct and pinned that leg. The whole movement loosened his chokehold and I didn't waste time rolling over and slamming my elbow across his jaw.

Mayhem erupted around us.

"Get the fuck away," Ange shouted.

Unlike the first time I tried to escape from Orlov's deadly ground game, I went on all fours into a turtle position, keeping my limbs tight, head down, mostly to catch my breath as well as pump back blood and oxygen into my brain. Those few heartbeats restored clarity and I anticipated his attack. When his hand touched my side, I spun, twisted, and flipped him over. This time, I had his waist in a leg lock and crossed my ankles squeezing.

Orlov roared and choked and growled.

He was on top of me, wide open with disbelief on his face. At close enough range, I delivered two rapid punches to his face and released him.

I scrambled to my feet and bounced away.

Orlov rose unsteadily, swaying, eyes groggy, lips curled back in a snarl. We squared off. I shifted my cocked arms upwards, and the second his eyes followed that movement, I spun and back-kicked him on the head, twisting his body around.

Orlov dropped to the mat.

The referee ran to check on him, but swiftly called a knockout. He raised my arm as the victor.

It was over.

I faced my corner. Dom, Natalya, and Ange were rushing toward me.

I headed straight for Natalya. She jumped onto me, and I caught her under her ass while she wrapped her legs around me.

"You won! You won!" she screamed.

The adrenaline and power of the fight thrummed through me. Instead of lowering my wife, I flipped her over my shoulder. The adrenaline had sharpened my senses, and I caught sight of someone I hadn't seen in years, my mind making rapid-fire connections that my wife had once again used subterfuge and put her life in jeopardy.

"Luca, where the hell are you going?" Dom yelled.

I could hear Natalya shouting at me. *Oh, tesoro, I will deal with you later. I'm looking forward to it.* My eyes focused on the red-haired man dressed in commando gear, standing at the edge of the crowd looking like event security, but he wasn't.

He was smiling at me. The fucker.

I reached him and lowered Natalya.

"Bristow," I snarled softly.

His smile widened into a shit-eating grin.

I punched him.

"Are you done?" Dom asked while holding an ice pack to his jaw.

I'd punched three people since Orlov.

Dom, Matteo, and Hank Bristow. All three conspired with Natalya to take down Carmine, who had met his bloody end on the floor of the building right across from where the fight was held. My wife had severed his femoral artery. I looked at her now, wearing an oversized sweatshirt—clothes that weren't hers, but there was blood spatter on her jeans and the tip of her sneakers. And she was calm about the kill. She truly was my queen.

We were back in the penthouse. Natalya was sitting beside Sera, who was tending to Matteo's cut lip.

"The shoe isn't so nice when it's on the other foot, is it, Zio?" Sera was pissed at me. "At least we gave Natalya a choice."

"You asked her to lie to me," I snapped.

"I wasn't lying!" Natalya protested, but I speared her a look and she shut up.

"Are we going to argue omission versus lying?" I cut a glance at Matteo. That asshole knew what I was talking about. He nearly lost Sera because of it.

I was breathing hard, and it wasn't from the fight. It was because my blood pressure went through the roof again after I discovered what my wife had done. I hadn't even come down from my high stemming from the match, and the adrenaline spiked once more. All eyes watched me like I was a wild animal on the prowl.

At the penthouse were Dom, Matteo, and Sera. This operation was part of the Archer Syndicate. It was an organization I'd heard rumors about but never could confirm its existence.

Many times Dom had hinted he wanted me to be a part of something big, but I'd always declined. Now they'd dragged Natalya into it, and I had no choice but to listen to their bullshit.

Which wasn't really bullshit because they kept the underworld in check.

Ange and Dario were both listening with interest. The three of us had conversations about the organization before that originated with the De Luccis.

Madone, my niece was married to the head of the Archer Syndicate, and I must admit, I was fucking proud of her.

I glanced at the person I wanted to tear apart the most. Hank Bristow was standing beside Trevor, who I knew worked with Matteo and was ex-military like Bristow.

"Let me get this straight, so you're involved with the Archers?" I asked Bristow.

"Doriana's network tapped their group for extractions," the ex-Navy SEAL said. "Carmine killed Doriana two years ago, right around the time of the mission that exposed Natalya."

"Tell me now why I shouldn't kill you for getting my wife in trouble."

"It wasn't his fault." Natalya rose from her seat, and this time she didn't quake under my glare. "Carmine had been playing Doriana all along and was feeding her information about Orlov's human trafficking operations to gain her confidence. She suspected she'd been compromised. That's why she didn't want me to transfer the money."

I wagged my finger between Natalya and Bristow. "And you two were communicating behind my back?" This was what I couldn't fathom, and it pissed me off the most. "We had this understanding after New York, *tesoro*. No more secrets."

She hung her head. "I know, but Detective Voss…"

Dario straightened from where he was enjoying the show. "Detective Voss? How is he involved?"

"He's a buddy from my special ops days." Bristow grinned his infuriating grin again. I pictured him missing a couple of teeth, courtesy of my fist. But then I registered what he had said. Dario beat me in voicing the conclusion.

"That day when he confronted us," my consigliere said. "He made up that bullshit, didn't he? He didn't have evidence about our activities." Dario glanced at Natalya. "He handed you a card."

My wife looked like she wanted to disappear into the floor. "Yes. It was a message from Bristow and it's a way for us to confirm our identities online since we weren't trusting each other. I didn't want to risk it, but they made me believe they had something on the *family*." She squinted her eyes at Bristow.

"We had to blackmail you somehow to get you to help us take down Carmine," Bristow said. "Voss played along and confronted you guys. He thought it was a brilliant fabrication. Little did he know I wasn't bluffing."

Ange came forward. "Are you saying you have proof?"

Bristow handed him a flash drive. "It's all there. No copies anywhere. Chicago PD never got their hands on it. Like I was saying, Voss thought I made it up."

"It wasn't blackmail," Natalya added. "He gave me references to prove who he was, otherwise I wouldn't have gone along. Both of you worked a mission years ago to stop human traffickers in Vegas. And he's best friends with your stepsister's husband. We're practically family."

Bristow snorted. "I wouldn't go that far."

I wouldn't go that far either, but Natalya wasn't far off the mark. And the reason I hadn't gone apeshit over this whole operation was because Bristow belonged to a group that regularly went rogue against red tape and pulled off miraculous results. In this case, I was the red tape.

"Did you know where Natalya was this whole time?" I asked.

Bristow shook his head. "I tracked her down a few months before you found her. And by the way, your hackers aren't *that* good. I planted those traffic cam sightings that led you guys to the town of Grafton." He looked me directly in the eye. "Just so you know, Carmine was the one who told Orlov that Natalya had his money. I was already part of his crew of mercenaries then and Carmine was counting on Orlov to offer up the Game of Bosses as payback."

"That's when he came clean to us that he was The Friar," Matteo interjected. "The Archers worked with The Friar often particularly with my cousin Ronan McGrath who was the only one who knew The Friar's real identity. You know the McGraths, right?"

Bristow chuckled. "Of course he does. Luca gatecrashed the McGrath's barbecue a couple of years ago."

I rolled my eyes when everyone started snickering.

"We inserted Trevor as our own man inside so he could communicate with Dom and ensure Natalya's safety." Matteo splayed his hands. "And that's how everything went down."

Surprisingly, I was okay with the high-level information of the op and didn't need the nitty-gritty details. Bristow could be a useful associate because he had legal access to government databases and infrastructure. I didn't want to burn any bridges over this. I was opportunistic if anything and could ask a favor in the future.

I turned to Natalya. "I still don't understand what happened to you after Carmine burned the house down."

She compressed her lips before dipping her chin and shot me a wary glance beneath her lashes, as though the revelation would make me lose my shit.

The long seconds that passed only agitated my adrenaline-infused wrath, but I still gritted, "The truth. All of it."

"It was sad, really, or maybe it was fortunate…for me at least," she started saying. "Carmine entrusted me to the second capo who turned against you. Then the capo entrusted me to one of his crew. The man felt sorry for me and took me to the St. Louis women's shelter. Apparently, it wasn't the first time he'd been doing this whenever he felt sorry for women who'd become victims of violence. I think he was planning to skip town."

"Russian outliers ambushed this guy," Ange said. "Remember that incident, Luca? One of our men was slain on I-55."

"I remember. That interstate runs straight into St. Louis," I said grimly. "So in short, Carmine misplaced you." I stated it in a deadly calm voice that was a far cry from everything I was feeling.

Natalya took tentative steps toward me, sensing an impending explosion. I held up a finger to stop her progress because she wasn't wrong. I'd reached a breaking point. Words failed to take form. I had to turn away from everyone, needing to push down the bubbling rage with alcohol. I walked to the bar and grabbed the scotch, poured it into a glass, and gulped it down.

No one said anything.

I poured another drink and stared at the glass. It wasn't calming me down.

My jaw clenched. I was done holding it together.

I detonated.

I hurled the glass against the wall. It shattered, and the amber liquid marred its pristine surface.

Everyone was still quiet.

I stared at the bottle in my hand.

"That's good scotch," Ange commented. "It's better to—"

"Everyone out!" I snarled. "We're done here."

Dom approached cautiously. "We still need to discuss—"

"Not tonight. You guys are staying for another few days." I glared at Bristow. "If you rope my wife into one of your schemes again…"

"I'll keep you in the loop."

Fucker. I tipped my chin in acknowledgement. I wasn't a total tool. If it wasn't for him, we would have never found Natalya.

My eyes homed in on my wife. She was about to leave with everyone.

"Where are you going?" I barked, stepping in front of her.

"I'm going to get Elias," she squeaked.

"He's with your parents and Martha. He's fine."

"But…"

"Just you and me tonight, *tesoro*." The endearment dripped with sarcasm. I was still livid about the whole thing. She had the rest of the night to make it up to me.

I clasped her biceps firmly and kept her to my side.

And as my family congratulated me again on winning the fight, the guys could barely hide the amusement from their faces. They knew there was only one thing that would tame the fury. Sera was the last one to say goodbye and gave me a hug. "You were magnificent tonight, Zio." Her tone was full of affection and it reminded me how much I missed her. Then she looked at Natalya with an impish grin. "Go easy on her. She did badass shit tonight." She winked at my wife.

"Don't encourage her," I groaned. "And tell Carlotta we won't be down for breakfast tomorrow, but we'll see you in the afternoon."

Natalya froze. My fingers tightened on her arm.

The elevator doors closed. We stood and stared at it for a while.

Finally, I turned to my wife and said softly, "Run."

CHAPTER
Forty~Seven

NATALYA

"What?"

My panties had been drenched since the fight, and I think I'd been having mini orgasms ever since. Being plastered to a sweaty, aggressive male was so arousing, I despaired we couldn't shake everyone around us. My husband was annoying because he passed up an opportunity for hot sex in favor of finding out what happened. But Luca wasn't ruled by his dick as he had often informed me. And I should be swooning that his concern for me came first.

I'd been anxious for everyone to leave, but now that they had, I didn't know what to do with the man in front of me.

His whole body said "don't fuck with me," yet my body was screaming "take me, take me."

Instead of answering, Luca tipped the bottle of scotch to his mouth, all the while not taking his eyes off me.

His eyes were wild and heated.

Like he wanted to eat me alive.

I backed up a step. I didn't know what to do. He told me to run.

He lowered the bottle. "I'm giving you a seven-second head start."

I couldn't help it. I laughed. "Where will I run to? It's a big penthouse but—"

He erased our distance, and his nose touched my neck. He breathed me in. Then he nuzzled its curve and traced a path to my cheek and inhaled some more. I spasmed between my legs and grew wetter.

"I smell your arousal. You want to fuck."

I burst into a brief, nervous giggle. "Isn't that what you want?"

He backed up a couple of steps. "Yes. But I want to do other things."

Other things? What other things? He continued to back away until he was by the wall. His fingers hovered over the light panel of the penthouse. "Tonight, you made me feel helpless. I just got you back, and then I thought I lost you and it would have been all my fault. Because of my ambition, Carmine was still out there."

"I'm sorry, Luca, but it had to look real and—"

"I understand that." He cut me off. "A few days from now, I might even think it was brilliant. But tonight, you're going to give me back control."

I swallowed. "What?"

"Your surrender. I don't want you to give it to me easy. I know I have to fight for it. That's the only way to tame the aggression inside me. To be worth it. You'll always find a way to defy me if you think it's for my own good. It would always drive me crazy, but that's who you are." His mouth tipped derisively. "And I will enjoy it every time I remind you that you are mine."

"So, what do we do now?"

His smile was feral. He touched the light controls. I startled when the penthouse fell into shadows and drew the blinds. The lights of Chicago peeked through the vertical blinds so we weren't in total darkness, but still…

My husband stood motionless, like a predator playing with its prey. "Run."

I took another step back, deciding to take the hallway that led to our bedroom even as arousal twitched wetness between my thighs, and my clit felt swollen. "Do I hide?"

"Six seconds. Run."

His last "run" was more forceful, more guttural like he was more beast than man. It triggered a flight response in me. I spun away from him, nervous laughter trapped in my chest as my feet began to move, relieved I was wearing sneakers and in less danger of breaking an ankle.

I ran.

With each step that pounded toward our bedroom, my excitement rose, my vision became sharper, and my skin burned. There were three rooms in this section. I bypassed our bedroom and dove into the unused guest room, knowing that the bathroom was attached to another room. I could escape from there and loop back through the apartment. At the back of my mind, I wondered if it was unlocked.

Dammit, why was I so nervous?

My sneakers skidded on the tile, making a cringy loud squeak. I threw myself on the adjoining door. Locked. Why was it locked? Hysterical laughter bubbled inside me. This was a stupid game. I ran back into the bedroom and stopped.

Luca darkened the doorway. The white T-shirt he wore after the fight was like a beacon in the shadows.

I scrambled around the bed and put it between us.

"This is stupid," I said, through heavy panting. "I mean, where is there for me to run? You saw me come into this bedroom."

"It's not stupid, because I'm having fun," he drawled. He took a step into the room. "Are you afraid of me, Natalya?"

"What? No!"

"Good." He took another step. "Because I feel this is going to be our game."

I focused on his movements more than his words. He was going around the bed slowly. I could jump over it and escape him and run the length of the penthouse to the other wing. I laughed lightly. "This cat and mouse?"

"No." Another step. "That I will always chase you."

He lunged.

I screamed and jumped over the bed. I was almost at the door when his arms came around me and lifted me up against his hard body.

"Luca!" I screeched.

He threw us on the bed like he was still in a caged match, stealing the air from my lungs. Pinning me on the bed, his mouth came crashing down on me, but the kiss was brief and I lost sight of him because he dragged the sweatshirt over my head. Then, while straddling my legs, he unbuttoned my jeans and dragged down the zipper.

"I wish you'd worn a skirt," he growled.

I pummeled his shoulders. "What? And make it easy for you?"

He had to get off me to remove my jeans, so I twisted around and tried to leave the bed, pumped and drunk on euphoria and getting into our primal play. The sudden chill over my ass told me he'd taken off my panties along with my jeans. By this time, my head and arms were dangling over the edge of the mattress, but he put an end to my attempts to escape him and hauled me back onto the bed. I grappled for leverage and pushed up on all fours, but his mouth hit my pussy, taking broad swipes, sending exquisite pleasure racing between my legs. His head moved under me and he gripped my thighs to drag me down.

I was sitting on his face and he continued to eat me like I was his last meal.

"Oh my God," I moaned. My clit was so swollen. "Can you breathe down…"

I didn't finish the sentence. A growl vibrated at the same time he sucked my sweet spot and it throbbed with orgasmic pulses. I screamed and surrendered, pushed against his face, because, oh God, sometimes I felt murderous toward Luca, but if he wanted to suffocate, then he could do it while giving me an orgasm.

While I was still reeling from the massive climax, he flipped me over and drove into me. My body arched. Two weeks of no sex and he was enormous inside me.

His face appeared, triumphant and vibrating with leashed power. I saw the split second he lost all restraint. He hooked my legs over his elbows and spread me wide and rammed into me over and over.

"I love you. I love you," he chanted, teeth bared, completely feral. He fucked me forever. He fucked me like he hated me. He fucked me like I was his whore. Pulling out, he flipped me over again and grabbed my hips, dragging me to all fours, and slammed back inside me. And this time, he thrust with abandon. And I reared into him and met him thrust for thrust. Because despite his roughness, despite the way he dominated me, it gave me power that I could do this to him and make him lose complete control.

His arm went under me, made me spread my knees further, and then his fingers circled my already sensitive clit and another blinding orgasm shook me.

I cried out again, and my breathing became labored. "Luca… enough, please."

I was begging, and he was grunting, growling, and guttural. With one last thrust, he exploded inside me. Slick wet heat made me slicker and dripped down my legs. He continued pumping as though he hadn't just claimed and wrecked my pussy.

Finally, he folded over me. We collapsed sideways on the mattress, and while wrapped all around each other, he kept my back plastered to his chest.

"You're still inside me," I murmured.

"You feel so good. I think I'll stay in you for a while," he returned. "Don't move, baby."

"We're going to sleep like this?" I laughed into the pillow. "We both need a shower." He hadn't washed off the fight, and I hadn't washed off the day either.

He snuggled deeper inside me. "Hmm...we fuck filthy. I love filthy."

I did too.

Sometime in the early morning, we returned to our bedroom. We showered and indulged in a bath. Luca made slow love to me afterward, and we fell asleep. I didn't know how many times he reached for me in the night, how many times he cleaned me between my legs, but I gave my husband what he needed. And he gave me what I craved.

The morning sun was high in the sky when I finally found the strength to open my eyes. My limbs ached. I was thoroughly loved and satiated.

The bed beside me was empty, and I wondered what time it was. I padded to the bathroom to freshen up, and I walked out just when the doorknob was turning.

Elias barreled through and hit my body full force. "Mamma!"

My mouth fell open, and my gaze flew back to the door. Luca was holding a breakfast tray. "Did you prep him to say that?"

Luca smiled sheepishly. The bruises from the fight were more apparent this morning. There was a cut on his brow. "It appears I had to make waffles for him to tell the difference."

"So what is this, Mr. Moretti? Breakfast in bed?"

"Yes. Why don't you get back under the covers while your son and I serve you?"

"Aw." I did as I was told. Elias crept into the bed at my side while his father balanced the breakfast tray with my waffles, bacon, and orange juice. There was even a little glass vase with a daisy in it.

"This is all so sweet, Luca."

He sat beside us. I cut up the waffles and gave a bite to my son. I grabbed a piece of bacon and munched on it. I was starving.

"You okay?" Luca brushed my hair aside.

"I'm fine." I touched his face. "How about you, *caro*? Any aches or pains?"

His mouth twitched. "I should ask you the same."

I leaned into him. "I'm deliciously sore."

"Mamma, b-con," Elias chattered. I handed him a piece, which he put in his mouth.

"He's gonna be a big man like his papà when he grows up." I nudged Luca. "Where's everyone?"

"They're in Sera and Matteo's unit, having breakfast."

"Oh my goodness, I feel like a terrible hostess."

"Stop." Luca put a finger on my lips. "That's why I told them we wouldn't be seeing them until the afternoon." He looked at Elias. "I want it to be just us." His eyes softened. "The three of us. Elias, do you remember what I asked you to do?"

I split a look between my boy and Luca. "What are you two up to?"

Elias made a big oh with his mouth as if he remembered something he forgot. Then he gave a big smile and reached for the end of the tray and grabbed a folded paper.

He handed it to me.

Curious, I opened it and laughed.

"Will you marry Papà?"

I glanced at Luca. "We're already married."

With a gaze too intense for morning breakfast, he picked up my left hand and ran his thumb over my bare ring finger. "This is telling me we aren't."

I never thought about my rings since I came back, but Luca was still wearing his.

"I'm going to have new ones made," he said fiercely. "I want to say my vows again. Will you marry me again, Natalya?"

I hugged Elias and told his father, "Yes."

Epilogue

Natalya

"What are you doing here?"

My mother's panicked voice made me smile. I was in the bridal room of the church near Tralestelle. Unlike the first time we got married, the renewal of our vows was a smaller affair. More intimate. Before the ceremony, I escaped into this room because I heard the rumble of thunder. I wanted to look out the window and watch the storm clouds roll in.

I glanced over my shoulder.

"Relax," I told her. "My makeup is on point."

And appearances were all Elena Conte cared about. The relief on her face was predictable to the point it almost made me laugh.

Luca and I had moved back to Tralestelle soon after his fight in Chicago while we left Mamma and Papà in the city. They visited us on the weekends, and vice versa. Whatever Luca told Elena two months ago seemed to stick, but even without my husband's help, I could've handled Mamma on my own. The two years I'd spent away from everyone had given me tremendous confidence I didn't think I had, and Luca, despite his overprotectiveness, his belief and pride in me, helped me thrive.

"You look beautiful, Nattie." The smile on her face was genuine. It was genuine because it was unfamiliar and it made my heart squeeze for the young girl who would have appreciated that smile. I quickly dispelled those feelings because today was not a day for regrets. There was too much joy in my heart.

"Thank you, Mamma." She stood behind me and we looked at the full-length mirror. Unlike my wedding, I wasn't wearing a voluminous gown. I was wearing a modern ecru maxidress cut from light crepe fabric. I loved the one shoulder neckline with feather trim along the cuff of one-sleeve and its asymmetrical hem, which hit just above the ankles. Apparently, I had a thing for asymmetrical hems. I thought back to the tango festival, and I looked forward to dancing at the party.

Mamma brushed at my sleeve, and her eyes dropped to it. "I know you and I haven't had a good mother-daughter relationship." I braced myself for her next words, but when she lifted her eyes, there was an apology. "You are smart and beautiful. I was only admired for my looks, and because of my jealousy, because I wanted to feel better about myself, I became a terrible mother."

I didn't say anything. Now that I had Elias and knew how a mother should feel, I was done making excuses for her behavior.

She dabbed at her eyes. "Look at me. I'm going to ruin my makeup." She exhaled raggedly. "But know, daughter." She touched her chest. "That after so many years, I can truly say from the bottom of my heart, that I am so proud of you."

Her words were said with all sincerity, and I had no reason to doubt her.

I turned to her. We smiled at each other and hugged.

We emerged from the bridal room to see Luca stalking toward us. His brows were furrowed and his jaw clenched. My mother froze. She even stuttered a step and a distressed gasp escaped her lips.

I felt sorry for her. My husband seemed to terrify her with just a look.

But when Luca saw my face, the lines between his brows smoothed and a sexy smile tugged on his lips.

"There's my beautiful wife." He dragged me into his arms. "Are you ready?"

"I am," I breathed.

"Good, because our ring bearer is getting impatient."

I laughed. Sure enough, Elias was getting pouty. Nessa seemed to calm him. Our son was in a sleek little suit, and I could just see him wear them like nobody's business when he grew older. Just like his dad. I looked forward to those years.

"Mamma. Mamma! Hurry!"

We invited only close family. And I seriously felt close to them after what we'd been through in the past few months.

Sera, Matteo, Dom, Carlotta, and most of the De Luccis were there.

Ange was in the front row with his daughter and wife, a wife I'd never met. Apparently, they'd been estranged for a while, but had now reconnected.

Dario was with a date.

I was glad Martha made it because she was also overseeing the catering at the house where everyone would celebrate. Of course Tony and Rocco. Among Luca's soldiers, they were the ones who I trusted with my family's lives.

Luca led me to the top of the aisle with our son in front of us.

Instead of a sea of white roses, variegated colors of peonies filled the aisles. From scarlet, to coral, to hot pink and white. It symbolized the colorful life I expected to have with Luca.

Without waiting for the piano to signal the start of our march, Elias started walking down the aisle.

Luca and I exchanged a fond shake of our heads and a smile. There was no question our son was born a leader like his papà.

So we followed his lead.

In front of the priest, with Elias between us, Luca said, "God has given me this second chance. I'm not wasting it. The past two years only proved how miserable I was without you. You left me Elias, the only light that made me hold on through those dark years. I couldn't imagine another day without you in my life. Never leave me again, *tesoro*. I will not survive it. In front of family and friends, I pledge to put you, Elias, and our future children first. And from the bottom of my heart that only beats for you, I vow to cherish, love, and protect you for the rest of my life."

It wasn't the words, but the fierceness with how he said them that left me speechless. They wrapped around my heart with so much love for my husband.

The church was quiet except for sniffling. I wasn't the only one affected by my husband's vows.

My eyes burned with so many emotions, and my husband's stormy gaze packed so much intensity behind his words.

"Luca." I inhaled raggedly. "I didn't prepare beautiful vows like yours."

Everyone laughed.

He caught my hands in his and dragged me closer. "Tell me simply. That's all I want to hear."

"I love you so, so much." I suppressed a sob. My heart was just brimming with happiness. "To you and Elias, I promise to be the best wife and mother."

"You already are." And then he kissed me deeply and sweetly.

The priest cleared his throat.

Laughter went around the church again.

"Papà. Papà." Elias lifted the rings to us.

Luca chuckled and took the new rings from our son, and then he slipped them on my finger.

~

Five months later, Paris

Luca

We delayed our second honeymoon. Why? Because my wife loved rain and December was the rainiest month in Paris.

After standing in line to get ice cream at Berthillon, we were walking across Pont de la Tournelle, the arched bridge that spanned the width of the river Seine, when the first raindrop hit my face.

"Oh my goodness," Natalya breathed. Her expressive brown eyes danced with excitement. "Not even a full day in Paris and it's happening." We stopped at the center of the bridge and watched the gathering nimbus cumulus clouds cloak the city in an enchanting gray filter. I was seeing Paris through the filter of my love for

Natalya and couldn't believe how love could be so fulfilling once I surrendered to its power.

I'd been an idiot, but I was an idiot no more.

"Rain already." Natalya's impatience made me laugh. She gathered her coat around her. It was nuts to eat a cold treat in forty-five-degree temperatures, but I couldn't deny my wife. I went behind her to shield her from the frosty breeze and keep her warm.

"Baby, eat your ice cream." It had melted all over her hand. "We're staying here for two weeks. Odds are we'll do it many times."

"Are we talking about walking in the rain or something else?" She leaned sideways so she could shoot me that saucy look I'd grown familiar with, and my own eyes hooded. We were such a combustible pair, and I liked the games we played in the bedroom. My cock hardened at just the thought of having her to myself. I loved my son, but it surprised me how obsessed I was with my wife, and there were times I was jealous of the attention she gave him.

I grabbed her hand with the cone and licked her ice cream. "That and something else."

"Hey, eat your own ice cream." She glanced at the sky again and a big drop of rain fell on her face. "Ugh, it's such a tease."

"Like you?" I murmured. I turned her around to face me and planted a kiss on her sweetened lips. She tasted like decadent chocolate and temptation. I finished my own before the impending rain.

"Well…" Natalya took a sultry swipe of her cone with her tongue.

Yep. Tease.

"Oh, here it comes." She finished the rest of her ice cream so fast, I worried for a second that she was going to get brain freeze or choke.

"Careful, baby, that's the wrong thing to choke on."

She rolled her eyes but laughed. Innuendos between us were nothing new, but it only escalated the sexual tension when we got on the plane to Paris.

And as the sky finally opened—thank God it wasn't a washout—the steady rain slowly fulfilled my wife's wish of walking in Parisian rain with her husband.

She lifted on tiptoes and kissed me. "Thank you."

"You're welcome, baby." I slipped our hands together, and we walked over the bridge.

"Brrr…it's getting really cold."

I put my arm around her. "It *is* December."

"What are we going to do when we get back to the duplex?"

"I thought it was obvious." Depending on what came first, it was either the hot tub or fucking.

She rolled her eyes again. "Obviously. But after."

"Whatever you want."

She snuggled closer to me. "You're very warm. I can feel your heat through your trench coat."

"I aim to please."

"How about we watch *Casablanca*?" she suggested.

"It depends. Are you going to ask me a tough question again?"

She laughed into my chest before raising her eyes to mine. "I don't care if you're my hero or villain. I love you just the way you are."

"That's good. Because I'm never letting you go." I leaned over and kissed her lips. "I love you so much, *tesoro*."

Can't get enough of Luca and Natalya? Signup for my newsletter and grab three bonus scenes that include a deleted super spicy scene, Elias's third birthday, and a glimpse of our couple three years in the future.

scan here for bonus scenes

Nico and Ivy are next in a sizzling enemies-to-lovers romance, Scorned Love.

Curious about Bristow? Check out my romantic suspense series, Rogue Protectors.

Afterword

Scorned Vows put me through so much emotional stress. Though I love putting my heroes through the wringer, I hate doing that to the heroine, but I had to because it was important for readers to experience Natalya's heartache. I wanted you all to hate Luca, but not too much that he's beyond forgiveness. This book was the hero redemption I wanted to write. The way I weighed what made a good grovel vs. a bad one was almost a thesis. Grand gestures or expensive things are cop outs, and what I really wanted to see was hero karma and his anguish for having caused the heroine pain. So, yes, there were still grand gestures, but I had to weave in the hero's regret at what he had done and led to his changed behavior. Also, the premise where Natalya got amnesia and the bad memories came back first? I was cackling and excited about writing Luca's frustration. Hopefully, I redeemed him in your eyes. Let me know!

As usual, I had a fantastic team behind me.

Thank you, Becca aka The Fairy Plot Mother. You always asked me the right questions to fuel my intellection process to solve plot and character issues. Our weekly calls kept me accountable to reach my internal deadlines.

Erica of Erica Edits. I love your timely and fabulous edits to my manuscript and appreciate your professionalism in all things. Your feedback on my work is always uplifting.

Sue, I don't know what I would have done without your amazing beta read. Your eye for detail is amazing and you always go above and beyond. I know Luca and Natalya caused you a lot of angst, and I'm happy you powered through the words to witness Luca's redemption and loved it!

Amy, thank you for going through my pre-edited draft. I love what you suggested that improved the flow of the plot.

Judy of Judy's proofreading. Thank you for being my final eyes on the manuscript!

Mandy, thank you for being a good friend and being a message away. I know I've built up and teased Luca a lot. I hoped he lived up to your expectations.

To my Very Important Paige readers. Thank you for your support.!

To the amazing world of booktokkers and bookstagrammers. Thank you for your support of my books and my ever-growing TBR.

And finally, to hubby and my furbaby Loki. Both of you are always so patient when my mind is in creating worlds and characters. I love you both to the moon and back.

Connect with the Author

Find me at:

Facebook: Victoria Paige Books
Website: victoriapaigebooks.com
Email: victoriapaigebooks@gmail.com
FB Reader Group: Very Important Paige readers

facebook.com/victoriapaigebooks

tiktok.com/@vpaigebooks

twitter.com/vpaigebooks

instagram.com/victoriapaigebooks

Also by Victoria Paige

Scorned Fate

Scorned Heir

Scorned Vows

Scorned Love (June 2024)

Rogue Protectors

The Ex Assignment

Protector of Convenience

The Boss Assignment

Her Covert Protector

The Wife Assignment

Bristow's book (October 2024)

Guardians

Fire and Ice

Beneath the Fire (novella)

Silver Fire

Smoke and Shadows

Susan Stoker Special Forces World

Reclaiming Izabel (novella)

Guarding Cindy (novella)

Protecting Stella (novella)

Always

It's Always Been You

Always Been Mine

A Love For Always

Misty Grove

Fighting Chance

Saving Grace

Unexpected Vows

Standalone

De Lucci's Obsession

Deadly Obsession

Captive Lies

The Princess and the Mercenary

* All series books can be read as standalone

Printed in Great Britain
by Amazon